Sheila O'Flanagan's books, including *Stand By Me*, *The Perfect Man*, *Someone Special* and *Bad Behaviour*, have been huge bestsellers in the UK and Ireland; they are all available from Headline Review. Sheila pursued a very successful career in banking, foreign exchange dealing and treasury management before becoming a full-time writer based in Dublin. In her spare time she plays badminton at competition level.

Praise for Sheila O'Flanagan's bestsellers:

'A great read and the perfect escape from those dreary winter evenings' *Sun*

'Sheila O'Flanagan is one of the blinding talents on the female fiction scene' *Daily Record*

'A big, comfortable, absorbing book . . . bound to delight fans and guaranteed to put O'Flanagan on the bestsellers list – yet again' *Irish Independent Review*

'Hugely enjoyable' *Best*

By Sheila O'Flanagan and available from Headline Review

Suddenly Single
Far From Over
My Favourite Goodbye
He's Got To Go
Isobel's Wedding
Caroline's Sister
Too Good To Be True
Dreaming Of A Stranger
Destinations
Anyone But Him
How Will I Know?
Connections
Yours, Faithfully
Bad Behaviour
Someone Special
The Perfect Man
Stand By Me
A Season To Remember
All For You

Sheila O'Flanagan

All For You

headline
review

First published in 2011
by HEADLINE REVIEW
An imprint of HEADLINE PUBLISHING GROUP

First published in paperback in 2012
by HEADLINE REVIEW

1

ISBN 978 0 7553 4397 3 (A-format)
ISBN 978 0 7553 4387 4 (B-format)

Typeset in Galliard by Palimpsest Book Production Limited,
Falkirk, Stirlingshire
Printed and bound in Great Britain by
Clays Ltd, St Ives plc

HEADLINE PUBLISHING GROUP
An Hachette UK Company
338 Euston Road
London NW1 3BH

www.headline.co.uk
www.hachette.co.uk

Acknowledgements

Regular readers may now be as familiar with the people I thank after each book as I am. But that's because they are there behind me for every one and they deserve their place between the covers!

And so, once again, many thanks to:

My super-agent Carole Blake
My lovely editor Marion Donaldson
My fantastic translators, copyeditors and publishers in Ireland, the UK and around the world
And, of course, booksellers everywhere!

No matter what I do I always have the support of my wonderful family and friends, thank you so much. Colm, of course, has been with me on more than the book journey and helps me not to take things too seriously, so – for the fun times – thanks again!

In writing *All For You* I had to do a lot of research, which was made all the more enjoyable because of the fantastic people who were so forthcoming with their time and expertise.

At Met Eireann enormous thanks to Gerald Fleming, Head of Forecasting, for his time and his knowledge, and especially for allowing me to stand in the studio and pretend I was presenting the weather – it was a very sunny day by the time I'd finished with it so they should let me do it more often . . .

In Monterey, I met some warm and generous people who shared so much about their town and its history. A big thank you to Karen Nordstrand of the Monterey County Film Commission for pointing me in the right direction; to Jeanne McCoombs and Dennis Copeland of the Monterey Public Library who unearthed so many gems for me; and to Jean Richards for her extensive information on the Women's Movement in the area. Special thanks to Diane Mandeville of the Cannery Row Company and Brenda Roncarati, Mentor of the Boys & Girls programs, for the wonderfully informative and fun breakfast in Monterey. I hope I've treated your lovely town with the respect and accuracy it deserves.

As always, thank you so much to my readers who have created a community around my books, who keep in touch with me and who spur me on. It's always great to hear from you. You can reach me through my website www.sheilaoflanagan.com or my Facebook Fan page. And you can follow me on Twitter too!

If you want the rainbow, you've got to put up with the rain.

Dolly Parton

Prologue

Meteorology: the study of the atmosphere and its interaction with the earth's surface, oceans and life in general

She was never sure whether it was a memory or a dream. It often came to her when she was drifting off to sleep. Or sometimes just before she woke, like a YouTube clip in her head. She was watching it even though she was part of it, which was an odd feeling. She could see the scene: a small wooden house with a blue and white striped awning over the narrow deck; a green and yellow hosepipe snaking across the flagstoned yard; a small wheelbarrow full of hedge clippings with a rusted rake perched precariously on top. She could feel the warmth of the air too, hot and muggy but with the occasional tiny wisp of breeze. She could hear people talking inside the house, voices muted, suddenly raised, clearly angry, and then muted again. She didn't know what they were saying, but the flashes of anger worried her. And then she was in the scene herself, still a child, sitting on the bleached steps outside the house, a collection of brightly coloured building bricks on the ground in front of her. She was arranging them into piles. Most of them were in an orange pile. Fewer in a blue pile. Fewer still in a yellow pile. She was dividing them carefully, the tip of her tongue peeping out of the corner of her mouth.

She placed the last brick on the blue pile. And then she felt the sudden drop of rain on her arm. A big drop. Warm.

She looked up at the sky. It had been grey all morning. Big, lowering, bruised clouds covering its previously brilliant blue. And now the clouds were unleashing a deluge on the dried earth below. She held her hands up to the rain, enraptured by the feel of the warm, heavy drops on her skin, letting it soak through her pretty lilac and white checked dress.

She heard the adult voices raised again and then someone say, 'Where's the child?'

There was the sound of chairs scraping against tiles, of footsteps drawing nearer. And then a short exclamation, and she felt herself scooped up into his arms. Warm, comforting arms. She could smell the spicy scent of aftershave and she could feel the swift kiss to her forehead.

Then women's voices asking was she all right and him replying, although she wan't quite sure what he said.

They all clustered around her.

And then, as always, the clip faded.

Chapter 1

Nimbostratus: a dark grey featureless cloud producing lots of rain

The first thing Lainey did when she woke up on the morning of the wedding was to listen for the sound of rain. For the briefest of moments as she lay there, burrowed beneath the duvet with her arm lightly across Ken's sleeping body, she thought that she'd been wrong, and her heart leaped. And then she realised that the relentless drumming against the roof wasn't part of the dream after all. It was real. It was raining. Chucking it down, just as she'd predicted.

She snuggled closer to Ken as she listened to the gurgle of the water cascading through the pipes outside the window. The truth was, she hadn't ever doubted that it would rain. She'd pretended to be uncertain for everyone else's sake, but she was never wrong about wet weather. She had an instinct for rain. And badly as she felt for Carla and Lennart (but especially for Carla, because she'd be the one in the long white dress, and long white dresses didn't go well with slick wet pavements and sodden muddy gardens), she couldn't help feeling just a little bit pleased with herself that her instincts – as well as her powerful forecasting programmes – had been right this time too.

Despite the fact that she was right, though, the downpour was as disappointing for her as for everyone else. She'd been looking forward to today ever since Carla had announced her engagement, and had been almost as excited about the wedding as her friend. She'd wanted clear blue skies and warm south-westerly breezes so that they could pose for pictures in the grounds outside the old stone church and on the sand at Ballyholme beach (although, in fairness, even glorious sunshine couldn't make an Irish beach look quite as glamorous as those on Barbados, which apparently had been Lennart's suggestion for the wedding location).

But as she'd studied the weather in the fortnight leading up to Carla's big day, Lainey had realised that grey skies were much more likely than blazing sunshine. So when she met her friend for coffee a few days beforehand, she told her to be prepared for the worst.

'What's the worst?' Carla asked.

Lainey broke the news about the probability of heavy downpours.

'You've got to be kidding me!' Carla wailed. 'It's July, for heaven's sake. Surely I should be entitled to a dry day and a bit of sunshine in July!'

Lainey was tempted to remind her that the last couple of Julys had been total washouts, and that planning for a dry day in an Irish summer was an exercise in hope over experience, but she simply looked at her friend in sympathetic silence.

'It's fabulous now.' Carla gestured in frustration at the china-blue sky, which looked so calm and settled, with its scattered streaks of ethereal white cirrus clouds. 'You can't possibly tell me that this will be gone by the weekend.'

Lainey knew it would be gone by the following day. It was always hard to accept, sitting in balmy sunshine, that the grey clouds would come rolling in, but she knew that they would. They weren't all that far away even now. She opened the meteorological chart she'd brought from her office on the table in front of her. Carla, who was tipping brown sugar into the foamy latte that the waitress had left with them a couple of minutes earlier, looked at it intently.

'You see this front? Coming from the Atlantic?' Lainey pointed at the chart, placing a saucer on the corner to stop it lifting in the summer breeze. 'That's the big problem. It's the tail end of the hurricane that hit the Florida coast earlier this week. My bet is that it's going to be sitting slap bang on top of us by tomorrow evening. And that's why it'll probably rain. And keep raining. All the same . . .' she tried to sound optimistic and encouraging as she pushed her sunglasses on to her head and looked at Carla from her dark blueberry eyes, 'you know forecasting is about probabilities. I could always have got things completely wrong and the weekend might be an absolute scorcher.' Although if she believes that, Lainey said to herself, she's either totally blinded by love or I'm a more convincing liar than I ever thought.

'You're never wrong,' conceded Carla glumly as she added more sugar to her coffee. 'In that case, I suppose we'd better rethink the photo shoot on the beach. Being soaked to the skin isn't my idea of a good look, and I'm certainly not going to ruin my gorgeous Pronuptia dress by dragging it over wet, seaweedy sand. I should've listened to Lennart and gone to Barbados after all.'

'Actually,' Lainey said comfortingly, 'you might have been just as badly off. There are more tropical storms due there this week.'

Carla laughed. 'Oh well! I suppose the weather isn't the most important thing anyway.'

'Of course not.' Lainey's voice was cheerful. 'The most important thing is that you're marrying the man you love.'

'And a man who's single and solvent and without any emotional baggage,' Carla told her with a grin.

'A rare and wonderful combination,' agreed Lainey. 'I'm looking forward to meeting him.'

'I can't wait for you to meet him too,' said Carla. 'I've so struck it lucky, Lainey. I really have.'

'Looks like we all have,' said Lainey. 'Val and Nick. You and Lennart. Me and Ken.'

Carla looked at her in surprise. 'You and Ken? Are you . . . have you . . . ?'

'Nothing definite yet,' said Lainey quickly. 'But . . . well, I really think that this time I've found Mr Right at last.'

'You do?' There was the merest hint of concern in Carla's voice.

'Absolutely,' Lainey said.

'Well, that's great.'

'I mean it,' she told Carla. 'This time it's different. This time I'm sure I've got it right.'

She understood why Carla was a little sceptical. Lainey had been sure she'd got it right twice before. Unfortunately, in both cases, despite having become engaged to first Ross and then Denis, she'd never made it as far as the altar. Admittedly the last time she'd had a ring on her finger had been five years earlier; she'd been twenty-six then and utterly certain that she'd found the man of her dreams. But the engagement had only lasted four months. It had taken her almost a year to get over it. Denis had told her that he cared about her a lot but, in all honesty, he'd come to realise that she was a bit too high-maintenance for him. And he couldn't commit his life to a high-maintenance woman. She'd asked what high-maintenance meant, and he'd said that if she didn't know, then he couldn't help her.

Lainey had been deeply hurt by Denis's remarks, but there was a part of her that knew she hadn't handled being engaged to him very well. That, in reality, it had taken her over. She'd accumulated folders and binders and all sorts of brochures about hotels, car hire, flowers and everything else wedding-related, and it had been her main topic of conversation whenever they were together. She understood that Denis might have been overwhelmed by her control-freaky plans and incessant wedding chatter. After he'd broken it off with her, she'd tried to explain to him that she'd lost the plot a little and that she'd get it all together for the future. But it was too late. The next time she'd seen him had been in a bar, and he'd been chatting animatedly to a petite blonde who was laughing at one of his jokes. It was hard to tell if she was a high-maintenance girl or not.

I used to laugh at his jokes too, Lainey had thought, as she did an about-turn and left the bar. I didn't realise our engagement was about to become one. And I never thought this would happen to me a second time.

She'd been twenty-one when she'd first got engaged. It had been two weeks before Christmas and she and Ross were walking home late one night from a party. He asked her what she'd like for a Christmas present and she snuggled up to his heavy jacket and said, 'You.' He kissed her and then she said half jokingly, 'And maybe a diamond ring too.'

On Christmas Eve he'd handed her the jewellery box with the ring nestling in the soft red velvet and she'd shrieked with delight and covered him in kisses before allowing him to slide the ring on to the third finger of her left hand. She loved the idea that someone cared about her enough to want to be with her for ever. And she loved Ross too. He was cute and kind and she was always happy to be with him. She reckoned that they were ideally suited. But by New Year's Day, after she'd told all her friends, shown them the ring and arranged three different engagement parties, he'd begun to wonder if they were rushing things. They were still at college, he reminded her. They weren't equipped to get married. He, in particular, wasn't ready yet. He was sorry for thinking that he had been. And so maybe it would be better to put it on hold, take a breather from each other and think about it for a bit longer. He hadn't said anything about her being high-maintenance. But after Denis's comments five years later, she wondered if her enthusiasm for everything wedding-related had seemed high-maintenance to Ross too.

She'd asked him if what he wanted was to be engaged without setting a date for the wedding, and he'd looked uncomfortable. It was then she realised that what he really wanted was to break it off altogether. That getting engaged to her in the first place had made him rethink their entire relationship and find it wanting.

Lainey had handed back the ring and told him that if he was unsure about marriage, it was absolutely the right decision. She'd waited until she was at home and locked in her bedroom before she burst into tears. When he heard about the broken engagement, her grandfather had murmured drily that the Christmas decorations had lasted longer, a comment that had caused her grandmother, Madeleine, to poke him in the ribs and tell him to shut up and keep his views to himself.

Two engagements, but no husband. Even though she'd been hurt each time the relationship hadn't worked out, Lainey reminded herself that they were worthwhile experiences. She'd learned from them, she told her grandparents. And her friends.

She'd said that to her mother too. (Well, the first time she'd simply told Deanna that it had been a silly mistake born from the romance of Christmas. The second time she'd said that she was the one who had doubts. She didn't want her mother to think that she'd been dumped again; that would have been too pathetic for words.) Deanna had sighed deeply on both occasions – although probably, Lainey thought, with relief – and told her that she should have more sense than to want to get married in the first place. She reminded her that nearly seventy per cent of divorces were initiated by women and that many of them said that they wanted to regain their self-identity in the process. She pointed out that men were possessive about women, especially beautiful women, which was probably why both Denis and Ross had wanted to put a ring on Lainey's finger and brand her as their own, regardless of how short-lived the branding was. And then she said that Lainey was very lucky to have escaped both times. Being considered beautiful, she reminded her, was a curse, not a blessing. It was important to keep that in mind.

* * *

People had always said she was beautiful. Even now, she remembered adults looking at her as a child and cooing over her with delight, murmuring that she was the loveliest girl they'd ever seen. It hadn't really made any impression on her back then. It just seemed natural. Later on (and whenever she was around to comment), Deanna would remind her sharply that most of the people who said she was pretty were just being polite. As well as which, she would add, beauty came from within and so counted for nothing if you weren't an intellectually curious person with it. Lainey was fairly sure that having a daughter who was considered beautiful rather than one who was famed for her intellectual curiosity was one of the biggest disappointments of her mother's life. And she agreed with Deanna (perhaps the one thing in life they completely agreed on) that being regarded as beautiful truly wasn't all it was cracked up to be. Besides, she didn't consider herself to be as beautiful as all that. When she looked in the mirror she always saw the flaws that other people seemed to miss.

Lainey Ryan was five foot eleven tall, and slender. (Too tall, in her opinion. It made her noticeable, and Lainey didn't like being noticed; however, she conceded that having a good figure was an asset, because she liked her food and it was nice not to be on a constant diet like some girls she knew.) Her hair was a glossy russet and fell in loose curls to her shoulders, framing a heart-shaped face with dark blue eyes and a rosebud mouth. (Hair: a bit unmanageable and always tangled first thing in the morning. Face: OK but prone to occasional dry patches, and, of course, there was the tiny silver scar over her eye that she'd got the day she'd jumped from the roof of the garden shed for a dare and cracked her head on the concrete path below. She was five at the time. Mouth: there was no denying it was sexy. Which wasn't always a good thing.) She had to admit that the whole package wasn't unattractive. The problem, though, was that being beautiful was a burden as much as a blessing. She read books and saw films in which the awkward, ungainly and plain girl (well, less pretty; it was Hollywood after all, and their view of plain was skewed beyond measure) always got the man in the end, because even though she didn't have the looks, she had a good heart. She would feel sorry for the prettier one then, doomed always to be unlucky in love because she didn't have a good heart and couldn't help her vanity. So Lainey also tried very hard not to be vain. She realised that there was no point in complaining about her height or her hair or even her scar, because her friends would snort and tell her that she was gorgeous and had nothing to worry about and then go on to complain about their own beauty problems. She had to learn to live with her looks. There was no getting away from them.

She'd had experience of dealing with them early on, because she'd been the butt of jealousy from some of the girls at her school, where she was regularly called Lanky Lay and where various cliques made it their mission to stop her getting too big for her boots by telling her that boys would only ever go out with her for one thing, because they didn't fall in love with gorgeous girls, they wanted ones with good personalities. Lainey wasn't sure how good her personality was, but she hoped that deep down it was OK, although it was hard to tell because she was quiet by nature, and despite her looks, she wasn't asked out on dates by the guys who swarmed around the less pretty but certainly more popular girls. (You're out of their league, Val, one of her small group of friends, told her. They're afraid of you. Val was averagely pretty, averagely intelligent and easy to get on with. She'd gone out with a few boys, but, she told Lainey with a sigh, none of them were as much fun as she'd expected. Boys were quite boring really. It was just that nobody considered you were anyone until you'd got off with one. Lainey had to take what Val said at face value back then. It wasn't until she went to college that she started dating properly.)

When she learned about the bullying, Deanna was angry. But Lainey couldn't help feeling that her anger was directed at the fact that the girls at school were caught up in caring about what the boys thought rather than the fact that they were making Lainey's life miserable. 'I despair,' Deanna had said, 'at how society moulds women into submissive beings at such a young age. And those damn brain-candy magazines that tell you how to make boys like you should be banned!'

Lainey didn't think her classmates were submissive at all – rather the opposite, in fact – but years later, after she'd studied Deanna's work, she understood what her mother meant. Not that it had been much use to her at fourteen. Back then, all she did was try to be liked by not drawing attention to herself and her looks, so she tied back her glorious hair, didn't attempt to make boys like her, and studied hard.

Later in life she decided that she'd probably applied herself to her studies to keep her mother happy too, and to prove to her that she really was as intellectually curious as Deanna wanted. She had to admit that it hadn't had the desired effect, because Deanna never seemed to consider that she'd done well enough. No matter how successful Lainey was, Deanna always remarked that she could have done better. And she was perpetually disappointed by the fact that her daughter's essays were marked down for lack of arguments, or for undeveloped thoughts.

Although she didn't excel in essays or in school debates, Lainey had a greater talent for subjects like maths and statistics that required definite answers rather than opinionated discussion. She chose to study physics at college because physics was a route into working in weather, and weather was something she truly loved.

In fact, weather fascinated her. She was intrigued by clouds and cloud formations, by the unexpected chill of a breeze on a sunny day, and by the sudden fog that sometimes rolled in from the sea. She liked finding patterns in warm and cold fronts, knowing that they could predict how the days ahead were going to be. And regardless of everything, she was still Deanna's daughter. She wanted a job that relied on how she was inside, not out. She had no intention (despite the suggestions of some of her college friends) of getting a portfolio of photographs and asking to be taken on by a modelling agency. She knew that she wouldn't be able to flaunt it the way women like Kate and Naomi and Erin and Claudia did. And she didn't want to anyway. She was happy to lose herself in warm and cold fronts, in isobars and isotherms, in things that she could understand even if she couldn't control them.

From the moment she'd started studying meteorology, Lainey had felt herself relax into her life in a way she hadn't done before. She liked knowing in advance whether skies would be clear or grey, and enjoyed being the one to tell other people to prepare for rain or sun. She was delighted when she started her job at Met Eireann, and she got on with the people she worked with. Even when she felt tense and uncertain inside, she'd learned to project a confident exterior, especially when it came to making forecasts. She enjoyed discussing weather with her colleagues and was happy that they accepted her opinions as worthwhile. Over the years she'd learned that people mistrusted beautiful women, assuming that they could be beautiful or brainy but not wanting them to be both. At work, they didn't seem to notice her looks; as far as they were concerned, it was her ability to interpret the data in front of her that was the most important thing about her. (Carla, one of her best friends since her college days, said that it was because nerdy meteorologists preferred graphs to gorgeousness. They don't notice your contours, she said; they're too obsessed with the ones on their charts.) However, Lainey accepted that it was the way she looked as much as her skills as a meteorologist that had led to her being on the roster of forecasters who presented the weather on TV. She wasn't naive enough to think otherwise.

When her department head had asked, almost a year earlier, for more staff who would be interested in being on the television weather roster, and Lainey hadn't bothered answering the email, he'd come to her and talked to her about it.

'I really don't think it's for me,' she said. 'I'm not into the idea of standing up in front of millions of people and making a fool of myself.'

'You won't make a fool of yourself,' said Martin.

'I don't like being the centre of attention.' She looked uncomfortable.

'They'll help you out,' he told her. 'You'll get training.'

'Even so.' Lainey shook her head. 'It's a lot harder than people give credit for.'

'You don't want to do it because it's too hard?' Martin

Browne looked puzzled. He'd always thought that Lainey liked new challenges. She was usually quietly determined in getting on with projects that interested her and firm about the resources she needed to complete them.

'It's not that,' she said hastily. 'It's just that there are plenty of others who are properly interested and who'd be way better at it than me.'

'But you'd look great.' Martin tried not to sound defensive.

'You want me because of how I look?'

'Not just that,' said Martin hastily. 'I think you'd be good at it.'

Her looks had never really helped her before, thought Lainey. They'd landed her in hopeless relationships and kept Deanna away, they'd worked against her when she wanted to be taken seriously and they'd set her apart from people all her life. This time maybe it would be different. This time being pretty was giving her an opportunity, even if getting a job because of her appearance seemed to be against every principle that had been drilled into her. And yet in a world obsessed with beauty, perhaps she was ridiculously old-fashioned. Maybe Deanna had always been wrong. Maybe it was time that she used every asset at her disposal to get ahead.

So she told Martin that she'd do the screen test and see how it went but that he wasn't to be surprised if they rejected her as being beyond help because she knew that not everyone could actually multitask in the way that you had to be able to to give a good weather forecast. Besides, she might be pretty, she added darkly, but she was also renowned for her ability to trip over her own two feet. So it was entirely possible that she'd reduce the studio to rubble and be written off as utterly hopeless.

But she wasn't hopeless. She didn't trip up. The camera loved her gentle voice and her easy way of building the weather story. Easy on the eye, easy on the ear, easy on the brain, she'd heard one of the cameramen say. A natural in front of the camera. She couldn't help feeling a little bit pleased at that. Although she wondered how Deanna would feel when, and if, she ever saw her on screen.

Lainey knew she looked good on TV. And suddenly she didn't mind. It was fun to make the most of her appearance, nice to chat to the make-up artists about various products, many of which she'd never used before. It was OK to read the beauty pages in glossy magazines and wonder about different looks. Because it was part of her job now. Not as important as actually getting the forecast right, of course. But being on TV gave her permission to be beautiful. And she couldn't help liking it.

It had been shortly after she'd started doing the broadcasts that she'd met Ken. At the time she'd been at the in-between stage of getting over another messy break-up (though thankfully not another engagement!) yet feeling that she should be making a bit more of an effort to get out and meet people. Carla and Val, still her two closest friends, had been nagging at her to start socialising instead of asking them over to her apartment for girlie evenings in, and she knew they were right. (She missed flat-sharing with them, because they'd been great every time she'd broken up with someone. But with Val now married and Carla dividing her time between Drogheda and Stockholm because she worked for a Swedish company with an Irish base, Lainey had been left to find somewhere by herself. She'd thought about moving back home, but her grandmother had very firmly told her that she had a life of her own now and should stay independent. Which was why she was renting the one-bed apartment in Laurel Park, a short distance from the Met Eireann offices.) But being alone was miserable when you'd broken up with someone, so when Alva Brennan, one of the other forecasters, told her about the exhibition of weather photography in a city centre gallery and mentioned that a few of them were going along, Lainey had said that she'd come too. And she was glad that she had, because that was where she'd met Ken, who'd wandered in quite by chance, simply because the gallery was near the office where he worked and his attention had been caught by the wonderful photograph of a double lightning strike in its window.

They'd started to talk when both of them were standing in front of a magical photo showing hoar frost on trees. Ken had remarked that it looked like something out of a fairy tale. And that 'hoar frost' sounded like a name from *The Lord of the Rings.* Or Harry Potter, he added. Certainly a magic spell of some description. Lainey told him that it was a result of the direct sublimation of water vapour in the ambient air. And when he'd looked at her blankly, she'd grinned and said it was just frozen dew. After they'd walked around the rest of the exhibition together and she'd explained some of the photos to him, Ken had asked her if she'd like to go for a drink and talk some more about meteorological terms. He liked the way she said words like 'vorticity' and 'anticyclone', he told her. He liked the fact that she knew what they meant. When she'd told him that it was her job to know, he'd smacked his forehead with the palm of his hand and wondered aloud how he hadn't realised before who she was.

The last time Lainey had gone for a drink with a man, the discussion hadn't touched on weather at all. Richard Hanson had dumped her over a glass of chilled white wine and left her sniffing into her tissue. She hadn't actually cried until after he'd left. But she'd nearly choked with the strain of keeping her eyes dry while he told her that he'd met someone else. Someone a little less high-maintenance.

High-maintenance again! Lainey had been swamped by despair. Why did they all think she was high-maintenance? She wasn't the sort of person who needed to be bought presents or taken on expensive dates. She was happy with relaxed nights in the pub, or going to the cinema and sharing a bucket of popcorn. But Richard told her she was looking at the wrong things. She was too possessive. She wanted to know what his plans were all the time. She wanted them to be constantly in touch with each other. She kept thinking of them as a unit instead of two separate people, which, he said, was very high-maintenance indeed. Plus, he added as he got up to leave, it was weird to date someone who preferred walking in the rain to lying out in the sun. (Which wasn't even true. She just found rain interesting, that was all. And strangely comforting.)

Walking through St Stephen's Green with Ken after the exhibition, she couldn't help admitting to herself that the last few years had been a relationship disaster for her and that she should really steer clear of men for a while. At least until she managed to work out how to be as low-maintenance as they wanted.

But she'd gone to the pub with Ken anyway and they'd hit it off instantly, finding a common interest in music and film – they both liked rock and roll and action movies, but also admitted to each other a secret fondness for power ballads, which Ken said he usually sang to himself when he was competing in triathlon events. Helped him to keep a good rhythm, he told her. (He worked in a sales office, but, he said, triathlon was what motivated him.) Lainey was impressed by his fitness – and very impressed with the ripped body that went with it – and also by his encyclopaedic knowledge of Hollywood blockbusters. It was late by the time they left the pub, and Lainey realised that for the first time in ages, she hadn't been thinking about the fool she'd made of herself over Richard Hanson. As she and Ken strolled down Grafton Street she wondered if he'd want to see her again. If tonight was the start of something important. Something that might lead to . . . well, no point in rushing things. No point in dreaming the dream too early. Not like she usually did. So if Ken Morgan asked her out again, she promised herself that she'd take things slowly. She wouldn't obsess over him. She wouldn't be demanding. She wouldn't phone or text him without a proper reason. And she'd keep her freaky interest in rain over sun to herself.

Ken phoned her the next day. He told her that it must have been fate that had made him go into the gallery that evening when he'd never bothered going in before. And that he wasn't one to fly in the face of chance. His words warmed her. Maybe, she thought as she hopped into a taxi taking her to the opposite side of the city to meet him, this relationship will be very different from the others I've had. And maybe he'd be different too. Maybe Ken would turn out to be the one. Maybe (no matter how much she tried not to let herself think it) this was a day she'd remember for the rest of her life, looking back on it in years to come, recalling how they'd met by chance and how it had been the start of something wonderful.

And her relationship with Ken *was* wonderful. He seemed to want to be with her as much as she wanted to be with him. Although she felt embarrassed at first, Ken never minded when people recognised her and asked her what the weather would be like the next day. He would smile at her afterwards and squeeze her waist and tell her that whatever the weather, she gave him a warm front. He made her join the same gym as him, where she'd pedal at a relaxed pace on a bike while he went at the cross-trainer with a fierce intensity. Being honest with herself, she found the gym incredibly boring. But she liked the idea that it was something Ken wanted to share with her.

However, she liked being alone with him most of all. She was happiest sitting in his townhouse in Rathmines, watching downloaded movies and eating microwave popcorn before making slow, languorous love to him in his mezzanine bedroom. Eventually she'd built up an accumulation of her own things there so that it had become a home from home. She had begun to wonder whether Ken would broach the subject of her moving in with him altogether. He'd made a few light-hearted comments about her taking over his place, but when she apologised and said that she'd bring her bits and pieces home again, he'd told her not to worry; they were fine where they were. She'd felt a warm glow when he said this, but at the same time she made sure not to increase the pile of her stuff. She wasn't going to have him thinking that she saw them as a unit instead of two people. Even if she was beginning to feel that way herself.

She loved Ken. More than she'd ever loved Richard Hanson. Or Ross or Denis or, indeed, any of her previous boyfriends, all of whom, sooner or later, had left her nursing a bruised heart and wondering if there was any such thing as true love and, if so, whether she had the remotest chance of finding it. This time, she told herself happily, this time she really had.

She wriggled from beneath Ken's arm and sat up in the bed. He groaned slightly and then rolled over so that he was lying on his back. She allowed her long hair to brush his face. In return, he pulled her close to him. He was definitely the one, she thought, as their lips met. The one, she thought with a sudden frisson of anticipation, who was coming to her best friend's wedding with her, and who didn't mind his name being linked with hers on the invitation and who'd even bought a new suit for the event. Which was a definite step forward, because men and weddings (certainly weddings in which they weren't the key player) were a notoriously tricky combination. But not today. Not for her and Ken. Which meant that they were going to have a wonderful time.

Lainey loved weddings. She loved the romance and the hope and the glamour and she'd loved them ever since she was five years old and had been a flower girl for her cousin Bethany. The invitation to be a flower girl had been down to her grandmother, who loved putting Lainey into pretty dresses, even though her granddaughter favoured shorts and dungarees, which were much more suitable for climbing the apple tree in the garden (and the garden shed from which she'd leaped so calamitously a few months earlier).

But Lainey had unexpectedly fallen in love with her pastel-pink satin dress and its wide cream sash, her matching cream ballet pumps and the pink and cream flowers threaded through her long, shining hair. She'd felt very important walking up the aisle as part of the bridal group and scattering her rose petals around the altar. She'd loved the photographs afterwards and she'd even enjoyed the reception, although she'd fallen asleep in the corner of the room when the dancing had started. Lainey knew that being a flower girl at Bethany's wedding had sown in her heart the seed of having the perfect wedding of her own, regardless of her mother's very definite views on the subject. (Afterwards she'd learned that the flower girl episode had caused a massive row between Deanna and Gran. She was glad she hadn't known anything about it at the time.)

There had been other weddings since then, though she'd never had an official part in the proceedings. But she'd still loved every minute of every one of them. There was something about weddings, Lainey thought, that made you feel that there was hope for the world. Something uplifting and enchanting. And that was why she wanted to get married herself.

Her own first engagement had been made and broken before she went to the next wedding, which was that of Val and her long-time boyfriend Nick. Val had known him since her schooldays and they'd been friends before eventually starting to go out together. Lainey always thought that Val and Nick were two of the most suited-to-each-other people she'd ever met. They'd married in a civil ceremony, which, naturally, had been much more low-key than Bethany's traditional church wedding. And although it had been lovely, Lainey knew that she herself preferred the whole bells and whistles, princess-for-a-day approach, which was in complete contrast to the way she normally lived her life.

She knew that there were probably ridiculous and complex reasons why she wanted a fairy-tale wedding of her own, although she had no intention of thinking it through and figuring out what they were. She knew that being married wasn't the most important thing in the world. She was well aware that life wasn't all about finding some mythical Mr Right. She also reminded herself that her mother would be disgusted to think that she had recurring wedding fantasies, and that this was probably the one thing in her whole life that Deanna was totally right about. But she couldn't help daydreaming. She couldn't help stopping outside a church for a glimpse of the bride whenever she realised that a wedding was taking place. And she couldn't help hoping for a big white wedding of her own. No matter how silly it was.

'We'd better get a move on.' Ken walked naked out of the bathroom. His wet hair stood up in spikes on his head but it was his lean, fit body that grabbed Lainey's attention. She told herself that she'd been lucky to find someone as drop-dead gorgeous as Ken. And that he'd look fabulous in his tux, though there was a lot to be said for looking at him the way he was now.

'I'll be ready soon.' She turned back to the mirror and carefully stroked her mascara wand through her already long lashes. Ever since starting to do the TV broadcasts, she'd got better at make-up. The girls at the TV studios had shown her tricks with creams and powders that had taught her how to make the most of her looks when the occasion warranted, although most days she stuck with tinted moisturiser and lip gloss.

'You look great,' Ken told her warmly. 'You could go like that.'

She grinned at his words. 'I don't think my friend and her family would approve if I sashayed into the church in nothing more than my bra and knickers.'

'You'd probably divert attention from the bride all right,' he agreed. 'But it does seem a shame to cover them up.'

Ken had bought her the lingerie set – dark red lace with tiny silk rosettes – for her birthday. They hadn't been going out for very long at the time and she'd been both shocked and gratified by the intimacy of the gift. (And by the fact that he'd got her size, 36B, exactly right.) She'd worn it that night for her birthday dinner in the intimate bistro round the corner from Ken's house. They'd gone back to his place as soon as the meal was finished and he'd removed it from her body. Which had been fun.

It was perfect for wearing underneath the dress she'd bought for Carla's wedding. It had taken her two Saturdays of intensive searching in Grafton Street, the Dundrum Town Centre Mall and some quirky side-street boutiques – as well as a large chunk of her monthly salary – to find one that she thought was just right; but she knew that the soft red dress with its detail of black flowers on the skirt fitted the bill perfectly.

Just about managing to ignore Ken's attempts to divert her from the dress, she put it on and stood in front of the mirror again. This time she began to work her thick curls into a loose up-do. Lainey would have loved poker-straight hair that she could have pulled into an elegant chignon, but she accepted that chic sophistication was never going to be her look. Her beauty was the untamed sort and nothing that she did would ever turn her into someone smoothly styled and groomed.

She watched Ken's reflection in the mirror in front of her as he got dressed and she worked on her hair, acknowledging that she'd been right about the tux. He looked very handsome. We are, she said to herself, going to be a gorgeous couple today. Like Brangelina were in their prime. Only a bit less flaky. Obviously. And right now Ken is by far better-looking than Brad ever was!

She opened the wardrobe door and took out a pair of shoes.

'You're not going to wear those, are you?' There was a note of concern in his voice.

'Well . . . yes.' She dangled them from her fingers, black with high heels and a tiny red bow on the front, which she knew would go perfectly with the red dress. She'd practised wearing them over and over again so that she could walk without tripping, which was always a bit of a worry for her when she was in heels. She didn't wear them regularly enough to stride out with confidence.

'I thought you were planning on your red sandals with that dress,' said Ken.

'They were an option,' she agreed. 'But they're not half as stylish. Besides, in case you'd forgotten, it's pissing rain. I'm going for a combination of dry feet and style.'

Ken looked at the black shoes again. 'You're going to fall,' he warned. 'You always fall when you wear high heels.'

'Not always,' she protested.

'You fell down the stairs last week,' Ken reminded her.

'Not because of my shoes,' she said defensively. 'I was wearing my trainers then.'

'I suppose you didn't bother bringing the sandals because you knew it was going to rain?'

She nodded.

'Sometimes a little knowledge is a dangerous thing.' Ken quoted Einstein at her. 'You'd be safer in flatties.'

She stuck her tongue out at him. The sandals were pretty but the shoes were perfect. Besides, having left the sandals at home, they were the only shoes she had with her that went with the red dress. Her other footwear consisted of the trainers she'd worn on the drive from Dublin to Bangor and the flat ballet pumps she'd planned for the trip back the following day. (The rain should have stopped by then. She was expecting a bit of watery sunshine.)

She slid the shoes on to her feet. Then she inspected herself in the long wardrobe mirror. She looked good. She still would have liked a sleek hairdo (her own reminded her too much of a darker version of Tilda Swinton's do as the Wicked Witch in *The Chronicles of Narnia*), but her dress was fabulous and the shoes were perfect.

Ken stood behind her. Immediately she realised what was really bothering him. The high heels, teamed with the added height of the Wicked Witch hairstyle, meant that she was at least a couple of inches taller than him. In her delight at having such a good dress-and-shoe combo, she'd completely forgotten precisely how tall the heels would make her. She patted her hair in an effort to flatten it down a bit, but it was held in place by industrial quantities of gel and spray and didn't budge.

'You look sensational.' He slid his arms around her and she exhaled slowly in relief. Obviously it would be stupid of him to be upset about her height, but she could understand how he might be. After all, most men liked to be tall and protective beside the woman they were with. She would've preferred him to be taller than her too. But there was nothing she could do about it now.

He kissed the nape of her neck and she shivered with pleasure.

'What's especially nice,' he murmured, 'is that everyone will look at you and think how lovely you are, but I'm the only one who can unwrap the packaging.'

She giggled.

'And I intend to do just that,' he said. 'Right now.'

'We might have time,' said Lainey doubtfully, 'but not if you mess my hair and make-up.'

'That'd be a total crisis, would it?' he joked.

'Absolutely,' she assured him. 'I don't want to be the cause of us arriving late and for people to think I'm a wanton slut.'

'They won't know we've been doing wanton things,' said Ken.

'I bet they will,' murmured Lainey as she turned to kiss him anyway.

Chapter 2

Isobar: a line of equal atmospheric pressure drawn on a weather map

Carla's older brother, Roy, and his wife, Hazel, were waiting in the foyer of the hotel when Ken and Lainey eventually made their way downstairs. Lainey was hoping that her flushed cheeks and bright eyes would be put down to make-up and excitement over Carla's big day, and not because the sex with Ken had been absolutely great. He was good at urgent sex, she thought. He managed to make it exciting and arousing and she was totally turned on by the quickness of it all. Whatever people said about taking your time and making it sensual (and there were nights when she definitely wanted the whole scented candles and mutual massage regime), there was something thrilling about sex in a hurry.

As they walked across the foyer, she cleared her mind of thoughts about sex with Ken. She wanted to focus on being the perfect girlfriend today. Not the tarty madam who was already wondering when they could do it again.

The original plan had been to stroll from the hotel on the

outskirts of Carla's home town of Bangor, in Northern Ireland, to the small stone church ten minutes away. But with heavy rain sheeting from the ever-darkening sky and a stiff wind whipping up the water of the marina, walking wasn't an option.

'Did you ever think it would be this bad?' Hazel looked enquiringly at Lainey, who shrugged helplessly.

Although Carla's two sisters, Sharon and Jodie, had occasionally called to the flat in Dublin, Lainey had never met her brother and his wife before. Roy had introduced himself the previous night when she and Ken were in the hotel restaurant. He said he'd recognised her straight away and asked them if they'd like to join him and Hazel for a drink after their meal. Like Carla, Roy had moved from his home town and was now living and working in Glasgow, so he and Hazel were also staying in the hotel. Over a couple of drinks in the bar they'd discussed the unseasonal weather, lamenting the fact that Carla had picked this week instead of the previous one for her wedding and staring at Lainey as though she could magically make the clouds disappear.

'It wasn't looking great,' Lainey admitted as they waited for the taxi that Ken had ordered. 'But you always hope, I guess.'

'Poor Carla. She planned everything so carefully,' said Hazel. 'It's terribly bad luck to have this kind of day in July.'

'I know.'

'This is such a lovely location when the sun is shining,' added Hazel. 'They could have had photos outside the church and at the marina . . .'

'She wanted some on the beach,' remarked Lainey.

'If she'd wanted a beach she should've gone somewhere

with guaranteed weather,' said Roy as they peered out of the hotel's double glass doors.

'How long before the taxi arrives?' Hazel looked anxious.

'I think this is it now,' replied Ken as a blue people carrier pulled up. He went outside and then gestured to them. Although it was only a few yards from the shelter of the building to the car, the ferocity of the rain meant that they got very wet.

They got wet again as they scurried up the winding pathway to the church. Lainey was just behind Hazel when she slipped on one of the cobblestones. She managed to stay upright for half a second, her arms flailing wildly, before she landed with a thud that jarred every bone in her body.

She was too shocked to get up straight away and felt the rain from the stones seep through her red dress as she sat on the ground. It was Ken who grabbed her by the hand and dragged her to her feet.

'You clown,' he said. 'I warned you. You know I did. Are you all right?'

'Yes. I think so.' But Lainey's wrist hurt from where she'd tried to break her fall, she'd scraped her knees and twisted an ankle; while a lock of her hair, rigid with hairspray, had come free of its clips. She tried to pin it back into place, wincing as the pain from her wrist shot up her arm.

'You can do that inside,' said Ken impatiently. 'C'mon, Lainey, we're drowning out here.'

She was limping as he hustled her into the church. They stood at the back while she took her right shoe off. The heel had come loose. As she examined it, it came away in her hand and she looked at it in dismay. There was a large damp patch on her red dress too, which was streaked with dirt. Lainey wanted to cry but she didn't let herself. She was quite wet enough already. And she didn't want to add mascara tracks on her cheeks to her by now bedraggled look.

'Anything broken?' asked Ken.

'No bones,' she said as she flexed her wrist gingerly. 'But the heel has come off my shoe.' Her voice wobbled.

'Well there's nothing you can do about it now.' Ken was looking at her with an expression of exasperation mixed with concern.

'I'm such an eejit.' She couldn't keep the frustration out of her voice. 'I shouldn't be let out.'

'Don't worry about it. Nobody will take any notice of you. It's Carla they've come to see.'

He was right, she knew. But it didn't make her feel any better.

'Come on,' he said as he took her by the arm. 'Let's find our seats. You'll be safer sitting down.'

Sliding into a pew near the front of the church was some consolation for hobbling up the aisle, Lainey decided, although she wondered what the Carmodys were thinking of her as she took her place in her bare feet. She liked Carla's mum, Jayne, who was relaxed and easy-going and who had a reasonable relationship with Carla's father, whom she'd divorced ten years earlier. Carla's dad had brought his new girlfriend to the wedding (the one element of the day that had stressed her friend) and Eilis had shaken hands with Jayne, which Lainey knew would keep Carla happy.

The relentless drumming of the rain could still be heard over the background organ music, which was gentle and calming. Lainey felt herself begin to relax as she listened to it. Ken was right. Nobody was here to look at her. It was all about Carla. Hardly anyone would have noticed her tumble. She brushed some drying bits of clay from the side of her dress and wriggled in her seat so that she wasn't sitting directly on the damp patch.

She glanced around her and spotted Val and Nick, who'd driven from Dublin that morning rather than coming up the night before. She waved at her friend, who was looking gorgeous in a pale yellow suit. Yellow was a colour that didn't really suit Lainey's slightly Mediterranean complexion, but it looked fabulous on her blonde, fair-skinned friend. And, of course, it had the added advantage of being clean and dry!

The church looked fabulous too. Carla had spared nothing when it had come to the flowers on the altar and the posies at the end of each pew, which brought warmth and colour to the rather austere grey brickwork of the interior. If it had been a better day, thought Lainey, if the sun had been shining as Carla had wanted, then the altar would have been illuminated by coloured light from the narrow stained-glass windows. But as it was, the flowers, and the congregation, were doing all the work.

There was no sign of the groom. Lainey hadn't yet met the single and solvent Lennart Soderling. Carla had kept the relationship quiet, not even mentioning it to her two best friends until they came to Stockholm to visit for a long weekend. They'd stayed with her in the small apartment provided for her by the company and had enjoyed themselves tremendously in the glorious sunshine of early summer.

It had been while they were having lunch in a waterside restaurant that Carla had pointed at an elegant building on the other side of the canal and told them that her boyfriend lived there.

'Boyfriend?' Lainey allowed her fork to drop on to her plate in surprise. 'I didn't know you were seeing anyone.'

'Have been for a few weeks now,' said Carla.

'Is this serious?' demanded Val.

'It could be,' admitted their friend.

They were still surprised when she announced the engagement, and a little peeved that they hadn't yet been introduced to the man who had apparently swept her off her feet. But Carla said he was tremendously busy and that they'd eventually get to see him, but that she could promise them he was the man of her dreams.

They'd been in Val's house that night, Carla having come back to Dublin for a few weeks.

'And is he coming to Ireland?' asked Lainey as she nibbled on some Pringles. 'Does he need to check out your heritage?'

'He's been to Bangor already,' admitted Carla. 'He met Mum and Dad and did the whole asking for my hand in marriage thing.'

'No!' Val's blue eyes danced.

'Absolutely,' said Carla. 'He's quite old-fashioned.'

'I can't wait to meet him,' said Lainey. 'He sounds such a pet.'

Three men walked past the front pews and stood at the altar on the groom's side. The Swedish contingent at the wedding was quite small, but easily identified, because almost all of them were stereotypically blond. Lainey knew that one of the three men had to be Lennart, but she wasn't sure which of them it could be. They were all tall (one was positively lanky), but none of them quite matched Carla's description of broad-shouldered and definitely handsome.

She checked her watch. The ceremony had been due to start fifteen minutes ago but of course the bride was always allowed to be late. She wondered how she'd deal with that herself. She was a punctual person at heart and didn't like being late for anything. She knew she'd be itching to walk in the door of the church exactly on time, which would make her appear far too eager!

The background music changed abruptly to Handel's 'Arrival of the Queen of Sheba' and there was a rustling at the back of the church. Then Carla began her walk up the aisle, holding the arm of her father and smiling at the assembled guests.

As she drew closer, Lainey could see the happy, expectant smile on her friend's face. Carla was striking rather than pretty, with caramel hair and grey-green eyes. Today, though, she truly was radiant as she walked by with a swish of her narrow-bodiced Tudor-style dress. Its extravagant full skirt, adorned with pearls and trimming, which Lainey reckoned had cost a fortune, skimmed the red carpet. Sharon and Jodie, the bridesmaids, were also wearing Tudor-style dresses, decorated in green and gold.

Lainey felt her eyes well with tears and she bit her lip hard to stop them from falling. It was too early to cry, for heaven's sake. She should at least wait until the ceremony had actually started! But still . . . She sniffed and took a tissue out of her tiny black bag. Carla was her best friend. It was OK to cry at her best friend's wedding.

Carla and her father stopped at the top of the aisle and the vicar welcomed them. Then the shortest of the three men at the altar took Carla by the hand. Lainey's eyes widened in surprise. She hadn't thought that the least prepossessing of the three would turn out to be the single, solvent groom, the man who Carla called 'my ideal husband'. She looked over at Val and could see an expression of surprise on her face too. Was this why Carla hadn't introduced them to Lennart before now? Because she would have seen their surprise? And because she would have had to answer their inevitable question, which was how much older than her he was. Not that it mattered, of course. Age wasn't important. Love was. Perhaps he wasn't that much older anyway. All the same, Lainey thought, if Lennart Soderling was under fifty, she'd be very surprised indeed.

The rain was still falling heavily when they left the church after the ceremony. The photographer abandoned his plans for shots in the carefully tended gardens of the church, as well as the pictures on the beach that Carla had wanted. Instead, she and Lennart immediately got into their limo for the short drive to the hotel. Other guests who'd driven to the church sprinted to their cars. Val and Nick went with one of Carla's aunts; Ken and Lainey (who was walking barefoot over the cobbles and wincing with every step) were offered a lift by a cousin. They squashed into the back seat of Stephen's Ford Ka and were grateful that the drive was a short one.

The champagne reception back at the hotel quickly banished the guests' disappointment at the dismal weather. Lainey left Ken sipping a glass of bubbly and chatting to one of the other guests while she went up to their room to repair the damage from her fall. Her dress had dried out, but there was a large stain where she'd landed and there was no way she could wear it for the rest of the day. She pulled it over her head in frustration. She'd spent ages searching for the perfect dress and it had lasted less than an hour! As for her shoes – well, Ken had been right. She was hopeless in high heels, and not just because she towered over him.

She opened the wardrobe door and took out her Kate Moss skinny jeans. She had nothing else to change into. She couldn't believe that she was about to wear a pair of two-year-old jeans and a purple wrap-around top to her best friend's glamorous wedding reception. She put on her ballet pumps, retouched her make-up and tidied her hair, which, despite the hairspray, now looked like Narnia's Wicked Witch after she'd stuck her finger in an electric socket. She sighed as she stared at herself in the mirror. Still beautiful. Nothing could change that. But not elegant. Nothing like she'd hoped.

There was a tap at the door and she hurried to open it. At least Ken had come to see how she was getting on. That was why she loved him.

But it was Val who was standing outside.

'What the hell happened?' she asked. 'I saw you in the church. You looked as though you'd been run over by a combine harvester.'

'Thanks,' said Lainey wanly, and explained about the fall.

'You dope.' But Val's words were warm. 'Honest to God, I don't know why you persist with heels. It's not like you need them.'

'I know, I know. Ken was pissed off at me wearing them because they made me taller than him. But I thought I looked good. I guess pride comes before a fall and all that.'

'You don't need killer heels to look good,' said Val. 'Have you got anything else to wear?'

'Only what I've got on now.'

'I wish I could help out,' said Val. 'But I don't have a change of clothes with me, and besides, there's no direction in which any of my stuff would fit you.' Val was seven inches shorter than her and had always been curvy.

'Never mind,' said Lainey philosophically. 'I'll load on a bit more make-up; might distract them from the jeans.'

'Attagirl.' Val patted her on the back. 'Anyway, people will be sympathetic. It could've happened to anyone.'

'Unfortunately these kind of cock-ups usually happen to me,' said Lainey as she took out her lip gloss and began to apply it.

As soon as she came downstairs again, Ken put his arm around her and told her she looked great.

'I look like a gatecrasher,' she replied.

'Don't be so silly,' he said. 'You'd look fab in a sack.'

His words of comfort made her feel a whole lot better, even though she couldn't help rueing her clumsiness.

'I'm surprised I didn't end up on my ear too.' Eilis Gaffney, who'd left Carla's dad talking to her mum and was looking a bit lost, stood beside Lainey. 'I'm wearing knock-off Louboutins and I can hardly put one foot in front of the other. I'm so crippled I don't know how I got up that path myself.'

'The things we do for style,' said Lainey.

Eilis chuckled. 'You'll definitely be the most comfortable of us all later. We'll be bursting out of our dresses or nursing our blisters and you'll be right as rain.'

'I take it you're a silver-lining sort of person,' said Lainey.

'Have to be,' said Eilis pragmatically. 'Girlfriend of the bride's da. Here only because of intense family negotiations.'

'I think it's nice that you managed to come to an agreement.'

Eilis's expression was half-hearted. 'It's really because of Lennart. Both his parents have divorced and remarried and are here with their partners. So Carla and her mother felt they couldn't say no to me.'

'Did you actually want to come?' asked Lainey curiously.

'It was important to me,' confided Eilis. 'I didn't want to be sitting at home while Andrew was here. I suppose that makes me sound pathetic.'

'Not really.' Lainey considered it. 'You've been with him for a good while now, haven't you?'

'Over a year,' confirmed Eilis.

'Are you going to get married?'

'Million-dollar question,' replied Eilis. 'I don't know.' She glanced over Lainey's shoulder to where Ken was talking to one of Lennart's family. 'How about you?'

Lainey felt the little trip of her heart that always happened when she thought about marrying Ken. 'Plenty of time yet.'

'True,' said Eilis. 'After all, Lennart waited till he was fifty-one.'

So he was exactly twenty years older than Carla. Not that age mattered so much these days, Lainey thought, but it was still a big gap.

'I told her that she was taking on a big task. An unbroken-in man. He hasn't been married before, you know.'

'So I heard,' Lainey said. 'Carla never mentioned his age when she was telling us. Not that she had to, of course, but . . .'

'I guess it doesn't matter if she's happy.'

'Most important thing,' agreed Lainey, and then the bell rang for dinner and they all went to the dining room.

* * *

The ceremony at the church had been an Irish one, but the hotel dining room had been decorated in the Swedish colours of yellow and blue, and the meal was a Scandinavian-style buffet. Lainey, who'd acquired a taste for the food in college thanks to the nearby Swedish deli, loaded her plate with meatballs in creamy sauce and tucked in happily.

Carla's father opened the speeches with one in praise of his daughter, then Lennart spoke, telling the assembled guests that he'd never imagined he'd find someone like her in his life. Carla spoke too, saying that she'd known from the moment she met him that Lennart was the man for her.

'I bet,' murmured Ken to Lainey. 'He's loaded, you know.'

'He's the MD of the company Carla works for, so I suppose he's well off,' agreed Lainey. 'Carla told me she was glad to find someone single and solvent.'

'More than solvent,' said Ken. 'He's worth a few million.'

'Really?' Lainey looked at her boyfriend in surprise. When Carla had talked about Lennart, she'd concentrated on his qualities as a person – his kindness, his good humour, his ability to make her laugh (and, she'd said, winking, a reasonable ability in bed too). She hadn't breathed a word about millions in the bank.

'So his brother told me,' said Ken as he dipped a prawn into Lainey's meatball sauce. 'He's the financial success of the family as well as the patron of a children's charity in Sweden, so he has a social conscience too.'

'Very worthy,' agreed Lainey.

'It seems your friend has landed on her feet,' said Ken.

'Indeed it does,' said Lainey as, in keeping with tradition, another one of the Swedish guests stood up to make a speech in honour of the bride and groom.

* * *

Later in the evening, when most of the guests were dancing, Carla came and sat beside her. Except for a quick word of congratulation, Lainey hadn't spoken to her all day. She told her that she was having a great time, that the food had been wonderful and that the band was fantastic.

Carla rearranged the Tudor-style dress so that it fell neatly around the chair. 'And there hasn't been a brawl or a massive misunderstanding and someone flouncing out in tears yet either.'

'Were you expecting one?'

'You know how it is,' said Carla. 'Someone drinks too much and says what they really think to someone else, and the next thing you know there's a family feud that lasts for generations. Also, with both Eilis and Mum here, I was a bit worried that sparks might fly.'

'That would have been a bit of a drama all right. I'm glad it didn't happen.'

'Me too. The only glitch was your fall in the churchyard. Are you all right? Ken told me it was quite a crash. He was afraid you'd really hurt yourself.'

'Only my pride,' said Lainey. 'But it doesn't matter. I'm glad to be here. It's a great day.'

'Sorry you didn't get to meet Len beforehand.'

'So am I.'

'I'm sure you were a bit surprised,' said Carla.

'Oh?' Lainey was nonchalant.

'Get over yourself, Ryan.' Carla punched her gently in the arm. 'He's probably not what you were expecting.'

'He's the man of your dreams and that's the most important thing.' Lainey's tone was sincere.

'Too right,' said Carla. 'His own house, his own hair and his own teeth. A total dreamboat.'

'Carla!' Lainey laughed.

'He's mature,' said Carla. 'An adult. I'm so fed up with juvenile, self-obsessed men.'

'I can understand that,' agreed Lainey.

'I met him and I realised that this was a man who I could be happy with.'

'And who would be head-over-heels in love with you. And you with him, of course.'

'You're such a hopeless romantic, Lainey Ryan!'

'But it *is* romantic,' Lainey protested. 'His speech was wonderful, all about thinking that the chance to meet someone had passed him by and then finding you . . .'

'Well I found him, to be honest,' said Carla. 'It was hard work getting it to the stage where he asked me to marry him.'

Lainey stared at her.

'A fifty-year-old unmarried man!' Carla grinned. 'He's had a lot of experience of not getting caught by women. It took a lot of effort to nail him, I assure you.'

'But . . . but he loves you. And you love him.'

'Whatever love is,' said Carla wickedly.

'What d'you mean?'

'Well, even though I say it myself, he's acquiring a very presentable wife. And I'm getting a man who has a successful career, three houses – although one is just a cabin in the forest really – a decent pension plan and money in the bank. The way I look at it, it's a perfect recipe for love.'

Lainey looked startled.

'Oh, come on,' said Carla as she watched the changing expressions flit across her friend's face. 'You've been engaged twice. You can't possibly believe in it all being about moons,

Junes and romance. There's more to marriage than a warm glow and good sex.'

'You can't mean that!'

'Of course I do,' said Carla firmly. 'I thought about it a lot when I turned thirty. I went through all my past boyfriends and wondered why on earth I'd wasted my time on any of them. I reckon modern society has totally lost its way when it comes to marriage. All of this searching for true love. You can make anyone love you. But they won't stay in love. The old matchmakers were right. You need to base marriage on something far more secure than that.'

'Well, yes, but . . .'

Carla smiled complicitly at her. 'I know that people are thinking that because Len is quite a bit older than me I might be making a terrible mistake. But I'm not. I know what I'm doing and so does he. He's a businessman and he needs to have someone to support him socially. There comes a time when bringing a new woman to every event becomes more trouble than it's worth. He wants someone who'll be an asset to him. And I will.'

'You sound like someone from a Victorian book.' Lainey couldn't believe what Carla was telling her. 'Or from one of those "How to Be a Good Housewife" articles from the fifties that we laugh about now. I can't believe you're sincere about all this, Carla. There's a whole lot more to life than just being a wife. You know that.'

'Of course I do,' said her friend equably. 'But when you decide to get married, it's important to realise that marriage is a partnership. And that sometimes you're better off not being crazy in love with the person you're married to.'

'But you're in love with Lennart, surely?' Lainey was

confused. 'You sounded in love when you first told me about him.'

'Love is only a small part of it,' Carla replied. 'There are vastly more important reasons for marrying someone. Like money. And security. I get all of them with Lennart. I wasn't looking for Mr Perfect when I met him. I was looking for someone who was good enough for me. And Lennart is.'

Lainey was spared having to think a suitable response because Lennart himself came over to join them. He was taller than he'd appeared in the church, she realised, and he radiated authority and charisma. She realised why Carla found him attractive.

'Having fun?' he asked.

'Great wedding.'

'Excellent. We hope that when we get back from Tuscany, you and Ken will come to visit us. We will be spending a few months in Stockholm.'

'That would be lovely.'

'Wonderful.' Lennart held his hand out to Carla. 'Come on, Mrs Soderling,' he said. 'They're playing our song. Time for you to join me on the dance floor again.'

'Whatever you say, Mr Soderling.' Carla beamed at him. As he put his arm around her and drew her closer to him, she looked over his shoulder and winked impishly at Lainey, who was watching them, a bewildered expression in her eyes.

Lainey had always believed in One True Love. She'd believed in it from the time her grandmother started reading bedtime stories to her, filling her mind with images of Cinderella and Sleeping Beauty and Rapunzel, who had all triumphed over the obstacles in their way, found their Prince Charming and lived happily ever after. She'd believed in it when she read romantic novels as relaxation after her day's studies. She knew, of course, that romantic novels always ended happily and that in real life not everyone found the right person. And that even if you did, there was no guarantee that it would be right for ever. Her own family life had taught her that. But she believed that it *could* be for ever. And she wanted to believe that, for her, it would.

Clearly she hadn't got it right yet. Her two engagements were a testament to that. However, she knew that she was more mature now, and more realistic too, despite her longing for a fairy-tale ending. She knew that day-to-day living with someone was different from the sparkle and excitement of dating a new man. After all, she practically lived with Ken. She'd seen his dirty socks in the laundry basket and the mouldy cheese he frequently forgot about in his fridge. She'd even helped him unblock the drain in his shower. (She'd felt bad about that. The problem had been caused by her hair.) But she knew that if (when?) she and Ken got married, it would be because she loved him. Not because she thought that he was good for her in some practical way. Not because she thought she was good for him either.

So she was utterly stunned by Carla's admission that love was only part of the reason she was marrying Lennart Soderling. She was equally taken aback by the fact that Carla seemed to be perfectly happy to allow Lennart to be in charge in the relationship because he was the one who controlled the purse strings. Carla had always been a career girl before, interested in her work and scathing about women who relied on men for anything. Yet she'd changed utterly because of Lennart Soderling. And because of his money.

Lainey couldn't help feeling that she and Carla between them had somehow got love and practicalities very mixed up. Lainey wanted true love and romance, but she also wanted to have her career. Carla seemed to be lukewarm on the love and romance element but was prepared to make her marriage her career. Lainey wondered which of them was right.

She glanced at Ken, who was gyrating to the sound of the Bee Gees. She was perfectly sure that he wouldn't want her to give up her job at Met Eireann. She knew that he was proud of her and liked seeing her on the TV talking about the weather. He liked knowing that he was the one going out with a woman whom everyone in the country knew. Or thought they knew. He always texted her after her broadcast, whether she was coming back to his house or not. Reminding her about his warm front. He loved her, she was sure about that. She loved him too. Surely their relationship was far more solid than Carla and Lennart's? Because it was based on a better foundation.

Ken saw her looking at him and waved.

'Come on!' She made out the words he was saying although she couldn't hear him. 'Come on.'

She got up from her seat. Her ankle still ached and she knew that she'd probably make a fool of herself on the dance floor. But for the man she loved, she was prepared to take the chance.

Chapter 3

Arcus: a long, dark horizontal cloud running along the base of a storm cloud

She didn't feel as self-conscious as usual dancing, possibly because everyone knew she'd hurt her ankle and didn't expect much from her, but more likely because nobody else seemed to be self-conscious at all. Certainly not Carla's Uncle Jim, easily in his seventies, who was jitterbugging with one of her younger cousins, oblivious to the fact that his candy-striped shirt had worked its way free of his trousers and was flapping merrily above his generous pink belly. Nor Lennart's Aunt Marta, who was kicking up her heels with the best of them despite having no sense of rhythm whatsoever. In fact all of the guests had thrown any reservations they might have had about how they looked completely out of the window as they bopped the night away.

Eventually Lainey pleaded exhaustion and took herself back to the table, where she sat and sipped a sparkling water while propping her leg on an empty chair. Jayne Carmody, Carla's mother, joined her a moment later, saying that it was lovely to see her and asking how she was after her fall.

'I'm fine, thanks.' Lainey repeated the words she said to everyone who'd asked her how she was, even though her ankle was now throbbing and her scraped knees still stung from time to time.

'You'll have to wear flatties the day you get married yourself,' said Jayne. 'Can't have you throwing yourself around the churchyard in a wedding dress.'

'You're so right,' agreed Lainey, who had long since decided that flat shoes would be a necessity for her own nuptials. Especially if it all went right with Ken and he was the one. She wouldn't want to tower over him on their wedding day, after all!

'And is there any chance of a wedding on the horizon?' asked Jayne, glancing to where Ken was dancing with one of Carla's cousins, a slim redhead whose sense of rhythm was far superior to Lainey's own.

'Who knows.' Lainey tried to sound nonchalant, even though she'd been thinking of her own wedding for most of the day. 'Fingers crossed. If you're allowed to cross your fingers.'

'I'm sure you are.' Jayne got up from the seat. 'Oh, well, that was a nice rest, but I'd better circulate. The work of the mother-of-the-bride is never done.'

Lainey watched her go. She wondered how Deanna would enjoy being the mother-of-the-bride. Then she pulled herself together. She had to get real. Deanna wouldn't enjoy it at all. Not that Lainey had to worry, because no doubt her mother would boycott the wedding on principle anyway.

Ken eventually flopped on to the chair beside her. 'I'm wrecked,' he said. 'It's far more energetic out there than doing a triathlon.

More dangerous too. That woman Marta nearly took my eye out a couple of times with her elbow.'

'She's enthusiastic all right,' said Lainey.

'You didn't stay out there long.'

'I'm a bit tired myself,' she told him. 'And my ankle aches. I think I have a bruise on my bum too.'

'I'll have to check that out later.' He winked lasciviously at her and she laughed.

As soon as the band finally finished up for the night, the guests who weren't staying at the hotel began to drift home. Meanwhile all of the Swedish guests and a large group of the Irish too made their way to the residents' lounge to continue the celebrations. Carla and Lennart were among them. Carla said that she didn't want such a fabulous day to end and Lennart seemed perfectly happy to stay up all night if that was what she wanted. Jayne had gone to bed, though, while Andrew and Eilis had gone home.

Lainey and Ken sat side by side on a comfortable sofa. Both of them were drinking mineral water to rehydrate themselves.

'Well, Lainey!' Carla beamed at her from the opposite side of the room. 'What d'you think? A good day?'

'A great day,' Lainey agreed. 'Excellent. Couldn't have been better.'

'Except for the weather!' everyone chorused.

'Och, I didn't care about it in the end,' Carla said. She leaned her head on Lennart's shoulder. 'I married the man I wanted, that's all that matters.'

'And I married the woman I love.' Lennart looked fondly at her.

'That only leaves you, Lainey, out of the three of us,' Val piped up. 'What're the chances?'

Lainey shot a daggered look at her friend. Val was practically lying in an armchair beside Carla having clearly had too much to drink. Otherwise she never would have made the remark.

'Now would you stop putting ideas into her head!' Ken squeezed Lainey's shoulders. 'All this wedding stuff is great fun, but we have the perfect arrangement as it is, don't we, babes?'

She smiled at him. 'Sure we do.'

'Together when we want to be and the freedom to do whatever takes our fancy otherwise.' Ken chortled. 'Why in God's name would we change all that?'

'I was single for fifty-one years and thought I was happy. But one day being married beats all that.' Lennart looked self-satisfied. 'You should think about it too, Ken. It has its advantages.'

Lainey held her breath. Ken was never comfortable with being put on the spot, and this was a spot that she didn't want him feeling uncomfortable about.

'I don't want to mess up an ideal relationship!' Ken sounded horrified. 'And I know Lainey's very happy with things the way they are too. As she's told me time after time, hasn't she got a great apartment of her own just a stone's throw away from work? Why would she even think about moving in with me on the other side of the city and give herself all that commuter stress?'

Lainey saw Val and Carla exchange glances. She knew what they were thinking. Lainey Ryan would give up her single girl's apartment in a flash if it meant tripping up the aisle.

'If you get married—'

'Lennart, put a sock in it.' Carla sat up straight and frowned at her new husband. 'You're making them feel awkward.'

'Sorry. Sorry.' Lennart looked abashed. 'I have obviously got marriage on the brain right now. I didn't mean to upset you, of course, Ken. Lainey.'

'You didn't upset us,' said Lainey as casually as she could. 'Don't worry, Lennart.'

'Oh, good.' Lennart looked relieved.

'You see,' Ken said. 'Not all of us feel that we have to go down the marriage route. Some of us are freedom-lovers. That's why Lainey and I are a good couple. We both want exactly the same thing.'

It was an hour later when Ken and Lainey left the (now much smaller) group of diehards and went to their room. She slid her ballet pumps from her feet, took off the wrap-around top and shimmied out of her jeans. The she went into the bathroom, wiped off her make-up and cleaned her teeth. Finally she tugged a brush through her tangle of gelled curls and got into the double bed.

Ken went into the bathroom after her. He was careful about his skin and liked doing a cleansing and moisturising routine himself. But, Lainey thought as she lay in bed waiting for him, the results proved that he was right to take the time. She'd truly never gone out with anyone better looking in her life.

'I'm knackered,' he said as he got into the bed beside her.

'Me too,' she agreed. 'But it was a wonderful day.'

'They didn't skimp on anything,' he said. 'Though meatballs for dinner was a bit weird.'

She rolled over and he put his arm around her. 'What

would you have instead? A traditional turkey-and-ham kind of thing?'

'I haven't thought about it,' he replied. 'No intention of thinking about it either.'

'It was a bit embarrassing when Lennart started to talk about us,' she said cautiously.

'Fool. He doesn't know us.'

'No. But I suppose being at a wedding makes you think about it a bit,' she said.

'Are you thinking marriage thoughts now?' he demanded.

'Of course not,' she lied. Because of course she was. Her wedding day was her favourite feel-good daydream. Picking hymns, deciding on flowers, worrying about the guest list (she could while away hours worrying about mythical guest lists) . . . she loved all of it.

'Good,' he said. He yawned loudly. 'I know we're on the same hymn sheet about marriage. But I appreciate that being at a wedding can make even the best of girls go a bit gooey. I saw you sniffing in the church when Carla arrived.'

'Everyone was sniffing,' she said nonchalantly, wishing she'd never agreed with him (one night when she'd had too much to drink and didn't want to rock the boat) that marriage was the last thing on her mind. She said nothing for a moment and then spoke even more casually. 'All the same, I suppose one day in the future I might want to get married. Most people do. Don't they?'

'Maybe. I'd be lying if I said it didn't occasionally cross my mind, but then . . . it's constricting, isn't it? I like my life the way it is. Our lives the way they are. You coming and staying when I want and not being there when I need time to myself.'

'Sure. Yes. Absolutely.' There was a lump in Lainey's throat.

'I'm not ready to settle down. And why should you be? You've got a great career and you're practically famous. Definitely famous, in fact. Most of the guests knew who you were and everyone thinks you're an absolute stunner. I do myself,' he added warmly, pulling her even closer. 'I know you've said that you're not interested, but I bet you could pick up a TV game show or something no problems. Or one of those celeb-watch programmes. You're really, really good-looking, you know. Even in your scuzzy jeans you were way prettier than anyone else there.'

That was a compliment. She was sure of it.

'And you wouldn't want to marry me before I got my game show and became really famous?' she asked lightly. 'Just in case someone else came between us?'

'C'mere,' he said. He pulled her again so that she was lying on top of him. She could feel the warmth of his naked body beneath her. He drew her even closer. 'Now,' he said, 'no one can get between us.' He kissed her and she returned the kiss. Then he rolled over suddenly so that their positions were reversed. 'You're the hottest, sexiest, most desirable woman in the world,' he told her as he slid inside her. 'There's nobody better for me than you. And nobody better for you than me.'

He was right, she thought. Nobody could match him when it came to making love. Nobody ever would.

He stayed lying on top of her afterwards until eventually she had to push him away.

'Can't breathe,' she said. 'And need to use the bathroom.'

'OK.'

His eyes were closed when she came back to the bedroom.

'Are you awake?' she asked as she got into bed.

'If I was asleep, I wouldn't be able to answer that question.'

'Do you love me?'

He opened one eye.

'You know the answer to that already.'

'It's just . . .' She sounded hesitant. 'You hardly ever say it.' Which wasn't strictly true; he always said 'love you, babes' after sex. She just would've liked to hear it a bit more out of bed.

'Words not actions.' He winked at her. 'I showed you twice today already! And I'd show you again but I've run out of stamina.'

'I know you say it sometimes,' she agreed. 'But it's usually sort of jokey. I want to know you mean it.'

'You're being silly.'

'No.' She propped herself up on her arm. 'It's important to me, Ken. *You're* important to me. I need to know how important I am to you.'

'Oh, come on,' he said. 'It's late. We've had a great day. We've had great sex. I'm knackered now. Please don't let's get all serious and talky.'

'I don't want to get all serious,' she said. 'I just . . .'

'What?'

'I want to know where we're going. Where we're going to end up.'

'With about two hours' sleep if you don't lie down,' he told her.

'Ken!'

He groaned. 'Can't we leave this till tomorrow?' he asked. 'I'm tired. You should be tired too.'

'I need to know,' she said.

'Bloody weddings!' His voice was suddenly angry. 'Perfectly sensible women like you burst into tears and start dreaming of wandering around in an enormous white dress as soon as you see someone else in one.'

'I don't want an enormous white dress.' That was a massive lie. She wanted one of fairy-tale proportions.

'It's all such a sham,' he said.

'No it's not,' she protested. 'Are you saying that Carla and Lennart are a sham?'

'C'mon.' He yawned. 'He's nearly twice her age. And loaded. What do you think?'

'I never realised before how damn cynical you are.' Though Carla's words were still going round in Lainey's head and she knew that Ken wasn't entirely wrong.

'Not cynical, practical,' he said. 'You've always thought I was practical. And I am.'

'So what are you saying? A registry office wedding?'

'I'm not talking about weddings at all. Give it a rest, Lainey. Go to sleep.' He turned on his side and closed his eyes again.

She opened her mouth to speak, but caught the words in time. Leave it, she said to herself. He's tired and probably had too much to drink. You're tired too. He's right about weddings. They do make you turn into a romantic heap of slush. So forget it.

'Are you saying that you'll never want to get married?' It was as though somebody else had taken control of her voice. She hadn't been able to stop herself.

'Prob'ly not,' he mumbled.

'Then why are we together?' She couldn't help herself. 'What's this relationship all about?'

'Right now, it's about going to sleep,' said Ken.

'No.' Lainey was wide awake and couldn't even contemplate sleep. 'I've got to be sure.'

'Of what, for God's sake?'

'Of us. Of you.'

He sat up abruptly and stared at her.

'What the hell's with you?' he demanded. 'I thought everything between us was perfect just the way it is.'

'It is. But . . . but in the end there has to be a point to it.'

'Having fun is the point!' he cried. 'Enjoying ourselves. Having great sex.'

'And that's it?'

'Yes,' he said as he pummelled the pillow and flopped back down on it again. 'Absolutely it. Is that clear enough? Now can I please, please get some sleep before my eyes fall out?'

Chapter 4

Virga: a cloud where the precipitation doesn't reach the ground

Lainey felt as though she'd been punched in the stomach. As well as very, very stupid. What was wrong with her? Why was she suddenly pressuring Ken like this? Men hated being put under pressure. No matter what the subject. And marriage was a very delicate issue to pressurise anyone about. She knew that. She had experience of knowing it, for heaven's sake! Thanks to both of her previous engagements (how many people could start a sentence with those words? she wondered), she understood how fragile men were about commitment. In both cases she'd piled on the pressure almost as soon as she'd slid the ring on to her finger, going into overdrive about everything wedding-related. It had been her obsession with things like guest lists and wedding dresses that had made both Ross and Denis freak out. She should have learned her lesson. Even if Ken had wanted to marry her sometime in the future, subjecting him to a barrage of questions about when and how their wedding might take place was enough to make him clam up completely.

She lay on her back and stared at the ceiling. She'd done it again. She'd jeopardised a perfectly good relationship over the marriage question despite knowing better. She'd got it right with Ken until now. She hadn't been possessive or narky or clinging or control-freaky. She hadn't been high-maintenance at all. She hadn't even sat in the privacy of her apartment and practised writing her possible married name as she'd always done before. Lainey Somerfield, Lainey O'Hara, Lainey Kearns – and a whole heap of other surnames too. But she hadn't written Lainey Morgan at all. Well, she'd traced it on the steamed-up bathroom mirror once but that didn't count. Above all, though, she'd steered away from uttering the M word in front of Ken. Had always laid it on thick about how she was happy with her life and cherished her freedom.

Which meant that, until now, everything to do with her and Ken had been different. He'd been the one who'd made most of the running. It was him who'd texted her the morning after they'd first met, saying that he'd been thinking about her all night. She hadn't replied for seven hours, even though she'd been itching to send a message back. With Ken she'd cultivated her Lainey Ryan TV persona. Warm and friendly but just that little bit remote. Occasionally allowing him to see a little bit of her vulnerable side too. Telling him about her fondness for high heels but her inability to master them. He liked that. He liked being protective of her. And he loved knowing that other men looked at her when she was on the telly but he was the one who was dating her. He'd told her that lots of times. She'd felt secure knowing how much she meant to him and how much he enjoyed being seen in her company.

A few weeks earlier, he'd given her the key to his house

in Rathmines. Just for emergencies, he'd said. But she'd been really excited when he'd handed it to her. As far as she was concerned, that was the moment when it had truly become serious between them, even though she didn't make a big deal of it at the time. Giving her a key surely meant that he was prepared to move their relationship up a level. She'd been certain about that. It *had* been a big deal, no matter how dismissive his approach had been.

When she'd asked him to come with her to Carla's wedding, he'd agreed without even thinking. Lainey had been a bit nervous about it because she couldn't help feeling that the two of them at a wedding together was a sort of statement, but Ken said it would be a bit of fun and that he was looking forward to a weekend in Bangor with her.

Now the fun had gone out of it. She'd sensed that she was annoying him. And yet she hadn't been able to stop herself. Had kept digging the hole she'd unexpectedly found herself in.

She closed her eyes and listened to the rain. Tomorrow, she thought, I'll be bright and cheerful and I won't say anything about tonight. And maybe, like today's weather, it'll all blow over.

She slept fitfully and was wide awake again at seven thirty. She turned gently in the bed. Ken was sleeping on his side, his face away from her. He was snoring gently. It was far too early to wake him (and she wasn't going to do that anyway; he was pissed off enough with her as it was), but she knew she couldn't go back to sleep herself. She slid out from beneath the duvet and peeked through the narrow chink in the heavy brocade curtains. The rain had stopped. The sky was still grey but the clouds were thinner. It would be clear by the evening, she thought. Blue skies, a day too late for Carla and Lennart.

The water in the shower was lukewarm, and no matter how she twisted and turned the controls she couldn't get it any hotter, so she decided against washing her hair, which was still heavy from the gel and hairspray of the previous day. She brushed it vigorously and then tied it back from her face. She looked at her reflection in the mirror.

Her skin was dull beneath eyes that were red-rimmed from too much alcohol, tiredness and the tears that she'd shed while Ken was sleeping beside her. She didn't look beautiful this morning. She looked wretched.

Ken was still sleeping when she went back into the bedroom. She thought the sounds of her splashing around in the bathroom (and knocking the bottle of shower gel off its shelf and on to the floor) might have woken him. But he was lying exactly as she'd left him, still on his side, still snoring gently.

She got dressed in the jeans, top and ballet pumps again. She hesitated for a couple of seconds, then picked up her handbag and went downstairs to the breakfast room.

There weren't many people there and she sat at a table by the window. Everything about the day was calmer than yesterday and the sea – previously whipped into a white frenzy by the wind – now lapped gently against the shore. Hopefully things between me and Ken will be a bit calmer today too, she thought, as a waitress came over, took her order for coffee and then told her to help herself from the breakfast buffet.

Normally Lainey was a big fan of breakfast buffets. Despite her slender frame, she enjoyed her food and regarded buffets as a challenge to see how much she could pack away. She liked a cooked breakfast because it was something that in a million years she'd never bother with at home. Far too much trouble to do herself, she thought; great when someone else did it for you. But this morning she couldn't face the scrambled eggs, the sausages, the bacon, the mushrooms, the tomatoes or the black pudding. (Well, she wouldn't have had the black pudding even if she'd been feeling on top form. The whole concept of it disgusted her. Even though her gran loved it.) Instead she put two slices of bread into the toaster. They came out far too pale, so she popped them in again. The second time they came out scorched. She debated having another go but couldn't be bothered. She abandoned the toast and put a croissant on her plate instead. Just as she returned to her table, Roy and Hazel entered the breakfast room. Hazel spotted her immediately and the two of them came to join her.

'You're up early,' said Roy.

'So are you.'

'We have to leave before nine for our flight,' explained Hazel. She looked around. 'Is Ken still asleep?'

Lainey nodded.

'It was a great day, wasn't it?' Hazel looked at her enthusiastically while Roy asked the waitress to bring them a tea and a coffee. Then he told Hazel he was going to forage at the buffet. She asked him to bring her back whatever he could carry.

'Absolutely.' Lainey tried to sound equally enthusiastic as she responded to Hazel's remark.

'She's so lucky with Lennart,' added Hazel. 'He's a wonderful man.'

'Yes,' said Lainey.

'But you have a wonderful man yourself in Ken.'

'You think?'

'Absolutely,' Hazel said. 'He's a pet.'

'Talking about me again?' asked Roy cheerfully, as he returned with two plates of hot breakfasts.

Hazel beamed at him. Lainey got up. The smell of the bacon was making her feel sick.

Ken was in the shower when she returned to the bedroom. He walked out of the bathroom as she was putting her clothes in her small overnight bag. As always she felt her heart beat faster at the sight of his toned body. She gave him a faint smile.

'I gather you've had breakfast?' he said.

She nodded.

'I'm not going to bother with it myself.' Ken was dressing as he spoke, pulling on his Levi's and sliding a blue T-shirt over his head.

'Were you thinking of heading home right away?' asked Lainey.

'Yes.'

She wasn't sure what to say to him. She hated strained atmospheres. And the atmosphere between them was as taut as cling film stretched over a bowl. Their words were simply bouncing back at them.

'Well, I'm ready to go,' she said brightly.

'Right,' he said.

They left ten minutes later. He put the Toyota into gear and swung it out of the hotel car park. They'd passed Belfast before Lainey spoke.

'Last night,' she said.

Ken kept his eyes on the road ahead of him.

'I freaked you out. I'm sorry. I didn't mean to.'

'Forget about it,' he said.

'Forget about it?'

'I don't want to talk about it.'

Neither did she. But if they didn't talk about it, then where would their relationship be? Although, she wondered, where on earth would it be if they did?

'At least it's stopped raining.'

I can't believe I said that, thought Lainey. I can't believe I've just made a comment about the bloody weather!

'I've got a headache,' said Ken. 'I don't want to talk about anything at all.'

'Sure.' She sat back in her seat. The best thing to do was what Ken wanted and keep her mouth shut. She'd done enough damage already.

They were silent for the two hours it took to reach Lainey's apartment. Ken pulled up outside the electronic gates and Lainey fished in her bag for the zapper to open them, tutting with annoyance when she couldn't find it.

'It's all right,' said Ken. 'I'm not coming in anyway. You can use the pedestrian gate.'

She didn't need the zapper for the pedestrian gate. That only needed a key code.

'Look, Ken . . .' She turned in the seat beside him. 'I really am sorry. I didn't mean to nag you.'

'No need to be sorry,' he said. 'You were right to lay it on the line. We've been going out for a while and I understand that you might have wanted . . . well, something more. I thought that giving you the key to my place was enough.

I thought you were OK with that. I didn't realise that you were thinking about the whole relationship thing in massive detail, wanting to know exactly where we were going and why and all that sort of stuff.'

'I'm not,' she said despairingly. 'Really I'm not. It was just the whole wedding thing . . . You were right, it kind of got to me and I started thinking about it. But I don't want to get married either, Ken. Honestly. It's not me.'

He turned to look at her.

'I think it *is* you,' he said. 'I think you want the whole lifelong-commitment scenario.'

'How could you possibly get that idea?' She laughed, although she knew that it sounded brittle. 'You know I have a glam lifestyle, what with the TV and everything. I'm not ready to compromise that for a man. Even one as hunky as you.' She laughed again, a little more naturally this time.

'But if the right man came along you'd make it work, wouldn't you?'

'Of course. But—'

'And you want to get married one day, don't you?'

'Yes. But—'

'You're in a completely different place to me, Lainey,' said Ken. 'I love the time we have together, I really do. But I'm happy with where we are right now and I don't want to spend my life wondering when you're going to spring the marriage question on me again.'

'I didn't ask you to marry me!' she exclaimed. 'All I did was say that one day I wanted to get married. That's not such a big deal, is it?'

'Not to you, maybe. But it is to me. And if that's how you feel, then maybe we shouldn't see each other.'

How was it, she asked herself, that twenty-four hours earlier everything had been so right between them? They'd been in love, having fun, going to a wedding together as a couple. And now he was breaking up with her. What had changed? Really? Just because she'd asked questions about their future, questions that were perfectly OK to ask, he'd decided that their present was over. Even though they got on so well together. Even though they had fun together. Even though he thought she was the sexiest girl in the world. (He'd told her that over and over. As though he'd really meant it.) Was he really prepared to walk away from all that just because she'd mentioned marriage?

'Look, Ken—'

'I know you've got some stuff at my place,' he said. 'I'll drop it back to you.'

'Don't you think—'

'And you'd better give me back my key. If you can find it.'

She stared at him.

'Is this so easy for you?' she asked. 'Just to end it?'

'I can't cope with this right now. I really can't.'

'You're overreacting,' she said. 'Come into the apartment. Let's talk about it.'

'I don't want to talk,' he said. 'I need to get home. I've got training later today.'

She knew that she was close to tears. But she sure as hell wasn't going to cry. Not now.

'Here's your key.' She could always find his key in her bag. She kept it on a separate key ring. One with a little plastic heart. It had been a free gift in a magazine she'd bought the day after she met him. She'd thought it was symbolic.

'Thanks.' He dropped the key ring into the coin tray.

'Will you call me when you're bringing my things?'

'Sure.'

She didn't want to get out of the car. She didn't want yet another relationship to be over. But she opened the door.

'Goodbye, Ken.'

'Bye, Lainey.'

He was gone before she even turned away.

Chapter 5

Cumulus: fair-weather clouds usually appearing on sunny days

She sat in her fourth-floor apartment overlooking the communal garden. Leafy bamboos swayed gently in the afternoon breeze outside the window. Usually she found the gentle rustle of the long green leaves calming, but right now she was too upset for them to work their magic. She was wondering how it was that someone who was supposedly as intelligent as her managed to so spectacularly mess up her relationships every single time. So much for being beautiful as well. Beauty didn't keep men with you when you got it wrong. And she couldn't stop getting it wrong. If there was a right choice and a wrong choice to make in a relationship, she unerringly picked the wrong one. The way she looked at things now, she might as well forget the idea of sharing her life with anyone, because she was clearly totally unsuited to being part of a couple. Other unmarried thirty-something women joked about being found dead with their cats. Lainey was quite sure she actually would be. If she had a cat. Although the cat would probably leave her too.

She closed her eyes and rested her head in her hands. She was utterly, utterly hopeless and she was a failure yet again.

This time was even worse than the broken engagements. She'd been young and foolish when it came to Ross and Denis. She'd rushed into wanting to make a statement with them because it seemed important to her to publicly state that she was in love and that she was loved in return. It seemed important to show that the relationships weren't frivolous, that they were going somewhere. Her mother had always despised frivolity, and although Lainey knew that Deanna's views could be extreme, she understood what she meant. You didn't let men mess you around when it came to relationships. Either it was about something important, or you walked away. You didn't let them string you along.

Deanna had said all this to her on a number of occasions and Lainey had taken her words to heart, even though her grandmother, Madeleine, would tell her that Deanna had warped views and that there was nothing wrong with a bit of frivolity from time to time.

'In clothes and make-up, yes,' Lainey replied. 'But you shouldn't mess with people's feelings.'

Madeleine had agreed but told Lainey that she didn't have to take it all as seriously as Deanna did. Because, she'd added, Deanna hadn't always got it right, had she? Lainey, as she grew older, agreed that as a role model her mother had her flaws. Nevertheless, she couldn't help hearing Deanna's words every time she went out with someone new.

But they didn't really make a difference. When she'd met Ken, she'd tried really, really hard to be the perfect girlfriend, because she'd felt a stronger bond with him than any of the others. She'd told herself to be a bit more frivolous and low-maintenance. Yet in the end, she'd still been left with nothing. She had to accept that when it came to dating men, she just didn't know how to deal with it. She didn't know what she was meant to do, how she was meant to behave. She always seemed to drive them away, even when they seemed to be happy with her. It didn't matter whether she was laid-back or intense or cheerful or moody – sooner or later it all went horribly wrong, and somehow it was always her fault.

She shouldn't have brought up the subject of marriage. Especially in the middle of the night when he was tired and a little bit drunk and when Lennart had already undoubtedly irritated him by raising it in front of other people. And the stupidest thing she'd done, she thought miserably, was going back to the subject after they'd made love. She should've left well enough alone. It was even more humiliating that he'd told her he'd no intention of marrying her a few minutes after making love to her. Or having sex with her, which was all it was really if he'd never meant a word of 'love you, babes'.

Fool, fool, fool! She shouted the words out loud and threw a flip-flop across the room. It flew out of the open patio window, bounced off the balcony handrail and sailed through the air towards the garden below.

She was about to groan over the fact that she couldn't even throw something across the room properly when she heard the cry.

Oh bloody hell, she thought in a panic, I've clocked one of the neighbours. I hope it wasn't Annie.

She jumped up from the sofa and leaned over the balcony rail. To her relief, it wasn't the elderly woman who lived in the apartment below who'd been struck by her footwear. She recognised her victim. The tall, fair-haired Shay Loughnane, who lived in the apartment block directly opposite her, was holding the flip-flop and rubbing his head. Shay had moved into his apartment earlier in the year, but (as with the majority of Laurel Park's residents) she'd never spoken to him. However she did feel that she knew him slightly, because he rarely bothered to close the curtains on his windows, so she sometimes saw him in the evenings lounging in front of the TV with his feet propped on the coffee table in front of him, or sitting upright with a game controller in his hand. Usually there was a pizza box on the table too, or the foil containers of a takeaway meal. More often, though, he had a girlfriend with him, all of whom seemed very groomed and very classy, although he didn't seem to have an exclusive relationship with any of them. His preferred method of home entertainment for women seemed to include sitting on the balcony sharing a bottle of wine, before disappearing into the apartment. On those nights the curtains were firmly closed.

He was looking around him now, the flip-flop still in his hands.

'Hey,' she called apologetically. 'It was me. I'm sorry. I hope I didn't hurt you.'

'You got me on the side of the head. With force,' he told her. 'Of course it hurt.'

'It was an accident.' She leaned a little further over the balcony, her hair tumbling around her face. 'Do you need to go to hospital or anything?'

He grinned. 'It was only a low-flying flip-flop. I hope I'm tougher than that.'

'I'm glad you're OK,' she said.

'Startled more than anything. Is this your way of getting to know the neighbours? I'm Shay, by the way.'

It occurred to her that at any other time in her life she'd probably think this was meant to be. That the circumstances of their meeting were a story she'd always treasure. 'Remember the day I hit you over the head with a flip-flop?' she'd say. 'And you asked me out. And we fell in love.' He'd look at her and smile. They'd kiss. It would be wonderful . . .

But not today. Today, possibly for the first time in her life, her imagination wasn't running away with her.

'Lainey,' she introduced herself. 'Glad to meet you, but I threw it outside by mistake.'

'Oh, I know you,' he said. 'Nice to talk to you, though. D'you want me to throw it back?'

'Can you manage?' She was on the fourth floor after all.

He looked offended. 'Of course I can. I've played basket-ball.' He stood back and threw the flip-flop neatly upwards.

She caught it with her right hand. 'Thanks!'

'So it's safe now, is it?' he asked.

'Safe?'

'To walk through the garden without fear of injury?'

'Of course.'

'Well, nice to have finally spoken to you, Lainey. See you around.'

'See you,' she said and went back inside again.

She sat down on the sofa and closed her eyes. She really should think before she acted. It was lucky that her flip-flop hadn't actually hurt someone. It would've undoubtedly become a matter for the residents' association. Although in fairness, Annie Dwyer, the woman she feared she'd hit, was the president of the association and a bit of a pet. She was also the source of Lainey's information about fellow residents, and how she knew Shay's name, as well as the names of the people in the apartments either side of her. Nevertheless, hitting her on the head could've made a bad day even worse. And this was a rotten day already.

She was on her own again.

And for the first time in her life, she wondered if she was meant to be.

She was back on the sofa, staring blankly into space, when her phone rang. She looked at the caller ID for a moment or two, debating about accepting the call, thinking that she didn't have the mental strength for it right now. Anyone else in the world, she thought, as it continued to shrill annoyingly. Anyone. But there was no point in putting it off. She took a deep breath and hit the accept button.

'Hi.' There was a faint American twang in the voice. 'I was beginning to think I'd have to leave a message.'

'I was busy,' lied Lainey. 'What's up, Deanna?'

'I thought I'd let you know I'm coming back to Ireland for a while. At least a month, maybe longer.'

'Oh.'

'You sure sound thrilled with that news.' Her mother's voice, through a sudden burst of static on the line, held a hint of sarcasm.

'Just surprised,' said Lainey. 'Why are you coming?'

'I'm putting together a major TV documentary,' said Deanna. 'I'm visiting half a dozen European countries.'

'Best to keep busy,' said Lainey.

'It's an excellent opportunity,' Deanna said. 'It's quite some time since I worked outside the States.'

'Congratulations.'

'So . . . I'll be in touch when I arrive, huh?'

'That'd be good, yes.'

'OK then.'

'OK,' said Lainey and ended the call.

She stared at the grassy bamboos again and sighed from the very depths of her being. Deanna was coming back. Just as she'd thought things couldn't get any worse.

The sun was shining as she freewheeled down the Old Finglas Road the next morning to the iconic Met Eireann building at the start of Glasnevin Hill. One day, when she'd still been at primary school and her grandparents had brought her to the nearby Botanic Gardens for a summer treat, she'd asked them about the four-sided pyramid clad in bronze, certain that it had been built by aliens. Her grandmother had told her that they studied the weather there, and she'd looked at her and asked if that meant rain. And her grandmother had replied rain and wind and sun and snow, and as far as Lainey had been concerned, she'd made up her mind there and then that that was where she wanted to work.

A weather anorak, her grandfather had said once, but with a certain level of pride in his voice. Even before she'd begun her studies seriously, Lainey had bought books on weather phenomena, watched TV documentaries about storm chasers and found out as much as she could about why it could be sunny at seven in the morning and disappointingly cloudy by ten. (The sun heated the ground, she discovered, and warmed the air up. The warm air, carrying moisture, rose, then cooled, and the changing moisture caused clouds. Irish air, being very moist, tended to make a lot of clouds.)

But not today. Today was bright and clear and the air was dry, so she knew that there would be nothing to mar the panoramic view of the city from the south-facing forecasting offices. And the brightness of the weather had helped to lift the heaviness in her heart. She was still miserable, but it was impossible to let it weigh on her so utterly when the sun was warming her shoulders and lighting up the day. She left her old-fashioned bicycle in the basement and then took the lift up to the fourth floor.

Michael Loh and Stephanie Childs, who'd been on the night roster, smiled at her. And smiled even more when she handed them two frothing cappuccinos from the café up the road, which had fitted neatly into the basket on the front of her bike.

'You're a lifesaver,' said Stephanie, removing the lid and stirring the coffee. 'It was a boring night. Not helped by him,' she added, pointing at Michael.

'Why? What did you do?' asked Lainey.

'He was telling me about his bloody car,' replied Stephanie in a voice laden with disgust. 'Droning on while I was trying to look at a new type of precipitation graph. But he kept blathering about engines and camshafts and . . . well, who knows? I stopped listening after the first hour.'

Lainey chuckled. Michael was a classic-car freak. He was currently restoring an old Morris Minor.

'How many times do I have to say "not interested" for him to listen to me?' asked Stephanie plaintively.

'Never mind,' comforted Lainey. 'I'm sure you can think of something equally mind-numbing to bore him with.'

'I keep my obsessions to myself,' said Stephanie cheerfully. 'Here, look at this. Interesting storm mid-Atlantic. Won't reach us, but a right little belter all the same.'

Lainey sipped her own coffee (double chocolate macchiato) as she looked at the computer-generated graphic. She nodded approvingly. She liked storms. She loved their energy and their power.

'So how was the wedding?' asked Stephanie when they'd finished looking at the screen. 'Totally washed out?'

Lainey gave her a rundown on the day, leaving out the fact that she'd been dumped by Ken and making a joke about her fall.

'After spending all that time looking for a dress.' Stephanie's voice was full of sympathy. 'That was unfortunate.'

'Oh well, I survived,' said Lainey as philosophically as she could. 'And I'm sure the dress will be grand once I get it cleaned. Can't think of when I'll ever wear it again, but I suppose it'll be good to have in the wardrobe.'

'I'm sure hunky Ken will bring you somewhere you need a great dress.' Stephanie finished her coffee and threw the waxed cup into the bin.

'Uh, maybe.' Lainey didn't want to talk about her break-up with Ken in front of Michael, who was listening to their conversation even though he hadn't taken part in any of it.

'Everything all right with love's young dream?' asked Stephanie, who'd already guessed from Lainey's expression that it wasn't.

'We had a bit of a row.'

'Oh, everyone does that at weddings,' said Stephanie cheerfully. 'It's all those love hormones and stuff fizzing round the place. You'll be fine.'

Lainey gave her a half-hearted smile and said nothing. She was afraid she'd cry if she opened her mouth.

'I'd better finish off the stuff I was working on,' said

Stephanie. 'Then I can go home and close the blackout curtains.' She turned back to her keyboard, while Michael took some charts to the photocopier and began copying them.

Lainey released the breath she'd been holding. She'd tell people about Ken soon enough. But not quite yet.

By later that morning, the comfort of her daily routine had settled her. There was still an aching gap in her heart, but compiling forecasts for the radio bulletins as well as specialised forecasts for the people who contracted them had kept her busy. (Today's forecasts were the sort that cheered most people up. It would be warm and sunny for the rest of the week.) The truth was, though, that no matter how busy they were, the air on the forecasting floor was always one of quiet industry. Even though the computer screens were showing a variety of moving graphs and charts and the printers clattered throughout the day, the atmosphere was studious rather than frenzied.

One of Lainey's old college friends, who worked in the trading room of an international bank, had brought her to see it shortly after he'd started. She'd been driven almost demented by the hubbub of noise, the incessant shouting and the constant flashing of lights. She didn't know how Cormac could think in such a place, let alone work. But he assured her that he could, and that he liked it. She'd been glad to get back to the sanctuary of her charts, which could also predict uncertainty and turmoil, but in a much quieter way.

Because of her seven o'clock start that morning, Lainey was finished by early afternoon, and she decided to call to her grandmother rather than going straight home. It took her thirty minutes to cycle to the cottage-style house in Killester where she'd lived for most of her childhood. The cottages had been built for soldiers returning from the Second World War and had originally been small and basic. But over the years almost everyone in the area had renovated and extended them so that they had become the darlings of estate agents everywhere, with their large gardens and distinctive style. The pavements and roads around the cottages were narrow, and every time Lainey visited her grandmother she felt as though she was stepping back in time.

Madeleine Ryan's house was on a corner site, which meant that it had an even bigger garden than her neighbours. Although Madeleine and her husband Edmund had renovated the cottage a number of times over the years they'd lived there, they'd kept their extension of the property to a minimum, which meant that there was still plenty of garden for Madeleine to indulge her love of growing things. Even as she stood on the doorstep and rang the bell, Lainey caught the sent of lilac and roses drifting through the air.

She waited patiently for Madeleine to answer. Five years earlier, her grandmother had fallen and broken her hip. She'd had it replaced (honestly, she'd said at the time, isn't modern medicine wonderful – shouldn't I think about getting a few other bits replaced while I'm at it?), but ever since then she'd been slower on her feet, and in the last year or so she'd taken to occasionally using a silver-tipped black cane to help her get around.

Lainey heard her grandmother's footsteps in the hallway, and waved at the spyhole set into the door. She heard the bolt being drawn back and then the door swung open.

'Hello, sweetheart! It's good to see you.' Madeleine gave her a hug and ushered her into the kitchen and dining room at the back of the house. This was the extended area, cleverly built to take full advantage of the sun.

'Good to see you too, Gran,' said Lainey. She looked at the older woman expectantly.

'Yes, yes, I have cupcakes.' Madeleine grinned and her granddaughter hugged her.

The cupcakes were Madeleine's speciality, light and golden and generously topped with creamy icing and sprinkles. Whenever Lainey bit into one, she felt about five years old again.

'You get the cakes and I'll make the tea.'

This was another tradition.

Lainey filled the kettle. While it boiled, she set the table with two pale pink china cups and saucers, and matching side plates. She took paper napkins (white with a pattern of pink forget-me-nots) from a drawer in the tall dresser and set them, along with silver knives and cake forks, beside the plates. While she made the tea in the pretty china teapot, Madeleine placed a cake in the centre of each plate.

Today's cakes were topped with white icing and multicoloured sprinkles.

'Gorgeous, Gran,' said Lainey as she bit into hers. 'You should go into business. Cupcakes are the in thing these days. Bakeries charge an absolute fortune for them.'

'I like making them for people I love,' said Madeleine. 'I couldn't do it for money.'

Lainey smiled. None of the Ryan family had ever done anything for money. At least, she amended as she glanced around the room and caught sight of the photograph of her mother, not initially.

Her gaze switched back to her grandmother, who was busying herself with stirring her tea.

She hadn't got her height from her gran. Madeleine Ryan was tiny, just over five feet tall. But what she lacked in height she made up for in presence. Lainey would have liked to have inherited Madeleine's quiet elegance and economy of movement instead of her unknown father's height and dark good looks. The older woman was sitting upright in her chair, her shoulders back so that her spine was straight. Her silver-grey hair was caught up into the elegant chignon that Lainey could never manage to wear. Her violet eyes were still sharp and alert in her rather narrow face. (Lainey was hoping that she had actually inherited her grandmother's smooth complexion, which meant that, despite her seventy-three years, Madeleine had fewer wrinkles than many younger women.) She had always looked younger than her age and enjoyed flirting with the latest fashions, although she would tell Lainey that she never wanted to turn into mutton dressed as lamb. Age-appropriate, she said, was important. But not ageing. Today she was wearing a pale lavender dress that buttoned down the front. As always, thought Lainey, her grandmother looked cool, poised and in control. Not someone who'd push a guy too far about marriage and throw flip-flops out of her apartment window because she'd been dumped. Not someone who'd let herself be dumped in the first place.

Madeleine placed her spoon neatly on her saucer and gazed dreamily at the empty chair in the corner of the room. Then she turned back to Lainey.

'Did you enjoy Carla's wedding?' she asked.

Lainey had been preparing for the question ever since she'd

arrived. She knew she'd have to tell Madeleine about her break-up with Ken, but she needed to build up to it.

'It was good,' she said. 'Rained all day, unfortunately.'

'That was a pity,' agreed Madeleine.

'And I fell.' Lainey was able to make a real joke of this now. 'Graceful as an elephant, as always.'

'Did you hurt yourself?'

'Sprained my ankle and wrist. Skinned my knees. And the heel came off my shoe,' said Lainey. 'But it was mostly my pride, to be honest.'

Madeleine tut-tutted sympathetically, then glanced at the empty chair again.

'What else?' she asked, returning her steady gaze to her granddaughter.

'Huh?'

'Grandad says there's more.'

'Gran!' Lainey frowned. Ever since her grandfather had died two years ago, Madeleine had used his name any time she wanted to find out things that Lainey didn't want to tell her. She would say that Edmund wanted to know, even though it was Madeleine herself who was consumed with curiosity. Sometimes Lainey thought that her grandmother genuinely believed that her late husband was sitting in the armchair, asking questions. She wondered if, when she wasn't there, Madeleine still talked to the empty space and still left the chair for his exclusive use as it always had been. She didn't feel able to ask.

'Your grandfather always knew when you were upset,' said Madeleine. 'Much more than me.'

Which was true. Grandad was the one Lainey would run to when she needed comfort, burying her head in the security of his rough Aran jumper, needing to feel his strong arms around her. After she'd cried about whatever it was that had upset her, her grandfather would always rub the top of her head and tell her that she'd be better before she was twice married. Which, she'd thought as she got older, wasn't a hard call for him to make.

'Ken and I split up,' she said.

'Oh, Lainey.' Madeleine's eyes flooded with sympathy.

Lainey felt her lip wobble. 'It was for the best,' she said.

'I thought you two were getting along well together,' said Madeleine. 'You've been going out such a long time.'

'We *were* getting along. It was just that I wanted a bit more than he was ready to give me.'

Madeleine looked at her speculatively. 'You didn't ask him to marry you, did you, dear?'

'Gran!' But Lainey blushed. Her grandmother knew she'd been the one who'd asked Ross to give her a ring as a Christmas present.

'Did you mention the M word?' asked Madeleine.

Lainey looked uncomfortable, and Madeleine sighed.

'Are you all right?' Her tone was gentle.

'I will be,' said Lainey, although her voice wobbled. 'I've got a lot of practice in getting over broken hearts.'

'That's because you give your heart away too easily,' said her grandmother.

'I know. But this time was different.'

'So was last time.'

Lainey shook her head. 'Not like with Ken. Honestly, Gran. We just seemed to click.'

'You said that about Richard, too. And Denis. And—'

'I know. I know. But I was so sure with Ken, I really was.'

Madeleine sighed. 'It's our fault, of course.'

'Huh?'

'Me and your mother. Conflicting views. Left you with mixed-up ideas about men.'

'I wasn't mixed up about Ken.' Lainey blew her nose in the paper napkin.

'You don't have to marry everyone you meet,' said Madeleine.

'I don't try to.'

'Don't you?'

'No!'

Two broken engagements meant that her grandmother had a point, Lainey conceded mentally. But it wasn't that she wanted every man she'd ever dated to marry her. The problem was that whenever she went out with someone new for the first time, she couldn't help wondering if she was going out with her future husband.

'Oh well,' said Madeleine brightly. 'You're still young. Plenty more fish in the sea.'

'Not really.' Lainey sounded glum.

'Which part?' asked Madeleine.

'Well, I'm thirty-two,' Lainey told her. 'Which is, of course, the new twenty-two but according to health magazines is actually old, biologically speaking. Did you know that eleven per cent of couples over thirty-five are infertile? And that goes up to thirty-three per cent when they're in their forties.'

'Do you want to have a baby?' Madeleine looked aghast. 'Is that it? Are you broody?'

'No!' cried Lainey. 'I mean, I'd like to have a baby sometime, but not yet. And not with just anybody.' She looked at her grandmother from beneath her sweeping dark lashes.

'Let's face it, Gran, I know that being the product of an unstable relationship isn't the best start in life. I just want to keep my options open.'

'You know what your problem is?' asked Madeleine.

'What?'

'You think you can have everything. But you can't.'

'Don't start,' said Lainey. 'Don't give me a lecture on Having It All. I know it's impossible and I don't want it all. But I think having a baby is something I'll want some day. So if that's the case I should really be looking for the right person now. Let's face it, you were in your early twenties when you had Deanna. And she was only nineteen when she got up the duff with me.'

'Please don't use that revolting expression,' said Madeleine.

'That's what it was,' said Lainey practically. 'And I don't blame her for not being happy about it. I wouldn't have been either.'

'We seem to be wandering off the point a bit,' said Madeleine. 'Which is that when it comes to men, you pin your heart to your sleeve and you let them take potshots at it. You should be far more analytical, Lainey.'

'You sound just like Carla.'

'Oh?' Madeleine looked interested. Lainey related Carla's confidences to her grandmother, who looked approving. 'Didn't think young girls thought that way any more. Fair play to her, she's dead right. You never get your ideal man. You have to compromise. Love isn't everything.'

'Gran! You're terrible. You married Grandad because you loved him.'

'Hmm, yes,' admitted Madeleine grudgingly. 'But I would've preferred someone who could do a decent tango.

And I wouldn't have tied the knot with him if he hadn't had a good income.'

'I don't believe you for a minute.'

'It's perfectly true,' said Madeleine. 'I wouldn't have gone out with him in the first place if he hadn't met my requirements.'

'You had requirements?'

'Absolutely. Financial security was number one on the list.'

'You and Carla both.' Lainey looked astonished. 'I can't believe that in more than half a bloody century things haven't changed.'

'People change a lot less than you think,' said Madeleine. 'The trouble with your generation is that you expect too damn much. It leaves you horribly confused and exhausted. Leaves the men confused and exhausted too,' she added. 'Poor Ken, he probably has no idea what he really wants either.'

'Oh, Ken knows what he wants all right,' said Lainey darkly.

'What's that?'

'No commitments.'

Madeleine nodded. 'It's a problem with men. A commitment is like growing up. And they find it hard to do that.'

'Did Grandad?'

'It was a different time.' Madeleine glanced at the empty chair again. 'They didn't have any choice. But,' she added with a smile, 'he still did some stupid things, didn't you, pet?'

Lainey wondered if she should get a health professional to talk to her grandmother. Madeleine seemed perfectly normal most of the time, but listening to her asking questions of a chair was disconcerting. She wondered if it was just that

Madeleine was lonely. After all, she'd been with Edmund for fifty-two years. And now she was living by herself. Perhaps I should offer to move back, thought Lainey. Maybe she needs proper looking after. Maybe she shouldn't be on her own.

'Has your mother been in touch with you?' Madeleine changed the subject.

Lainey exhaled slowly. 'Mmm.'

'She's arriving next week. She's staying with me. At least a month, she thinks.'

'That's what she told me. Bloody hell, though. A month of her, you'll be driven round the bend!'

'Language, Lainey.'

'If Deanna's here, you'll probably hear a lot worse than that!'

Madeleine laughed. 'I suppose so.'

'She said she'd be in touch with me when she arrived.'

'Don't worry,' said Madeleine. 'I'm sure she'll be fine.'

'I'm not worried.' Lainey shook her head. 'It's just – oh, you know what she's like.'

'Still,' said Madeleine, 'given that she's staying with me, you have one less thing to worry about – your poor demented gran going quietly nuts all on her owney-o and talking to the chair.'

Lainey put her arms around her grandmother. 'You're an aul' codger, Gran,' she said. 'And you know me too well.'

'Of course I do,' said Madeleine. 'And I love you to bits. Now, would you like to share another cupcake?'

Chapter 6

Pileus: a horizontal cap cloud appearing briefly on the summit of another cloud

Deanna Ryan was stretching her legs by walking around the cabin of the Airbus 330 when the Fasten Seat Belts sign was switched on. She wasn't surprised by this – the turbulence had been getting steadily worse as the huge plane travelled across the Atlantic Ocean. Deanna didn't mind turbulence – she thought of it like a roller coaster, and she'd always been a fan of roller coasters – but airlines didn't like their passengers being bumped around. And they certainly didn't like them being out of their seats when it was even marginally bumpy. Terrified, she supposed, that someone would get hurt and sue them.

It was all so different to the flights she'd taken years ago, when flying was more adventurous. Passengers could haul whatever they liked on board as hand luggage, smoke in the cabin and make love in the toilets. (She'd never actually made love in the toilet of an aeroplane, and couldn't help thinking that it would be extremely uncomfortable, but nevertheless she liked the idea of people behaving outrageously.)

'Excuse me, madam.' The stewardess spoke politely but firmly. 'The seat belt sign is on. You have to return to your seat.'

'I'm doing that now.' There was a time when Deanna would have snapped at the girl to stop treating her like a moron, but she didn't do that any more. She had an image to maintain. And though that could often be feisty and aggressive in public, she knew better than to be feisty and aggressive in private.

She walked to the front of the economy cabin and through the curtains that separated it from business class. Splashing out on business class for herself, paying for it out of her own pocket, had been a luxury. But a luxury that she could afford and a luxury she felt she deserved. She was fifty-one years old, and her days of looking for the cheapest possible option to get from one place to another were over. Besides, long-haul travel was tiring enough without having to sit beside an inconsiderate oaf taking up half her seat as well as his own and snoring through the night. (It had been her placement a few years earlier beside such an oaf, reeking of BO and stale tobacco, that had ended her desire to mix with the masses.)

She sat down, fastened her seat belt and reclined the seat as far as it would go. Then she closed her eyes. It was two years since she'd last been in Ireland. That had been for her father's funeral, which naturally hadn't made for a very enjoyable visit. She was hoping that this would be a more pleasant experience. But she wasn't exactly betting on it.

The plane touched down at 9.30 in the morning, bumping through a swathe of light grey cloud until the land was visible below. Deanna had stared out of the window during the descent, not entirely sure how she felt about being in Ireland again. She didn't think anyone could ever really dismiss the country of their birth, no matter how hard they tried and no matter for how long they were away. She always thought she had. Until she saw the silver light reflecting from the water of the Irish Sea, the jumble of boats moored in Howth Harbour, the vibrant green of north Dublin and the silver thread of the railway line running across the Malahide estuary. And then she knew that she was home. Even if she didn't consider it home any more.

Everything about Dublin was smaller and more intimate than the States. Than almost anywhere else she'd ever been, which she knew couldn't really be true, because she'd been to smaller places. But the familiarity made Dublin different. Made it special despite everything.

The airport was busy and she was jostled by a younger woman with a rucksack, running at breakneck speed along the corridor, oblivious to the people around her. Deanna tutted with annoyance, especially when more young people came running in the wake of the first girl. They were laughing and shrieking. They didn't really notice her. But then, she thought, young people never really noticed older people. Young people lived in their own bubble, in the here and now, without baggage from the past adding to the rucksacks on their shoulders.

Not, of course, that she was old. Fifty-one wasn't old. But she knew she'd lost a certain innocence about the world and her place in it. A place that hadn't turned out exactly as she'd expected, though she knew nobody's ever did. That was something she'd learned through experience. And she was OK about it now. The place she'd eventually found hadn't turned out to be so bad after all.

She diverted into one of the washrooms and stood in front of a mirror. The woman who looked back at her was very different from the naive girl who had first left Ireland with her very own rucksack. This woman was mature and definitely not naive. Deanna Ryan was medium height, with grey hair cropped short. Her aqua-blue eyes could harden in a way that told whoever was looking at her that she was a woman who took no nonsense. Good skin, although maybe a little more tanned than was recommended, because she was never able to stay out of the California sun. She was wearing a pair of stone-washed Calvin Klein jeans. A plain white shirt. A black leather jacket. A large handbag, also black leather, was slung over her shoulder and she carried a briefcase. Brown, this time. Didn't quite go with everything else. But it was a good briefcase. Besides, Deanna didn't think that everything should match. The fact that her jacket and handbag did was simple coincidence.

She put down the briefcase and rummaged in the handbag for lip salve. She'd used it regularly during the dehydrating flight. Now she rubbed it across her lips again. She replaced the salve and took out a brush. She didn't really need to brush her wiry hair. The cropped style meant that it stayed in place easily enough. But she always fixed her hair before arriving anywhere. She put the brush back into her handbag. Then she picked up the briefcase and went to fetch her baggage.

When her large navy case appeared on the carousel, she grabbed it and made her way into the arrivals hall. She wasn't expecting anyone to meet her. She'd told Madeleine not to even think about it, and Madeleine had replied that there wouldn't be any point in her coming to the airport because she didn't have a car any more. No need, she'd added. I have a free bus pass and I can take taxis if I want to go anywhere special. Much more economical than worrying about cars.

Edmund had been the car fan in the family. He'd loved driving. Madeleine had always seen it as a means to an end, but Edmund had enjoyed it for its own sake. Deanna remembered Sunday-afternoon drives in their grey Ford Cortina when she was younger, aimless meanderings along narrow leafy roads. A Drive in the Country. A Drive to the Seaside. A Drive into Town. Sometimes, when they reached their destination, they didn't even get out of the car, just turned around and drove back home again. These days, of course, driving for its own sake was almost a criminal offence. And probably far too stressful to bother with anyway. Deanna herself drove a Prius. She'd bought it because of its green credentials, even though deep down she preferred the Corvette she'd once owned. Part of her wanted to drive a car like that again and to join the groups who claimed that driving old cars was more environmentally friendly because you weren't contributing to the detrimental effects caused by new manufacturing. But she'd needed a new car. So she'd succumbed. Which proved, she thought as she exited baggage reclaim, that everyone has their tipping point, even me!

She strode through the arrivals hall without stopping and joined the queue for taxis just outside the terminal building. (No sign of a Prius among them, she noted with wry amusement.) There were a lot of businessmen in snappy suits ahead of her, but she waited patiently for her turn. The taxi – an old Mercedes – smelled strongly of pine air freshener, which made her feel nauseous. She opened the window a chink and sat back in the seat. The driver asked her how she was, where she'd come from and if she'd been away for long. Deanna told him that she'd give him a twenty per cent tip if he didn't talk, so he remained silent for the rest of the journey.

Like Lainey, Deanna also felt she was stepping back in time when she pushed open the gate of the house in Killester. Memories came flooding back as she walked up the path – chasing friends along the narrow roads; playing hopscotch (which they'd called 'beds') outside the house, the squares drawn with chalk; climbing the apple tree in Mrs Moriarty's garden next door because it was bigger than the one in her own . . . Back then, the area had seemed noisier and friendlier. There were no children playing on the streets now, even though it was the height of summer. She wondered where they all were. Or if everyone who lived here now was retired, like her mother.

The front door opened before she got the chance to ring the bell.

'Welcome home,' said Madeleine, and kissed her on the cheek.

Deanna had been seventeen when she'd left, a few weeks after her Leaving Certificate results had come through. Nobody had doubted that she'd had the potential to do well in her exams, because she had a quick mind and a keen interest in the world, but she was restless and impatient and hated sitting at her desk studying, which meant her results didn't always reflect her abilities. At the parent–teacher meetings that

Madeleine and Edmund always attended together, Deanna's teachers called her strong-willed. And rebellious, they'd often add, although not necessarily with regard to school rules. Deanna didn't mind observing rules, they said. But she argued constantly, always wanting to know why something had to be done a certain way, always querying the conclusions drawn in class, making it difficult for teachers to get through the curriculum and disrupting other students.

'She's extremely bright,' Mrs Fallon, the vice-principal, told Madeleine. 'But she's very difficult.'

Madeleine knew that Deanna was difficult. She'd been that way even as a baby, always active, hardly sleeping and very demanding. And as she'd grown older, she'd remained difficult simply because she never took anything she was told at face value and wore Madeleine out with her perpetual questions.

'But why?' was one of her favourites, followed very often by 'It's not fair.'

Deanna had a keen sense of fairness. She believed that everyone should have the same chances and opportunities. But (as she would go on to say many times in the years that followed) not everyone took their chances and made the most of their opportunities. And if you didn't, she said grimly, then you had to accept that you'd been the one to allow them to pass you by and you shouldn't moan about it.

She was eleven years old when she realised that not everyone had the same sense of fairness as her, and that girls sometimes took the brunt of unfairness. Until then she'd happily played football on the green outside her house with some of the boys (she was friendlier with the boys than the girls, mainly because she preferred active games like football to pretending to be married and having children like so many of the girls). But when Mr Traynor, father of Billy and John, decided to form a local football team and enter a junior league, he told Deanna that she couldn't play.

'But why?' she demanded. 'I'm a better striker than Billy.'

'You're a girl,' Mr Traynor told her with finality. 'Girls can't play on a league team.'

'But I'm better!' she protested. 'You know I am. He knows I am too.'

Billy, standing just behind his dad, looked sheepish.

'That's not the point,' said Mr Traynor. 'You can't play on the team.'

Deanna told Mr Traynor that she hoped they'd lose. Billy and John, who she'd considered to be good friends, said that she had to understand that boys played football but girls didn't. She headbutted Billy, kicked John in the shins and went home to sulk.

'Never mind,' Madeleine had said. 'We'll go shopping together and I'll buy you something nice to wear and you can forget about silly football.'

'You don't understand,' Deanna said through gritted teeth. 'They think they're great just because they're boys. They're not that great. And they're stupid. It's not fair.'

It was the start of a realisation, as far as Deanna was concerned, that boys always thought they were better than girls, that somehow they seemed to get more opportunities than girls too, and that no, it wasn't fair.

She was persuaded of the rightness of her viewpoint when she went to see Mrs Carthy, the careers guidance teacher, to discuss her future prospects.

'Perhaps you'd like to be a teacher,' Mrs Carthy said as

she looked through a sheaf of Deanna's reports. 'You're curious about things and I'm sure you'd be good at imparting knowledge.'

'You suggested teaching to Michelle Johnson, Amy Waller, Trudy Taylor, Sandra O'Connor and Chloe Fitzpatrick.' Deanna listed off five of her classmates. 'Surely there are other jobs?'

'Well, there's nursing, of course, but I'm not sure you—'

'Teaching, nursing and the civil service,' Deanna said. 'They're the choices you've given everyone! Isn't there anything else I can do?'

'Well, what are you interested in?' Mrs Carthy sounded miffed.

'Travel,' said Deanna, who'd decided years earlier that Ireland was a backward country, a barren rock on the edge of Europe with no culture and no ambition, and that she needed to broaden her horizons.

'That's a great idea,' said Mrs Carthy. 'You could become an air hostess. That way you'd get to see lots of interesting places.'

Deanna looked at her dubiously.

'And who knows,' Mrs Carthy beamed, 'you might even marry a captain.'

'Is there a reason you didn't suggest I could *be* a captain?' demanded Deanna. 'D'you think I couldn't fly the plane myself?'

Mrs Carthy took a deep breath. This was the first year they'd decided to offer careers advice in the school. She'd been persuaded to take on the role. But she wasn't entirely sure she was equipped for it.

'I'm sure you could do anything if you put your mind to it, Deanna,' she said. 'The thing is, your mind is usually all over the place. Which wouldn't be good for flying planes.'

* * *

Deanna didn't consider herself to be a feminist or a women's-libber or any of the terms that were generally used to describe mouthy women who wouldn't keep their opinions to themselves and had an apparent aversion to shaving their legs. (She regularly got rid of her body hair, especially on her legs, where it was dark and unflattering.) She didn't think any of her beliefs were radical or even very progressive. But she did feel that there was an underlying injustice in the way women were treated in society. Not just because most people seemed to believe that – regardless of what career a woman chose or how bright she was – what every girl really wanted was to meet the man of her dreams, marry him and live happily ever after. It was simply that women weren't taken seriously enough by the people that mattered, who, ironically, were mostly men. Women were supposed to be grateful for whatever was given to them. They were supposed to be thankful for being born in a modern age, when they could vote, instead of a century earlier when they were fighting for that right. But what was the point in being able to vote, she wondered, if none of the things you could vote about were issues that were important to you? And it was wrong that society was set up in a way that made it hard for women to be part of the country's decision-making processes. Deanna wanted, in some way, to change things. But she couldn't help thinking that Ireland was light years behind the rest of the world when it came to how women were treated. And that it would take more than someone like her, with an ill-defined sense of injustice, to do anything about it.

Madeleine was more worried about Deanna's job or college prospects than her concerns about the rights of women generally. She wanted Deanna to make up her mind about either applying to college or looking for a job. Deanna herself, however, had other plans.

'What sort of plans?' asked Madeleine warily.

'I've decided to take time out and travel the world,' said Deanna triumphantly. 'Along with Julie and Maya. I'm going to learn about other countries and other people, I'm going to see how women are treated there, and when I come back, I'll have lots of experience.' She gave her mother a self-satisfied look. 'I'm going to the University of Life.'

Years later, when the concept of a gap year became more common, Madeleine realised that it could have its uses. But back then she was angry with her daughter. Drifting around the world (backpacking, Deanna had said, something Madeleine had never even heard of) seemed a wasteful way to spend her time. Especially drifting around with Maya and Julie, who, Madeleine thought, were two of the most irritating and unattractive girls she'd ever met in her life. Madeleine knew that being a woman wasn't all about being sweet and simpering and wearing make-up. But she couldn't see the harm in a bit of lipstick from time to time. Deanna's friends, however, were totally against it, saying that women shouldn't have to paint themselves to attract men. And Deanna had begun to say the same thing, adding that most men weren't worth attracting anyway.

'That's such nonsense,' Madeleine would say when Deanna started to rant. 'Your dad is a wonderful man, a hard worker and a great father. He likes me to look my best, and I don't see anything wrong with that.'

'Sure, Dad is great,' conceded Deanna. 'But I don't need to live like you, Mam. I don't need a man to provide for me. I don't want to be beholden to anyone.'

'I am *not* beholden to your father!' Madeleine was furious. 'We're a partnership. We both bring different things to our marriage. That's what you don't understand.'

Deanna looked dismissive.

She came home with information on her year's travelling with her friends. They were buying InterRail tickets for trains around Europe and they planned to get work as casual labour on farms or restaurants, she said. They would stay in hostels or farmhouses, wherever they could.

Madeleine was wrecked with worry about her going away. She worried about her safety, she worried about the places she'd visit, she worried that when Deanna returned she'd have lost out on job opportunities in the city. She'd been wrong about that, she conceded eventually, but not wrong about other things.

Deanna, Julie and Maya had taken the ferry to England a few weeks later. In an age before mobile phones and when telephone calls were prohibitively expensive, Madeleine was totally out of touch with her daugher's life. Every so often a postcard would arrive: from Paris or Lyon, from Rome or Madrid, and Madeleine would tell herself that this would be good for Deanna in the end. That it would help her to settle down. She understood the need for young people to spread their wings. She would have loved to spread hers a little wider when she was younger herself. But she still worried all the same. And she still thought that flitting from country to country, earning money by waitressing or picking grapes, was a sad waste of Deanna's talents. She couldn't understand how someone who hadn't wanted to be pigeonholed into a 'girlie' job suddenly seemed to think that being a waitress was the best fun in the world.

Madeleine had been absolutely stunned to get the postcard from California. She hadn't known that the girls were thinking of going to America. As far as she was concerned, it was a place that many of her friends had emigrated to and never returned from. She felt a hard lump in her throat as she deciphered Deanna's scrawl.

Having a whale of a time. You'd laugh at my job but I'm earning good tips. Great life.

When she got that postcard, Madeleine wondered what in God's name Deanna was working at now. And if she'd ever return.

Deanna had wondered if she'd ever return too. Travelling through Europe had been exciting and fun, but being in California was like being in a different universe. She loved everything about it: the light, the lifestyle, the people and their enthusiasm . . . It was a million miles away from grey, miserable Ireland, which seemed to Deanna to be all about hard work and getting by and nothing about the joy of living. But California was all about fun. And for the first time in her life, Deanna felt as though there was a reason for being alive. It wasn't just about getting up in the morning and getting through your day of hard, unappreciated work before going to bed at night; it was about filling your hours with enjoyment and laughter.

She and Maya and Julie had come to the US after meeting two Californian girls in Tuscany. Lexy and Fawn were 'doing' Europe (they'd also bought InterRail tickets) but were looking forward to getting home.

'You should come,' Fawn told Deanna. 'You'd love it.'

Deanna said that they hadn't planned on America and that they didn't have visas. Fawn had smiled conspiratorially and told her not to worry. Her dad worked in the Diplomatic Corps, she told Deanna. Visas wouldn't be a problem.

'In that case . . .' Deanna beamed at her new friend. 'I'm in. And I bet the others are too.'

They were, although Julie had only stayed for a month before going back to Ireland because her father had taken ill and she was needed at home to help look after him. (Deanna wondered why Julie's brother Tom, who was living at home, couldn't help with looking after his father instead, but she kept quiet. There were times to argue, she'd learned, and times when it was better to say nothing.)

She was working in a dog-grooming parlour in Monterey, which was Lexy and Fawn's home town. Deanna, who'd always felt she was more of a big-city person than a small-town person, nevertheless fell in love with its easy charm and ocean-side location. She loved the diversity of its people; having come from Ireland, where almost everyone who lived there had been born there too, it was exhilarating to meet people whose heritage was Spanish or Italian, Chinese or Japanese.

She'd seen the job advertised in the window of a local shop and knew the idea of dog-grooming would have everyone back home in fits of laughter at the foolishness of the profligate Yanks in paying to have their animals washed. Back home, washing the dog meant turning the hose on him in the back garden. K9s Dog Parlor was an entirely different proposition. When people came into the salon with their dogs, they were treated as valued clients and not freaks with more money than sense. (Though in all honesty, Deanna thought that was what they were.) But she enjoyed working there because it was relaxed and cheerful and her boss, Mindy, was very easy-going. She liked the fact that the work was physical and fun. She felt that she could be herself, Deanna Ryan, happy with who she was, and not Deanna Ryan, waiting for a man to marry her and whisk her off to something better.

When the girls in her class at school had suddenly taken an interest in boys and started experimenting with their clothes and make-up in order to attract them, Deanna had been horrified. She couldn't see why on earth anyone as smart as Emily Courtney would want to attract some of the moronic boys around their neighbourhood. Boys should be grateful, Deanna thought, to know Emily. And yet Emily and the rest of her classmates spent hours poring over magazines in order to find the best look to suit their colouring and the best way to behave on a first date. It was demeaning, Deanna thought, and girls who allowed themselves to be suckered into thinking that boys were God's gift to womenkind were delusional. She didn't get involved in the discussions about boys, or indeed in trying to meet boys at all, but grew her friendships with girls like Maya and Julie who thought the same way as her and considered Emily Courtney and her friends to be utter airheads, even though they also seemed to be incredibly popular. Deanna felt an anger, too, that women were judged more on how they looked than on what they knew, and she deliberately didn't bother with make-up and the latest fashions as a result.

Yet here, in Monterey, that anger had dissipated. Maybe, she thought, it was because everyone she met was so relentlessly self-confident and positive that she felt (even though her career was currently limited to washing poodles) there were great opportunities waiting for her. She still bristled when she read the papers and watched TV and realised that the social agenda was being set by men, but she was sure that it would change and she was quite certain that the change would happen in America before anywhere else. Monterey was used to change, having gone from boom to bust and urban renewal again over the past fifty years, and the women of the town had been part of that change.

In the glory days of the 1920s and 30s, when the town had been known as the sardine capital of the world, and the fishing boats had come into harbour laden with their silver cargo, it was the women who had rushed to the canneries to process the fish. Women had held things together when the fishing industry had stalled and women continued to be active on town committees – although Deanna reckoned they should have even more prominent roles.

But there were still things to fight for. There was a massive pay disparity between what men earned and what their female counterparts took home for the same job, no matter how progressive the town or the state or the country proclaimed itself to be.

However, she was happier than she'd ever been. She shared a small wooden house in Oak Grove with Maya, Lexy and Fawn. The four of them sat on the deck drinking beers, had frequent barbecues down at the beach and generally enjoyed lives that were free and easy and fun.

Deanna particularly liked heading at weekends to the Pillow Theater cinema, where you brought your own pillow, flopped down and watched movies in a bohemian atmosphere that was a million miles away from anything that Dublin had to offer. She would often meet the girls for cocktails in the Outrigger too, even though the food there was terrible and the windows were almost too grimy to see through. But it was a thrill for Deanna, because there wasn't a chance in hell that she'd ever have drunk a cocktail in Killester and it seemed like a sophisticated sort of thing to do.

The town's changing times offered opportunities for people who wanted to take a chance, and the two Californian girls decided to open a craft shop on Cannery Row, selling pottery, glassware and other bits and pieces that they either made themselves or commissioned artists to make for them. They set it up with a loan from Lexy's father because the local bank hadn't been keen to advance money to two young women, even though Lexy had drawn up a business plan and had brought samples of their work for the bank manager to see. Deanna had been angry on Lexy's behalf, but the older girl had simply said that her father could afford it because he was a hotshot legal guy and he was happy to support her. Deanna felt there was something intrinsically wrong with this, but she wasn't entirely sure what. It made sense for families to support each other. But it shouldn't have to be that way.

Lexy and Fawn didn't mind that the money had come from Mr Steiger. The shop was in a great location and it wasn't long before it was a popular destination for tourists and locals alike. Lexy said it was turning into a good investment for her pop. And with interest rates at about six per cent, better that he should make money from it than the bank!

Regardless of how well the situation had worked out for

everyone concerned, Deanna still felt aggrieved on Lexy's behalf. But she was trying to be a calmer person these days, more in tune with the laid-back California lifestyle. She told herself not to get frazzled by things she couldn't change.

And then she went to the café.

It was on Alvarado Street, and the nearest one to K9s, but she'd never bothered going in before. After all, there was a coffee machine as well as a water cooler in the grooming parlour, so there was no need for her to go out. And she normally went to Breakwater Cove at lunchtime, where she would eat as she watched the boats come in and out of the harbour. But this day had been exceptionally busy, because one of Mindy's best clients had come in with her four dogs and Deanna hadn't had time to grab a coffee or anything to eat. The sign for the café, swinging gently in the breeze, had attracted her, and she'd made the decision to get coffee and a cake there.

It was busy. She realised that most of the space was taken up by a group of women who'd pushed tables together so that they could sit around them and talk. The women seemed to be of all ages, and their conversation was loud and animated. Deanna sat at a table on the opposite side of the room, but she couldn't help hearing what they were saying. And what she heard jolted her. Because they were talking about the injustices that women had to put up with in a patriarchal society. They were complaining that women didn't get the same opportunities as men. They were angry about the portrayal of women in advertising. They were saying all the things that Deanna believed in and that angered her too, even though in her months of travelling she'd put her anger to one side, and even though she couldn't help feeling that women were far more progressive in the US than in Ireland.

She wanted to join the group but she didn't have the nerve. She wondered who they were and why they were meeting in the café. She eavesdropped shamelessly on their conversation and ordered an extra coffee just so that she could hear one of them, middle-aged and white-haired, talk about the kind of life she wanted for girls yet to be born into the world, and how she would fight to get it. She would have stayed as long as they did, but she couldn't keep drinking coffee and staring at them. So, after an hour, she left. The next day she went in and asked about them. The café's owner (an affable, balding man in his mid-fifties) said that they were a group called the Light Fighter Feminists and that they met in the café every month.

'I'm sure they'd be happy to have another convert,' he said. 'Though frankly, honey, there are better things you could be doing. You're far too pretty to get involved with that lot.'

She bit back a sharp reply and made a note in her diary to call into the café again in a month's time. She wanted to be part of that group. She liked the way they talked.

But she missed the next meeting of the Light Fighter Feminists. She missed it because she'd met Jorge, and meeting him changed her life for ever. She met him on a sunny afternoon when she called to the craft shop after work. It was warmer than usual for January, and Jorge was sitting on the steps outside the shop, basking in the welcome heat. He looked at her and smiled, and took her breath away.

Jorge had soulful dark eyes in a tanned, bearded face. His hair was longer than was then fashionable, but the look suited him. He was wearing a tan suede jacket over a red cotton shirt and wide-legged jeans. If Deanna had been asked to imagine the man she'd most like to date, Jorge would have been that man. Normally she never imagined men she'd like to date because she was too angry with them to care. For a moment she was angry with Jorge too, sitting on the steps, in her way. But then he smiled.

It was a lazy, languid smile. It made his eyes crinkle. It was a smile that embraced her, cheered her and made her feel good.

'Howdy,' he said.

'Hello.' She'd never been tongue-tied in the presence of a man before. But she wanted to say the right thing to him. She knew that she was blushing, which was embarrassing. She was annoyed with him for making her feel that way, and yet she couldn't help herself.

'Am I in your way?'

'Sort of,' she said. 'I was going into the shop, but . . .'

'Great store,' he said.

'Yes.'

'Jorge.' He said it slowly, emphasising the Latin-American phrasing.

'Deanna.'

'You're not from round here, Deanna, are you?'

'Are you?'

She was surprised at the way she spoke to him, surprised at the playful tone of her voice. She hadn't known she could speak like that.

He grinned. 'Nope. Just driftin' through. How about you?'

'Living here.' She said it proudly. 'For the time being.'

'Well, now.' He looked at her appraisingly. 'I might just

have to reconsider my moving-on plans, Deanna. What d'you think?'

Afterwards, what she thought was that she'd lost complete control of her senses. She certainly lost her heart. She'd lost it the moment he'd spoken. No man had ever had that effect on her before. She spent every moment she could with him, much to the amusement of Lexy and Fawn but the annoyance of Maya, who hissed to her one night that she was behaving like some slutty tart, waiting for her man to call. Deanna had been annoyed with her friend and told her that it wasn't like that, that she and Jorge thought about life the same way, that he loved her and respected her. That they shared the same ideals. That he thought women should be free to pursue their dreams. That it was wrong to think of girls as loose and men as people who should sow wild oats. Sexual freedom cut both ways, she said. Besides, Jorge was different from other men. He understood.

'The only person who understands what it's like to be a woman is another woman,' said Maya forcefully. 'You should know that by now, Deanna. You know you should.'

Maybe she'd been wrong, thought Deanna. Maybe the reasons she'd felt the way she did were nothing to do with how women were treated by society as a whole, but how she was treated herself. She hadn't been particularly popular in school. But maybe that was because of her, not because of the other girls. Maybe it was because she'd stupidly refused to embrace her femininity and been judgemental about the girls who did. Maybe she'd been wrong about all men being egotistic, bombastic, selfish bastards. Because Jorge was none of those things. Jorge, who was laid-back and carefree and who played the guitar with a sensitivity that touched Deanna's soul, was the best thing that had ever happened to her. And she was totally and utterly in love with him.

Discovering she was pregnant was the biggest shock of her life. She'd never even considered the possibility, because every single time they'd made love they'd used condoms (available in Ireland only on prescription; the country was a total and utter back-water. She would have happily taken the pill, which was readily available in California too, but it gave her blinding headaches). At first she didn't realise why she was suddenly racing to the toilet every morning and chucking up before she'd had her cup of coffee and cigarette on the deck outside the house. But when it finally dawned on her, she turned the taps on full and the shower radio to its loudest whenever she rushed to the bath-room to be sick, so that the sounds of her body-racking vomiting would be muffled. She didn't want Maya, Lexy and Fawn to know that she was pregnant. Not yet.

But she had to tell Jorge. She asked him to come to the house one night when she knew the girls would be out. He sat on the rickety swing chair beside her and she took a deep breath and broke the news. He said nothing.

'What are we going to do?' she asked eventually. She didn't like having to ask; it made her seem whiny and dependent, and that wasn't the way she was. It wasn't the way they were.

'Hey, baby, I don't mind what you do.' Jorge took a drag from the joint he was smoking and handed it to her. She shook her head. 'I have plans, though.'

'What plans?' Afterwards she thought how stupid she

was to assume that his plans were for her and their unborn baby.

'I'm heading south,' he said. 'I've been in Monterey too long. I'm thinking of going to Mexico for a while.'

'Mexico!' She was taken aback. 'You never said anything about Mexico before.'

'I don't talk about what I'm gonna do,' said Jorge languidly. 'I just go do it.'

'But it's different now,' Deanna told him. 'You can't just go where you like any more, Jorge. We've got a baby to think about.'

'*You* have a baby to think about,' said Jorge. 'How do I know who the daddy is?'

She stared at him. She couldn't believe what he was saying.

'You know,' she said eventually. 'Of course you do. I haven't been with anyone else since you. I love you and I thought you loved me. Otherwise . . .'

'Gimme a break,' he said. 'It's not like we're married or anything, Deanna. I told you, I'm a drifter. You said you were a drifter too. We were having a little fun, is all.'

'Maybe. But this changes everything.'

'Not for me.' He stood up. 'I'm sorry things haven't worked out how you expected, honey, but you can't tie me down with a baby that could be anyone's.'

'You know it's yours!' She'd never been angry with him before. But she was very angry now.

'Sweetheart, we used protection.'

'I know. But something went wrong and now you have to face up to your responsibilities!'

'It's not my responsibility.' He shook his head.

'Yes,' she insisted. 'It is.'

But he simply shrugged his shoulders and walked away. And he didn't come back.

She couldn't believe it. She'd done everything she'd planned not to do. She'd fallen for a man and she'd believed in him and she'd got pregnant and she was only nineteen years old.

She was a fool. She'd managed to ruin her life before it had even started.

Chapter 7

Supercell: a thunderstorm with a deep rotating updraught

Lainey rarely called her mother by anything other than her given name, and Deanna never referred to herself as Mum or Mam or Mom. In a million years Lainey would never have put Deanna into the same box as the mothers of her friends, and, she supposed, in a million years Deanna wouldn't have wanted to be put in that box either. She'd discovered, when she was in her teens, that her reasoning had pleased Deanna, who once said that despite everything, she supposed Lainey wasn't turning out to be a total loss after all. Lainey had been surprised at how satisfied she'd felt when her mother said this, even as she told herself that she didn't need praise from someone who was such a fleeting presence in her life. She felt it was wrong, somehow, to get a greater glow from Deanna's words than from anything that Madeleine ever said to her, even though she had a warm and loving relationship with her grandmother.

But every girl has a difficult relationship with her mother, she reminded herself, as she picked up the phone to call her a couple of days after Deanna's arrival in Dublin. It's just that most of them are difficult because they know each other too well. Not because they don't know each other at all.

It was Deanna herself who answered.

'Hi,' said Lainey. 'I thought I'd better ring you.'

'It's good to hear from you.' Deanna's American accent had faded over the last forty-eight hours, as it always did when she was back in Ireland. 'How are you keeping?'

If you really gave a damn, thought Lainey, you'd phone me or email me more often.

'Fine,' she said blithely. 'Not a care in the world. And you?'

'I'm good,' said Deanna. 'Busy, of course. And I expect to be busier once I get on my tour circuit.'

'Of course,' repeated Lainey.

'I wanted to talk to you about my documentary,' said Deanna.

'Huh?' Lainey was surprised. Deanna normally didn't want to talk to her about anything to do with her work.

'I thought it might be interesting to look at your career and your choices as part of it. It would be good research for me.'

You've got to be kidding, thought Lainey in horror. The idea of her mother dissecting her choices was appalling.

'I'm sure I'm not interesting enough for you,' she said evenly.

'You could be,' Deanna told her. 'We won't know till we talk.'

'Right.'

'Coffee? Dinner?' asked Deanna briskly, ignoring the doubt in her daughter's voice.

Honestly, thought Lainey, I'm closer to the people at work than I am to this woman. I might as well be meeting a complete stranger really.

'Either would be lovely,' she said politely.

'In town? Or is there anywhere local you fancy?'

'Town works for me.'

'When?'

'I'm off on Wednesday.'

'Anywhere special suit you?'

They arranged to meet in the Westin, as Deanna had a lunch date there followed by a meeting, and it would suit her not to have to move.

'See you then,' said Deanna.

'See you.' Lainey hung up and looked at her computer monitor. There was another storm beginning to form in the Atlantic Ocean. It looked as though it was heading straight for the west coast of Ireland. Which meant more bad weather ahead.

Deanna always felt dissatisfied after talking to Lainey. There was an underlying judgement in her daughter's voice and she knew that Lainey was basically telling her that she'd failed as a mother. Deanna readily accepted that she hadn't been a good mother. She hadn't been cut out for it in the first place. So it wasn't surprising that she'd made such a hash of it. But it annoyed her that Lainey made her feelings so clear. She'd done her best for her daughter, after all.

When she realised that Jorge had left her, she'd also realised that she was going to have to do it all on her own. She'd faced up to her responsibilities in a way he hadn't. In a way, she thought, that all women faced up to responsibilities when men left them in the lurch.

It was Lexy who first saw her with her head down the toilet and it was Lexy who realised, straight away, why. Lexy was the one who offered to help her too. She said that if Deanna wanted an abortion, she knew the best place to go. 'You have your whole life in front of you,' she told Deanna. 'Do you want to ruin it just because of a stupid mistake with a guy who wasn't worth a minute of your time?'

That was how Deanna felt about it too. The idea that she was pregnant with Jorge's baby was terrifying. Both because she didn't want to have the baby at all and because it would be a constant reminder of the fact that she'd let a man take advantage of her. Not by sleeping with her, of course. She'd wanted to sleep with him, and women were as entitled as men to sleep with whomever they chose. But she'd been fooled by letting him trick her into thinking that there was something between them when the truth was that all he was looking for was sex. And she didn't like being made a fool of.

The warnings of the nuns in the convent school kept coming back to haunt her. She remembered them telling a classroom full of teenage girls to keep their self-respect so that men would respect them in return. Never to do anything they'd be ashamed of. She wasn't ashamed of sleeping with a man. But she was ashamed that the man had been Jorge. She was ashamed that her own judgement had been so spectacularly wrong. She'd thought that she was a good judge of people. She'd thought she knew everything. And the truth was, she'd known nothing.

She also knew that she couldn't have an abortion. Despite the fact that she was able to ignore the nuns' words when it came to having sex, she couldn't ignore their views on getting rid of the baby. It was a sin. And no matter how dated, stupid and misogynistic she thought the Catholic Church was, she simply couldn't bring herself to abandon a lifetime of its teaching. She told herself that she'd be doing the right thing by getting rid of the unwanted child, but she couldn't persuade herself to go through with it. And so she went ahead with her pregnancy and gave birth to her baby daughter on a day when a savage storm swept through California with 90 kph winds gusting across the country and furious waves crashing on to the shore.

Deanna had listened to the raging winds and pummelling rain against the hospital windows as she'd held her crying baby to her chest. She couldn't believe that somewhere out there Jorge was still drifting aimlessly around, finding other girls to have a bit of fun with, while she was now responsible for this bawling scrap of humanity, which was just as much a part of him as it was of her. It wasn't fair. It wasn't right. And it wasn't that she didn't want the best for her baby daughter, but she had a horrible feeling that her best was never going to be good enough.

She phoned home the day after Lainey's birth.

'What's wrong?' asked Madeleine immediately.

'Why does anything have to be wrong?'

'We haven't heard from you in months. No letters, no cards. And now a phone call?' Madeleine knew that she sounded tetchy, but she couldn't help that. She was tetchy. And anxious.

'I have some news for you.'

Madeleine's grip tightened on the receiver.

'You're a grandmother,' said Deanna. 'I had a baby girl yesterday. We're both fine.'

Edmund could see that Madeleine was in shock. At first he thought that something terrible had happened. He was relieved when, having taken the receiver out of her hand, Deanna told him about the baby, even though he was horrified that she hadn't told them about her pregnancy at all. And he was also horrified that she'd had a relationship with someone they didn't know and who wasn't on the scene any more. He wanted to shout at Deanna and ask her how it was she'd managed to forget the type of upbringing she'd had. But he didn't. He simply said that he hoped she was all right. And that the baby was too. Afterwards he reminded Madeleine that the birth of a baby wasn't terrible. It was joyous. Even on this occasion. But he knew that Madeleine, once again, was worried about Deanna. From the day her daughter had taken the ferry to England, she'd never really stopped.

Edmund and Madeleine flew to California two weeks after Deanna's call. The storms had passed by then and the West Coast sun was shining brightly when they finally arrived at the house in Monterey. Deanna was sitting on the swing seat on the deck, the baby in her arms, when the cab pulled up. Madeleine could hear the sound of the baby's crying before she even stepped out of the cab that had brought them the final mile to her daughter's home. Despite her exhaustion from the long flight and the tiring bus journey from San Francisco, she pushed open the garden gate and hurried up the wooden steps while Edmund paid the cab driver. She sat down on the seat beside Deanna, put her arms around her and told her that she loved her. Then she asked if she could hold the baby.

As soon as Madeleine picked her up, Lainey stopped crying. Her contorted dark eyes relaxed and opened and fixed on the woman in front of her. Madeleine kissed her granddaughter gently on her forehead. Edmund, who'd joined them on the deck, stroked her cheek with the tip of his finger. Lainey gurgled with pleasure.

'Is she hungry?' asked Madeleine.

Deanna shook her head tiredly. 'I fed her already. I think it's wind. She always seems to yell just as much after she's been fed as before.'

'You were a bit like that,' said Madeleine. 'You settled down, though.'

'Eventually.' Edmund allowed the baby to grasp his little finger. 'Oh, she's a real dote, isn't she?'

Deanna didn't reply. Madeleine looked at her appraisingly.

'You're exhausted,' she said. 'You need some rest. Why don't you go to bed and we'll look after Lainey.'

'What, before you give me the lecture on what a fool I've been and how ashamed you are of me?' said Deanna.

'We're not going to lecture you,' Madeleine told her. 'What's done is done. We want to help you.'

None of this had been what Deanna had expected. But the thought of someone looking after Lainey while she slept was so beguiling that she didn't say anything. She got up from the seat and went inside without another word.

Five minutes later she was asleep.

She woke up four hours after her parents had arrived, the longest uninterrupted sleep she'd had since giving birth. She pushed the sheets to one side and got out of the bed. She stood silently for a moment in her oversized maroon college T-shirt, listening for the sound of her baby crying. But everything was silent.

She walked out of the bedroom and on to the deck. Her parents were sitting in the sun, Madeleine reading a magazine and Edmund puffing on his favourite pipe. The baby was sleeping in the crib beside them. It was, thought Deanna, like an American Dream image. Mom, Pops and baby. Only, of course, that wasn't how it actually was. And that wasn't how it was going to be either.

Madeleine and Edmund told her that she had to come back to Ireland. Deanna said that she was happy in California and that she wanted to stay. Besides, she added, my daughter is an American citizen. She has a right to be brought up in her own country.

'I'm fed up with your silliness now.' Madeleine spoke to her more sharply than she'd done in years. 'You're being bloody selfish, Deanna. That child needs a loving family around her, and you can't provide that, can you?'

'I have great friends who'll help me out. They'll take her when I need it.'

'Oh, come on!' Madeleine was impatient. 'You're talking about a baby here. You can't just farm her out to complete strangers. She's not one of your grooming parlour clients, you know.'

'Don't patronise me,' said Deanna. 'Don't talk at me as though I'm stupid.'

'Well it was stupid to get pregnant, wasn't it?'

'I knew you'd say that eventually!'

'It's the truth.'

The two women glared at each other.

'I didn't intend to.' Deanna wavered first.

'I don't know whether I'm glad to hear that or not,' said

Madeleine. 'I thought I brought you up better than to sleep with the first man who came along. I thought you were smarter than that too.'

'Who says he was the first man to come along?' Deanna looked defiant.

'Even worse,' retorted Madeleine angrily.

'I made a mistake.' The fight went out of Deanna's voice. 'That's all. I made a mistake.'

'But you can't treat your daughter as a mistake,' said Madeleine. 'She's not an appendage to your life. She's part of it.'

'I know that,' said Deanna. 'You and Dad have one view about how a family should be. I have another.'

'And your view is that one baby and lots of friends works?' Madeleine was incredulous.

'Yes,' said Deanna.

Madeleine sighed. Her daughter had always been headstrong. She'd thought that it was a good quality in a person. Now she wasn't so sure.

Edmund had only been able to remain in the States for a week, because he didn't have the time to take off work. Madeleine said that she'd stay a bit longer. The unspoken pact between her and her husband was that she'd stay until she got Deanna to come home with her. In the meantime she'd help her with the baby, because so far Deanna's maternal instinct hadn't really kicked in and she was utterly hopeless. But, Madeleine told Edmund, sooner or later it would. Sooner or later Deanna would realise that being a mother was the most important job in the world.

Deanna had to admit that Madeleine was a million times

better than her at looking after the baby, which was crazy really, because it wasn't as though her mother had all that much experience. Unusually for her time, she'd only had one child – not, Madeleine had once told her, because they didn't want any more, but it simply hadn't happened for them. But despite her limited experience, Madeleine was adept at looking after the baby and Deanna conceded that Lainey was much happier in her grandmother's arms than in her own.

She wanted to reclaim her life. So a few days after Edmund had left, and while Madeleine was pushing Lainey in her pram along Ocean Avenue, Deanna called to the grooming parlour. She was surprised to see a man, in his early twenties she guessed, giving a bath to Bobo, a Labrador who was brought regularly to K9s. She went into Mindy's tiny office. Her boss was going through a sheaf of invoices.

'Hi, Mindy,' she said.

'Oh, hello.' Mindy looked surprised to see her. 'How are you?'

'Well, I've had my baby.' Deanna beamed at her. 'Though it'll be a while before my body gets back into shape. Still, I'm sure that being back at work will mean losing the fat fairly quickly.'

Mindy looked at her as if she was bonkers and told her that she'd had to get someone else while Deanna was off work.

'Yes, but I stayed for as long as I could,' said Deanna. 'I told you I'd come back.'

'I had to have someone straight away,' said Mindy. 'I couldn't wait for you.'

'I've only been gone a month! A couple of weeks before the birth and a couple of weeks after.'

'I know. But business doesn't stop while you're having a baby. And Todd is a great worker.'

'You're saying I wasn't?'

'Of course you were,' said Mindy. 'But it's different now, isn't it? It's not your main priority any more.'

As if washing dogs ever was a priority, thought Deanna angrily as she walked back to the house and the fish stew that Madeleine was preparing for dinner. I'm made for better things than that!

Madeleine agreed that Mindy's treatment of her was wrong and that one day it would surely be illegal to throw a woman out of work because she'd had a baby. But right now, she told Deanna, your baby needs you. You have to look after her. And I'm begging you to come home with me, because in the end, that's the best solution for both of you. Deanna said she'd think about it, but she didn't want to think about it. She wanted things to be the way they were before.

The next day she walked past the grooming parlour again and saw that the Light Fighter Feminists were meeting in the café. She went inside and ordered a coffee. The women were talking about a demonstration they were going to hold outside the county offices, protesting at double standards in employment. Deanna reckoned the protest was practically meant for her. She asked the white-haired woman who seemed to be chairing the group about it. She wanted to know if anyone could come, and Patsy Fuller, taken with the determined set of Deanna's mouth, said the more the merrier. She invited her to join the rest of the meeting, and Deanna pulled up her chair and, for the first time in her life, really got stuck in to a conversation. These women were on her wavelength, she thought. They understood that not everyone believed that life for a woman was about creating the perfect home and marrying the perfect man and raising the perfect family. What, Deanna asked them during a lull in the conversation, was the point in being educated and well-informed if all they were going to do with their education was raise children? Children were important, of course, but if raising them was your only aim in life, what was it all for? To make them educated and well-informed too? For them to then just raise other children? Was it all about the continuation of the species and nothing about enlightenment in your own life? The women nodded in agreement and Deanna felt welcome in the group.

She loved the march and the protest too. She got a thrill from shouting 'The personal is political!' and shaking her placard. She had never felt as alive as when an official tried to break up their protest, causing a minor scuffle, which ended for her when someone else's placard banged her on the head and she had to sit down on a low wall to recover.

Madeleine nearly had a fit when Deanna returned to the house sporting a black eye as a result of her encounter with the placard.

'You told me you were going to see some officials about work,' she said angrily. 'Not that you were taking to the streets!'

'We did see some officials. And we did talk about work,' said Deanna as they watched footage of the protest on the evening news. 'They know how we feel.'

'And did any of them give you a job?' asked Madeleine.

'I wouldn't work with that gang of sexist pigs even if they did,' said Deanna.

Madeleine said nothing. Things were not going according to plan. But then with Deanna they never did.

It was Lexy who changed her mind about everything. Lexy had come to her and said that it had been OK having her mom stay for a week but that it was a big strain having her there for longer. And that it was a bit of a strain having a baby in the house too. It was interfering with their lifestyles. They hadn't had a party in months. And they were afraid to smoke pot with either Deanna's daughter or her mother around.

'You've got to find somewhere else,' said Lexy. 'I'm sorry, Deanna. We're friends, I know. But we can't have your entire family in permanent residence. Things have changed. You've got to accept that.'

She was wrong and everyone else was right. Her life had changed. She didn't want it to be that way. But there was nothing she could do about it. She'd allowed Jorge to ruin it for her. And no marching or slogans or shaking of placards could change the fact that she was the one with the baby and she was the one who had to make decisions about it.

So she told her mother that she'd come back to Ireland. But she cried when the plane took off from San Francisco. Lainey cried too. And Madeleine wasn't sure which of them needed comforting the most.

Chapter 8

Stratocumulus: low-level patches of cloud with a well-defined clumpy base

Lainey was putting together the evening TV forecast in the Met Eireann office at the television studios. She was looking at the graphics in front of her, deciding that the outlook for the next few days was mixed – not exactly an unusual occurrence in Ireland. The country's location meant that it was continually affected by competing weather fronts.

It would rain later that evening, she decided, but the following day would be dry and sunny. Not warm, unfortunately, because the prevailing winds were coming from the north and would add a bit of bite to the air. Which wasn't really what people wanted to hear at the height of the summer. But it was what they were going to get all the same.

She leaned back in her chair and gazed at the monitors without really seeing them. She was thinking about Ken. It had been a habit to drop in to him after her shift in the television studio ended. When they ended up in bed together, as they nearly always did, she'd give him a running commentary of meteorological terms as he explored her body. They both found it funny. And surprisingly erotic, too, which, whenever she thought about it, made Lainey chuckle. She wondered how many people were turned on by hearing the words 'a warm front is on its way' or 'the wind-chill factor will make it seem colder'.

She missed him. She missed his company and his way of making her laugh. A hundred times since they'd said goodbye her finger had hovered over his speed dial on her phone. She had a legitimate reason to call him after all. He still hadn't returned the stuff she'd left at his house. She'd sent a text about it a couple of days after their return from Belfast, and he'd replied to say he'd be in touch. But he hadn't called. So she was perfectly within her rights to phone him instead. And maybe, she thought, with a bit of water under the bridge, he'd change his mind about everything.

She twirled a curl of hair around her finger. But would he? He might change his mind about not wanting to see her again (he always said that her long legs never failed to get to him every time) but would he change his mind about the future of their relationship? About where it was going? Which, clearly, from his point of view, was as far as the bedroom and no further.

Dammit, she muttered, as she sat up and concentrated on the screen in front of her again. I have to stop thinking about him. I have to get over him. I've had enough practice. I know that it gets easier over time. Only this time, she thought, I don't want it to get easier. I don't want to lose him. I don't want to have to start all over again.

She pulled a magenta-pink jacket over her ivory top and made her way to the weather studio. The meteorologists had their very own studio, a small room just down the corridor from the office where they prepared the forecasts. She'd been astonished the first time she'd been shown it, always having thought that the forecasters hung around the news set until it was time to do their broadcast. But they didn't. They waited in the small self-contained studio, surrounded by equipment and standing in front of a camera that was remotely activated.

She was completely alone in the room. There were no cameramen or technicians around her. The cameras and sound systems were already set up. Realising that she had to deliver the forecast on her own had scared her, at the start. Not everyone could cope with the fact that you presented it in a vacuum and that you were responsible for getting everything right. You watched the clock to know when to start. You watched the clock to know when to finish. You stood in front of the blue screen with the clicker in your hand and you tried to make the weather presentation both interesting and informative. But you never truly knew how good a job you'd done because there was nobody to give you any immediate feedback. Of course there were sometimes letters or emails (and occasionally even Twitter streams) devoted to the weather forecast but she didn't get to read them until much later. Quite often they were critical, not of the forecasting itself, but of how the forecaster had looked. The viewers commented on their clothes or a new hairstyle or shade of lipstick. (There had been a barrage of mail when Lainey had her hair cut shorter than usual. Most of it from people telling her to let it grow again.) But very few people commented on the actual weather.

Lainey took off her shoes as she got ready to do the forecast. She always did it barefoot because she was afraid of catching her heel in something as she walked between the taped lines that marked the edges of the camera's vision.

There was nothing to catch her heel in, but she preferred to be barefoot anyway. It was her thing. Other people had things of their own, rituals that they adhered to before they went on air. Complying with a ritual, doing the same thing every time, gave you a sense of control. And even if it was tentative at best, it helped you feel confident.

She stood in front of the camera and rolled her head from side to side. She could see the visual that was being projected on to the blue screen behind her. The fact that everything was projected on to the screen determined what she wore for the presentations. No blue; that would blend with the screen and give her a disembodied look. Lainey favoured pinks and purples, which suited her colouring. Tania, one of the other forecasters, liked pale greens and browns. Some of their clothes hung on a rail at the side of the room. They often left their preferred outfits there.

'. . . And now to the weather, with Lainey Ryan.'

She smiled her big, wide smile at the camera and began to talk. It came easy to her, marrying her commentary with the graphic screens, allowing the weather story to unfold. Most people thought the forecasters were reading from an autocue. But they didn't do it that way. They told the story themselves, using the graphics to guide them through it. When she'd first started, she was afraid of drying up in front of the screen, of forgetting what she wanted to say. But it had never happened, because she liked talking about the weather and she knew the story she needed to tell. As she spoke, she always imagined people planning their days. Staying in bed late because of the rainy start. Taking the kids out because of the sun. Remembering to bring fleeces because of the wind.

'. . . And that's the weather. A very good night.' She smiled again and waited until the light on the camera had gone out. Then she slipped on her shoes again and went to the office to collect her things. She wondered if Ken had watched the forecast. And if he was missing her at all. Somehow, she doubted it.

And then she wondered if her mother had watched it. Would she bother? Unlikely, thought Lainey. Not for something as trite as the weather.

Tonight she felt as though nobody had seen her at all. As though she'd given her forecast to a blank wall.

On the days when she was doing the night shift she didn't cycle to work, and the walk usually took about forty-five minutes. There was already a hint of the rain to come in the air, and she strode briskly along the pavement so that she'd make it home before it arrived. She'd put Ken temporarily out of her mind and was instead thinking about her forthcoming dinner with Deanna. She was focusing on how to deflect her mother's inevitable questions about her career and her prospects for advancement. Deanna would want to know what promotions she was in line for, or what potential opportunities she should be chasing in commercial weather companies (Deanna had researched everything to do with careers in meteorology when Lainey had informed her what she was planning), or what the chances were of her becoming the head of a department or the entire network. Lainey tried to explain that she was currently a state employee, so she couldn't exactly storm the walls of a boardroom to become a weather whizz, but Deanna took no notice of that.

Most of her friends complained that their mothers took

too much interest in their love lives. Val and Carla both had mothers who'd vetted their boyfriends on a regular basis and dished out advice or criticism about them. But in Lainey's case it was different. She didn't think her mother had ever asked her a question about boyfriends or dating. All she wanted to know about was career and success. The answers to which, Lainey murmured to herself, must be very disappointing for her. I love my job and I know I'm good at it, but delivering the forecast on TV simply doesn't cut it as a resounding success in her eyes. And it's probably just as well she doesn't ask about the men, because I couldn't blame her for counting me as a failure at that too. Although from Deanna's perspective, the failure is because I'm the one that's being dumped and not the one doing the dumping. The renewed memory of Ken's abrupt dumping of her made Lainey feel miserable again.

A few drops of rain had begun to fall as she keyed in the entry code to the pedestrian gate of her apartment building. The gate swung open and she walked along the narrow path that divided the two main blocks of the complex. Lainey had been living there for nearly three years, and she liked its convenience for work as well as for the city. It was generally quiet and relatively peaceful, although it was hard to get to know people, as most of the residents, like her, were renting and tended to stay for a couple of years at the most. Lately Madeleine had been asking her if she'd thought about buying a home of her own, but it wasn't something that appealed to Lainey. Not yet, anyway. She knew that many people thought of houses as investments. But when she bought somewhere, she wanted to buy it as a place to live. She wasn't into the notion of moving every few years. Besides, buying somewhere of her own would be making some kind of statement. It would be saying that she was a single girl and happy about it. That she had her own place and her own stuff and that she didn't need anyone else in her life to be happy. Despite the break-up with Ken, she didn't know if she was ready to make that statement yet.

The thing is, she thought, when I'm on my own without a boyfriend, I'm perfectly happy. It's just that when I meet someone, when the whole romance thing suddenly starts to fizz up, I lose all sense of proportion. Maybe if I had a place of my own, I'd stop thinking about someone to share it with. Maybe then I'd be like my mother, too. Single, solitary and satisfied with my life.

She heard footsteps on the path behind her and glanced over her shoulder. Shay Loughnane was walking along the path. His latest girlfriend followed half a step behind him. Slower, no doubt, because she was wearing spiky-heeled shoes, which, Lainey knew, just had to be crippling her. Lainey registered the fact that without the heels the woman wouldn't have reached her neighbour's shoulder. She wondered what it would be like to be small and dainty. Would people think of you differently, treat you differently then? Would they think you were cuter or more vulnerable because you didn't tower over them like an Amazon?

She veered towards her own apartment and then heard her name. She looked back.

'Hey, Lainey. Accurate forecast.' He gestured towards the grey skies.

'We do our best,' she said lightly, thinking that at least one person had seen her tonight and so she hadn't been talking into the void after all.

He waved. She opened the door to her block and, deciding she'd done enough walking for the day, took the lift to the fourth floor. She went into her apartment and hung up her jacket. She didn't bother switching on the lights, because her curtains were open and the steady glow from the garden lights was enough to guide her to the sideboard, where she slid her iPod into the docking station and switched it on.

She flopped on to the sofa to the voice of Enrique Iglesias. She was pretty sure that liking Enrique's music was cheesy, even for an occasional-power-ballad girl, but she didn't care. She didn't play her R&R music at night; she reserved that for cycling, or for when she was cleaning the apartment, when she'd dance around the place with a duster in her hand, playing air guitar.

Across the garden she noticed the light to the apartment opposite come on. She saw Shay walk across the room and open the doors to his balcony. His girlfriend followed him. They stood on the balcony for a while, and then he leaned towards her and she leaned towards him and Lainey couldn't help watching as they kissed each other. She wondered if he cared about the women he brought back to his apartment. Or if he, like Ken, didn't want to get involved, despite the kisses and the overnight stays. Were most men like that when it came down to it? Was she truly an incurable romantic who hadn't got a clue what real life was like?

She got up and closed the curtains. She didn't know how much of Shay's love life was going to be on display, but she didn't really want to see any of it. Deanna was right. Men weren't worthy of your attention. Not worthy of your love.

Her mobile vibrated and she looked at the incoming text message. It was from Ken. Her fingers trembled as she opened it.

Sry not in touch b4 now. Will drop your stuff over soon.

She stared at the phone. He hadn't completely forgotten about her after all. He'd texted her. He would be calling to her apartment. He would have her things. Maybe, she thought, he'd seen her on the TV that evening and remembered the nights of passion they'd had after her broadcasts. Maybe, deep down, he still loved her. And dropping over her stuff was an excuse to see her.

Or maybe he was simply doing exactly as he'd said. Returning her things. Cutting her out of his life. She didn't know what to think. But she did know that the idea of seeing him again was making her heart beat faster.

Chapter 9

Duplicatus: a cloud formation with more than one layer

Ken still hadn't returned her stuff when, a few days later, Val called and asked if she'd like to come over for dinner. Nick was in Cork, she said, and wouldn't be back until the following day, so perhaps they could have a girlie night together?

It was a while since she'd had a night in with her friend, and Lainey was delighted to have the opportunity for a bit of light-hearted gossip. She regularly kept in touch with both Val and Carla through emails or Facebook, but it wasn't the same as actually talking to them in person. Carla's most recent email had naturally been full of information about her fabulous honeymoon in Italy and how wonderful it had been. She'd added a link to a photo album that had included photographs of her and Lennart posing by Lake Garda looking blissfully happy. Seeing it, Lainey couldn't really believe that Carla had only married Lennart for security. The two of them seemed madly in love. Lennart's arm was around Carla, holding her tightly to him as she gazed adoringly at him. Carla's email had also suggested that Lainey might think about a visit to Stockholm soon, and she'd replied that she'd love to come. It would be good for her, she thought, to get away for a few days. Her last break had been at Easter, when she and Ken had gone to Portugal for a week with some of his friends. It seemed a lifetime ago.

Men may come and go, but friends stay for ever, she thought as she waited for the bus to take her into the city centre, where she would transfer on to the Luas tram which left her a mere five minutes from Val's house in Dundrum. And I'd be lost without mine. I really would.

It was a warm evening and had been a fine day, but the intermittent heavy clouds they were continuing to forecast at Met Eireann had begun to darken the sky. Lainey had added a telescopic umbrella to the canvas bag over her shoulder before leaving her apartment. She glanced up at the clumpy grey stratocumulus above her and hoped that it'd hold off with the rain at least until she got on the bus. But it still hadn't arrived before the first drops began to fall. She took the bright red umbrella out of the bag and told herself that it was good to be prepared.

She was looking impatiently at her watch and wondering what on earth had happened to the bus when a blue Volkswagen Golf pulled up just past the stop. The driver rolled down the passenger window, leaned out and called to her. She was startled by the sound of her name, because she didn't know anyone with a blue car. And then she realised that it was Shay Loughnane, telling her that he was going into town and that he'd give her a lift if she wanted.

Does he think he has to be nice to me all the time now just because we've spoken to each other? she wondered. I'm sure he's driven past me hundreds of times before. And again the thought flitted into her head, but disappeared almost as quickly. Remember the first day we met? You picked me up at the bus stop in the rain . . . but that wasn't strictly accurate, because the first time they'd actually spoken was when she'd hit him on the head with her flip-flop. You're such a fool, she muttered to herself as she collapsed her umbrella and hopped into the seat beside him. You really need to get hold of yourself.

'Thanks very much.' She fastened the seat belt.

'You're welcome. No need for you to get soaked.'

'It'll stop soon,' she remarked, 'but it's nice not to have to wait for the bus.'

'Where to?' he asked.

'Anywhere,' she told him. 'I'm visiting a friend on the south side.'

He grinned. 'Got your passport?'

She smiled in return. 'Up to date. I'm getting the Luas, so if you're heading near a stop that's fine, otherwise whatever suits you.'

'I'll drop you at Dawson Street for St Stephen's Green,' he said. 'I'm heading there myself.'

'Perfect, thanks.'

'Not doing the forecast this evening?' he asked after she'd stayed silent for a minute or two.

She shook her head. 'I've done my days for this week. And now I'm off till Friday.'

'Oh, right,' he said. 'You have to work weekends, of course.'

'I like it, though.'

'I'm working at the weekend too,' he said.

'What d'you do?'

'I'm a physiotherapist,' he told her. 'I'm attached to a sports clinic near Drumcondra.'

'I know it.' Since she'd started going out with Ken, she knew almost every sports clinic in Dublin, because he'd been to most of them. She wondered if Shay had ever treated Ken.

'Hopefully you'll never need us.'

She doubted it. Keeping fit had been fairly irrelevant to her lately. She hadn't been to the gym since before Carla's wedding, when Ken had given her a routine to tauten her arms and stomach. She'd been conflicted about what to do since, thinking that it might be a good place to bump into him casually but scared that he'd simply blank her, which would have been impossible to take. Besides, her body was heavy and lethargic, weighed down by the misery she felt inside. She didn't think she could possibly do anything energetic.

'I hope you warm up and down properly,' he added.

'Excuse me?' She glanced at him, startled.

'I've seen you heading off in your tracksuit,' he told her. 'So I took you for a gym bunny.'

'I do go to the gym, yes,' she said, deciding not to get offended by his description. 'And I know how to warm up.'

'Ah, but do you actually bother?' he asked. 'Most people do a few pathetic little stretches for about five minutes and then launch themselves into a mad spinning class or something. End up injured, of course.'

'I don't get injured,' she said, although she acknowledged to herself that he was probably right. Her warm-ups were minimal. And her lack of injury was more to do with the fact that she never really did anything too energetic because, except for the opportunity it had given her to be with Ken, the gym bored her rigid. I'm so bloody shallow, she thought glumly; I adapt my interests to suit my boyfriends. Deanna would be disgusted with me!

Shay said nothing in reply to her and drove in silence until they turned on to the Quays and were stopped in some heavy traffic. The rain was falling patchily now and the wipers squeaked as they moved across the windscreen. He switched them off.

'I really appreciate you driving me,' she said as they moved forward again.

'You're welcome,' he said. 'Any time you need a lift, let me know.'

'That's a rash offer if ever I heard one,' she told him in amusement.

'Possibly. You could be one of those party animals who're out every available moment.'

'Not as party as you,' she said.

He looked at her. 'And what's that supposed to mean?'

'Well, you're out a lot, aren't you? And when you're in, there's usually a girlfriend with you.'

'Excuse me?'

She knew she'd put her foot in it. 'I see you sometimes,' she admitted. 'In your apartment.'

'Huh?'

'Not that I deliberately look,' she said hastily. 'But sometimes I go out on to my balcony and your lights are on and I see that you've got a woman . . .' She broke off. 'I'm sorry, that sounds voyeuristic and moralising all at once, and I don't mean to be.'

'You don't?' There was an edge to his voice.

'Of course not. And I'm not spying on you,' she emphasised. 'I just . . . notice sometimes.'

'I see.'

Lainey was hot with embarrassment.

'I've seen you too.' He flicked the wipers across the windscreen.

'What?' She had cream voile as well as drapes on her windows, so it never occurred to her that anyone could see inside.

'Sure. With that pumped Adonis you bring back sometimes. He sure does like himself. Meet him at the gym, did you?'

'No, I didn't. Do *you* watch *me*?' she demanded.

He shook his head. 'Nope. But like you said, if you're in and the light is on and the drapes aren't closed . . .'

'There isn't much privacy in apartment living in Dublin,' she said, resolving to make sure her curtains were tightly closed in future.

'No,' he agreed. 'Which is something both of us should probably keep in mind.'

'Absolutely,' she said. Not that she really had to worry about closing her curtains. There'd be nothing worth seeing through her apartment window for a long, long time.

It had stopped raining by the time he dropped her outside the Dawson Street car park, and she thanked him again before hurrying to St Stephen's Green to catch the Luas. A tram had just pulled in and she hopped on it straight away, pleased with her good fortune.

Twenty-five minutes later she was outside Val's house. She walked up the short driveway and rang the bell.

Val opened the door almost immediately and gave Lainey a welcoming hug. She told her she was delighted to see her, thanked her for the bottle of wine she'd brought and ushered her into the living room, which led on to a conservatory the size of Lainey's entire apartment.

Val and Nick's house had originally been his family home. As Val had told Carla and Lainey when they'd moved in five years earlier, they'd never have been able to afford it if his parents hadn't downsized and sold it to them at a generous price. They'd been redecorating it room by room (a delicate process according to Val, because she didn't want to offend the Stauntons, whose taste in interior design was stuck somewhere in the eighties) and now they'd almost completed the transformation. The conservatory, Val said, would be one of the last things she'd worry about. Her priority had been the kitchen, bathroom and living room, followed by two of the four bedrooms.

'It's looking good,' said Lainey as she sat in one of the big armchairs and tucked her feet beneath her. 'Oh, but I wish I had this sort of space.'

Val handed her a glass of wine.

'I love it myself,' she admitted. 'And I love being able to walk in the garden, even if it is in a shameful state. I'm expecting the residents' association to come knocking at the door any moment, complaining that my unmown grass is lowering the tone of the neighbourhood.'

Lainey chuckled. 'The joys of suburban living. Different sort of pressures to apartment living. I nearly did the whole banging on the wall thing the other night, because the neighbours were having a loud and long party and I was on the early shift. When I hear myself wondering why they can't keep the noise down and sit around having nice conversations, I realise I've turned into my gran.'

'There are worse women than your gran,' said Val, who'd known Madeleine since childhood.

'That's true,' said Lainey. 'And not that I'm putting her

into the worse-than-Gran category, but guess what – my mother's come back for a visit.'

She told Val about her imminent meeting with Deanna and the documentary she was planning.

'And she wants to interview you for it?' asked Val.

'I doubt that very much.' Lainey drained her wine glass and allowed Val to refill it immediately. 'I think she's just looking at me for background material.'

'I'm sure she's interested in you for more than just background material,' said her friend.

'It'd be a bit weird, don't you think? Being interviewed by my mother?' Lainey asked. 'Not that I suppose she'd make a big deal of that fact.'

'I think it'd be cool. What's it all about?'

'I'm not sure of the exact theme,' said Lainey. 'But obviously it's something to do with feminism, and I really don't think I fit into her definition of a feminist.'

'Why not?' Val looked questioningly at Lainey. 'You're a modern woman, you live alone, you do a brilliant job and you're the face of the weather on TV.'

'You say the nicest things,' Lainey told her. 'But from Deanna's point of view I hardly advance the cause. After all, weather girls aren't exactly considered at the forefront of the feminist movement.'

'You've told me a million times that you're a meteorologist, not just a weather girl,' said Val firmly. 'I know that you had to study hard to get your job. So no false modesty.'

'I'm not trying to be modest,' Lainey assured her. 'People who simply present the weather do a perfectly good job. I'm saying that I'm nothing special. Not to Deanna.'

'You're very successful.' Val was obstinate. 'And with all this climate change stuff, meteorologists are in big demand.'

'That's not a bandwagon I want to jump on,' said Lainey. 'It interests me, of course, but to be honest, I just like doing forecasts. I'm not going to make a difference to the world.'

'And that's how you define success?' asked Val. 'Making a difference to the world?'

'It's certainly how Deanna does.'

'But you?' Val spoke seriously. 'How do you define it, Lainey?'

Lainey looked thoughtful. 'I don't know,' she said eventually. 'I suppose I've always felt the same as Deanna about it. That you have to make a difference.'

'Just because she's some mad overachiever who loves the sound of her own voice doesn't mean you have to be too.' Val was scathing. 'And making a difference doesn't have to be about success either. Nor does it have to be global. What about those charity walks you've done? That's making a difference.'

'Not quite the same thing,' said Lainey.

'So what? Anyway, you're as successful as Deanna, just in a different way.'

'Now you're being really silly,' said Lainey. 'Nobody could live up to her achievements! Critically acclaimed books on feminism, most of them *New York Times* bestsellers; worthy TV documentaries; speaking engagements all over the world. Anyone who knows anything about the women's movement knows about her. Even people who don't have heard of her! It's just unfortunate for her that she's my mother. Unfortunate for me too, because she's a hard act to follow.'

'I'm sure she's very proud of you,' said Val.

Lainey shook her head. 'I don't think so. And I don't blame her for that,' she added hastily. 'I realise she's a . . . a special sort of person and I have to accept that her standards are different to everyone else's. And what she wants for me would be different from what a normal mother would want for her daughter.'

'I'm sure she wants you to be happy,' said Val. 'That's all my mum cares about.'

'I don't honestly know about that,' Lainey said. 'Deanna isn't someone who seems to think that happiness is important. Doing something useful with your life – as a woman, of course – is what floats her boat.'

'Poor Lainey.' Val looked at her sympathetically. 'You think you have to live up to her, but you don't.'

'That's not true,' Lainey said. 'After all, hardly anyone knows she's my mother, so it's not as though I'm constantly being compared with her.'

'Odd, that,' remarked Val. 'You'd think someone would have picked up on it. They know she has a daughter, surely?'

'Not so much,' said Lainey. 'She'd never get away with it now, what with the internet and everything, but back when Deanna was making her breakthrough, nobody knew anything about me. Not in the States, anyway. And the people that knew in Ireland couldn't have cared less. So I faded into the background as far as she was concerned. Which suits me just fine,' she added quickly.

'It would be tiresome being constantly linked to her all right,' agreed Val.

'You know, I've decided it's because of her that I can't hold down a relationship,' Lainey said. 'I've mulled it over a lot, and she has to be the reason. Whenever she was around, she was always so horrible about men that I must have loads of issues buried deep inside.'

'But you love men,' Val pointed out. 'You've had lots of boyfriends. And you have Ken now.'

'Ho hum.' Lainey swallowed hard and told her friend about the break-up. She'd deliberately avoided phoning Val and crying down the phone immediately after the event. She'd wanted to wait until she could say Ken's name without dissolving into tears.

'Oh no.' Val immediately filled Lainey's wine glass again. 'I'm so, so sorry. I liked Ken.'

'So am I,' said Lainey. 'And I thought I loved him. But the thing is, I've broken up with so many men I thought I loved that it has to be me, not them.' Suddenly, even though she was finished with tears, she began to cry. 'Sorry.' She sniffed. 'Don't mind me. You know how I blub at the slightest thing.'

'Come on.' Val got up from the chair. 'Let's have something to eat. You can't be upset on a full stomach, as my own mother likes to say.'

The aroma in the kitchen was warm and comforting. Val – who hadn't even known how to switch on the oven when they'd shared a flat – bustled around with the food and put a portion of piping-hot lasagne in front of her friend.

'You are quite horribly Marta Stewart-ed now,' observed Lainey, who had recovered her equilibrium. 'And the worst of that is that I think it's a good thing.'

Val grinned as she passed some warm focaccia bread. 'I'm just showing off. Lasagne is my stand-by dish. D'you think Carla will get the domestic bug now that she's married?'

'Good question.' Lainey looked thoughtful. Then she told Val what their friend had said about her reasons for marrying Lennart. About security being as important as love. 'Or maybe more important,' Lainey added. 'I got the impression talking to her that Lennart being rich was the key factor in their marriage.'

Val raised an eyebrow. 'How very un-Carla.'

'So you'd have thought,' agreed Lainey. 'I swear to God, though, she was like a different person; someone who'd made a list and checked it twice!'

'It was a bit of a shock to see him,' said Val. 'I didn't expect him to be a middle-aged man.'

'It's not as though age matters that much, but it's still a bit weird.'

'She seems to know what she wants.'

'They did look pretty loved up in the honeymoon photos.'

'Everyone looks loved up in honeymoon photos,' Val said. 'Things would be bad if they didn't.'

'I guess so.'

'I hope it all works out for her.'

'D'you think it won't?'

'Who knows,' said Val. 'Maybe she's worked it out perfectly. Is she staying on in the company?'

'As far as I know.'

'We need to keep in contact with her,' said Val. 'I'm sure it's all very well being Mrs Lennart Soderling and having her houses in London and Stockholm, but will that do her any good on a bad hair day?'

'Probably,' Lainey said. 'She'll just pick up the phone and call someone to fix it.'

'You could be right.' Val nodded. 'She might embrace the whole being-rich thing with enthusiasm.'

'She's not really that sort of person,' said Lainey as they returned to the living room with a second bottle of wine. 'But you know, Val, I can't help feeling left behind now.'

'In what way?'

'You're both Smug Marrieds and I'm still the Sad Singleton.'

'I'm certainly not smug and you're absolutely not sad.'

'Well, I'm still sad about Ken,' admitted Lainey. 'I'm sad that I handled it so badly.'

'Maybe if you didn't want to get married so much . . .' Val looked thoughtful. 'I know you've said she's given you issues about it, and feel free to hit me if I'm wrong . . . but is the real reason you want to march up the aisle just to spite your mother?'

'Val Staunton!' Lainey looked affronted.

'Well, you're so different to her in so many ways,' said Val. 'Carla and I wonder sometimes.'

'You do?'

She nodded. 'You see those pictures of Deanna Ryan and she looks so stern and forbidding, and although she's not unattractive, she's certainly not at all . . . not at all feminine. And then there's you, Lainey, and you're the most feminine person I know. It seems impossible that you two are even related.'

'It seems impossible to me too,' agreed Lainey with a smile. 'But how I look and live my life – excluding my complete failure with men – has nothing to do with my mother. I was brought up by my gran, and she's the most feminine person I know.'

'True.'

'But maybe you're right.' Lainey sighed. 'Maybe on some weird internal level I want to prove to Deanna that it's possible to be pretty and happy and in love and not be a sad loser as a woman. Only thing is . . .' she ran her finger around the rim of her wine glass, 'I haven't exactly proved that point yet. And I'm not sure I ever will.'

Lainey was still thinking about her evening with Val when she walked into the Westin the next day to meet Deanna for the first time since her grandfather's funeral. She hadn't left her friend's house until after midnight, getting a cab home and feeling somehow happier than she'd done ever since her break-up with Ken. It had been nice to share her worries and insecurities with someone who understood her. She felt lucky that she had a friend like Val. Like Carla too, of course. They'd spent quite a bit more time talking about Carla and her new husband, wondering if she was being sensible about her marriage or if she'd regret putting security over true love. They hadn't managed to come to a satisfactory conclusion.

As she walked up the stairs to the hotel's atrium, Lainey knew Deanna would be horrified at the idea that someone like Carla – bright, intelligent and hard-working – would get married for security. Women were their own security, her mother always said. They had to look out for themselves. In the end, men would always let them down. (Lainey always thought her mother's comment was a bit rich – after all, Deanna didn't allow men into her life at all, so what did she know really? It wasn't fair to make sweeping generalisations based on the fact that her father had been a shit.)

Deanna was sitting at a corner table scanning the newspaper through a pair of small reading glasses, a silver teapot and china cup in front of her. She was wearing a charcoal-grey tailored suit, a pinstriped blouse with sharp collar, and black leather shoes. Her iron-grey hair was short and neat. As Lainey stood looking at her for a moment, Deanna glanced up, her blue eyes immediately meeting her daughter's. Lainey walked over to the table and stood opposite her.

'Hello,' said Deanna as she took off her reading glasses, folded the paper and put it on the table. 'It's good to see you again. You look well.'

Lainey had spent a lot of time on her appearance before coming to meet her mother. She wanted to look her very best when seeing her for the first time in two years. As always, she was wearing a lightly tinted moisturiser, but today she'd also done her eyes in the smoky shadows that emphasised them. She'd applied mascara to lengthen her lashes and rose blusher to the apples of her cheeks. Her lips were glossed and her hair was carefully brushed, even though it fell in the usual tumble of loose curls around her face. She was wearing a layered Monsoon skirt in shades of rose, and a dusty-pink wrap-around cardigan over a mauve vest top. Her jewellery was coloured rhinestones and a collection of bracelets jangled on her arms. Her nails, thanks to an after-dinner manicure from Val, were pale pink. On her feet she wore purple sandals with pink sequins. She knew that she appeared young and pretty and bohemian, a look that suited her and one which she knew Deanna had never gone for.

'You seem well yourself.' She sat down opposite the trim, businesslike figure of her mother, not leaning forward to kiss her because she knew that Deanna didn't like public affection.

(Actually not even private affection. Deanna wasn't a tactile person.)

'Thank you,' said Deanna. 'Your grandmother is insisting on feeding me up.'

Lainey smiled. 'That's what she does all right.'

'I'm not sure how long I can stay with her before none of my clothes fit me any more,' observed Deanna.

'I'm sure you have plenty of self-discipline,' Lainey said.

'Your grandmother doesn't always listen to reason,' Deanna remarked.

'And you've got to remember that the TV adds ten pounds,' added Lainey. 'Tell her that!'

'I'm more interested in how good the documentary is than a random ten pounds,' said Deanna. 'My appearance is irrelevant.'

'Of course,' said Lainey quickly. 'I'm sure it'll be brilliant.'

'I've got a great team. I hope so.'

'It must be very exciting for you.'

'You could sound as if you mean it,' Deanna said.

'I do mean it!' cried Lainey. 'Of course I do. It must be very exciting to put a whole project like that together. But probably not as exciting as visiting the White House or getting whatever prize it was you got from the French President last year.'

'It would've been far more exciting to visit the White House if Hillary had been in the Oval Office,' remarked Deanna.

'I bet you wish you could have voted for her.'

'I voted for Mary Robinson when she was elected President of Ireland,' said Deanna. 'That was a great day to be Irish. I was proud to come home and vote then. It made such a difference to how women could see themselves.'

I'm here a few minutes and somehow we're already talking about politics and women's issues, thought Lainey glumly. And I started it! We never have a conversation that isn't about some bloody issue or another.

'How do you think Gran is?' she interrupted Deanna, who had spun off into a diatribe about Irish politics and the patriarchy that was the Dail, saying that the downside to having had female presidents was that the government believed it was progressive when it came to women in politics, whereas in fact it was still a club where those who shouted loudest advanced the furthest, regardless of their qualifications, and the loudmouths were usually inadequate men.

'Gran?' repeated Lainey when Deanna didn't answer.

'Fine, I guess.' Deanna was irritated at being dragged away from the issue of the under-representation of women in politics.

'You guess?'

'She appears good to me,' said Deanna. 'The same as always, in fact. Trying to organise me, chivvy me about, make me eat stuff I don't want to.'

Lainey quite liked the fact that Madeleine could make Deanna do things she didn't want to.

'Have you noticed her talking to Grandad?'

'What?' Deanna was startled.

'She talks to him,' Lainey told her. 'Well, to the chair where he used to sit. She does it a bit when I'm there and I'm convinced she does it even more when I'm not. I worry about her.'

'She lives on her own,' said Deanna briskly. 'She needs to verbalise her thoughts. That doesn't mean she's losing her marbles, you know.'

'I know that,' Lainey retorted. 'I just want to make sure that she's all right. She's in her seventies after all.'

'I'm perfectly well aware of her age, Lainey. She's my mother.'

'But I've lived with her longer than you.'

Deanna looked at her watch. 'Fifteen minutes,' she said.

'Huh?'

'Fifteen minutes before you reminded me that I abandoned you to your grandmother's care. Not bad. Sometimes you manage to mention it within the first two.'

'Oh, for heaven's sake!' Lainey spoke impatiently. 'I'm not having a go at you.'

'That's a first.'

'You're impossible,' said Lainey. 'You *want* me to argue with you! You goad me, you really do!'

Deanna laughed suddenly. 'I like to see you animated and analytical,' she said. 'Though not always with me as the object of your ire.'

Lainey leaned back in her chair. Her mother did this to her all the time. Wrong-footed her. Made her feel as though she was being led through hoops of Deanna's own design.

'So how long will you have to stay here?' she asked, trying to move away from the personal, and reckoning that if her grandmother needed to be checked out medically, she herself would be the one to get it done.

'At least a month in Ireland,' Deanna said. 'I'll be hopping back and forward to the UK and Europe too. Hopefully I'll wrap the Irish segment up fairly quickly, but I've added time for a few lectures and other publicity work. Then I'm going to Strasbourg. I'm scheduled to address members of the European Parliament.'

'So what exactly is it all about, this documentary?'

Deanna took a sheaf of papers from her bag and handed it to her daughter.

'Whether feminism has served today's women well, and how they've responded in return.'

'What if you discover it hasn't?' asked Lainey.

'If it hadn't been for women like me, you wouldn't have been able to go to college and get your degree so that you can stand in front of the camera and talk about the weather with confidence,' said Deanna. 'So feminism has certainly served you well. How today's women serve feminism is a question yet to be answered.'

'Right.' Lainey couldn't think of anything to say in response.

'I worry about them,' said Deanna.

'Women?'

'Young women. The infantilisation of them. The sexualisation of them. The current vogue for saying that it's a personal choice to have a dress that starts below your breasts and ends above your knickers.'

Lainey smiled.

'We worked so hard to stop women being sex objects,' said Deanna. 'Now they seem to want to be.'

'Some of them have made successful careers of it,' observed Lainey.

'Which, quite frankly, revolts me.'

'You gave them a choice. You can't blame them for the ones they've made.'

'Hmm. We were hoping that the choice would drag them out of the sex-toy arena. And out of the Barbie-lookalike arena too. Though they're not helped by the fashion and cosmetic industries, who promote eternal youth as a right and the image of a fairy-bloody-princess as a lifestyle choice. What have princesses ever done except look pretty on the arm of a prince? However, I'll deal with it in as objective a manner as possible and try not to mention hair extensions and cellulite tyranny either. Anyway, more importantly, how is your own career progressing? I saw you on TV. You looked well.'

'Thank you.'

'And, as I said before, confident. Although I wish you wouldn't wear pink, it's so clichéd. Also, you smile a bit too much at the end. As though you're trying to ingratiate yourself.'

'I like pink. It suits me and looks good on screen. And I'm not trying to ingratiate myself. I don't smile too much.'

'This is constructive criticism,' said Deanna. 'You've got to be able to take constructive criticism. That's a problem women still have. They personalise everything.'

'I'm not personalising it,' objected Lainey. 'I'm just saying I don't smile too much.'

'My opinion,' amended Deanna. 'Maybe other people like it.'

Lainey said nothing.

'Anyway,' continued her mother, 'I'm sure there must be other opportunities for you within your chosen field. There are a lot of grants in the climate change area for example.'

'I know. But I like what I do.'

'You've got to be looking forward,' said Deanna. 'Onwards and upwards. Don't let other people push you into the background.'

'I'm on national television,' said Lainey as mildly as she could. 'Hardly the background.'

'You know what I mean.' Deanna sounded impatient. 'I want you to fulfil your potential, Lainey. I want you to succeed.'

'Why?' asked Lainey. 'Surely what matters is that *I* feel I've fulfilled my own potential.'

She saw a flash of irritation in Deanna's eyes and waited for the onslaught. But her mother held back.

'I hope you're doing anything you do to the best of your ability,' said Deanna eventually. 'And I want you to succeed for your own sake, not for me. You have, of course, been relatively successful in your career. Which is why I'd like you to participate in the documentary. You're in an area where many of the women are seen to be airheads. The weather girl has had a bad press as far as brains are concerned. Fortunately you're a professional, which I'm very thankful for. Most of the information is in the papers I've given you.'

'I'll read it. But are you really sure you want me in it? It's your work, after all.' Lainey couldn't help being surprised that Val had been right about Deanna including her.

'I want to involve women from a variety of traditional and non-traditional jobs. The decision is yours, of course. I don't want to influence you.'

But you've always influenced me, thought Lainey as she looked at her mother. I've always wanted to do what you wanted. Even if you never realised it. And even if I didn't realise it until now either.

Chapter 10

Barometric pressure: the pressure on the surface of the earth exerted by the air

On her return home from America almost thirty-three years previously with her mother and her daughter, the first thing that struck Deanna was how insular Ireland was. Closed in, not just by its geographical size but also by the mentality of its people. And by its down-at-heel look too. Dublin city, referred to by locals as 'dear ol' dirty Dublin' was indeed both expensive and dirty, its buildings grimy from years of smog, its streets strewn with litter and its people grey and unprepossessing. A postal strike had paralysed the country, while PAYE workers were protesting vehemently about the amount of tax they paid. The only bright spot, as far as many people were concerned, though certainly not in Deanna's view, was the imminent visit of the Pope to the country.

Deanna had no time for the religious fervour that seemed to have gripped everyone as a result. Her view was that the Pope should stay in Rome. He was a man, first and foremost.

And he was the head of the most patriarchal institution in the world. Additionally, he'd consider her to be a fallen woman, unmarried, not even knowing now where the father of her child was. If there was a God, and if he turned up to see his earthly representative (*his* representative, she thought; why do we have to think of God as *he*? A woman would surely have made a better job of being a deity), and if she was among the throngs who went to the Phoenix Park to see him, she was pretty sure she'd be hit by a well-aimed bolt of celestial lightning. Because she wasn't sorry that she'd had sex. She was just sorry that she'd had sex with a man who'd messed up her life by leaving her with a child she was so badly qualified to take care of. She wanted the best for Lainey. But she was quite certain that no matter how much she cared, her daughter deserved a lot better than her as a mother.

The reaction in her neighbourhood to her return was one of quiet sympathy for Madeleine. Most people had always considered Deanna Ryan to be too cocky for her own good, but they were sorry for her now. Some of the gossip suggested that Madeleine had been too lenient with her daughter in the past, and that her leniency had brought the chickens home to roost. But most mothers were secretly grateful it was Deanna and not their own daughters who'd been unfortunate enough to get pregnant, allowing themselves a gentle sigh of relief whenever they saw her pushing Lainey along the road in her pram.

Deanna found it very difficult to settle back into life in Killester. She missed the clarity of the Californian sun, the sound of the Pacific Ocean pounding on the shore and the cheerful optimism of the Monterey people. She missed the Light Fighter Feminists, who'd organised a conference called 'Any Woman Can' in the Monterey Peninsula College the day after she left that had sounded exciting and progressive. She hated the begrudgery that seemed to stalk Irish life and the resentment of other people's good fortune if you yourself hadn't struck it lucky. Not that many people had the opportunity to strike it lucky when the economy was scraping along and most of the workforce was just about doing the same. But if by any chance you did well, there was always someone around to remind you where you came from and make sure you didn't get too big for your boots.

She, of course, had no opportunity to get too big for her boots any more. Every day she would get up and feed Lainey (bottles; not for a moment had she ever considered breast-feeding her). Then she'd take her for a walk, usually down leafy Castle Avenue as far as the seafront, where she'd let the easterly wind whip through her hair. Lainey seemed to like being outside – even if she wasn't sleeping, she would be quite happy being pushed along in her pram. But taking her for a walk was more for Deanna's own benefit than her daughter's. She had to get out of the house and away from her mother, who was full of information about how she should look after her baby and who was constantly thrusting knitting patterns at her and suggesting that she take up the hobby, which she insisted would be both therapeutic and useful.

'I'm not a doddery old grandmother yet,' Deanna would retort, and Madeleine would then remind her that she wasn't doddery either but as a grandmother she was doing her best for her granddaughter. And she would also remind Deanna that Lainey was now Deanna's number one priority and that she had to get her head out of the clouds and start being realistic about her life.

The problem was that Deanna didn't like facing the reality of a demanding baby in a dismal country. She knew that she hadn't been able to cope with her in California either, but she still couldn't help thinking that if only she was back in Monterey, everything would be so much easier. She felt far more at home in the States than she ever did in Ireland, even though there was nobody to help her with Lainey there. Lexy had made it perfectly clear that it wouldn't be possible to live in the house with a baby, which would have meant having to move out and find somewhere by herself. Deanna understood that. If it had been any of the other girls, she would have felt the same way. Children, even little babies, were demanding and you had to change your life completely to accommodate those demands. She couldn't begin to think of what it would be like when Lainey was older and able to articulate her needs and desires. Which, Deanna supposed, would be dolls and stuffed toys and God knows what else, none of which interested her in the slightest.

She briefly met up with Julie, who was back living with her parents and who'd recently begun working in a bank. Her friend's hair was now styled in a fashionable poodle perm and she'd taken to wearing thick mascara and gloopy lip gloss. She told Deanna that it was important to have a groomed appearance when she met customers every day because first impressions counted. Julie's father had recovered from his heart attack, although he had taken early retirement from work, something, Julie said, that was both a blessing and a curse for her mother, because although she was pleased that her husband was less stressed, she wasn't used to having him under her feet all the time.

'By the way, I've met someone.' Julie didn't sound at all shamefaced as she imparted the news. 'We've talked about getting married.'

'Oh,' said Deanna.

'Well,' Julie said, shaking her head so that the curls bobbed around her face, 'we all have to grow up sooner or later, don't we? What's important when we're kids isn't what's important when we're older.'

As she sat on one of the benches overlooking the seafront one Monday morning, Deanna tried to recall her own early childhood and what had been important to her. She couldn't remember it all that clearly. She knew that her mother had always been there, and that Madeleine had been a source of comfort when she'd fallen and scraped her knees or when she'd got into a fight with some of the other children on their road (a fairly regular occurrence), but she was completely unable to say what things had made her happy and what she'd enjoyed doing as a small girl. All she knew was that she was miserable now.

Lainey whimpered in the pram and Deanna adjusted the pale pink woollen blanket (a gift from Martha, their next-door neighbour) around her. She gazed at her daughter, seeing in her already pretty face a marked resemblance to Jorge, which made her clench her fists in rage. He had been a handsome man but she didn't want to be reminded of him and his desertion of her every time she looked at the baby. It was so wrong and so unfair that men could wreak such havoc in someone else's life and then just walk away. They were such bastards. All of them.

Lainey began to cry, and Deanna gritted her teeth. She couldn't understand why her daughter seemed to cry so much. Not a day went by without her screwing up her face and wailing at something. Deanna never really knew what it was she was crying about. Madeleine would say that she was just seeking attention, and Deanna would complain that she got nothing but attention – didn't all their lives revolve around her? What more did she want?

'She'll settle,' Madeline would tell her. 'Just give her time.'

But how much time? Deanna wondered. How much time before the cranky baby turned into a person who could have a rational conversation? How long could she be expected to jump every time Lainey cried? When would she have a life of her own again? What was the point, she asked herself, in all those hours she'd put in at school, learning to use her brain, getting an education, if all she was going to do was run around after someone else?

Lainey stopped crying and Deanna took the newspaper from the carrier bag attached to the pram. There was a feature on one of the inside pages about Ireland's first female airline pilot, Grainne Cronin, who was smiling out from a black and white picture. Grainne clearly hadn't had a careers guidance counsellor like Mrs Carthy suggesting that she should be an air hostess and marry a captain. She was obviously a woman with a mind of her own. Deanna wished that she herself was featured in the newspapers for doing something groundbreaking for women everywhere. But she didn't begrudge Grainne her success at all. She was elated by it. Good on you, girl, she murmured to herself as she read the story. I bet it's hard being there among all those macho men. You probably have to put up with all sorts of sexist comments. But stick with it. For the sake of women everywhere!

She clenched her jaw as she remembered Mindy and how she'd given her job away just because she'd had a baby. Mindy was a woman, but she'd betrayed Deanna by replacing her with a man. At a crummy dog-washing job! It wasn't fair. It wasn't right. Women needed protection in the workplace. From other women as well as from men. They needed to make that point as forcefully as possible. With a protest. Deanna recalled the thrill of going on the protest with the Light Fighter Feminists. Women who believed in a better life for themselves and for other women too. A life where they could get ahead and achieve things on their own merits. These were women who wanted success. Women who didn't think that you should succumb to the almost sacred belief that being a mother was the most important job in the world.

Maybe it is if you want it to be, she said under her breath as she looked at her now sleeping baby. Maybe for some women it's all they ever want. But it isn't for me. Which clearly makes me the very worst mother in the world. And likely to stay that way.

She could feel her eyes welling up with tears, but she didn't know whether she was crying for herself or for the baby who was depending on her. And who, she couldn't help feeling, was going to be let down over and over again.

Madeleine didn't know what to do about Deanna and Lainey. She was worried that her daughter hadn't bonded with her granddaughter, that the link between them seemed to be so fragile. She couldn't understand how Deanna seemed to be so fretful about the baby and so irritated by her. She knew that babies could be annoying and time-consuming, but for her, there was always the moment when you took them into your arms and they looked at you so trustingly and so helplessly that you couldn't but feel your heart crumble with love for them. She was concerned that Deanna didn't seem to feel the overwhelming rush of emotion that she'd felt herself the moment she'd given birth. She didn't know if it was because of Lainey's unknown father; a man who Deanna insisted on calling 'the cheating bastard' even in front of Edmund, who had never allowed words like that to be used in the house before.

'You'd better get used to it,' Deanna said. 'Because Lainey's father was a bastard and that's what people will call her too. A bastard child of a loose woman.'

Edmund had been truly shocked at Deanna's words and Madeleine (unforgivably, she told herself afterwards in shame) had actually slapped Deanna's face, leaving her daughter speechless.

The atmosphere in the house was like a tinderbox and Madeleine was afraid that somebody would say something that would fan the flames of a row they'd never be able to forget. She worked really hard to keep everyone happy, but she could feel the strain of Deanna's misery and Edmund's anger plus her own concerns weighing on her more and more heavily every day.

She wanted Deanna to be happy. She wanted her to fall in love with her daughter and to see that her life wasn't over. But she knew that Deanna wasn't thinking like that. She knew that Deanna saw herself as a failure for having come home with her baby and having to rely on her parents for help. Deanna had always been an independent spirit, and now her spirit was broken. Madeleine had no idea how to fix it. Which made her feel like a failure herself.

Edmund and Madeleine had set up a college fund for Deanna when she'd started secondary school. When she didn't go to college, they kept the money in a bank account 'for when she might need it most', Edmund said. After she returned home with Lainey, her father had given her the deposit book and told her that it would help her with the baby's expenses. Deanna had looked at it and swallowed hard. She knew that her parents must have made sacrifices to accumulate such a sum for her and she felt that she'd let them down badly. They'd expected to have a bright graduate in the family by now. But instead they had a loser like her. She didn't deserve the money. But she needed it.

Two months after she'd come back from America, Deanna went into the Aer Lingus sales office in the city and, offering up a sigh of thanks to Fawn's father for her unlimited visa, bought a one-way ticket to San Francisco. After handing over the money, she went to Davy Byrne's pub and ordered a Bacardi and Coke, which she sipped slowly while she looked at the printed ticket. She knew that Madeleine and Edmund would be both devastated and disappointed. But she also knew she didn't have any choice.

At first Madeleine didn't realise that she'd left. The day before she went, Deanna said that she'd be going out early the following morning. Madeleine hadn't taken any notice, because she often went out early. She suspected it was a way for Deanna to have time to herself, leaving the house before other people were out and about and while Lainey was still asleep. So she thought nothing of it when she heard the front door open and close.

She thought nothing of it either when Deanna didn't get in touch all day. Years later, when she got to grips with mobile phones and email and internet chat over the computer, Madeleine wondered how everyone had coped with being unable to contact friends and family by multiple means at all hours of the day or night. But back then, not hearing from someone for twelve hours didn't set alarm bells ringing. Not being in touch was perfectly normal. So she didn't start to worry until after their evening meal, when she realised that there was still no sign of her daughter and she had no idea where she was.

She asked Edmund if Deanna had said anything to him about her plans for the day, and he replied that she hardly ever talked to him these days, so no chance of that. Both of them agreed that it was silly to worry. But an hour later both of them were very worried indeed.

'I'll kill her when she gets in,' said Edmund. 'She might have a child of her own but she's still nothing more than a child herself.'

'She's twenty years old now,' Madeleine reminded him. 'Hardly a child.'

'Not an adult either,' retorted Edmund.

'I suppose not,' agreed Madeleine, who sometimes thought that Deanna actually behaved like a ten-year-old.

She went into her daughter's room to see if she could find any clues as to her whereabouts. And that was when she saw the envelope propped up on the dressing table, with 'Mam' carefully printed on the front. Her hands were shaking as she picked it up. She knew Deanna was depressed about being home in Ireland. She knew that she wasn't coping well with the responsibilities of her baby. But she was suddenly terribly afraid that she was looking at her daughter's last words to her, and she felt sick.

She ripped open the envelope even as she flopped on to the single bed that had been Deanna's ever since she was four years old. And she read the letter that her daughter had left her.

Dear Mam & Dad,

I'm sorry. I'm no good at this. I'm an embarrassment to you and to myself. I don't want to be in Ireland and I don't want to be an unmarried mother. I know that you'll probably say things like I've made my bed and I have to lie in it, but the truth is that I can't. I was made for better things than this. And I need to aim for them. So I've gone back to California. I feel so much more alive there. I love it. It's my home now. It always will be. I'm so sorry for doing this to you. And to Lainey of course. But it's better for everyone. I'll be in touch in a few weeks.

Lots of love,

Deanna.

Madeleine walked into the kitchen with the letter in her hands. She dropped it in front of Edmund, whose eyes darkened as he read it.

'The selfish little trollop!' he roared when he'd finished.

'Not so loud!' Madeleine spoke in an urgent whisper. But it was too late. Lainey, who'd been as good as gold in her pram all day, began to cry.

Madeleine lifted up her granddaughter.

'You're all right, honey,' she crooned. 'Everything's all right. We'll look after you. Your mother knew that. That's why she left you with us.'

Deanna probably had a point, thought Madeleine. It was for the best.

But it still didn't make it right.

Chapter 11

Altocumulus: mid-level layers or patches of cloudlets

The sun had broken through the light covering of cloud and the afternoon was warm and bright, so when Lainey got home from her coffee with Deanna, she sat out on the balcony of her apartment. Two small boys, both wearing Arsenal kit, were playing football in the garden below, happily ignoring the signs that prohibited ball games in the complex. Lainey knew that Annie Dwyer would eventually emerge from her apartment and tell them to stop. The ban on ball games was to protect the flowers and the bamboos, but the children didn't even notice them (in fact they were using two bushy bamboo plants as goalposts). Regardless of the threat to the foliage, Lainey was enjoying the sounds of their happy laughter as they kicked the ball around.

She'd enjoyed playing football when she was a kid too. She used to play with the boys on the green outside the house, because she was taller and stronger than most girls of her age. She'd been fearless in tackling them and winning the ball right up to her seventh birthday, when Pearse

McMahon had lunged at her, sent her flying and broken her leg. It had been absolute agony and had put her off playing football for life, although she enjoyed watching international matches on TV. She remembered Madeleine accompanying her to the hospital in the ambulance and waiting with her in A&E until her leg was set. Afterwards she'd felt brave and slightly proud of her injury as she hopped around the neighbourhood on her crutches, but at the time she'd been howling with pain. Madeleine had comforted her, though, and told her that it was a badge of honour to have broken something. She herself had broken her arm as a little girl when she fell off a haystack on her grandfather's farm. Then she'd taken photographs of Lainey in her cast and sent them off to Deanna, observing that she'd clearly inherited her mother's talent for kicking a ball around.

Madeleine had always been there for her, thought Lainey, as she gazed unseeingly from the balcony. She'd been the one to pick her up when she'd fallen, the one to praise her for her achievements and the one to kiss her good night. She was the only one who had a right to comment on her choices and advise her on her life. Deanna, for all of her remarks about what she expected from her, had no rights whatsoever.

Lainey wasn't sure when exactly she realised that there was a difference between being looked after by a grandmother instead of a mother. She'd always called Madeleine Gran or Granny, but even so it wasn't until shortly after Madeleine had enrolled her in the local playschool that she realised her situation wasn't the same as other children's. Her grandmother had sat her down and explained to her that her mother lived in a different country and that was why Lainey couldn't see her every day. But, Madeleine added, Deanna thought about her all the time.

'Is she dead?'

Carol-Anne Baker's mother had died a few weeks earlier. They'd all been told that Mrs Baker had gone to heaven and that she would still be watching over Carol-Anne and her brother even though they wouldn't see her any more.

'Of course she's not dead.' Madeleine had been horrified.

'So she can come to see me?'

'She's in a far-away country. But she will. And she has seen you, Lainey. She saw you when you were born and she saw you when you were two years old and she loves you very much.'

Lainey didn't remember seeing her mother when she was two years old. But Madeleine had shown her photographs of them together on a beach. Deanna was wearing shorts and a T-shirt and her cropped hair was sticking up in spikes on her head. Lainey was in shorts and a T-shirt too, her dark curls tousled by the sea air. She was in her mother's arms and smiling broadly. Lainey kept the photographs in a box in her bedroom, and every so often she would take them out and look at them, desperately trying to grab hold of the memory, unable to believe that she couldn't recall a day that seemed to have been such a happy one.

The earliest memory she had of Deanna was of her visit when she was five years old. Her grandmother had sat her down and told her that her mother was coming to stay for a while. She'd been almost sick with excitement at the thought of meeting her at last. She hadn't been able to sleep the night before she arrived and had lain in bed thinking of how the two of them would be best friends for ever and how Deanna would be the one in future who would bring her to the doctor or the dentist, or for a special shopping trip into town.

She'd got up at six in the morning and had her breakfast (a glass of milk and a slice of bread with a generous dollop of Nutella) alone in the kitchen, imagining what it would be like when her mother saw her for the first time in so long. She bubbled with excitement at the thought of it. She wondered if Deanna was bubbling with excitement too.

She was kneeling on a kitchen chair washing her plate over the sink when Madeleine came into the kitchen and asked her why she was up at the crack of dawn when it was usually so hard to get her out of bed. And she remembered telling her that it was because her mother was coming home and she had to get ready. Madeleine had replied that Deanna wouldn't be here until much later, but Lainey hadn't cared. She wanted to be ready as soon as possible. She couldn't wait to finally meet her mam.

She'd wanted it all to be wonderful and exciting, but of course it hadn't been like that at all. With the benefit of hindsight, it would never have matched up to the expectations she'd had of it, but she couldn't forget the moment her heart froze when Deanna strode into the arrivals hall at Dublin airport, saw Madeleine and Edmund, waved at them and then, before saying hello, launched into a rant about the idiot man in the seat beside her who'd patronised her during the entire flight and who hadn't shut up about his expenses-paid trip to the States as part of his job in an insurance company.

'I swear to God,' Deanna had said, 'you'd think that he was running the effing company. Which he couldn't have been, because otherwise he would've been in business class and not economy with the rest of us.' Then Deanna had looked at Lainey with a puzzled and almost apprehensive expression on her face and told her that she'd grown.

Lainey had brought flowers for Deanna, freesias and asters picked from Madeleine's garden. She handed them to her and said (as she'd been practising all night), 'Welcome home, Mam. It's lovely to see you.'

Deanna took the flowers and hunkered down beside her. She hesitated, then pecked Lainey on the cheek and said it was good to see her too. She told her that her name was Deanna, not Mam or Mum or anything like that. Lainey had thought about saying that everyone called their mother Mam, it didn't matter what their actual name was. But there was something in Deanna's manner that stopped her from speaking. And something in her manner, too, that stopped her from wrapping her arms around her like she'd intended.

They made their way to the car park and got into Edmund's Fiesta. Lainey and Deanna sat in the back together. Lainey wondered would it be OK to take her mother's hand, but Deanna was leaning away from her and looking out of the window.

'It's still so bloody dreary,' she said as they turned on to the main road. 'You know there are loads of Irish people coming to the States now all looking for work. I keep telling myself how lucky I was to have met Lexy and Fawn.'

Madeleine turned around in her seat.

'Yes,' she said. 'This country has gone to the dogs. It makes me wonder about the future.'

'Me too,' said Deanna shortly as she continued to look around her.

Lainey didn't try to slip her hand into her mother's. She didn't think the time was right.

Things were a little different when they got back to the house in Killester. The sight of her family home, with its familiar photos on the walls and furniture in the rooms (even though it had been redecorated since she left), seemed to soften Deanna somehow. Lainey followed her as she walked along the corridor to her room and then stopped.

'You're sleeping here?' She turned to Lainey.

'It's my room.'

'It used to be mine.'

'I know. Gran told me.'

'You're in the spare room, Deanna,' called Madeleine.

'So I see.'

'But you can have mine if you like,' said Lainey quickly. 'If you'd rather stay in it, I don't mind.'

'It's OK,' said Deanna. 'I wouldn't dream of putting you out of your room.'

'It was yours first,' Lainey told her.

'And it's yours now.' Deanna picked up her bag and walked into the next-door room. 'Thank you for offering, but don't worry, Lainey. I'll be fine.'

Deanna was always fine, thought Lainey now, as she gazed at the fair-haired boys, who had stopped kicking the ball and were sitting side by side on the grass. She was fine because she didn't feel things like normal people. She was able to distance herself from the emotion of what was going on in her life and analyse it. She was able to remove those emotions and decide what the best course of action in any given situation should be. When Lainey had asked her if she was going to stay in Ireland now that she was home, Deanna had spoken to her as though she were an adult, not a five-year-old, and told her that it wasn't practical for her to stay here, that she had a job in America and that it was important to her.

'More important than me and Gran?'

'Not more important personally,' Deanna had replied. 'You and Gran are my family and so that makes you important. But what I'm doing now is important for lots and lots of people.'

'I don't care about lots of people.' Lainey was sulky. 'I care about us.'

'That's a silly attitude,' said her mother. 'If we didn't care about other people, the world would be a very sad place.'

Lainey had felt, after her conversation with Deanna, that it would be her fault if the world turned out to be a sad place, because she wanted her mother to stay with her and have fun with her instead of going back to America to do whatever was so important there. Although, over the weeks that Deanna stayed in Ireland, she did wonder how much fun they might have had together, since Deanna, unlike just about every other mother she knew, didn't really seem to do much by way of fun things. She was constantly reading newspapers and going to libraries and getting involved in 'research' for the various projects she was apparently working on.

'They've given me funding to produce this study.' Lainey overheard Deanna and Madeleine talking together in the kitchen one afternoon. 'I can't walk away from it. And I don't want to stay away from the US for too long either. I'm lucky that I can go back to the college, but I don't want to jeopardise everything by staying away longer than I have to.'

'Why can't you do the research here?' asked Madeleine.

'You know that's not possible.'

'I know that Lainey needs a mother.'

'She needs *someone*,' Deanna agreed. 'But that someone isn't me. It's you, Mam. You know that. You're her rock. You protect her. Anyway, you'd hate it if I came back and took her from you.'

Lainey had crept back to her room and sat on her bed after hearing her mother's words. She wanted to feel upset, but the truth was that what she actually felt was a little bit relieved. She wanted to love Deanna. She really did. But she wasn't the mother she'd dreamed about. She wasn't a person who'd bring her to the movies or read her bedtime stories like Madeleine. She didn't want to bake cupcakes or sing songs or watch TV with her. And although Lainey could tell that Deanna was fiercely intelligent (she seemed to know everything about everything), she wasn't easy to like. She felt very guilty whenever she thought this, as though it were somehow her fault. As though she was a disappointment to Deanna in a whole heap of ways.

So, even though she cried when her mother left to go back to America, she was pleased too. She could stop having to talk about being a good student and beating the other kids. She could wear her pink T-shirts and put her butterfly clips in her hair again. She could take Mr Ted out of her bedside locker and leave him on her bed every day as she used to. With Deanna gone, things went back to normal. And Lainey felt an awful lot happier.

The entire balcony was now bathed in warm sunlight. Lainey stopped thinking about the past and began to think about the present instead. Deanna's return to Ireland for longer than a week was unusual. She wondered how her mother and her grandmother would cope with being in the same house together for a protracted period, although she supposed that if Deanna was out and about working on the documentary it might not be too bad. At the same time she resolved to keep on top of things. She didn't want Madeleine getting fussed because of Deanna. She didn't want to get fussed herself, if she could help it. She thought that she'd handled today pretty well, despite her mother's edginess. The thing with Deanna was that edginess was part of her whole reason for being. She wasn't Deanna Ryan unless she was coming up with a quip or a quotation that could be used in an interview. There were pages of her quotes on the internet. But she forgot, sometimes, that her family just wanted to chat.

Lainey got up from the lounger and retrieved her laptop from the living room. She pulled the lounger so that it was in partial shade and opened her web browser. Then she typed in Deanna's name.

There were hundreds of search results covering all aspects of her career. Wikipedia called her a radical feminist who had brought sexual politics to a whole new wave of women. There were lots of biogs of her, and all of them included her most famous cry, 'Get off your back and on to your own two feet', which had propelled her to public consciousness in a US TV interview after she'd been arrested at a rally for pushing a policeman. *Get Off Your Back* was also the title of her first book, described as 'an excoriation of the patriarchal society'. It had brought Deanna to the attention of the media on its publication, but it was her second book, *Tit Power*, that had been her breakthrough, reaching the number 1 slot on the *New York Times* bestseller list and raising Deanna's profile among the general public.

Lainey had read *Get Off Your Back* when she was in her late teens but she'd found it hard going and had been very much taken aback by her mother's view throughout the book that heterosexual relationships disenfranchised women and therefore should be avoided at all costs. It wasn't clear from Deanna's writing whether this meant she favoured homosexual relationships instead, and Lainey spent a lot of time wondering uneasily if her mother was actually a lesbian. But Deanna didn't seem to have a special woman friend in her life. She didn't seem to have many close friends at all. Lainey would have thought it was sad, except she perfectly understood why it would be difficult to get close to her mother. As far as she could see, the only person who'd ever achieved it had been her father. And nobody dared mention him in front of Deanna, ever.

Lainey had, of course, asked Madeleine about her father. She'd sympathised with her grandmother, who'd looked uncomfortable as she'd said that he and Deanna had split up. It must have been tough, she thought, for Madeleine to have to say this to a child who wanted more than anything to have parents the same as everyone else. But Madeleine had simply said that he and Deanna hadn't loved each other enough and that they hadn't wanted to get married. Lainey wanted to know if her father had loved her, and Madeleine had said that he hadn't really known her. It was only later that she learned he'd walked away from the pregnant Deanna. That had been the one time she'd felt truly sorry for her mother and angry with her unknown father. When she was older she'd gone through a phase of fantasising about him, imagining that he'd had a change of heart but hadn't been able to find her because Deanna had moved and she was in Ireland, but in the end she'd come to realise that she'd been an unimportant part of his life. It was wrong, she thought, that men could walk away from their responsibilities so easily, but the bottom line from her point of view was that she had a father who didn't want to know and a mother who was too busy to care. And even though she tried to rationalise it all and tell herself that they were a product of their times, she couldn't help occasionally resenting the fact that they'd pretty much abandoned her.

When she was being pragmatic about it, she would remind herself that life with two egocentric people (which they certainly had to be) would have been a nightmare, and if it hadn't been for Madeleine she'd have grown up a bigger basket case than she sometimes already thought she was. But other times she wished it had all been very different. She wished that her father had loved her mother to bits and had married her. And she wished that they'd all lived happily ever after in the wooden house that she sometimes saw in her dreams.

By six o'clock, the residents of the apartment blocks had begun to return home. Lainey always enjoyed this time of day on sunny evenings because the air would be filled with chatter as everyone pulled chairs out on to their balconies and took advantage of the evening sun. Most of the time the complex was quiet, with only the rectangular blocks of light from various windows indicating that people actually lived in the buildings. But summer evenings were different. She could even smell the aroma of a barbecue that someone had set up, which made her mouth water. She was thinking about cooking something for herself when the entry buzzer to the complex sounded.

'It's me. Let me in, the entry code has changed.'

Lainey's heart skipped two beats. Her mouth went dry and her fingers trembled as she pressed the release button for the gates. Ken was here. Without having called her first as he'd promised. He'd just turned up to see her. Damn!

She hurried into her bedroom, peeled off the T-shirt and shorts she'd been wearing on the balcony and replaced them with a light top and multicoloured skirt. She ran her fingers rapidly through her hair, glossed her lips and sprayed herself with her Nina Ricci. She looked at herself in the mirror. Pretty good considering. The intercom buzzed again, which meant he was now outside her block.

'Come on up,' she said.

She opened the apartment door and waited while he climbed the stairs. (Ken always bounded up the stairs; he never bothered with the lift.)

'Hi.' He stood in front of her, a brown paper carrier bag in his hand. 'I brought your things.'

'Thanks.'

'Sorry I didn't get around to it sooner.'

'Do you want to come in?' she asked hesitantly.

'Just for a second.'

He stepped by her and walked through the apartment with an easy familiarity. He put the carrier bag on the low coffee table near the patio doors that led to the balcony.

'Everything's in there,' he told Lainey, who'd followed him. 'Your hair products. Deodorant. Moisturisers.' His expression was perplexed. 'I always knew girls used all that stuff. I just didn't realise how much. And I thought you weren't too much into it.'

'Not really,' she agreed.

'I washed your clothes,' he added.

She could feel herself blush. She'd kept some bras and knickers as well as a few T-shirts at Ken's house. She wondered if he'd remembered them on her body as he threw them in the washing machine. (And she wondered too if he'd put them on a hand-wash cycle or if he'd simply chucked them in with his sports tops and smelly socks.)

'Thank you.'

'Was it because of me that all the entry codes have been changed?'

'Huh?'

'The gates? The door to your building? None of the old numbers work.'

'That was just a general security change,' she said. 'Nothing to do with you.'

If the management company changed codes on the gates and doors every time one of the residents split up, Lainey thought, they'd probably be different every second day!

'I'm sorry, you know.' Ken stepped out on to the balcony and shielded his eyes from the evening sun with his cupped hand.

'Sorry?' she asked as she joined him.

'We didn't end up well.'

Lainey held her breath.

'It was the wrong place and time,' he said.

'I pressured you,' she told him. 'I made you feel trapped.'

'Yes, you did.'

'So I'm sorry too,' said Lainey.

They looked at each other.

'I'm not ready to get married yet,' Ken told her.

'I know that,' she said. 'I knew it all the time.'

'I've missed you, though.' His eyes crinkled in the way

she loved. 'Especially when I was packing up your bits and pieces. Everything reminded me of you.'

'I missed you too.'

'I thought you'd call me.'

'Why?'

'You called a lot before. It was weird when you stopped.'

She hadn't called him half as many times as her previous boyfriends. She'd been trying to be low-maintenance, after all.

'I don't want to lose touch completely,' he said.

She could feel relief wash through her.

'Perhaps I might give you a buzz sometimes?' he added

'That'd be great.'

He held out his arms to her. Then he kissed her. And they went back inside and he made love to her in her bedroom as he'd done so many times before.

He left shortly afterwards and, feeling happy and relaxed, Lainey poured herself a glass of sparkling water and brought it out to the balcony. The sun was sliding towards the horizon but the air was still warm. She sat on her cushioned chair and thought about Ken's visit. She remembered the feeling of his lips on hers and the gentle touch of his fingers as they'd traced patterns on her body. She remembered the feeling of joy as she'd lain beneath him on her bed. She'd thought then that perhaps he wouldn't go. She'd imagined him saying that all the stuff about not wanting to get married was rubbish, washed away by the pleasure of being with her again.

But after lying with her for about twenty minutes, he'd got up and told her that he was really sorry but that he had things to do and had to get home. She hadn't stopped him.

She didn't want him to feel as though she was trying to cling on to him. If they were going to get back on track it would be done slowly.

She glanced back into the apartment and saw the brown carrier bag with her things still sitting on the coffee table. Leaving stuff at his place had probably made him feel trapped, even though he hadn't objected. She wouldn't make the same mistake again.

She'd just drained the glass of water when she saw Shay Loughnane walk on to the balcony opposite. He looked over at her and waved. She waved back, and then she saw the two small boys who'd been playing football earlier join him. She was surprised by that. She'd never seen children in his apartment before. Shay knelt down and put his arms around the boys. He gave them a big hug and she could hear them laugh. Then a woman walked out on to the balcony. She spoke to the children, who went inside. She leaned on the iron railing and gazed south, towards the Dublin mountains. Shay stood beside her and rested his hand on her shoulder.

This was new, thought Lainey. Shay and a woman with children. What had happened to the tiny brunette? It was only a few weeks since she'd replaced a very glamorous blonde. Lainey was intrigued by her neighbour's rapid turnover of girlfriends. Maybe he'd changed his ideas about what he wanted in a woman. Perhaps he'd decided it was time to settle down. Although going for a ready-made family might be a step too far. And it wasn't fair on either the mother or the kids to string them along. If, of course, that was what he was doing.

I need to stop judging people and their personal lives, she muttered to herself as she turned back into the shade of her own apartment. It's impossible to know what's going on in them really. It's easy to look at other people and criticise their choices. But you don't know why they've made them.

She didn't usually criticise other people's choices. She frequently reminded herself that unless you'd walked in someone else's shoes you couldn't judge them. But sometimes it was hard not to. And she had judgemental genes, after all. Deanna's career was based on making judgements. Very critical ones. If her mother was judging her now, Lainey thought, she wouldn't be at all impressed at her allowing Ken back into her life. That was because of her trenchant views on the general uselessness of men, but Deanna didn't really know anything about relationships. How could anyone who hadn't had a relationship with a man in thirty years know what it was like these days? So no matter how crap I am with them, Lainey muttered to herself, my mother is a million times worse! And I need to remember that. She resolved to try very hard not to allow herself to get rattled by Deanna's criticisms while she was here. She would try to let it all roll over her. And she would get on with her life so that, from the outside at least, anyone looking at her would think it was absolutely perfect. Which, with Ken reappearing, maybe it very soon would be.

Chapter 12

Noctilucent: the highest clouds, appearing as blue-white ripples against the night sky

Lainey was back to work at the weekend, although the Met Eireann office wasn't exactly frantically busy, owing to the fact that the weather had settled into a glorious stretch of clear days and warm nights. She was delighted to present the TV bulletins wearing pretty summer dresses to reflect the seasonality of the weather. Her smile was wider than ever as she told viewers to stock up on the Factor 30 because there was going to be some hot sunshine to enjoy. She only had the mornings to enjoy it herself because she was in the studios from 1.30 p.m. to 10 p.m. But she didn't mind. Getting up and knowing that the sun was shining was motivating, and although she avoided the beaches, knowing that they'd be crammed with families out for the day, she was quite happy to walk to the seafront at Clontarf and lie on the springy grass with a book in her hand.

She wasn't alone at the seafront. The area was crowded with people walking, skateboarding, cycling and jogging as well as those who, like her, simply wanted to sit out beneath the blue skies.

She was lying on her back, her head propped on her book, when Carla rang to tell her that she'd be in Dublin for a few days later in the week and hoped Lainey and Val would be able to meet up with her. Lainey said she'd be delighted and that she'd call Val and set something up. She'd just put the phone back in her bag when Madeleine called to say that Deanna had headed off to Brussels and would then be going to Galway for a few days, and asking if Lainey wanted to come to tea that afternoon.

'I can't today,' Lainey said regretfully. 'I'm on the telly later. But Monday would be great.'

She was looking forward to seeing her grandmother on her own again. Madeleine would give her all the gossip about Deanna. They'd be able to sit outside in the flower-filled garden and gorge on cupcakes while they nattered about her hectic schedule and name-checked the famous people she'd met.

It's the name-checking that makes me feel so inadequate beside her, Lainey realised as she buried her feet in the cool grass. The fact that she's met so many important people. That everyone knows who she is, and they respect her.

'Hey, Lainey!'

She glanced up. A woman she didn't know, dressed in jogging shorts and a cropped vest, was waving at her.

'Great weather!' the woman called. 'Glad to see you're enjoying it too.'

'Yes, I am,' said Lainey in return.

'Loved the dress you were wearing last night!' the woman added. 'Very pretty.'

'Thank you.'

The woman jogged off and Lainey felt a warm glow envelop her. OK, it wasn't the same as being Deanna Ryan and being invited to the White House and stuff, but people knew her too. Maybe Val was right. Maybe she was a success after all.

After she'd finished the bulletin and had changed out of her dress into a pair of jeans and a cotton blouse, she sat in the studio reception and waited for her cab to arrive. Getting across town at that hour was too awkward for public transport but didn't take too long by taxi. She was sitting on one of the leather seats, thinking about the tropical storm forming off the Florida coast, when Feargal Wright, one of the station's biggest stars and presenter of a TV arts and culture programme as well as a morning talk show on radio, sat down opposite her. Feargal was known as the thinking woman's beefcake, and he had a commanding on-air presence. He was well built, with light brown hair and penetrating blue-grey eyes. He was a skilled interviewer, both on radio and TV, and had high audience ratings, even for the TV show, which was more highbrow than his radio programme. Lainey wondered why he was still in the studio, given that his TV show had aired already that week, and then she remembered that he was working on another TV project, a type of intimate chat show, although it had yet to be broadcast.

In her two years presenting the weather, Lainey had never met any of the station's stars. As with everyone (me as well, I suppose, she thought in sudden amusement), Feargal Wright looked less impressive in real life. He was actually shorter than he appeared on screen, and his face had significantly more lines. Without the added weight added by the camera, he looked thinner, although he was still a very attractive man. He was, she knew, in his mid-forties and had broken up with his long-term girlfriend, Sadie Parsons, a few months previously. They'd been together for ten years and there had been a few stories in the tabloid papers saying that the split was because he'd refused to get married. The headlines had dubbed her 'Sadie-in-Waiting' because of rumours that she'd told him to make a commitment before the end of the year.

The implication in the stories, as far as Lainey remembered, was that Feargal had left her, saying that he wasn't going to be pressurised. She recalled thinking at the time that all men were the same and reminding herself not to fall into the pressurising trap with Ken herself. She'd failed spectacularly at that, of course. As always.

Lainey smiled a brief acknowledgement at Feargal, who looked at her for a moment before recognition flared in his eyes and he said, 'Lainey Ryan, right? The weather girl?'

'The meteorologist, yes.' She didn't mind being called a weather girl by her friends, but she wanted the station's heavy hitter to know that she was more than just a presenter.

'Of course.' He nodded quickly. 'You're not having to do much work these days, are you?'

'It's nice to have a settled spell,' she agreed.

'It'll still be fine for the weekend?'

'Yes,' she said confidently. 'I know it's hard to believe, but we reckon it'll be warm and dry until the middle of next week.'

'That's good news for me. I'm having a summer party at my house on Saturday evening,' he told her. 'You're very welcome to come along. Any time from seven. It's casual.'

She looked at him, startled. Her first conversation with a star and he was inviting her to a party!

'There'll be a lot of people there,' he said. 'Not all from television. Some politicians, journalists . . . it'll be fun.'

'Thank you for asking,' she said, wondering if he was just being polite in issuing the invitation. 'I'm not sure . . .'

'No problem if you don't make it,' he told her easily. 'But if you're not doing anything else, it would be nice to see you there.'

He lived in Killiney, on the south side of the city, but she didn't know his address. He handed her a business card on which he scribbled it.

'Thank you.' She put the card in her bag, unsure whether she'd actually turn up or not, still uncertain if he was really genuine about the invitation. She saw a taxi stop outside the building and she stood up. At the same time another of the station's employees hurried into reception. Lainey didn't recognise the woman, who beckoned Feargal to follow her.

'See you on Saturday, perhaps,' he said as he walked towards the studios. 'Bring someone with you if you like.'

'Um . . . right,' said Lainey. 'Thanks. Maybe I will.'

Despite the fact that it was past eleven o'clock at night, there were still a good number of Laurel Park's residents sitting outside their apartments. The sounds of laughter and clinking glasses wafted through the air as she keyed her entry code into the pad beside the pedestrian gate. While she waited for it to swing open she heard someone approach behind her and she turned slightly.

'Hello again,' said Shay Loughnane. 'We've got to stop meeting like this. How're you?'

'Grand.' She stepped through the gate and he followed her.

'Saw you doing the weather earlier,' he said.

Lainey was never quite sure what she was supposed to say when someone told her they'd seen her presenting the forecast. She wondered if they wanted her to ask them if she'd been any good, so that they could criticise her. Or if they were hoping for an extra insight into the weather just for them. (I know I said warm and sunny to the rest of the country, but watch out for a big fat cloud over your house at 11 a.m.)

'I'm really enjoying what you're providing for us now,' he added. 'It's so great to be able to wander around in T-shirts and shorts as though we were all living the Mediterranean lifestyle.'

'Unfortunately I can't take the credit for the sun,' she told him. 'Just as I hate being blamed when it's cold and grey.'

'You should always take credit when it comes,' he advised her. 'Even if it's not really due.'

'Well, thanks. The good news is that it'll stay fine for a bit longer. Which is lovely,' she added. 'I do like being able to be outside in the evenings without bundling up.'

'Want to join me for a late-night drink tonight?' he asked as they neared their respective blocks. 'It'd save you having to look over at me.'

She glanced at him, wondering if he was making a joke at her expense.

'I'm going to sit on the balcony for a while,' he told her. 'It'd be nice to have company.'

Two men in one night issuing invitations! That had never happened before. Not that either Feargal or Shay was thinking of her as a potential girlfriend obviously (although with Shay, who knew? As far as she could tell, he wasn't exactly the one-woman type). Nor was she thinking of them as possible husbands either. She realised, as this thought flitted through her mind, that she never thought of men as potential boyfriends. She always cut straight to the chase and imagined them waiting for her as she walked up the aisle. Which might, she acknowledged, be part of the problem she had with them. However, neither Feargal nor Shay triggered the walking-up-the aisle picture in her head. In fairness, she told herself, not every man she met did. Only the ones she dated.

She wondered why Shay was on his own tonight and what had happened to the woman with the children. Too much trouble, she thought. So is he asking me for a drink because he thinks I'd be an easier bet? Short-term anyhow.

'Lainey?' His voice held a hint of amusement. 'You seem to have gone into a trance there. Would you like to join me for a glass of wine?'

Even if he was a womaniser, she couldn't help liking Shay. He seemed relaxed and easy-going and it would be nice to sit out in the warmth of the night and have a drink with someone easy-going. But would he expect it to lead to something else? She wasn't stupid, but she didn't think a drink invitation should necessarily mean sex afterwards.

And what about Ken, for heaven's sake? Hadn't they got together again? Sort of? But he hadn't called since coming to her apartment. Not that she'd entirely expected him to, and yet there had been a part of her that had hoped . . . They'd made love, for heaven's sake! Surely she was entitled to something more than 'I've got to go. Be in touch'.

'I didn't realise it was such a difficult question.' This time there was even more amusement in his tone. 'I'm not a vampire character. I don't bite, you know.'

'I'm sorry. I was distracted,' she said. 'I . . .'

'I'm only offering a glass of wine,' he said, 'lest you've got a very bad impression of me. We get so few evenings like this in Ireland that it's a shame not to make the most of them.'

He was right. But if she went home now, she could call Ken and maybe he'd come over . . . although maybe he wouldn't. And surely it would be better not to be the one who called . . . Perhaps it would be a good idea to have a drink with someone else so that she wouldn't be sitting in her own apartment wondering about Ken, wishing he was with her and then giving in and pressing speed-dial and making him think she was checking up on him again.

'Well thanks,' she said finally. 'A glass of wine would be lovely.'

'Great.' Shay looked pleased.

She followed him into his block and they took the lift to the top floor. He unlocked the door to his apartment and led her inside.

It was bigger than hers. The living room was more spacious and there was an additional dining area that she didn't have. The kitchen was wider too, and the stainless-steel hob and oven gleamed with a shine that made her think they weren't used that often.

'Head on outside,' he said. 'I'll bring the bottle and glasses. White OK for you?'

'Absolutely.' She opened the huge patio doors and stepped outside. Shay had covered his wrap-around balcony in decking and lined it with a variety of potted shrubs and flowering plants. On the south-facing side was a glass-topped cane table and cushioned chairs. She'd seen him sitting at it with his girlfriends even in cold weather, when they were muffled up in coats and fleeces.

No need for such clothing tonight as the warm breeze brushed against her skin. She sat on one of the chairs and gazed up at the clear sky. The outside lights meant that only a few of the stars were visible. Her grandfather had taken her deep into the countryside when she'd been younger, away from the light pollution of the city, and she'd looked up at the array of stars in absolute astonishment.

'You're a time traveller now,' he'd told her.

'How?'

'The light from the stars takes hundreds and thousands of years to reach us,' he explained. 'By the time you see it, the star might already have faded and died. You're looking at how things were, not how things are.'

She remembered his words every time she looked at the night sky; remembered, too, how it had felt to snuggle up beside him and be warmed by the presence of his strong, comforting body. She missed her grandfather. He'd been the one man in the whole world she'd never had to second-guess.

'Here you are.' Shay came outside and handed her a glass of cold wine. He'd filled her glass but had only splashed a small amount into his own. He'd also brought out a dish of olives and peanuts, which he put on the table between them. He took a handful of peanuts before sitting opposite her and glancing upwards. 'Pity we can't see the stars,' he said.

'I was just thinking the same thing.'

'I guessed.'

'Huh?'

'I've seen you sometimes,' he said. 'Standing on your balcony looking upwards. I thought at first you were checking for clouds, but as you never seem to do your sky-gazing during the day, I thought you might be a bit of an astronomy buff too.'

She grinned at him. 'Not really, to be honest. I just like looking at them.'

'Me too,' he said. 'My father has a telescope. I still enjoy using it.'

'Hard to see much in the city,' she said.

'Our family house is in Carlow,' he told her. 'Off the beaten track a bit. So he sees more than us. When we were kids, he used to make us identify the planets. I loved looking at Saturn and Jupiter. You could see Saturn's rings and Jupiter's moons through Dad's telescope and it always gave me a thrill. It was amazing to think that you were looking at something so very far away . . .' His voice trailed off and he gave an embarrassed laugh. 'Sorry. Getting nostalgic for my youth.'

'Oh, we all do that,' she said. 'I used to stargaze with my grandfather too. Sometimes when I look up at them now I wish I was still a kid, safe and protected by him. Silly, I know.'

'Not really.' He sat back in the chair. 'Where are you from, Lainey Ryan?'

'Not far.' She told him about her grandmother's house in Killester.

'Did your whole family live there?' he asked. 'Parents too?'

'I was pretty much raised by my grandparents,' she told him. 'My mother lived a lot of time in the States and my father . . . well, I never got to know him.'

'That must have been tough. Not knowing your dad.' Shay's voice was gruff.

'It never really bothered me,' she told him.

'Did you ever meet him?'

She shook her head.

'Did you want to?'

She pulled at a loose thread on the sleeve of her blouse. 'He was just someone who got my mother pregnant and then left her. If he couldn't be bothered to know me, why should I want to know him?'

'Doesn't every child want to know its parents?'

Lainey shrugged. 'Maybe it depends on the child.'

'Maybe it does. Or maybe it depends on the parents.'

She glanced at him. He was staring ahead, not really noticing her. She wondered what sort of relationship he had with his parents – relaxed and easy, or complicated, like hers. But she didn't ask, and quite suddenly she saw him as a person with problems of his own, not some good-time guy who worked his way through women as though he was shelling peas. She was visualising his girlfriends as peas in a pod when he turned to her and smiled. He had a very sexy smile, she realised. No wonder he was never alone.

'Sorry,' he said lightly. 'Went off into a daze there myself. So, weather girl, are you planning a big career in TV?'

It was strange how so many people seemed to think that everyone who appeared on TV wanted to make a career of it. She explained to Shay that it was weather, not TV, that interested her and that presenting the forecast was only a small and, as far as she was concerned, unimportant part of her job.

'I'm sorry,' he said. 'I should've known you weren't just reading it off an autocue. Wasn't there a hoo-ha a few years ago about getting rid of forecasters and replacing them with presenters?'

Lainey nodded. It was true that Irish people wanted qualified meteorologists delivering their weather forecasts on TV and there had been an uproar when the national station, RTE, had tried to bring in a raft of presenters to do the job instead. Style over substance had been the general view at the time, something Lainey thought was a little unfair, as presenters were perfectly capable of reading the forecast as though they knew what they were talking about. Nevertheless she agreed that having properly qualified meteorologists lent a certain authority. She said this to Shay.

'And you bring both style and substance.'

'Thanks.' She couldn't help feeling pleased at his words.

'But the weather is as much TV as you're ever going to do?'

'Absolutely.'

'I suppose we're so surrounded by the media culture that we expect everyone to be fascinated by it and want to be involved,' he said.

'Do you want to be involved in the media?'

'Only when I'm getting incensed about something.' He grinned at her. 'I listen to Feargal Wright's radio programme most days because it's piped through our centre, and I sometimes start shouting at the radio and thinking that everyone but me is a complete idiot and I want to ring up and rant. I don't watch the TV show that much – clearly I'm a total philistine, because I find all those high-culture people too boring for words. And he can be a bit of an arse too . . .' He trailed off. 'Have I now just made an idiot of myself? Is he a close friend?'

She shook her head. 'Not at all. But he's invited me to a party at his house next weekend.'

'You see,' he teased her. 'Despite what you've said, you're one of the celebrity set after all.'

'As if.' She told him how she'd unexpectedly met Feargal and how he'd invited her.

'I'm sure it'll be fun,' he said. 'You can name-check everyone who's there, see what they're really like.'

'I think just about everyone who's on telly is less impressive in real life.'

'Oh, I dunno.' He studied her for a moment. 'You're almost exactly like you are on TV. And you're quite impressive on it actually. Very natural.'

'That's because I only have to do one thing,' she said. 'And I don't give personal opinions. So nobody thinks they know me or anything. It's different with people like Feargal.'

'But people build up a trust with TV personalities,' said Shay. 'I mean, I trust you when you say it'll be sunny.'

She laughed. 'You're trusting my computer simulations.'

'Oh, don't burst the bubble,' he told her. 'I want to pretend you stick your finger out of the window and decide that the sun's going to shine or the clouds will come in or whatever.'

'I don't think that'd be very accurate.'

'But fun. D'you ever follow those nature forecasters? You know, the wizened old guys who say that it's going to be a cold winter because the acorns are yellow or something?'

'I don't dismiss them out of hand,' she said. 'But to be honest, a decent satellite picture is a better indicator than a dodgy acorn. I'm doing a project on long-term forecasting at the moment and I'm sticking with the computer models.'

'Technology. You've got to trust in it, I suppose.'

'Absolutely,' she agreed. 'I love my forecasting stuff. I could sit for hours looking at charts . . .' She broke off. 'Boring, sorry.'

'Not at all,' he said, though she was pretty sure he was just being polite. She knew she tended to get passionate about weather in a nerdy way that nobody else quite understood. Ken hadn't really understood it either. He liked her TV forecasting persona (he always liked to say she made his temperature rise), but when she got technical about it, he tuned out. Not that she ever blamed him. She tuned out whenever he started talking about his job too.

Perhaps she should ask Ken to come to Feargal Wright's party with her. After all, he liked the whole television thing and he'd be sure to love something like this. And it would be a good reason to call him, inviting him to a special event. It wouldn't be like her just ringing him and asking him to come for a drink. And then maybe she could find out whether or not they had some kind of future together, whether making love to him again had meant anything or not.

She exhaled slowly. Why did she always have to make it so bloody complicated? Why wasn't she better at casual relationships? Why did it always have to be so important to her? Just once, she thought, why don't I do something spontaneous and silly with a man and not expect it to turn into anything else?

'Would you like a top-up?' Shay's voice broke into her thoughts.

It took a moment for her to come back to the present. He was smiling at her enquiringly, the wine bottle in his hand. She realised that she'd almost finished her glass of wine while he hadn't touched any.

Was he trying to get her drunk? She looked at him pensively. Was that the reason he was plying her with alcohol while not having any himself? Was it his normal way of treating women?

'I'd join you in another glass,' he said as he observed the fleeting concern etched on her face. 'But this is my daily allowance.'

She stared at him. Was he an alcoholic? Although if that was the case, he shouldn't be drinking at all.

'Diabetic,' he told her. 'It's not a problem for me. I keep it well under control. But it limits the amount of booze I can drink. Which some people would say is a good thing anyway.'

Even though she didn't really want any more wine herself, she allowed him to refill her glass because she was feeling guilty for having been wrong about him.

He was a casual acquaintance, she told herself, her mind going back to her previous thoughts. A nice man, it seemed, but she didn't care about him and he didn't care about her. He might have some one-night-stand type of idea going with the various women he brought back to his apartment, but so what? He had plenty of other women in his life and she knew enough about him not to visualise him waiting for her at the top of the aisle. He'd been spontaneous about asking her to join him for a drink. Wouldn't he be a good person to practise being spontaneous with in return?

'Would you like to come to Feargal's party with me?'

As soon as she'd uttered the words she knew she'd made a terrible mistake. Shay was looking at her in complete astonishment.

'You want me to come to the party with you? That's a bit sudden, isn't it? What about the Adonis?'

'I . . .' The wine had very clearly gone to her head and made her do something stupid, not spontaneous. 'It isn't anything important,' she said rapidly. 'I just thought you might like to come and do some celeb-watching, that's all. For a laugh. As for Ken . . . the Adonis . . . we're not exclusive.'

'Right.' He was still taken aback. 'You've caught me by surprise. I didn't realise . . . I thought Adonis was more important to you than that.'

'Sorry if I sprang it on you.' She looked uncomfortable. 'I wasn't asking you because I wanted . . . It's not . . . What I meant was . . . I hadn't made up my mind about the party and then we were talking about it and it suddenly seemed like a good idea because I didn't think Ken . . . But it's OK. You don't have to come. I was blathering.'

'So you're not inviting me after all? In fact you're disinviting me?'

She thought he was laughing at her but she wasn't sure. This was obviously why women traditionally didn't do the asking of people on dates. They were crap at it! (And it's not a date, she reminded herself quickly, it's a . . . It was meant to be a spur-of-the-moment, do-something-different thing. Though obviously a damn stupid thing.)

'I'm a little confused,' said Shay when she didn't say anything. 'For a moment I thought you wanted me to come to the party with you. But if you don't . . .'

She'd never felt so embarrassed in her life. What the hell had come over her? Why had she accepted his invitation to a drink in the first place, and why had she knocked back wine on an empty stomach? Why hadn't she gone home and phoned Ken like she'd been thinking of doing instead of trying to be a different sort of person and now ending up having made a fool of herself ? Shay was still looking at her quizzically. He must think I'm a total nutcase, she thought.

'Come, why don't you?' She made herself sound decisive and dismissive all at once. 'If you've nothing better to do. It'll probably be desperately boring, though. I have a feeling that a lot of the luvvies who'll be there will be horribly self-obsessed. But it might be a laugh.'

Lainey took a large gulp from her refilled glass. Shay picked up the bottle to top it up again but she stopped him.

'I've had too much already,' she said. 'I didn't eat a lot today. It's making me light-headed.'

'You don't need to skip meals,' he told her with mock severity. 'You're thin enough.'

'I'm not thin,' she said. 'Just . . . the right frame, I guess. And I normally eat like a horse. I just got distracted today.'

'All those warm fronts?'

'Something like that.' She smiled, her embarrassment easing slightly.

'Are you doing the forecast tomorrow too?'

She shook her head. 'Day off.'

'Lucky you,' he said. 'I'll be stuck indoors massaging the legs of people who've pulled muscles because they've run too much or too hard or not drunk enough water or whatever. And in this weather half of them will be sunburnt too! Anything exciting planned for your day off?'

'Not really.'

He said nothing and she couldn't think of anything else to say either. Which usually freaked her out when she was with a man. She was uncomfortable with silence. She took a sip from her glass and put it on the table.

'I'd better go.'

'But you haven't finished your drink,' he protested.

'I'm tired,' she told him. 'I need my bed.' She winced.

Mentioning bed might not be a good idea. He might think she wanted him in it! Sweet God, she thought, I've lost it completely!

'Sure you don't want to stay a little longer?' he asked. 'It's so pleasant out here tonight.'

'Yes, I know, but I really have to get home.'

'OK,' he said. 'Though . . . Never mind. Right, Lainey Ryan, do you want me to walk you to your door?'

'I think I can manage that all by myself,' she said quickly. 'Thanks.' She stood up and swung her bag over her shoulder. 'And thanks again for the drink. I really enjoyed it.'

'So what about the party?' he asked. 'I'm happy to drive if you like. Do you want me to pick you up from your place?'

Would he expect to be invited in? she wondered. Would he expect . . . well, what would he expect? What had she done?

'Around six thirty?' He was looking at her curiously.

'That'd be great,' she said. 'Fine.' She didn't have to let him in. She could be ready to leave as soon as he called. She would be ready. Absolutely.

He showed her out of the apartment. She got into the lift and then walked along the cobbled path that linked her block with his. The wine was definitely having an effect, because she was a little unsteady on her feet. She walked to her window to draw the curtains. She could see Shay still sitting on his balcony. She opened the patio door and he looked over at her.

'Good night,' she called.

'Good night,' he replied.

She went back inside and closed the curtains. Then she

walked into her bedroom. She tossed her bag on to the bed and the contents spilled across the counterpane. She gathered them up, and then she realised that there was a missed call followed by a text message on her phone. It was from Ken.

Saw you on TV tonight. You looked great.

Her heart beat faster. He'd seen her. He'd contacted her. It hadn't been a one-off thing after all. She pressed the speed-dial button. It was OK to call him now, surely. He'd rung her first. But the call went directly to his voicemail.

'I got your message,' she told him. 'I'm glad you liked how I looked. Um . . . well, that's it. Talk again maybe.'

She ended the call and kept the phone in her hand, wondering if he'd ring back. But it remained silent. So eventually she put it back in her bag and went to bed.

Chapter 13

Stationary front: boundary between cool and warm air, in which neither is advancing

Lainey phoned Ken again during her break the following day. She realised that she was trembling as she waited for him to answer.

'Hi,' he said. 'I missed your call back last night. I was out.'

Out where? she wondered. It had been late when she'd phoned. Had he been at a club, chatting up other women? Which he was perfectly entitled to do, except . . . he'd slept with *her*.

'I just wondered was there anything particular you were ringing about?' she asked.

He chuckled. 'No. I'd seen you on the telly. You looked good. So I thought I'd say so.'

'Oh.'

'We should meet up again,' he said. 'If you've nothing else on.'

'Sure.' She tried to sound casual. 'When did you have in mind?'

'Not for a few days,' he told her. 'I'm heading down to Cork tonight. But I'll be back at the weekend. I might drop by.'

'OK,' she said hesitantly. 'Well . . . have a good time in Cork.'

'Doubt that,' he said. 'It's work. See you soon.'

She ended the call and stared unseeingly ahead of her. So . . . were she and Ken a couple again? Were they getting back together? And if so, would it be different from the last time?

'Hey, Ryan, what's up?' Alva Brennan was looking at her curiously.

'Oh, just taking some time out.' Lainey opened her eyes again and drained her coffee cup.

'You looked very thoughtful. Is everything OK?'

'Sure.'

'If you're not doing anything Saturday, I've got some spare tickets for the concert in Croke Park,' Alva told her. 'Would you like to come?'

She hadn't been out with the work crew in ages. But what if Ken dropped by on Saturday and she was out at the concert? Although maybe that would be a good thing. Keep him on his toes. And then she remembered that she had other plans for Saturday night. She was going to Feargal Wright's party and she'd invited Shay Loughnane to come with her. It had been a bad idea when she'd asked him. It seemed even worse now.

She told Alva that she couldn't make it to the concert. But she asked to be included in the next trip out. She wasn't going to let her social life revolve around one man in the future. She'd learned some lessons over the past few weeks. Hadn't she?

* * *

She met Val and Carla in the city centre the following Thursday. Her two friends were already in the tapas bar when she arrived, fifteen minutes late because once again the bus hadn't shown up on time.

'They're scarily punctual in Stockholm,' Carla remarked as Lainey flopped on to her chair, slightly breathless from having walked very briskly from the bus stop. 'In fact one time when a bus was late the woman at the stop beside me wondered if we should phone the authorities. She thought something might have happened to the driver.'

Val and Lainey shrieked with laughter at the idea of phoning the authorities because of an overdue bus in Dublin.

'More like you phone them if one actually arrives on time,' cackled Val.

'Is it nice or freaky to live somewhere so efficient?' asked Lainey, after she'd given her order to the waitress.

'Both,' admitted Carla. 'That's why we're buying somewhere here too. So's I can come back from time to time and embrace my shambolic Irishness. That's not to say Lennart won't come too. He likes my chaotic ways.'

'And how's married life treating you? You're home very quickly.' Val looked quizzically at her.

'I love being married to Len,' said Carla. 'We only went on honeymoon for a week because there are things going on in the company right now he needs to be part of. But we'll head away again later in the year.'

'Meantime you're going to be a dutiful housewife?' Lainey looked archly at her.

'I don't know why you've got it into your heads that I'm going to be sitting at home in my gilded cage.' Carla sounded mildly irritated. 'I'm still going to work, you know. Just not in the same area, because that would mean me having to come back to Dublin for good in a couple of months, and that's not in my game plan, obviously. I'm going to work in one of the other research departments after I finish my few weeks off.'

'I thought you said you were going to be looked after by Lennart,' said Lainey.

'I bloody hope so,' Carla told her. 'But I'll still be looking after myself too. A girl's gotta take care of herself. However . . .' she grinned, 'let's face it. Marrying him is a good career move in a whole heap of ways. I don't have to worry about climbing the greasy research pole any more. I can work for the enjoyment of it and not for the money, because I don't have to worry about money ever again.'

Lainey's dark blue eyes were troubled as she looked at her friend. 'Is that really the most important thing?' she asked.

'More marriages fail over money worries than anything else,' said Carla. 'Seventy per cent, actually, according to Relate. So I've taken that out of the equation.'

'I was surprised that he was so much older than you,' admitted Val.

'Age is irrelevant,' Carla told her. 'He's mature. It's what made a big difference to me. He's not a stupid guy who feels the need to impress. He's a grown-up and he acts like a grown-up. I don't have to play mind games with him.'

'Are you happy?' asked Lainey.

'Of course I am.' Carla dipped some soft bread into the green olive oil in front of her. 'Admittedly Lennart is very different to the guys I used to go out with. But I care about him a lot. He's kind and generous and he has a clear view of what he wants from life. He wanted to get married and the truth is that I wanted to get married too. I felt that the time had come to settle down with one person.' She looked directly at Lainey. 'You, of all people, can't criticise me for that. And, by the way, I'm really sorry about you and Ken.'

Lainey picked at a piece of bread. 'He's not entirely off the scene,' she admitted.

'What?' Both Val and Carla looked at her in astonishment as Lainey told them of Ken's visit to the apartment to return her stuff.

'You slept with him?' There was disapproval in Carla's voice.

'It's not like it was the first time,' retorted Lainey.

'But he broke up with you.'

'The break-up doesn't have to be permanent.'

Val looked doubtfully at her. 'But you were devastated when you called to see me. And I thought he said he didn't ever want to get married?'

'Maybe he's changed his mind. Anyway, I'm not in a rush one way or the other.'

Carla and Val looked at her wordlessly.

'Stop staring at me!' she demanded.

'We're just a bit worried,' said Carla.

'What about?'

'That you're getting back into a relationship with someone who doesn't want the same things as you.'

'You're an expert now, I suppose,' said Lainey. 'Having worked out exactly what you want and gone after it relentlessly.'

'We're not talking about me, we're talking about you.'

'Yeah, well, I'm fine. You don't have to worry. Or lecture me. Or whatever it is you have in mind.' Lainey's eyes filled with tears and she blinked them away.

'Hey, I'm sorry.' Carla took hold of her friend's hand. 'I didn't mean to be so harsh. If you and Ken really are right for each other and you're getting back together then I'm happy for you.'

'We just want to be sure you know what you're doing,' said Val gently. 'We don't want you to be hurt.'

'I won't be.' Lainey had recovered her composure. 'I won't make the same mistake this time. If we continue to see each other,' she added hastily as Val and Carla exchanged glances.

'You should do the same as me,' Carla told her. 'Make a list.'

'What sort of list?' asked Lainey.

'A list of what you want in a husband. See if Ken ticks the important boxes.'

'You didn't do that with Lennart, did you?' Lainey looked shocked.

'Of course I did.'

'And what was on your list?' asked Val.

'Financial security,' said Carla. 'Obviously. Generosity – and I don't mean just with money; I mean a generous nature. Lennart has that. Respect.' She waited for a moment before she continued. 'I've gone out with a lot of guys and I hated when they said they'd call but they didn't, or when they were late for a date, or when they came to the flat and used the last of the toilet roll and didn't say, or helped themselves to stuff from the fridge – I want respect for me and my stuff, and Lennart gives me that.'

Val nodded slowly.

'There were other things too,' continued Carla. 'I wanted a sense of humour – well, we all want that. I wanted someone adventurous. I wanted someone talented. And I wanted someone who was reasonably attractive.'

'Wow.' Lainey's eyes were wide. 'I didn't realise you had such high demands before.'

'I didn't,' agreed Carla. 'Not when I was dating Sam Purley or Conor Fitz or that total tosser Mick McDaniels! But when you've made mistakes you have to learn from them. And I did. That's why I drew up the list.'

'Are you sure that being in Sweden didn't just get to you eventually?' asked Val. 'Turned you into an organised person despite yourself?'

Carla grinned. 'I had a bit of time for list-making when I first arrived,' she said. 'But when I made it, when I realised what I wanted, then it was easier to make the right choices. It's no different to the girls in Jane Austen books. Their marriages were based on a whole heap of things, and love was pretty much at the bottom of the pile.'

'Yes, in historical novels!' cried Lainey. 'But not in the twenty-first century, for heaven's sake.'

'I'm not saying that the heart isn't part of it. Just that marriage is too important to be left to chance. Too important to be simply a product of being crazy about someone you hardly even know.'

'I married Nick because I was crazy about him,' Val reminded her.

'And you were lucky. But most of the time it's not that easy,' Carla insisted. 'How many books are there about finding the right man? Hundreds! And about making guys fall in love with you? Hundreds more! And about Men being from Mars and Women from Venus and how to understand them? Thousands! The thing is, we're all brainwashed into thinking that we have to be madly in love, but the truth is that we should be looking at it just like those women in history did. A business arrangement.'

'Carla!' Lainey was shocked. 'That makes it sound like prostitution.'

'I'm not saying sex in return for money,' Carla told her. 'I'm saying women bring some attributes to the relationship and men bring others, but because we all want to be crazy in love the whole time, we forget that these things are more important than the dizziness and the romance.'

'Well I'm not just focusing on dizziness and romance with an ex-boyfriend,' said Lainey, who felt as though Carla was lecturing her. 'I've plenty of other fish to fry.'

'Oh?'

She told them about Feargal Wright's invitation to his party and the fact that she'd asked Shay Loughnane to come with her.

'Feargal Wright!' Val looked excited. 'He's impossibly sexy, Lainey. I fancy him like crazy.'

'Shay Loughnane! The serial dater from your apartment complex?' Carla stared at her. 'What on earth made you do that?'

'You see.' Lainey jabbed an olive with her fork. 'You think you know all about me, both of you, you think you have me in a box marked "relationship loser", but I'm not.'

'I'd never dream of putting you in a box,' said Carla sincerely. 'But I'm certainly taken aback by what you've just said. So what's the story? Are they interested in you? Are you interested in them?'

'Hmm. That's a different issue altogether,' admitted Lainey. She explained how the casual meeting with Feargal had prompted the invitation, and how alcohol, coupled with a desire to be spontaneous, had spurred her into her unexpected request to Shay.

'We all know what Feargal Wright is like,' said Carla. 'And we sort of know about Shay too, because you've mentioned him before. But where are they on your potential husband meter?'

'Nowhere,' Lainey insisted. 'That's the fun of it. I'm just telling you about them to show you that I don't only see men as potential husbands.'

'That's a first,' said Carla.

'Ah, don't be like that.' Val spoke quickly, seeing a flash of irritation on Lainey's face at Carla's words.

'Hey, every man goes into Lainey's potential husband book,' protested Carla. 'And there's no reason these two shouldn't either. If they fit your requirements, Lainey. If you make a list.'

'I'm *so* not making a list,' said Lainey firmly.

'Why not?' demanded Carla. 'It's a good idea. You wouldn't do your weather forecast without making a list of the things you want to say.'

'I know what I have to say about the weather,' said Lainey.

'And you should know what you want in a husband too,' Carla told her triumphantly.

Lainey shook her head in resignation. 'Now that the list has worked for you, you want everyone to do it. But life and love aren't always like that, Carla. There really is room for romance. I believe that. I truly do.'

'And I think that dooms you to everlasting disappointment,' her friend told her. 'But we're two different people. So . . . I'll allow you to go the route of red-hot passion and romantic moments if you concede that I haven't ruined my life by marrying someone I like.'

'Of course I concede that,' said Lainey quickly. 'And I agree that it's really important to like someone as well as be in love with them.'

'Y'see.' Val looked relieved. 'Girls can always reach an agreement in the end.'

'Naturally,' said Carla. 'We're eminently reasonable. What I want to know, though, Lainey, is whether going to parties with media stars and bringing sexy neighbours with you is a change in strategy as far as you're concerned.

'I never had a strategy,' said Lainey. 'It's about having a fun night out, that's all.'

'Very different for you, though,' observed Val.

'Have I become so predictable that one night out is a matter for major discussion?' demanded Lainey.

'A night out with two new guys certainly is.'

'It's a party,' Lainey reminded them. 'There could be plenty of men there!'

'And if so, you should approach them all with the list in mind,' said Carla. 'Honestly, Lainey, it's worth thinking about.'

'You're impossible.' But Lainey smiled at her friend. And Carla clinked wine glasses with her in return.

Lainey was still thinking about Carla's obsession with lists of requirements for suitable husbands as she flagged down a taxi and got into the back seat. She knew that Carla didn't trust her relationship with Ken any more. Carla never believed that splitting up and getting back with someone worked. She always said it was compromising. But everyone had to compromise at some point, Lainey thought, and Carla herself had been prepared to compromise with Lennart in order to get what she wanted out of life. So they weren't all that different really.

But the idea of a list was stupid. It was taking everything that was wonderful about a relationship and putting it after security and common sense. Love wasn't about common sense. It was something else entirely. Something magical. It was part of what she'd felt on the day she'd walked with Bethany up the aisle, wearing her satin flower-girl dress and scattering rose petals in front of her. Love and romance belonged together. They could never be reduced to anything as boring as a list. Ever.

Chapter 14

Corona: an occasional optical effect caused by droplets or ice crystals when looking at the sun through thin cloud

The last time Deanna had visited Galway, she'd been fifteen years old. That had been for a one-month stay at an Irish-speaking Gaeltacht college. Sending children to Irish colleges during the summer had been (and as far as she knew still was) a popular practice for Irish parents, both as a holiday and as a way for children to become more proficient in their native language. The students stayed with local families, who spoke to them only in Irish and tried to integrate them into a rural way of life. Edmund and Madeleine thought that Deanna would enjoy the freedom of being away from them, although they weren't so sure if she'd appreciate the rugged wildness of the Connemara countryside and its more sedate pace. 'She's not known for her sedateness,' Madeleine murmured to Edmund as she read the brochure extolling the virtues of getting teenagers out of the city for a while. 'Knowing her, she'll probably try to rally them to some cause or other.'

In fact, Deanna had been horrified by her Gaeltacht experience. As far as she was concerned, rural Ireland in the 1970s was even more embedded in the Stone Age than Dublin. The house where she and her friends were staying, a ten-minute walk from the college, was big and draughty; the Bean an Tí (literally translated as 'the woman of the house'; how bloody patronising was that, raged Deanna) was brisk and unsympathetic, and her idea of varied meals was bacon, cabbage and mashed potatoes one day followed by Irish stew the next. Deanna was used to Madeleine's more adventurous cooking and baulked at the Bean an Tí's offerings. But most of all she disliked the unwavering assumption that all the girls staying in the house would one day get married and have a household of their own to look after; whenever the Bean an Tí spoke to them, it was always about housework, knitting and needlework.

'Is there any chance at all that these women could be dragged into the twentieth century?' Deanna used to demand every day – at least until she was finally caught saying it in English outside the college and docked points for her use of the language, which meant she was prohibited from going to the Friday night disco, the only bright spot in an otherwise bleak social scene. Her memories of Galway, therefore, weren't good ones, and she was surprised when she arrived in the city after her brief trip to Brussels to see that it was now as bustling and cosmopolitan as any she'd ever visited. More bustling than some, in fact, because Galway had become a favoured destination for artists and students as well as tourists, and this was reflected in the quirky shops and cafés that jostled for space in the narrow city streets. It was still low-rise, of course; Ireland didn't do skyscrapers in any of its major cities. But there was a vibrancy and buzz about Galway that she'd never experienced before, and it delighted her. What delighted her less was the number of girls and women who strode through the streets in full make-up and the latest fashions, looking, Deanna thought grimly, like refugees from Rodeo Drive as they tottered precariously on the sort of heels that resembled instruments of torture rather than footwear. Deanna hated high heels. Women were helpless in them.

While she waited to check in at her hotel, she observed a large group of young women all wearing low-slung pink velour tracksuits with 'Bootie' emblazoned in silver script across their bottoms. Deanna couldn't help asking herself if the right to have 'Bootie' on your arse was what she'd been fighting for when she'd demanded that women get off their backs. When she saw the girls face-on, she noticed that they were all wearing pink T-shirts too. The message on the T-shirts was that they were part of Tania's Hen Night. Tania herself was wearing one that said 'Learner Bride'.

Don't judge, Deanna told herself as she handed over her credit card; don't judge, and remember that, unlikely as it seems right now, they might all have important, high-powered jobs and they're entitled to a bit of fun. But she really and truly wished that they didn't have to wear so much damn pink when they were doing it.

The members of the audience for her talk in the university building were more soberly dressed; a large contingent of women her own age had turned up to hear her speak, and many of them, like Deanna herself, wore jeans and blouses, often accessorised with chunky jewellery. Deanna was comfortable with them and pleased that they asked questions about the issues she raised in her books. More difficult for her was the interview she did afterwards with a pretty young journalist who seemed to think that anyone who called herself a feminist was an anachronistic old hag who hadn't yet made it out of the Dark Ages. Deanna worked hard to keep her fiery temper under control while at the same time remembering that she'd had more or less the same thoughts about the Bean an Tí when she'd stayed in the Gaeltacht all those years ago.

'It is, of course, possible to be a feminist and enjoy looking beautiful,' she told the journalist. 'My worry is when being beautiful is considered more important than anything else.'

'There's nothing wrong with wanting to look your best.' Philippa Moriarty flicked her poker-straight blond hair from her eyes. Porn-star hair, Deanna called it. A style and colour regularly favoured by lookalike wannabes and women who wanted to marry into celebrity.

'Absolutely not,' she agreed, wondering how the journalist managed to use a keyboard with the acrylic nails she was sporting, 'but it shouldn't get in the way of more important things in life.'

'If you look good, you feel good,' said the journalist firmly with another flick of her hair. 'I can't understand why some women don't see that. There's simply no need to look tired and careworn. There are millions of great beauty products out there. And fabulous hair colours too.' She faltered slightly as she realised that Deanna clearly didn't colour her hair and didn't seem to care that natural grey was ageing. Deanna didn't say anything in response to what she considered to be a lecture about her appearance, but she did wonder if women were more grateful for the choice not to have to go grey than for anything the women's movement had done for them.

She fared slightly better when she met a reporter from one of the national newspapers, who was older and less ruthlessly groomed than Philippa, and who congratulated her on provoking an interesting discussion. They both agreed that there was too much emphasis on style over substance these days, but also agreed that it added another layer of difficulty for women – now, as well as having to work twice as hard as men for half the pay, they also had to look like they'd spent the morning with a make-up artist and stylist.

'Sometimes I think we've gone backwards.' Deanna sounded disapproving. 'But other times . . . I look at the Forbes list of the most powerful women in the world and I know that we've made progress. There wouldn't have been a female CEO of a nuclear power plant thirty years ago. Or a woman speaker in the House of Representatives. Or two women presidents of Ireland in a row! All these things are great achievements. The problem for me is that I see the other side of it, the women who become famous or powerful because they marry into it and it becomes their lives. The women who'd be nothing if they weren't Mrs Somebody. The women who think that being famous for being famous is an actual career. And that terrifies me.'

The reporter had written a good piece after talking to Deanna and there had been a lot of feedback on the newspaper's website, although some of the comments were of the 'get back to the kitchen woman and make me a cup of tea' variety. But overall she felt she'd done a good job.

After her talks, she chatted with the production team for her documentary and got on to the other side of the interviewing table. She met with a couple of the region's best-known businesswomen as well as a number of college students to discuss what feminism meant to them. She was encouraged by the fact that the students felt that all doors were open to them, although she couldn't help thinking that one day life would deal them the blow of realising that the door might be open but they weren't necessarily going to be invited in. But she didn't say this to the girls sitting opposite her, who looked so confident and so hopeful (and so beautifully made-up), and who clearly believed that there was no need for women like her in the world any more because they already had it all.

Women like me, she thought later as she settled into the bar in the hotel and ordered herself a coffee before opening her twice-read copy of Natasha Walter's *Living Dolls.* Trying to keep the fight going even though too many people think it's already been won. A bit of a has-been in the eyes of many, no matter how successful I think I am. After all, I can sit here unnoticed and unbothered, reading my book and enjoying my drink. That wouldn't have happened twenty years ago. People would've come over to me then and talked about my appearance on *The Tonight Show*, because I was in their face then. Though not in Ireland, obviously. I'd have been left alone in Ireland then too. The Irish are good at not coming up to you. People think it's respect, but really it's just so's you know that you're not really important. We still believe in not letting you get too big for your boots.

She turned the page of her book and then looked up as she sensed someone in front of her. It was Tania, the Learner Bride she'd seen at reception earlier. Only now she was dressed in tight jeans and a cropped top.

'Hi,' said Tania brightly. 'I had to come over and say hello. I recognised you earlier. We have all your books at home.'

'How nice.' Deanna was flattered and immediately took back all the negative thoughts she'd had towards the Learner Bride.

'Can I have your autograph?' asked Tania. 'I know my mum would be thrilled to get it. To be honest, I think she thought you'd popped your clogs years ago, so this will be tremendously exciting for her. She loves your quote. You know, the one where you said that women need a room of their own and it might be outside their own home. She said that to me when she divorced my dad.'

Deanna smiled politely at Tania. She was going to correct her and tell her that it wasn't her quote and that the Learner Bride had got the wrong person. But the girl was already thrusting a pink notebook and a pink pen with silver feathers towards her.

'Can you sign it to Bella,' asked Tania. 'That's my mother's name. It'll mean so much to her.'

Deanna hesitated. Then she took the pen and wrote in the book: *To Bella, hope you found your own room, Germaine Greer.*

'Thanks so much,' said Tania. 'She'll be thrilled.'

'No problem,' said Deanna.

She took a sip from her drink. She didn't know whether to be insulted or not. Maybe it was the grey hair, she thought. Maybe one grey-haired woman looked the same as any other to a girl in her twenties. She allowed herself a wry smile. Vanity, she thought, can come in many different guises. And maybe I'm as bad as the rest of them. Maybe my whole life has been about my own vanity when it comes down to it. Even if I didn't think that way when I returned to America.

* * *

It had been a long journey. Deanna felt like a different person as she finally got off the bus in Monterey and hoisted her rucksack on to her back. The clear blue sky and the taste of the ocean in the air seemed to wrap itself around her as she stepped on to the warm street. She felt her body relax for the first time in months. It was good to be here again. California, not Dublin, was where her life was now. For her it was about places, not people. Even if that seemed weird to everyone else, and even if it meant leaving her daughter behind.

She crossed the street and began to walk. She wasn't going to the house she'd shared with Lexy and Maya and Fawn. She hadn't contacted them to tell them she was coming back. The person she'd called when she made her decision to return to the US was Patsy Fuller, the leader of the Light Fighter Feminists. It had been Patsy who'd encouraged her to join the march to the City Hall and Patsy she'd stood beside as they shouted at the officials inside. Patsy had given Deanna her phone number and told her to call her any time. Deanna knew that Patsy had meant any time she wanted to get involved in the Light Fighter Feminists' activities, but she thought that Patsy might be the one to help her all the same. Patsy, a big-boned woman in her early fifties, had been a lecturer in comparative literature at Stanford University, but was currently on a sabbatical and writing a book about the women's movement. She'd mentioned to Deanna, on the day they'd first spoken at the coffee shop, that she needed a research assistant. Deanna was hoping she hadn't found one yet.

It didn't take long to reach Patsy's house, a small single-storey building on Harrison Street. Deanna pushed open the green-painted gate and hesitated. For the briefest of moments she'd had a flashback to Dublin and her family home, and to how she'd sneaked out of the front door so many hours ago, leaving her baby daughter in the care of her parents. She'd stood over the cot for a few minutes before she'd left, gazing down at the sleeping baby, and her heart had contracted with an unexpected sense of loss. But even as tears flooded her eyes she blinked them away.

'I've got to be realistic,' she whispered to Lainey. 'You're better off here. I was never cut out to be a mother. I want good things for you, of course I do. But the best way I can do that is to go away and leave you with Mam. I know that she'll do a better job of bringing you up than I ever could. And while I'm away, I'll be working on changing the world, Lainey, so that when you're grown up you'll have choices that I haven't had. Nobody will tell you that the only jobs you can have are teaching and nursing and being an air hostess. Nobody will think that you're a loser because you don't have a boyfriend. Nobody will think that getting married should be the most important thing in your life. Or that you're a success if you marry someone rich. You'll be able to go to college and have your own success in your career. You'll be a well-educated woman with choices in her life. That's what I'll do for you while I'm away, and you'll thank me for it, because it's far more important than being there to wipe your nose or curl your hair or any of that stuff.'

She'd felt strong and determined as she'd walked out of the room and she hadn't regretted her decision for one second. There had been a brief moment, on the plane, when a baby a few rows back had begun to cry and she'd instinctively tuned into it, recognising it as the same hungry cry that Lainey made. Then she'd turned back to the magazine she was reading telling herself that crying babies weren't something she needed to worry about any more.

She hadn't thought about Lainey again until now, outside the door of Patsy's house. She was wondering how her parents were coping and if her mother had remembered to massage oil into the dry spot on the baby's arm. But of course she had, Deanna said to herself; wasn't Madeleine the one who'd noticed it in the first place? She'd never forget.

She rapped on the door and Patsy Fuller opened it. The older woman was dressed in jeans and a T-shirt and her shoulder-length white hair was held back by a thin black band.

'Hello, Deanna,' she said. 'It's nice to see you again. Come on in.'

Deanna walked into the open-plan L-shaped living room, which was piled high with books, newspapers and magazines. The walls were covered with drawings and photographs of women; well-known female icons like Sojourner Truth and Betty Friedan and Marilyn French, whose most recent book, *The Women's Room*, Deanna had read five times. In the smaller section of the room there was a big oakwood table on which a powder-blue portable Remington typewriter was surrounded by sheaves of paper and coloured folders.

'I work in organised chaos,' Patsy said as she observed Deanna looking round the room. 'Which can be good or not good. So let's talk.'

She gestured to Deanna to sit on one of the fabric-covered sofas. Deanna moved a pile of newspapers and told Patsy about her hopes and her dreams and her baby back in Dublin.

'You think you can change the world?' There was a note

of scepticism in Patsy's voice. 'You think that you'll give your girl a better chance in life that way?'

'She won't grow up stifled like me!' cried Deanna.

'And you're OK with her being with your folks?'

'Absolutely.'

Deanna looked anxiously at Patsy. From the moment she'd first heard the Light Fighter Feminists talk, she'd known that she wanted to be part of them. Allowing herself to become emotionally involved with Jorge had been a mistake. It had been as though she'd stepped outside herself, as though she'd been playing at being someone she wasn't. With Patsy, she felt sure that she had the opportunity to get her life back on track, to do the things she wanted to do and make her mark on the world again. She needed someone to believe in her, that was all.

'We'll give it a trial,' said Patsy. 'You can be my assistant for two months. I need someone – you can see that the organised chaos needs more organising. I have a guest room you can stay in during that time. After that, if you stay working for me, you'll have to make arrangements for living somewhere else. Even though I don't give a shit what people think about me personally, I don't want them making veiled references to older women keeping young girls in their homes.'

Deanna was startled.

'You're very naive,' said Patsy impatiently. 'Idealistic, too. Which can be as much a hindrance as a help.'

'I'll be a help,' promised Deanna. 'You know I will.'

'I think so.' Patsy's voice softened. 'You've a good heart.'

'And a good head,' added Deanna as she felt more weight fall from her shoulders.

* * *

The blue air-mail envelope landed on the mat three weeks after Deanna had left. Madeleine tore it open and unfolded the flimsy paper inside. She sat down at the kitchen table and read the letter, her eyes narrowing as she learned of Deanna's new job with the feminist author and her daughter's hopes for the future.

'No mention of us or of you,' she said to Lainey, who was propped up in her pram. 'No understanding of her responsibilities.'

Lainey gurgled.

'OK, OK, she does mention you,' amended Madeleine. 'She says that what she's doing is for the benefit of women everywhere. So that you'll grow up in a different world.' She tickled Lainey under her chin. 'However did I manage to have such a foolish daughter?'

Lainey chuckled.

'She'll come back sometime,' Madeleine promised. 'You won't be without her for ever.'

She showed the letter to Edmund when he came home that evening. Her husband was equally annoyed.

'Why couldn't she have gone to England if she wanted to be away from it all?' he demanded. 'At least she could have come home a little more often. But she can't afford to come home from America. And we can't afford to go there again either.'

'Maybe one day in the future it'll be easier,' said Madeleine. 'Maybe it won't always cost an arm and a leg to fly places.'

'You think?' Edmund snorted. 'More likely it'll just get more and more expensive. And she'll use it as an excuse to stay away for good. Though how anyone could stay away from someone as beautiful as this . . .' He picked the baby out of her pram. 'She's the loveliest child I've ever seen.'

'Her father must have been a good-looking man,' mused Madeleine.

'I don't care what he looked like. If I could lay my hands on him, I'd cut his balls off.' And Edmund, uncharacteristically crude, stalked into the living room with his granddaughter in his arms.

Deanna got back in touch with Maya, Lexy and Fawn. In her absence they'd got a new housemate, Sherilyn, who worked as a receptionist in a local auto dealership. The girls were surprised to see her and shocked that she'd left Lainey back in Ireland with her grandparents.

'You know what it's like,' Deanna told Maya as they sat outside on the deck. 'I couldn't go back.'

'Yeah, but your baby!' Maya tried to keep the disapproval out of her voice. 'How could you bear to leave such a beautiful baby?'

'Because she's better off without me,' replied Deanna. 'Besides, you agreed with Lexy that she was cramping your style.'

'Of course I did. We're a house of single girls. It was impossible for both of you to stay. But I don't know if I could've abandoned my—'

'I did *not* abandon Lainey!' cried Deanna hotly. 'I left her with people who love her. I'll know what's happening to her. Not like her father. Who used me and then disowned her.'

'Sorry. Sorry.' Maya was abashed.

'One rule for men and another for women. They take no interest in their children and nobody cares. But I leave my baby with someone who can look after her a million times better than me and I'm a bad mother.'

'I said I'm sorry,' said Maya.

'You meant what you said, though.'

'I didn't mean to upset you.'

Deanna took a deep breath and released it slowly. 'Probably not. We all rush to judge, but none of us is qualified.'

'Exactly,' said Maya, though she still felt that Deanna had made a terrible mistake and would one day regret it.

But Deanna knew she hadn't, even though she missed Lainey more than she'd imagined she would. She was absolutely certain she'd done the right thing. She was enjoying her job with Patsy, trawling through libraries and newspaper cuttings to find articles that would support the older woman's work. Patsy sent her to New York on a research trip too, and Deanna lost herself in the most cosmopolitan city in the world. New York was edgy and exciting in comparison with chilled, laid-back Monterey. Patsy also sent her to her old college, Stanford, where Lainey walked through the grounds and wished that she'd had the opportunities that had been open to Patsy. It was extraordinary, she thought, that the other woman was around the same age as Madeleine, and yet had so many different experiences behind her. Of course Patsy's family had been able to afford to send her to college, while Madeleine had been forced to leave school at fourteen. And yet, thought Deanna, as she sat on the manicured lawns of the campus, Madeleine was just as bright as the students here. She was an intelligent woman. She simply hadn't had the opportunities. Ireland was light years behind America. That was why she couldn't even think of going back.

Patsy's book was published a year later, to great critical acclaim. In the acknowledgements she lavished praise on Deanna for her 'unstinting work and intellectual curiosity'. Deanna was both pleased and embarrassed by Patsy's words.

'Don't simper,' Patsy told her. 'You deserve recognition for your hard work. Women are shocking about that. They blush and say, "It was nothing" when in fact it was everything. You think some guy is going to say that? Never. He's going to bang on about how much effort he's put in and how much praise he deserves as a result.'

She was right, Deanna realised. The men she knew never played down their achievements. If anything, they made things seem harder than they were.

'I've spoken about you to one of my old professors,' said Patsy abruptly. 'They're interested in offering you a scholarship.'

'What?' Deanna was utterly dumbfounded.

'I showed him some of your research notes,' she said. 'And the essays you wrote for me. He thinks you have potential.'

'College? Here?' Deanna still couldn't quite believe it.

'You deserve the chance,' said Patsy. 'Take it.'

Deanna flung her arms around the other woman.

'Thank you,' she said.

'Don't thank me,' Patsy told her. 'Prove me right. Realise your potential. Make a name for yourself.'

Madeleine and Edmund returned to the States for Lainey's second birthday, before Deanna started college. She'd moved back in with Maya, Lexy and Fawn after Patsy had agreed to keep her on full-time as her assistant. It suited everyone, since Sherilyn, who'd taken her place in the house, had decided to marry her long-term boyfriend. Deanna was horrified that Sherilyn – who was only twenty – was getting married at such a young age. But she was delighted to move back into Oak Grove.

She was very happy living with the girls again, even though she couldn't help feeling that she'd changed tremendously since the first time she'd shared the house with them. Then, she'd been the one in the so-called serious relationship. Now she was the only one who wasn't seeing someone. Not that she wanted to see anyone. Relationships with men subjugated you. She realised that now. She didn't want to be subjugated ever again.

Until she started college, she continued to work for Patsy, which was time-consuming but always interesting. So she didn't resent the nights she stayed in writing longhand notes for her employer while the others went to parties on the beach and came home in the early hours of the morning.

She was surprised and not entirely pleased when Madeleine phoned to say that she and Edmund were coming to stay for two weeks. In the last year and a half she'd put her parents, and Lainey, out of her mind, concentrating only on her work. She couldn't see the point in them coming to visit her, especially, as she pointed out, when she'd be moving to start college in the fall.

'All the more reason for us to see you first,' said Madeleine firmly. 'And you don't have to worry. We're not going to foist ourselves on you. We're staying at a hotel.'

'Oh. OK,' said Deanna. 'Well, call me when you get here.'

'See you next week,' said Madeleine and hung up.

She and Edmund arrived at their hotel in Monterey the following Friday evening, having driven a hired Mustang from San Francisco. With the confidence gained from the last trip, and more time to plan on this occasion, Edmund had decided to treat himself to the sort of car he'd always wanted to drive.

The hotel was a modern block building just outside the town. Their room was small but bright, painted in whites and creams, with louvred doors leading to a balcony that had views over the Pacific Ocean.

'I can see why she likes it here,' Madeleine remarked as she flopped on to an upholstered chair beside the big bed. 'It's spectacular.'

'Oh, I dunno.' Edmund eased his slip-on shoes from his swollen feet. 'Galway would give it a good run for its money.'

'Hungry.' Lainey looked at them both from her huge blueberry eyes.

'So are we all, sweetheart,' said Madeleine. 'Here you are.' She handed her a Jacob's cream cracker, which she'd robbed from the plane.

Lainey looked at it in disgust. She wanted more than a dry cream cracker.

'We'll have a little nap and then we'll get something to eat,' said Edmund.

Lainey's lower lip wobbled as an enormous tear welled up and spilled down her cheek.

'You're an awful fraud, Lainey Ryan.' Madeleine kissed her on the forehead. 'All right. We'll get something to eat and then we'll have a nap and then we'll phone your mammy.'

Her granddaughter beamed. She wasn't interested in either the nap or phoning her mother, but something to eat was definitely on her agenda.

They arranged to meet Deanna the following morning (because they were very tired and Lainey had already fallen asleep by the time they spoke to her) and were sitting in the garden of the hotel when she arrived.

Madeleine studied her daughter as she walked along the twisting path. Deanna's dark hair was cut short and she was dressed in a T-shirt and knee-length denim skirt. The slogan on the T-shirt read: 'If you're not angry you haven't been paying attention'. She didn't wear any jewellery or make-up, though her face was lightly tanned, with a smattering of freckles across her nose. Her look (even allowing for the message on the T-shirt) wasn't fashionable. Most of the women Madeleine had seen since their arrival in the USA wore their hair long, with big, bouncy curls; and they dressed in brightly coloured silk shirts with wide shoulders over narrow-waisted tight trousers.

'Mam. Dad.' She greeted them and then hesitated. 'Lainey.'

Deanna had known her daughter would have grown, but she hadn't expected to see a little girl in a navy blue dress with long dark hair held from her face by a velvet ribbon. In her mind, Lainey was still a baby. Two years old wasn't much after all. But she could see that Lainey was a person. Her daughter was looking solemnly at her.

'Hey, Lainey,' she said.

'Say hello to your mammy,' commanded Madeleine.

Lainey stood behind Madeleine's chair, holding on to the arm for support. Then she turned away.

'She's shy,' explained Madeleine. 'Well, just at the start. She'll be fine in a few minutes.'

Deanna pulled another chair up to the outside table and sat beside her parents.

'How are you?' she asked, while continuing to watch the toddler, who was peeking out from behind the chair.

'We're doing well,' said Madeleine. 'Still a bit tired.'

'Of course.'

'And you?'

'Excited about college.' Deanna's face lit up. 'It's a great opportunity.'

'Indeed.'

'Don't look at me like that,' said Deanna.

'Like what?'

'Like I'm letting you down somehow. You wanted me to go to college when I left school. Now I'm going.'

'I'm delighted for you,' said Madeleine sincerely.

'But your mother can't help wondering about your plans for Lainey.' Edmund's voice was hard. 'You walked out on her, Deanna, and you left your mother and me to take care of the mess.'

'You're far better able than I am to look after a baby!' cried Deanna.

'*Your* baby,' Edmund reminded her.

Deanna said nothing. Of course Lainey was her baby. She knew that. But there was no point in her father making her feel guilty about everything all over again.

'Did it ever occur to you,' continued Edmund, 'that your mother and I might have had plans for our life after you'd left school? That we might have had dreams of our own?'

'Edmund . . .' Madeleine put her hand on her husband's arm. 'This doesn't help.' She turned to Deanna. 'What your dad is saying is that walking out and not talking to us was immensely unfair.'

'I'm sorry,' said Deanna. 'I did what I thought was best.'

'I know,' said Madeleine.

'And it *is* best.' Deanna's voice was determined. 'It really is. OK, I messed up. But I have a chance now to make it all worthwhile. To do something with my life.'

'And Lainey's life?' asked her father.

'She looks happy and content.'

'She is,' said Madeleine.

'I can't take her now.' Deanna looked hunted. 'Not when I'm going to college. It just wouldn't be possible.'

Lainey watched her mother and her grandparents, a worried expression on her face. She knew they were talking about her. She just didn't know exactly what they were saying. She let go of her grandmother's chair and walked over to Deanna. She looked up at the woman she didn't know.

'Mammy,' she said.

Deanna told her parents that she'd spend the week with Lainey. They could have a holiday, she said, and she would look after her daughter.

'Is that what you want?' asked Madeleine.

'I always do what I want, don't I?' asked Deanna drily. 'Yes.'

So while Edmund and Madeleine explored California in the Mustang, Deanna spent time with her little girl. Lainey was quick and bright. She was into everything, Deanna realised, opening drawers and cupboards, disappearing the moment Deanna looked away from her and turning up at the other end of the garden or in the upstairs bedroom or in a thousand different places. It was a full-time job simply keeping an eye on her, and Deanna was exhausted after a couple of days.

The other girls were enchanted by her, and both Lexy and Fawn brought her presents from their shop – mermaid figurines, wooden boats and lots of ribbons and clips for her luxurious hair. Sometimes Deanna would see Lainey sitting in front of the mirror applying Fawn's lipsticks and eyeshadows to her face and she would shriek at her to leave people's stuff alone. She would also tell her that make-up was silly, but it didn't seem to make any difference. Lainey loved the various pots and tubes of colour that she found around the house and seemed to enjoy daubing them on her face.

'One day I'll get you to realise that what's inside is more important than what's out,' said Deanna as she looked at her daughter, who'd smeared Lexy's favourite eyeshadow all over her face. 'But I don't think today's that day.'

Lainey looked at her. And Deanna suddenly burst out laughing. Her daughter's expression was so serious and thoughtful behind the shimmering green glitter of the eyeshadow! She picked her up and kissed her. Which made Lainey giggle, and left Deanna herself with sparkles of silver and green all over her T-shirt, which today read: 'Women who seek equality with men lack ambition'.

Two days before Edmund and Madeleine were due to return to Ireland, they came to the house for lunch. Lexy and Fawn were at the shop, but Maya helped Deanna to get things ready for her parents. Deanna wanted everything to look perfect, so she spent the morning tidying the house and yard, clipping the unruly chuparosa and Californian lilac shrubs and raking up the debris before hosing down the dusty wooden deck. She glanced upwards as she worked. The sky was overcast but the air was warm, so she reckoned it would be OK to eat outside.

She and Maya set the table with the colourful mismatched

crockery they'd accumulated over the past few years. Deanna had bought fresh fruit, salads and cooked meats from the local deli, as well as bread from the baker, and she thought that whatever criticisms Madeleine might have about her life, at least her mother couldn't fault her on the food. She had local wine and juice too.

When Madeleine, Edmund and Lainey arrived, Maya left, saying that she had errands to run but that it had been lovely to see Mr and Mrs Ryan again and that she hoped to see them again soon.

'Thank you, dear,' said Madeleine. 'And I hope you come back to visit us in Ireland, too.'

Maya smiled at her and left the family to themselves. Deanna gestured them to sit at the table, lifting Lainey and putting her on to a chair with arms so that she'd be safe.

Madeleine started to talk about their trip to Carmel the previous day and how pretty the town was, and how she was convinced she'd seen Clint Eastwood walking down the street.

'She fancies Clint Eastwood,' said Edmund fondly. 'She wanted to see him!'

Deanna was about to tell her mother that Eastwood's movies objectified women when she stopped herself. She was enjoying lunch with her parents, the first time she'd truly enjoyed spending time with them since they'd arrived. It was nice not to pick over her life and her choices, to feel that they were constantly criticising her and finding her wanting. It was nice to actually laugh with them for a while. She couldn't remember when she'd last relaxed around her mother, and she wasn't going to spoil it by dissing her favourite actor.

She was in the middle of pouring coffee for them, while

chatting idly about one of Madeleine's neighbours, when the front gate opened.

At first she didn't recognise the man who was standing there. He was tall and thin and his face was clean-shaven. His dark hair curled to just above the collar of the red cotton shirt he was wearing over faded denim jeans. He stood and stared at them.

And then Deanna spoke.

'Jorge,' she said. 'What the hell are you doing here?'

Chapter 15

Undulatus: a cloud layer with a rippled appearance

Carla rang Lainey shortly after their lunch and told her that she hoped she hadn't felt as though she was getting at her.

'A bit,' Lainey said, 'but then you and me and Val always try to advise each other. The good thing is that we ignore each other's advice completely.'

'Not completely,' amended Carla. 'Sometimes we agree.'

'At least we're always here for each other if things go horribly wrong,' said Lainey.

'Look, hon, it's not that I'm expecting it all to go horribly wrong with you and Ken again, but—'

'Oh, please!' Lainey interrupted her. 'Of course you do. Carla, I'm not a fool. I know it mightn't work out a second time. But I have to give it a chance. I've invested a lot in me and Ken, and I need to believe that I wasn't a complete idiot.'

'Don't they always warn you that the value of your investment can go down as well as up?'

Lainey chuckled. 'Yes. And I know my stock with Ken is bumping along the bottom right now. But we do care about each other. He washed my stuff before bringing it back. He texted me to say he'd watched me on TV. There's more to us than just hopping into bed with each other, you know.'

'I do know that,' agreed Carla. 'I just don't want you to get back with him and think that everything will be fine if he has no interest in marrying you and that's what you want.'

'It's not the only thing I want,' said Lainey.

'Oh?' Carla sounded surprised.

'I know you all think my sole aim in life is to get another ring on my finger. But truly, Carla, only with the right guy.'

'I was thinking a bit more about that,' said Carla cheerfully.

'Really?'

'Yes. I think this party you're going to is an excellent opportunity to suss out possible substitutes for Ken – just in case it all goes pear-shaped again. I definitely think you should check out Feargal Wright. He's in the same boat as Lennart, after all, a self-made man with a good financial background and a lot to offer. He's excellent husband material.'

'He and Sadie Parsons broke up because he wouldn't marry her,' Lainey reminded Carla. 'So I don't think he's a shoo-in for my third fiancé.'

'She was just the wrong woman for him,' said Carla dismissively. 'So what about the Lothario from across the way? I'm still very impressed that you asked him to come with you.'

'A moment of complete madness that I regretted the moment I opened my mouth. On the basis that he's had more women in his apartment than I've had possible fiancés, I don't think he's in anything for the long haul either. In fact I'm beginning to wonder if any man is really in it for the long haul.'

'They all want someone to look after them,' Carla said. 'But marriage – well, it means growing up for them. And some of them don't have the grown-up gene.'

'That's what you like most about Lennart.' Lainey remembered what her friend had said about his maturity. She also recalled that Madeleine had said the same thing about marriage being a grown-up thing for a man to do.

'Absolutely,' said Carla. 'I know that in the modern world we're all supposed to be able to look after ourselves. But the truth is, Lainey, it's damn nice to have someone who's grown up enough to do all the looking-after for you.'

Lainey was still thinking of Carla's words when she hopped off her bicycle and pushed it up her grandmother's garden path the next day. She heaved a cloth bag full of shopping from the basket on the front and put it on the step while she rang the bell. She had her own set of keys, but she never used them when she knew Madeleine was home.

'Thank you,' said Madeleine when her granddaughter had put the various boxes away in the kitchen cupboards. 'I'm quite happy to wander down and get foodstuff myself, but washing powder and cleaning products are too heavy for me to carry home these days.'

'You should buy online,' said Lainey.

'Oh, I don't spend enough to make it worthwhile,' her grandmother told her. 'Though your mother agrees with you. She said internet shopping was the way to go.'

'She agrees with me? That's a first!'

'Don't be mean.' Madeleine filled the kettle and switched it on. 'She's doing her best. Though when she offered to do some shopping last week, she totally forgot that we don't have a car. She was horrified at the idea of walking along the streets laden with bags.'

Lainey laughed. 'I suppose most people would be surprised by our car-less state. She texted me from Galway – what exactly is she doing there?'

'She was part of a Women of the World festival or something, so as well as her own stuff, she went to a few other lectures and workshops . . . There's a piece about it in today's newspaper, and I saw another article about her too.'

Madeleine fetched it from the sideboard and handed it to her granddaughter.

Lainey sat down at the kitchen table and read the piece, noticing that the journalist had included the 'get off your back' quote even though it was so old. The article was balanced, saying that Deanna had been an inspiration for a generation of women, while wondering if there was a place in modern society for her form of radical feminism. 'Clearly many women still think so,' she concluded. 'Ms Ryan's words seemed to strike a chord with those who find modern feminism too light on dogma and too heavy on lipstick.' She added a note about Deanna's upcoming television documentary, as well as reminding readers of the many awards she had received.

'I guess she'll be happy with this.' Lainey folded the paper in half. 'When's she back?'

'She came back last night,' said Madeleine.

'Oh.' Lainey was startled. 'Where is she now?'

'She went out just before you called,' replied Madeleine. 'But she expects to be home before lunch. Are you going to wait around for her?'

'Is she in full lecture mode still?' asked Lainey. 'Because I don't have the strength for that, to be honest.'

Madeleine looked at her in resignation. 'A bit,' she admitted.

'Do you find it very tiresome?' asked Lainey. 'She's your daughter, after all, but she lectures you too.'

'She doesn't lecture me.' Madeleine's voice was suddenly flinty. 'She knows better.'

'Right.' Lainey got up from the table and made the tea.

'Cupcakes in the cake box,' said her grandmother.

Lainey placed them on a plate and put it on the kitchen table. Then she stood behind Madeleine and put her arms around her.

'You're the best grandmother in the whole world,' she said gently.

'Thank you,' said Madeleine. 'I hope that's not only because of my baking ability.'

'You know it's not,' Lainey told her. 'You know it's because of everything.'

Although she wanted to go home, she decided she should wait until her mother got back first. It was nearly an hour later before Deanna arrived. She looked surprised to see Lainey sitting in the garden with Madeleine.

'I didn't know you were calling over,' she said.

'I like spending time with Gran,' said Lainey.

'Why don't you sit down and join us, darling?' asked Madeleine. 'It's lovely out here.'

Deanna dragged one of the garden chairs into the sun and sat down.

'I read the review of your talk,' said Lainey. 'It sounded good.'

'Hmm.' Deanna's lips thinned. 'That journalist was nothing more than a child. I doubt very much that she knows anything about feminism. I'm sure she simply took out her laptop and Googled most of it.'

'That's what everyone does these days,' said Lainey.

'I guess so,' said Deanna. 'Which is why so many people know little snippets about everything and nothing much about anything.'

'But all that will change after your documentary,' said Lainey brightly. 'You'll bring good old-fashioned feminism to the masses.'

'That's not what I'm trying to do,' Deanna told her. 'I'm analysing the movement and its relevance. I'll be looking to see if things have really changed or if we only think they have.'

'Of course they have,' said Lainey confidently. 'I watched a clip of an old interview with Germaine Greer on YouTube recently. It was from before I was born and some interviewer was asking her questions about marriage and abortion and not letting her answer and being horrible and condescending. And if it was me I would've hit him. So things have changed, because no interviewer would treat a woman like that any more and no woman would take it.'

Deanna's eyes widened with amazement. 'You were looking at clips of Germaine Greer?'

'It was a link from a Google search I'd done of you actually,' said Lainey. 'I wanted to check up on all the things people say about you.'

'Why?'

'Family interest, I suppose.'

'And so in Googling me you decided to watch a clip of Germaine?'

Lainey grinned at her. 'Professional jealousy?' she asked.

'Oh, don't be silly. Germaine was always a heroine of mine.'

Deanna remembered Tania asking for her autograph and her jaw tightened.

'I've watched clips of you too,' said Lainey. 'There aren't as many of them, though. And of course you don't pop up on the telly quite so often over here.'

'I'm on American TV. But I don't want to be as populist as her. Or as popular either. I'm not at all keen on serious women becoming vox pop types.'

'I don't think she was very popular with the interviewer,' said Lainey. 'He was a real male chauvinist pig.'

'She put up with a lot,' agreed Deanna. 'But part of her problem was that she was pretty as well as articulate. They struggled with that.'

'Still do,' remarked Lainey.

'That's something we haven't ever managed to change.' There was frustration in Deanna's voice. 'We like to look at pretty women but we're always surprised when they say anything intelligent. As I'm sure you've found out yourself.'

'Sometimes,' admitted Lainey.

'And the cause isn't helped by all these plastic celebrity women.' Deanna's voice was suddenly scathing. 'Selling nothing except themselves. Pretending that they're good role models because they've made money out of getting their boobs done, slavishly following unhealthy diets and flaunting their hair extensions. And just because they're rich, people think it's OK.' She shook her head. 'Not one of them is well known for having a single original idea. It's pathetic and degrading. Women should—'

'Deanna, please!' Madeleine held up her hand. 'I'm old and I don't need to hear all this again. So could you park it and discuss something else instead?'

'This is important stuff,' said Deanna. 'These women make other women think that they have a right to be rich simply because they engineer themselves to look good. They're shockingly bad examples, and the worst of it is that impressionable girls think they're wonderful.'

'I agree,' said Lainey, and Deanna looked at her in surprise.

'I've always remembered what you told me,' Lainey said. 'About having to be intellectually curious. About beauty being superficial.'

'In your case . . .' Deanna sounded rueful, 'it's not just superficial beauty. I don't know how I produced you, I really don't.'

'I'm sorry,' said Lainey.

'What for?'

'Looking like this. Being a disappointment.'

'You can't help the way you look,' Deanna told her. 'And to be fair to you, you don't usually trowel on the make-up and wear ridiculous clothes.'

'Thanks,' said Lainey, who noticed that Deanna hadn't said that she wasn't a disappointment.

'Really.' Deanna was suddenly gruff. 'You've done well for someone who's been handicapped by her looks.'

Lainey couldn't help laughing. Nobody else in the world thought her looks were a handicap. Not even her grandmother.

'What?' demanded Deanna.

'You're priceless,' said Lainey. 'But don't worry about it. You'll never understand.' She exchanged glances with her grandmother.

'I don't know what the two of you are so complicit about,' said Deanna. 'I saw you winking at each other. I'm not a moron, you know.'

'Last thing in the world anyone would say of you,' Lainey assured her as she gathered her things. 'I'm heading off now, Gran. I'll call by again in a couple of days.'

'Have a nice time tonight,' said Madeleine.

'Off anywhere interesting?' asked Deanna.

'Oh, just to a friend's.' Lainey didn't want to seem part of a glamorous, air-headed media crowd in front of Deanna, although she'd talked about the party with Madeleine. Her grandmother was a big fan of Feargal Wright's and always listened to his radio show.

'You can tell me all about it next time you're over,' said Madeleine.

'I'll call you about the documentary fairly soon,' Deanna told her. 'I'm doing other parts of it first.'

The good bits, I'm sure, Lainey said to herself. And then felt guilty for thinking that way.

Lainey spent a lot of time debating what to wear to Feargal's garden party. The forecasters weren't part of the TV crowd and didn't normally socialise with them very much, so she had no idea if they'd glam up or dress down. She was sure the men would simply wear jeans and a casual shirt, but the dress code for women was far more complicated. A garden party certainly sounded like more effort than jeans and a T-shirt. At the same time it wouldn't do to make it look as though you'd gone over the top completely.

She looked at the selection in her wardrobe and eventually selected a shift dress in mocha brown silk, which she'd bought in H&M and which looked both casual and significantly more expensive than it had actually been. She teamed it with a pair of high-heeled gold wedges from the previous summer, which she hadn't worn very often because, like her shoes for Carla's wedding, they made her tower over Ken. But she didn't care this evening. She wasn't with him. And it didn't matter whether she towered over Shay Loughnane or not. Always providing he actually called for her, of course. She hadn't seen or spoken to him since she'd asked him about coming in the first place. There'd been no sign of him sitting on the balcony of his apartment (with or without any of the women in his life), or playing video games in his living room. She wondered now if he'd even remember. Maybe he hadn't taken her invite seriously which would be perfectly understandable given that she hadn't been very gracious about it in the first place. All the same, she muttered to herself as she stepped into the shower, it's bad enough being stood up by an actual boyfriend, but by a neighbour who's only coming along because I didn't have the nerve to change my mind about asking him . . . well, that would be a new low. Even for me.

She'd just got out of the shower and wrapped a towel around herself when the door buzzer sounded. Bloody hell, she thought. That can't be him already. There's still an hour to go!

She hit the button on the speaker.

'It's me,' said Ken.

'Oh.' She tightened the towel around her body.

'The gates to the complex were open, but can you buzz me into the building?'

'Well, sure, sure, hold on a second.' She hurried into the bedroom, pulled on a pair of leggings and a vest top and then hit the buzzer again. A few seconds later Ken appeared at her door.

'Is this a bad time?' He could see that her hair was wet and her face flushed.

'I was in the shower,' she told him unnecessarily. 'I'd only just got out when you rang. It was a surprise.'

'Sorry,' he said. 'I was training at Dollymount, running through the sand dunes. I thought it'd be nice to drop in and see how you were before I went home.'

'I'm fine,' she told him.

'You're sure looking that way.' His eyes moved apprais-ingly over her. The vest top clung to her still-damp body. 'Were you working out earlier?'

She shook her head. 'Over at Gran's.'

'How is she?'

'She's in good form. My mother is staying with her for a while.'

'I'm sure she'll like the company.' Ken really didn't know much about the history between the three Ryan women. It wasn't something Lainey talked about very much.

'Um . . . was there any other reason you called?' she asked.

'Do I need one?'

'Of course not. I'm just surprised to see you.'

'I miss you.' Ken moved closer to her. 'I really do, Lainey. I miss your smile and I miss your texts and I miss knowing that you're there for me.'

Hah! She couldn't help the triumphant feeling that washed over her. There was no need for her to compile lists after all. Carla Carmody-Soderling had totally misjudged Ken. He missed her. He cared about her. He loved her.

'Want to get back into the shower?' he asked.

She smiled as he led her into the bathroom and turned on the water. Then he made love to her in a way that made her certain that they were meant to be together for ever.

She'd almost dozed off in his arms, as they lay in bed afterwards, when she remembered Feargal Wright's party and that Shay Loughnane would be calling to the apartment soon. Her eyes snapped open and her heart started to beat faster. What the hell was she going to do now? Tell Shay that she'd changed her mind? Ask Ken to come instead? Well of course she'd ask Ken; he was here beside her, wasn't he? And hadn't he just whispered into her ear that she was the most desirable girl in the world? Nevertheless, it would be embarrassing to have to dis-invite Shay after all.

But before she could speak, Ken sat up and looked at his watch.

'Oh, shit,' he said.

'What?'

'I've got to get a move on. I'm supposed to be meeting George in half an hour.'

George Newbury was Ken's fitness trainer. He lived in Ashbourne, about twenty kilometres from Lainey's apartment.

'We're having a chat about my stamina,' Ken added. 'Though, quite frankly, after that, I think it's pretty damn good.' He gave her a smug smile.

She blinked a few times as he pulled on his shorts.

'I'm sorry, sweetheart,' he said. 'I didn't realise time was so tight. And you know what George is like, goes mental if I'm late.'

'Sure. Sure.'

'I'll call you soon,' he promised. 'Sorry I can't stay, but you know how it is.'

'Yes. I know how it is.'

'Love you.' He kissed her on the top of her damp hair and let himself out of the apartment.

Lainey stayed sitting on the bed, staring into space.

Fifteen minutes later, the buzzer sounded again. She jumped up, thinking that Ken had returned, but the voice through the speaker was Shay Loughnane's.

'Hi,' he said. 'Are you ready to rock and roll?'

'Um . . .' She didn't feel like going to the party now. Not after Ken's visit. And not after he'd left her feeling . . . well, the truth was that right now she was feeling used. Ken had dropped by, stayed long enough to go to bed with her and then left. She'd been feeling great about his arrival until the moment he'd mentioned George Newbury. From then on, she'd wondered if calling to her apartment had simply been a way to pass the time until he met George. It would certainly be a lot more convenient for him than going back across the city to Donnybrook. She couldn't really believe that was his only motivation in calling to see her. Yet . . .

'Lainey? Everything OK?' Shay's voice came through the speaker again.

'I . . . yes . . . absolutely . . . it's just that I . . .'

Perhaps the best thing to do was to tell Shay she was feeling sick. Which was the truth. But he'd wonder why on earth she hadn't said anything earlier. Why she'd allowed him to get ready and call for her . . . She couldn't back out now.

'I . . . fell asleep,' she said. 'I'm sorry. I'm running a bit late.'

'No worries,' said Shay easily. 'I'll wait in the grounds for you.'

'Sure?'

'Of course.'

She raced back into her bedroom and slid the mocha dress over her head, thankful that she hadn't left it lying on the bed earlier, where it would undoubtedly have ended up either creased or on the floor. Her hair was still damp and would take far too long to dry properly, so she twisted it up on to her head, thinking that the last time she'd worn it up had been at Carla's wedding. She'd sprayed it into place then, but she simply used lots of clips now. Then she applied her usual tinted moisturiser, a quick dusting of nude eyeshadow and a light coral lip gloss. Seven minutes after Shay had sounded the bell, she was ready to go.

'Sorry about the delay,' she said as she strode out of the apartment block.

'No problem. You look great.' He fell into step beside her. 'The sleep obviously did you the world of good!'

Or was it the sex? she wondered. Making love always left her eyes brighter and her cheeks pinker. How have I suddenly turned into a person who has sex with one guy and meets another one half an hour later? Me, Miss Lifelong Commitment? Am I now a modern don't-care woman?

'My car is in the underground car park,' he told her.

She followed him down the ramp, realising that, in the gold wedges, she was exactly the same height as him.

'I wasn't sure you'd still come,' she said as he unlocked the door. 'I thought you might have forgotten.'

'Of course I hadn't forgotten.' He started the car and eased it out of the tight space. 'Though I was half expecting a message from you saying that you'd uninvited me again. Especially when I saw Adonis call to you earlier.'

She felt her face flame red.

'He just dropped by,' she said. 'Nothing important.'

Except to sleep with me.

She adjusted one of the clips in her hair. She hoped it'd dry out OK. She wished she hadn't had to rush.

They used the sat nav to get them to Feargal Wright's house, as neither of them knew the area very well. It was almost seven thirty when they finally arrived, and although later than the time Feargal had given her, Lainey was hoping that they weren't too early. The punctuality concerns she had about turning up for her own wedding on time and thus creating a social faux pas were mirrored in her uncertainty as to what was the socially acceptable time to arrive at a function. Half an hour late would be ridiculously late for a wedding but seemed about right for a garden party. She hoped so. As they stepped out of the car, she could hear occasional bursts of laughter drifting across the garden, which was encouraging.

She entered the access code that Feargal had also scribbled on the business card he'd given her and pushed open the high wooden gate. They walked across the lawn until they were behind the impressive red-brick house with breathtaking views to the sparkling blue of the sea.

Top-flight presenters certainly do better than weather forecasters, Lainey thought ruefully as she looked around her. In a million years she never would have been able to afford a house as beautiful as this.

There were about two dozen people clustered round a trestle table laden with wine glasses; fewer guests than she'd anticipated, but enough that she didn't feel too obvious. Feargal himself was chatting to a small group; she recognised a newsreader and a sports presenter among them. He looked up as she walked across the grass and waved at her.

'Lainey, you came!'

He had a way of making you feel the most important person in the crowd, thought Lainey, as he greeted her with a kiss on the cheek. Which was probably why he was so successful. There was a warmth and forcefulness to his personality that she couldn't help responding to with equal warmth as she introduced Shay.

'Good to see you.' Feargal pumped his hand. 'Do you know any of these layabouts? No? This is Cliona Boyle, our most glamorous news anchor. And she doesn't mind me saying so.'

Cliona, a caramel blonde who had been reading the news for about four years and was constantly voted on to best-dressed lists, smiled indulgently at him.

'And this is Darren Price, our award-winning sports presenter.'

Darren was young and energetic, with spiky dark hair and a wicked gleam in his eye.

'I love your column in the newspaper,' Shay told him as he shook his hand. 'Very entertaining.'

'Thanks,' said Darren. 'Are you a sports person yourself?'

Shay started to talk to him about his work as a physio and Lainey suddenly realised that, in his own way, he was as passionate about what he did as Ken. Ken would've loved to have met Darren Price, she thought. He'd dreamed of being interviewed by him when, eventually, he won a triathlon event. If he'd stayed with her today, if he hadn't rushed off like that, she would have asked him to come to the party instead of Shay, and he could have met the reporter.

'Hello, Lainey.'

She recognised one of the researchers at the studio, a girl she sometimes saw when she went for coffee in the staff restaurant.

'Hi, Bonnie,' she said. 'How are you?'

'Great,' said the young researcher, who was wearing skimpy shorts and a vest top, which looked effortlessly pretty and perfectly suitable on her, although it would have been totally inappropriate on anyone older and less toned. 'Fab day, isn't it?'

'Absolutely.'

'Do you find good weather interesting or boring?'

'Oh, I love the sun as much as anyone,' said Lainey. 'I'm quite happy to be bored if it means being out of doors.'

'You've never been to one of Feargal's summer parties before, have you?' asked Bonnie.

Lainey shook her head. 'Truthfully, never even spoke to him before the other day.'

'Really? He talked about having you on the radio show once.'

'He did?' Lainey was surprised.

'For sure,' said Bonnie. 'Then he thought maybe it'd be more appropriate to have you on TV, although he couldn't figure out how to fit you into that programme. Reckoned that people liked to look at you as much as hear you. But perhaps his new one . . .'

Lainey looked horrified and Bonnie laughed.

'I'm surprised they haven't tried to get you to do something of your own,' she continued. 'Everyone says you're great on the box.'

'I'm glad they haven't asked me,' said Lainey. 'I really don't like being in front of the camera that much.'

'You all say that but you love it really,' Bonnie told her. 'You have to pretend to be so modest, but you've got to have some kind of showmanship about you, otherwise you wouldn't do it.'

Lainey wanted to say that it wasn't true, that she'd had to be forced into going for the screen test in the first place, but then she realised that the younger girl was probably right. These days she did like doing the TV forecast. She enjoyed the technical aspect of it, of having all her graphics exactly right and fitting her forecast into the allocated time-frame; she also liked knowing that people were watching her and believing what she told them. But that was because it was weather, and something she was interested in and confident about. It would be entirely different being involved in a different sort of programme. She wondered how Deanna felt about the documentary she was doing. Whether she liked being in front of the camera or not.

'Does Feargal have a party every year?' she asked to change the subject.

'Oh yes,' replied Bonnie. 'Though last year the weather was horrible – grey and cold – and he had it in the conservatory.'

Lainey glanced towards the house. The big glass conservatory stretched across the back of it.

'It was good fun all the same,' Bonnie continued. 'Sadie organised it for him. She used to organise everything.' She lowered her voice, even though there was nobody within earshot. 'Poor Sadie, she's such a nice girl. But Feargal really needs someone stronger to keep him in line.'

'Right,' said Lainey. 'Is he seeing anyone now?'

'Why, are you interested?' Bonnie raised an eyebrow enquiringly.

'Absolutely not,' Lainey assured her, even as Carla's words echoed in her ears.

'I suppose not,' agreed Bonnie as she glanced over at Shay. 'After all, you have a hunk of your own already.'

More people arrived and Lainey drifted into talking to different guests. But her mind kept wandering back to Ken and his appearance at her apartment. She wished she could put him out of her head, wished that she didn't feel so uneasy about his motives for having been there. Ken was a good person. She knew he was.

'Where's your boyfriend disappeared to?' asked Feargal Wright, joining her. 'I can't believe you're standing here all by yourself.'

'I wandered off to look at your gorgeous garden,' said Lainey. 'And he's not my boyfriend, just a friend.'

'Oh, really?'

'Yes,' replied Lainey.

'Well now, that's interesting.' His tone was enquiring. 'The talk at the studio was that you were going out with someone. That it was fairly serious.'

'There's talk?' She looked at him surprised.

'Hotbed of gossip,' he told her. 'About everyone.'

'I'm definitely not worth gossiping about,' she told him. 'I do have a boyfriend. But it's not Shay. He just came along today for moral support. And to meet Darren Price, I think,' she added as she glanced towards her neighbour, who was still talking to the sports presenter, although they'd been joined by a few other people. 'He's a bit star-struck.'

'There's some others who are star-struck by you,' Feargal told her. 'The guy who lives next door wants to meet you. He says you're the sexiest woman on TV.'

'I don't think the Met Eireann people want me to be

sexy,' said Lainey. 'I think they want me to get the weather right.'

'You did for today,' said Feargal.

She smiled slightly.

'Do people say that sort of thing to you all the time?'

'Pretty much.'

'Sorry. I hate being predictable.'

'So do I.'

He was turning on the famous Wright charm and she knew it, but she couldn't help responding to it all the same. She felt a sudden jolt of electricity, a connection between them. And the thoughts that so often came to her when that happened rushed into her mind.

Lainey Wright, she thought. The first day we met was in the TV studios. But I hardly noticed him then. It was at a party in his house when we realised there was something more . . . She shook her head mentally. This was crazy. She wasn't really interested in Feargal Wright. Thinking marriage thoughts already was plain ridiculous. Besides, they hadn't done Sadie Parsons any good, did they?

'Do you like my garden?' Feargal looked across the green lawn towards the sea.

'It's fabulous,' she told him. 'I'd love to have a garden like this, but I live in an apartment.'

If I married him, though, I'd have this garden for myself, I'd have this view every day. I want to live in a house with a garden, not an apartment. If I had a list like Carla, that would be on it. Someone who lives in a house with a big garden . . .

'It is lovely,' he admitted. 'I can't manage it myself, of course, though I'd love to take the credit. I have a gardener who comes in every fortnight.'

'He was here today.' Lainey gestured towards the perfect stripes on the lawn.

'Naturally,' said Feargal. 'Have to make everything look good for my guests.'

'And your sea views are fantastic too,' said Lainey.

A gardener to look after things, magnificent sea views . . . would they be on my list?

God Almighty, she said to herself, would you stop it! He's not someone you're actually interested in as a potential husband. And you're sizing him up like a commodity. You'd hate it if a guy did that to you!

'Even better from upstairs,' he told her. 'That's why I have picture windows in my bedroom.' He grinned suddenly. 'Better I should keep away from the topic of my bedroom. You could get the wrong impression of me.'

She grinned too, thoughts of the list and marriage banished from her head. And then Shay came over and joined them carrying two plates with cold meat and salads.

'Hey,' he said, putting them down on a nearby table. 'I thought you might be getting a bit peckish. So I brought you food.'

'Thank you.' She smiled at him. 'I was just talking to Feargal about his garden.'

'Pretty spectacular all right,' agreed Shay. 'I once had a bit of a garden myself. But it's apartment living for me now. I live in the same complex as Lainey.'

'I see,' said Feargal.

'I keep an eye on her,' Shay told him. 'Living opposite her, I know all her shady secrets. And she knows mine too.'

Lainey felt herself blush as Feargal looked speculatively at her.

'I don't have any shady secrets,' she said primly, which made both men laugh.

'I don't think I could live in an apartment,' said Feargal. 'I like my privacy and my garden too much.'

'Oh, I didn't have a choice,' Shay said. 'After the separation, she got the house and garden and I got screwed.'

Lainey looked at him, startled. She didn't know that Shay had been married. That wasn't information Annie Dwyer had passed on. Maybe not information the older woman was aware of.

Feargal patted him sympathetically on the back. 'Men are always the ones who get screwed,' he said. 'We lose everything but still have to pay for it. Far better to stay unhitched. Or at least sign a decent prenup.'

'Indeed.' Shay looked suddenly grim and Lainey could see that his eyes were hard.

'Ah well!' Feargal placed a sympathetic arm on his shoulder. 'Better to cut your losses than carry on in misery, that's what I say. Oh! Excellent, she came!' He turned, his attention caught by a sudden flurry in the throng of people. 'Deanna! Deanna! Over here!'

Lainey turned to follow his line of sight, wondering who the guest was who shared a name with her mother.

And then she saw Deanna herself striding purposefully across the lawn, dressed in her usual uniform of blue jeans and white blouse. She blinked a couple of times, not quite believing her eyes, as her mother came up to them, looked at her with equal amazement and asked her what the hell she was doing here.

Chapter 16

Vortex: a spinning, often turbulent, flow of air

When Deanna had asked Jorge the same question, more than thirty years earlier in Monterey, he'd hesitated before replying. He'd looked silently at her and at her parents, and most of all at Lainey, who was using a plastic fork to chase sweetcorn around the bright red bowl in front of her, oblivious to the fact that most of it was ending up on her lilac and white checked dress.

'Jorge?' said Edmund. 'You're Jorge?'

Deanna was still staring at him uncertainly. He looked, if possible, even more attractive than the last time she'd seen him, and with his face now shaved, she could see a startling resemblance to Lainey. Jorge's features were almost too fine for a man, his eyes almost too wide and his lashes almost too long. Those features were clear in his daughter and were what made her beautiful. Yet he was undeniably handsome.

'Yes,' he said. 'I'm Jorge. And I've come to see my baby.'

Edmund and Madeleine moved closer together, blocking his access to Lainey. He looked at them impatiently.

'I'm not here to harm her,' he said. And then, turning to Deanna, he added, 'I'm here to apologise to you. And to her. I should never have walked away like that.'

Deanna's legs had turned to jelly beneath her and she sat down abruptly on one of the blue-painted wooden chairs.

'I can't believe you're here,' she said. 'After all this time.'

'There's a part of me that can't believe you're here either,' he told her. 'I was afraid you might have moved.'

'I did.' She was oblivious of her parents, who were watching both of them anxiously. 'I went back to Ireland. But I couldn't stay away.'

'I saw your name,' said Jorge. 'In a book someone had left in a bar where I was playing. It was by a woman called Patsy Fuller. I picked it up and flicked through it and saw your name at the start.'

'I worked for Patsy,' said Deanna.

'Pretty well too, it seems,' Jorge told her. 'She said nice things about you.'

'Because of her, I have a scholarship.' Deanna still hadn't taken her eyes from his face. 'I start college in the fall.'

'That's great,' said Jorge. 'I know you wanted to get more education. I'm glad for you.'

'What about you?' she said.

'You're gonna laugh at this.'

'Am I?' She felt the edges of her mouth turn up in anticipation.

'I've got a job.'

'A job?'

'Yup. A brokerage in LA.'

'No!' She couldn't keep the astonishment out of her voice. 'You? In an office?'

'Absolutely. The opportunity presented itself and I took it. It was about time I started to earn my way properly.'

'But what about your music?'

'Me and a friend play Saturday nights in a little restaurant in Venice Beach.'

'Oh, wow.'

'So my life's good. I got my music and I got some money too. And I also got some sense, because I couldn't stop thinking about you and our baby, and I knew I had to come find you.' He looked over at Lainey again and his face broke into a wide smile. 'A girl. Can't imagine that I'm the daddy of a little girl.'

'Hey, listen.' It was Edmund who spoke, and Jorge turned to him. 'You haven't been much of a parent to this little girl yet. It takes more than biology to be a good father, you know.'

'Jorge, this is my dad, Edmund. And my mother, Madeleine.'

'Pleased to meet you folks,' said Jorge politely.

'We're . . . interested to meet you,' said Madeleine. 'My husband is right. You walked out on my daughter and her child and I really don't know what plans you have now.'

'Well,' said Jorge. 'I thought me and Deanna here would get to know each other again and I could get to know my little girl, and maybe, just maybe, we'd become a family.'

The Ryans stared at him.

'I think before you have any more ideas we need to have a long talk,' said Madeleine firmly. 'And I think we'll do that inside.'

Deanna didn't know how she should feel. On the one hand, seeing Jorge had inexplicably renewed in her every desire she'd ever had for him. Her body was vibrating with longing and she wanted nothing more than to reach out to him, run her fingers along his chest beneath the fabric of his shirt, feel the warmth of him, revel in the simple act of touching him. But she knew that these were simply physical urges. And that there was more to being with someone than mere desire.

Over the past two years she hadn't felt that desire at all. Every fibre of her being had been totally caught up in who she was herself. Caught up firstly in the disaster of her pregnancy and then, later, in her work with Patsy Fuller and her greater understanding of the feminist movement and what it stood for. She knew that the last thing any of her female icons would want was for her to fall into bed with the man who'd abandoned her when she most needed him. And they'd scoff at the idea of them becoming 'a family'. Who did Jorge think he was, coming here with that sort of proposal? And what did being a family actually mean? Living together? Getting married? What did he have in mind for them?

In any event, thought Deanna, as she sat on the faded settee and watched him carefully, being part of a family wasn't her ultimate goal in life. Perhaps if he'd made it an option two years ago, she might have jumped at it. But things had changed too much for that to happen now. She wanted to graduate from college and she wanted to work for women so that they wouldn't be reduced to thinking that their only choice was being married with children. Times had changed for her, and for other women too. It was the 1980s and there were opportunities out there. Opportunities that had been created by people like Patsy Fuller. The feminist movement might not be as radical as it had been ten or twenty years earlier, but women were beginning to think it their right to go to college, get qualifications and find good jobs. These opportunities were now open to her. Was she going to throw them away simply because Jorge had come into her life again and belatedly decided that he wanted to be a father? How dare he expect that?

But that seemed to be exactly what Jorge expected. He told her that he'd behaved badly and that he knew that walking out on her had been a selfish move on his part, but he was prepared to change all that. He'd gone into shock, he said, when she told him about the pregnancy and he hadn't been thinking straight. He'd had to leave but he hadn't stopped thinking about them – he'd even written a song for his unborn child. He'd realised that it was important for him to take responsibility for his actions, for her and for Lainey too. He'd made his decision to come see them again. He was relieved to have found them.

'And it took you two years to decide that?' interjected Madeleine, when Deanna said nothing.

'I had to do a lot of thinking,' said Jorge. 'My own situation wasn't clear cut.'

'In what way?' demanded Madeleine. 'Are you married already?'

'No,' said Jorge. 'But I had other things to think about. How I wanted to live my life.'

'Does your family know about Deanna and Lainey?' asked Edmund. 'Is there backup? Support?'

'Not yet.' A faint smile played around Jorge's lips. 'But they're gonna be so pleased when they find out.'

'It's not that simple,' said Madeleine. 'You have to—'

'Hey, this is between Deanna and me.' Jorge interrupted her. 'It's not up to you.'

'I rather think it is,' Madeleine told him. 'We've been the ones taking care of Lainey for the past two years. I think we're exactly the people who need to be consulted on her future.'

Jorge looked at Madeleine in surprise, and then Edmund told him that Deanna had left her daughter in their charge. He didn't say anything about her sneaking out of the house in Killester, leaving Lainey behind.

'In that case, you can understand how I felt,' Jorge told Deanna. 'It's a big thing, having a child when you're not ready for it.'

Lainey, who'd been playing with some coloured bricks from Fawn and Lexy's shop, suddenly started to cry. Edmund picked her and the bricks up and brought her outside. It had clouded over, but the air was hot and humid. He sat down on the deck with her and divided the bricks into colours. She began putting them in little piles. He walked back into the house again, although he kept an eye on her from his position inside the door.

'You can't just come here and order me to go with you to LA,' Deanna told Jorge.

'But I have rights regarding my child,' said Jorge.

'You forfeited those rights when you walked out on us,' Deanna told him.

'You might like to think so, but that's not the case.' Jorge's languid tones of earlier had changed, and his voice was suddenly crisp and clear. 'Anyhow, you walked out on her too. So I don't think you're in any position to be talking about what I can and can't do. If I want my child in my life, I'm entitled to have her.'

'For heaven's sake!' Madeleine's cheeks were pink. 'You

two are talking about her as though she's a commodity! She's a person. It's not about your rights, it's about hers!'

Deanna looked helplessly at her mother. 'I know,' she said.

'And I haven't heard you talking about anything other than her coming home with us the day after tomorrow,' said Madeleine.

'Home? She still lives with you?' Jorge looked surprised.

'Yes, she does,' said Madeleine.

'And where do you live?'

Both Edmund and Madeleine stared at him in amazement.

'Ireland, of course,' said Madeleine.

'Ireland!' This time Jorge was shocked.

'Where else?' demanded Edmund.

'You mean you don't live in the US?'

'Of course not,' replied Edmund. 'How could we possibly? I've lived and worked in Ireland all my life. We're only here for a holiday. To see Deanna and for her to see Lainey again.'

'So you hardly ever see her?' Jorge turned to Deanna. 'You hardly ever see her but you want to make rules about me seeing her? That's rich, Deanna, it really is.'

'I'm her mother,' said Deanna. The words sounded strange coming from her lips. She'd never said them out loud before, never thought of Lainey as her daughter in the way she was thinking of her now. 'I have to do what's best for her.'

'And you think that that's keeping her away from me?' demanded Jorge angrily.

'That's not what . . .'

A sudden roll of thunder stopped Deanna in mid-sentence, and almost at once the rain started to fall.

'Where's the child?' asked Madeleine. 'Where's Lainey?'

They all moved, but it was Jorge who was out of the door

quickest, and it was Jorge who picked her up and held her close to him. Lainey put her arm around his neck and rested her head against his chest as he brought her into the house again.

Deanna clenched her fists at her sides as she watched them. They were so very definitely father and daughter, it scared her.

'OK,' Jorge said as he stroked his daughter's back. 'We need to talk this through again. But first, somebody had better get her out of these wet things.'

They talked for a long time after Deanna had changed Lainey's rain-soaked dress for a clean T-shirt and shorts, but Edmund and Madeleine were adamant. They were going back to Ireland, Edmund said, and they were taking Lainey with them, because there was no other viable option. Deanna was starting college. It would be impossible for her to do that and live with Jorge in LA. And there was no way that they were giving Lainey to Jorge. He was a single man and nobody knew anything about his personal circumstances. How could he possibly look after a two-year-old child? Besides, it wouldn't be in Lainey's best interests for her to be with him. It wouldn't be in her best interests to be with Deanna either. Not that, until now, either of them had shown the slightest bit of interest in her anyhow.

'That's not true,' said Deanna. 'I care about her.'

'Oh, please.' Edmund looked at his daughter pityingly. 'The only person you care about in this world is yourself.'

'Which isn't a good advertisement for allowing her to keep our child,' said Jorge.

'What are you trying to do to me?' Deanna demanded of her father. 'Can't you be supportive?'

'I've been supportive for the past two years,' said Edmund. 'I still am. But the most important person in all of this is Lainey, and I want to support her most of all.'

'I know she's important,' said Deanna shortly.

'Well you didn't seem to think that when you sneaked out of the house.'

'That was then! I was upset.'

'Edmund. Deanna. Stop it.' Madeleine spoke quietly. 'We're all surprised and shocked by Jorge's reappearance. And I understand that he needs to feel . . . a connection with his daughter.' She turned her clear blue eyes to the tall, lean man who was watching Lainey, now sitting in the doorway of the house staring out at the pouring rain. 'But you've got to see, Jorge, that you can't just come here and make demands.'

'I want to know my daughter. And I was – am – prepared to make some kind of arrangement, understanding . . . oh, anything at all with Deanna. I thought maybe she still cared for me.'

'You walked out on me!' cried Deanna.

Lainey, distressed by the rising tension in the room, turned to Madeleine, who scooped her up and held her tightly. Lainey jammed her thumb in her mouth and began sucking vigorously on it, her dark eyes regarding the adults warily.

'Maybe I was being naive,' said Jorge. 'Maybe I was thinking that Deanna would be happy to see me and hear that my life has changed. And that she'd want to be with me.'

'I did want to be with you back then,' said Deanna. 'I thought I loved you. I was broken-hearted when you left – and don't forget, you told me that my baby could be anyone's!

You were far more selfish than I've ever been. But I got over you. In the last two years my life has changed too. And I've got opportunities to do things that I never had before. I can't turn down college to be with you when who knows how things might turn out between us? I hardly know you, Jorge. It was mostly sex as far as you were concerned.'

Edmund inhaled sharply, and Madeleine had to put a steadying hand on his arm.

'You two need to talk things through further,' she said to Deanna and Jorge. 'We're in the way. We'll go back to our hotel and take Lainey with us, because you can see that this is distressing her, and the two of you can talk.'

'That's fair,' said Jorge. 'But I don't want you guys disappearing with my daughter.'

'We won't,' said Madeleine. She gave him the name of the hotel. 'You know where to find us.'

She and Edmund got up. She was still holding Lainey in her arms.

'I'll call you later,' Deanna told her.

'Goodbye, sir, ma'am,' said Jorge as they walked through the door.

'Bye-bye.' Lainey lifted her head from Madeleine's shoulder and looked at him. 'Bye-bye.'

Deanna didn't know what to say to him. She was acutely aware that Madeleine was right about so many things. Deanna's new life didn't have room for Lainey. There was no question about that. And the truth was that she didn't usually spend a lot of time thinking about her or worrying about her. Not on a personal level. She did, however, think about her whenever she was working, always telling herself that what she was doing was making a difference, and that Lainey would benefit from that in the future. Deanna believed in the rightness of her decisions, believed that it was for the best both for her and for Lainey. What wasn't for the best, she thought, was having anything to do with Jorge, even if he was now a nine-to-five broker, a job that seemed utterly alien to her view of him.

'All I want is to be able to see my girl,' he told her after they'd argued fruitlessly for another half an hour. 'Why can't you understand that?'

'I do understand!' she cried. 'But what I can't see is how it could be remotely possible. Even if she was living here with me, it would be a trek for you to visit her on a regular basis.'

'She could spend time with you and time with me.'

'So we'd be passing her round like a piece of furniture,' said Deanna. 'That's impossible.'

'No it's not.'

'You're so selfish,' she told him. 'You've suddenly decided you want to be involved and you don't care what chaos that causes.'

'*I'm* selfish!' he exclaimed. 'I wasn't the one who sneaked out of the house and left her.'

'No!' cried Deanna. 'You walked away before she was even born.'

It was an argument that was going nowhere. They both knew it. Eventually Jorge said that he was leaving, that he needed to think things through. Consult with some people.

'What people?'

'My family. Legal people. Who knows? Because it's not right, Deanna. You shouldn't be the only one to say what happens to her.'

'I'm her mother.' Deanna spoke the words more forcefully this time.

'And that gives you all the rights?' He looked at her in disgust. 'That's not fair.'

'Now you know what it's like,' she retorted. 'In this world men have all the rights when it comes to just about everything else. You make the rules and we have to follow them. It's not so good when the shoe's on the other foot, is it?'

'Don't turn my daughter into one of your feminist battles,' he warned her.

'She's a girl,' said Deanna. 'She's going to have to face plenty of battles of her own in the future.'

Jorge shook his head. Then he walked out of the house and slammed the door behind him.

Deanna sat with her head in her hands. She was totally conflicted about the situation. She knew that she had no real right to make any decision about Lainey. The only people who should do that were her parents. But the law was different, and it would surely be on her side when it came to Lainey. Especially given that Jorge had deserted both of them. Except . . . if there was a legal battle and she was awarded custody of her daughter – then what? She couldn't help thinking that no matter what happened, no court would say that Jorge couldn't at least see Lainey from time to time. So that would mean that Lainey would have to stay in the States. What would she do then? How would she cope? What about her career? What about all the things she wanted to achieve? Would she have to sacrifice them all to look after her baby? When she'd already left her once to pursue them? How would the male-dominated courts see that? Would they think she'd deserted Lainey just as much as Jorge had? Would they blame her more because she was a mother? Would they be right?

I'm a bad person, thought Deanna miserably. Other women, other mothers would always have put their children first. And I want to. I really do. But I don't think I'm cut out for it.

There was a sudden clap of thunder overhead, and the rain cascaded from the sky again, drumming against the roof of the house, splashing off the deck and through the open front door.

I've made a mess of everything, Deanna said to herself as she stared out at the grey clouds. Even though I know I have to do what's best for Lainey, I'm really not at all sure what that might actually be.

Edmund and Madeleine phoned later that evening. Deanna told them that she hadn't heard anything from Jorge yet. Madeleine said that they still planned to return to Ireland the day after next with Lainey.

'I think that's best,' said Deanna. 'And if Jorge wants to do something about it . . . well, let's cross that bridge when we come to it.'

Deanna replaced the phone. Lexy, Fawn and Maya, who'd returned a short while earlier and had been told about Jorge's visit, looked at her sympathetically. But their sympathy, she knew, was tempered by the fact that all of them had totally fallen for Lainey and they couldn't understand for a single moment how she could bear to be parted from her.

The next morning, under the clear blue skies that had followed the previous day's rainstorm, she went to see Patsy

Fuller and told her what had happened. Pasty was the one person who understood how Deanna was feeling, the only one who could empathise with the conflicting emotions inside her.

'Wait till he contacts you again and tells you what he plans to do,' she said. 'Then come see me. We'll work something out.'

Deanna went back home. She'd left a note stuck to the door in case Jorge turned up while she was out, but it was still there, fluttering in the light breeze that always blew gently across the front of the house. She sat on the deck with a copy of Maya Angelou's *I Know Why the Caged Bird Sings* and waited for Jorge to come. She was engrossed in the book, but every so often she would look up, expecting to see the gate being pushed open and Jorge walking up the small path. But it didn't happen.

By evening she was totally on edge. She was worried that he'd gone directly to a lawyer and that she would be hauled into a courtroom to defend herself. He would say that she was an unfit mother because she'd given her child to her parents to rear. Which would be perfectly true. But he wasn't a fit father either. The most worrying thing of all, though, was that he was an American citizen and she wasn't. Maybe they'd ask her to leave the country. Without Lainey. She couldn't let that happen. She couldn't leave. Multiple scenarios, each more worrying than the last, chased each other round and round her head until it ached.

When the phone rang at six o'clock, she shot out of the chair to answer it. It was Madeleine, wanting to know what had happened.

'Nothing,' she said. 'He hasn't shown up.'

Madeleine sniffed. 'The heat of the kitchen was too much for him.'

'Maybe.'

'We're leaving tomorrow,' she said.

'I know.'

'Call me as soon as you hear anything.'

'OK,' said Deanna, and went back to the deck to wait for him.

She couldn't believe that he wouldn't come. Whatever else, he had seemed sincere about his desire to see Lainey. He said he'd written her a song, so she clearly meant something to him. It was irrational to arrive at the house and make such a fuss, then not return. His absence worried her even more than his presence had done. Yet she wondered what her concern actually was. After all, if he loved Lainey and wanted her to be with him, why should she stand in his way? Why didn't she simply say that her daughter should be with her father? Why did she so badly want to have control over Lainey's life herself?

Deanna couldn't answer her own questions. And that worried her even more.

The next day, the day that Edmund and Madeleine were due to depart for Ireland, there was still no news from Jorge. By now, Deanna was in a state of near panic.

'Well,' said Madeleine as they sat together at the hotel waiting for a cab, 'it's too late now. If he was going to stop us leaving, he would have done something sooner.'

'I guess so.' Deanna sounded doubtful.

'Maybe he's going to pull a stunt at the airport,' said Edmund.

'I can't see that,' Madeleine said. 'And the truth is . . .' she sighed, 'he seemed a genuine person. He cared about Lainey. I couldn't help believing that he wanted to be involved.'

'Perhaps he's changed his mind.' Deanna was watching Lainey running around the lobby. 'He walked out on me before. Maybe he's done the same again.'

They sat in silence thinking about Jorge. And then Edmund said that they'd better get going if they were to catch their flight.

'You'll call me if there's a problem at San Francisco?' asked Deanna.

'Of course,' said Edmund.

'Goodbye, darling.' Madeleine hugged her. 'Take care of yourself.'

'I will.'

'Say goodbye to your mammy.' Madeleine lifted Lainey.

'Bye-bye.' Lainey said the words automatically.

Somehow, Deanna thought, as she watched them get into the car, her daughter's farewell to her hadn't sounded half as heartfelt as the one she'd given Jorge. She knew she was probably mistaken. But that was how it felt. And that's why I'm doing the right thing, she told herself as she swallowed the lump in her throat. I can't give Lainey what she needs. She might be a baby, but I'm pretty sure she knows that too.

Chapter 17

Cumulus mediocris: a medium-sized convective cloud with little vertical growth

Lainey had gone to the bathroom in Feargal Wright's house. She'd needed a few moments on her own to get over the shock of Deanna's appearance, which had rendered her utterly speechless. She'd stared at her mother, unable to answer the question of why she was at the party. It was Feargal, looking at Deanna and then at Lainey, who actually spoke.

'Do you know each other?' he asked. And then, even as the words left his mouth, there was a dawning realisation in his eyes. 'Deanna Ryan. Lainey Ryan. Are you related?'

Lainey looked at Deanna, unsure of what to say. They had never been in a situation before in which Deanna had to publicly acknowledge that Lainey was her daughter. Lainey didn't know if that was what her mother wanted to do. Or if Deanna would shrug and say that, yes, they were related and leave it at that. Which would be beyond embarrassing.

'Of course we're related,' Deanna said. 'Can't you see the resemblance?' She stood beside Lainey and looked challengingly at Feargal, while Shay stood to one side and observed them, a slight frown creasing his brow.

'Now that you mention it . . .' Feargal nodded. 'It's in your eyes.'

Lainey was startled. Deanna had once told her dismissively that her eyes were like her father's, their dark blueberry his legacy. Deanna's own eyes were a lighter shade. But, she realised as she looked at her mother, they were the same shape, even if Deanna's had more wrinkles around them.

'So how are you related?' asked Feargal.

Lainey looked at Deanna. Deanna looked at Lainey. And then at Feargal.

'Lainey's my daughter,' she said simply, as though he should have known already.

Feargal couldn't suppress the surprised exclamation that came out of his mouth.

'I didn't know you had a daughter. I didn't know I *knew* your daughter!'

'You obviously didn't do your research properly,' said Deanna calmly. 'I presume you've done better research on my work, Feargal? Otherwise why did you ask me to be on your TV show?'

'That's different, of course,' said Feargal at once. 'I'm totally up to speed on your work. I thought I was totally up to speed on you too. I knew nothing about any daughter.'

'She's not part of my professional life,' said Deanna. 'Although she will be talking to me as part of the documentary . . .'

'She has a lot to live up to with you as a mother,' said Feargal. 'Though as she's one of the country's most popular weather girls, there must be a success gene in the family.'

Lainey couldn't help feeling that being a popular weather girl wasn't in the same league as being an award-winning feminist, but she wasn't going to argue. In fact she still felt totally unable to speak.

'You're talking about Lainey as though she isn't here,' remarked Shay casually. 'Which is a bit rude of both of you.'

'I'm used to that.' Lainey found her voice. 'Excuse me, Feargal. Deanna. I have to go to the bathroom.' And she walked away from them and into the house.

She stood in front of the mirror in Feargal's black and white downstairs bathroom and stared unblinkingly at her face. She didn't know for certain how like her father she actually looked, because she'd never seen a photograph of him. He hadn't been around long enough, Deanna had told her on one of her return trips to Ireland, to pose for photographs. But Madeleine had always said that she took after her father more than her mother, because none of her childhood photographs were in the slightest like Deanna's. She looked at her eyes. Wide and round. Striking, one of the guys at the TV station had once told her. Deanna's were striking too. But that was because when Deanna looked at you, it was always a forceful look.

Lainey shivered slightly, even though it was still warm. She opened her handbag and took out some mascara, which she applied to her already long, dark lashes. She was doing it for the comfort of the ritual more than anything else. And so that she had a reason to stay in the bathroom a little longer. Even though she told herself that it was ridiculous to want to hide from her own mother for no good reason at all.

She brushed her hair, added gloss to her lips and sprayed

herself with her Nina Ricci summer perfume. Then she took a deep, steadying breath, exhaled slowly and walked out into the garden again.

Deanna was still talking to Feargal. Lainey didn't know if she should join them or not, but was saved from having to make the decision by Shay, who detached himself from his spot near the barbecue and came over to her.

'Are you all right?' he asked.

'Sure.'

'I take it you were surprised to see your mother here.'

She smiled faintly. 'You take it right.'

'The two of you don't exactly get on?'

'It's a long story,' she said. 'Complicated.'

'I'm intrigued.'

'No need to be,' she told him. 'Deanna and I are totally different people.'

'I've heard of her, of course.' Shay's tone was dry. 'I didn't think she had a daughter.'

'It's not something she talks about. She didn't become well known until after I was born and living with my grandparents. So it never really came up. I suppose she wouldn't have got away with keeping me quiet if it had happened now, because nobody has a private life any more and something would probably be on the internet, but back then it was easier.'

'Do you mind being her secret?' asked Shay.

'I'm not exactly a secret,' said Lainey. 'Plenty of people already know I'm Deanna's daughter. My friends. Gran's neighbours. But it doesn't mean that much to them.'

Shay looked thoughtful. 'It's odd that nobody rooted it out, though.'

'Afraid to ask her too many questions,' said Lainey. 'Never occurred to them that it was a possibility.'

'True,' said Shay. 'She thinks all men should be castrated, doesn't she?'

Lainey shook her head. 'You're overexaggerating a bit there. She just thinks that the world would be better run by women.'

'More selfish and bitchy, maybe,' said Shay.

Lainey said nothing.

'Sorry.' He grimaced. 'I haven't had great experiences with women.'

'The broken marriage was all her fault?' Lainey voice held a touch of irony.

'Of course not. But afterwards . . . Oh, look, this isn't something I want to talk about right now. Not really the time or the place.'

'And my mother isn't someone I want to talk about either,' said Lainey. 'I'm sorry. This evening was supposed to be a bit of fun. Somehow it's managed to turn into something completely different.' She looked at him apologetically. 'I have the capacity to mess things up. I don't know how I do it.'

'Nothing is messed up.' Shay sounded forceful. 'Let's put your mother and my ex-wife into a locked room in our minds and raid the selection of vol-au-vents again.'

'Can you do that?' Her voice was unconvinced. 'Put it out of your mind?'

'Of course. Can you?'

'I can try,' she said doubtfully.

'Come on then.' He caught her by the hand and led her out of sight of Deanna and Feargal. But she still felt as though her mother's eyes were on her. And, in a way she couldn't fathom, that Deanna was worried for her.

She introduced Shay to Bonnie, who gave him a winning smile and told him he was by far the sexiest man at the party, which made him laugh. Lainey hadn't thought of Shay as being the sexiest man there until Bonnie's comment. Then she realised that the researcher was probably right. While she was thinking this, Feargal's neighbour approached her and asked if she'd sign a beer mat for him, which she did, telling him that she didn't think it would be worth much in the future.

'I have a collection,' Peter Donnelly, a balding man who looked to be in his mid-fifties, told her. 'Every time Feargal has a party, I get famous people to sign my beer mats. So you're taking your place in my beer-mat-of-fame stockpile.'

'Thanks.'

'I do like you on the telly,' he said seriously. 'You have a lovely voice.'

'Thanks,' she said again.

'And you speak so clearly. One of the problems today is that people don't talk properly. Or they do that American thing of raising their voice at the end of a sentence. So it sounds like a question?' He demonstrated what he meant, and Lainey nodded.

'I know,' she said. 'It's really irritating. Makes us all sound childish somehow.'

'Well you sound like a proper intelligent person,' he assured her.

Deanna would be glad to hear that, she thought as she thanked him. Peter's wife joined them and gently mocked her husband for getting another signature for his collection. But Lainey could see that she was tolerant of him and didn't really mind. Susan Donnelly was an attractive woman who was at ease with herself and with Peter. Lainey was sure they had a happy, relaxed marriage.

She wondered if she'd ever have a relaxed relationship and thought abruptly of Ken again, of his unexpected appearance at her apartment. She wanted to feel happy at the idea of him in her life once more, but the truth was, she actually felt unsettled. She'd never felt unsettled with Ken before. It was the very fact that she normally felt relaxed with him that had convinced her that this time she really had found the man she wanted to spend the rest of her life with.

Why were relationships so bloody complicated? she wondered. Why did the course of true love never run smoothly? For her, anyway. Other people seemed to cope perfectly well.

It was some time later before Deanna came over to her again.

'So,' she said. 'You said earlier you were visiting a friend this evening.'

'I am,' said Lainey.

'You don't know Feargal Wright,' Deanna told her. 'He told me he only invited you last week.'

'And?'

'You're hardly friends, in that case.'

'Does it matter?' asked Lainey.

'You should've said you were coming here.'

'Oh, for heaven's sake!' Lainey looked exasperated. 'I wasn't going to give you a blow-by-blow description of my evening!'

'You didn't have to lie to me, either.'

'I wasn't lying. I just couldn't be bothered to talk about it. I wasn't expecting you to turn up, Deanna. If I'd known you were coming, I wouldn't have come myself.'

'Wouldn't you?'

'No.'

'Why?'

'Because (a) we don't socialise together and (b) I wouldn't have put you in the position of having to publicly acknowledge me.'

'You think that bothers me?' Deanna asked. 'Really?'

'How can it not?' Lainey looked at her sceptically. 'Deanna Ryan, feminist icon, slept with the enemy. Wasn't sensible enough to use reliable contraception. Ended up encumbered by a daughter she never wanted. It must bother you deeply. For heaven's sake, Deanna, you've never, ever spoken about me in public before and I absolutely understand why. So I can't honestly think you wanted to talk about me now. Least of all here, as the guest of a famous broadcaster. Who will no doubt be itching to learn about the hitherto unknown relationship between you and me. Your secret love child, that's what they'll call me.'

'Stop dramatising,' ordered Deanna. 'You were always too dramatic for your own good. You're not my secret love child.'

'No? What am I, then? Oh, I know!' Lainey struck her forehead with the palm of her hand. 'I'm your secret child. No love involved at all. Between you and my dad. Or me either, come to that.'

Deanna was silent. Then Lainey turned around and walked away.

She wished she hadn't said what she had to her mother. She'd sounded as though she'd resented Deanna not loving her, and she didn't. It was just part of who Deanna was. Lainey didn't care. She had Madeleine, who loved her more than anyone. There was no question of her not being loved. She hadn't needed to sound whiny about it.

She walked the garden, looking for Shay. It was dusky now, and the garden was lit by a mixture of anti-mosquito torches and LED lights set into the wide sandstone patio.

'Hey, Lainey!' Feargal Wright put his hand on her shoulder. 'There you are.'

'Here I am,' she said.

'You seemed upset earlier.'

'Not at all,' she assured him. 'Just a little taken aback at seeing Deanna.'

He looked at her curiously. 'You two don't get along?'

'It's not that.' She absolutely wasn't going to discuss her personal life with Feargal Wright. 'I was surprised, that's all. I saw her earlier today and she didn't say anything about being invited here this evening. But then neither did I, so it was a surprise for both of us.'

'And the surprise for me, of course, was finding out that you're her daughter! There's nothing about you in all the publicity for her tour.'

'Why would there be?' asked Lainey calmly. 'The tour is about her, not me.'

'But there's never been anything about you ever,' said Feargal. 'I've done lots of research on her, you know. There's no mention at all of a daughter.'

'I dislike people who use their families as props,' said Lainey. 'I wouldn't expect her to talk about me.'

'She wrote about working mothers,' said Feargal. 'So she should've mentioned you then.'

'She was writing about the general, not the specific,' said Lainey.

'She's spent most of her life in the States.' Feargal's brow furrowed. 'I got the impression you've always lived in Ireland, though? Am I right? With your father?'

'I don't want to be rude, but it's not really any of your business,' said Lainey. 'I know that people who come on to your radio programme often talk at length about themselves, but it's not something I do.'

'I know that,' said Feargal. 'You have a reputation for being . . .'

'What?' asked Lainey, suddenly anxious. 'What sort of reputation do I have?'

'Being professional,' said Feargal. 'And self-contained. Nobody knows much about you.'

'I'm not employed by the station,' Lainey reminded him. 'I don't work with any of you. My friends are all in Met Eireann. They know plenty about me.'

'Is there some dark family secret?' Feargal was trying to sound light-hearted, but Lainey wasn't having any of it.

'Of course not,' she said. 'Just because Deanna and I don't . . . don't share everything like friends doesn't mean there's anything for us to hide.'

'You're right,' he said apologetically. 'I'm sorry if I seemed intrusive.'

'Not at all,' she said. 'It's perfectly fine.'

Which, of course, it wasn't.

It was Shay who rescued her from Feargal, appearing suddenly beside them and telling her that Bonnie had deserted him for strawberries dipped in chocolate.

'I'd better do a bit more circulating,' said Feargal. 'Talk to you later, Lainey.'

'I don't think so.' She looked grimly after him, then turned to Shay. 'I think he's eyeing me up as a potential story.'

'You or your mum?' Shay led her towards some empty chairs in a deserted area of the garden.

'She's going to be a guest on his TV show. It's supposed to be a cultural show, dealing with her work and upcoming documentary, but I guess the whole notion of her having a daughter that nobody's talked about would be too much to resist.'

'I still think it's amazing that she hasn't been quizzed about you before.'

'No real reason for it to happen,' said Lainey. 'I guess anyone who's ever rolled up to talk to her in the States has just seen her in her home, and it's clear that she lives alone. So I suppose they made assumptions and she never corrected them.'

'You've never said anything . . .'

'Why on earth would I? I don't associate myself with the public Deanna Ryan at all.' Lainey spoke dismissively. 'She's not a very important part of my life. Maybe nothing will come of it,' she added. 'After all, she's only famous in certain circles. It's not like she's a real-life celebrity, after all.'

'True,' Shay agreed. 'You won't be on the front pages of *Heat* or anything.'

Lainey looked at him in disbelief. 'Don't tell me you read *Heat*!'

'There's always copies of it lying around the waiting room in the sports clinic,' he told her. 'From time to time I decide it's important to know how many pounds some poor woman has been forced to lose in a week.'

'Thanks,' she said.

'For what?'

'Not making a fuss.'

'No problem,' he said. 'I've learned that making a fuss rarely fixes anything.'

Feargal had rigged up his iPod to an expensive sound system, and more and more people started to dance. Shay insisted that Lainey join the group, who were gyrating to Beyoncé. But she couldn't lose herself in the music, because she kept thinking about Deanna and the expression on her face when she'd told her that there was no love involved in any of her relationships. She wished she hadn't said it; it seemed unnecessarily harsh, and it had clearly wounded her mother. But it's not my fault, thought Lainey as she moved unenthusiastically to 'Single Ladies'. Just because it's hard doesn't mean it isn't true.

When the song ended, she pleaded exhaustion and made her way to an empty seat, where she watched the others continue to dance. Shay was a good mover, she thought, as he jived with Bonnie. He had a natural sense of rhythm. She wondered what had happened in his marriage. How the rhythm of his relationship with his wife had got messed up. And what had happened to make him so bitter about it. Because she could see that he was. Was that why he brought a procession of women to his apartment? she wondered. To get some kind of revenge on women for screwing up his life? She gave herself a mental shake. She was overdramatising again. He probably just liked the sex. Like most men.

Deanna was talking to Cliona Boyle. Or, from where Lainey was sitting, lecturing her, because she was speaking animatedly and wagging her finger in front of Cliona in a way that Lainey recognised from the clips she'd seen of her mother on American TV. She wondered how the experienced newsreader felt about being lectured by Deanna Ryan.

'Hey, everything OK with you?' Shay peeled away from the dancers and joined her.

'Sure.'

He followed her gaze towards her mother.

'Have you been talking to her?'

Lainey shook her head.

'She's got plenty of people to talk to rather than me,' she replied. 'Um, Shay, would you mind if we headed home now?'

'Are you sure?'

'Yes. I've had enough.'

'OK.' He was relaxed about it.

'Thanks. I feel bad about dragging you away, though. You seem to be having such a good time.' She glanced towards Bonnie, and he grinned.

'Far too young and fit for me.'

'I doubt that.'

'A man has to know his limitations.'

'I didn't realise men had any.' This time it was Lainey who grinned.

'Sadly, yes,' Shay assured her. 'Though mostly we'll never admit it. Come on, let's get going before I convince myself that I could possibly jive one more time.'

Chapter 18

Striations: grooves or channels in cloud formations

They didn't speak much on the drive back to Dublin. Lainey was thinking about Deanna, and Shay seemed caught up in thoughts of his own. Despite their physical proximity, they were miles away from each other, and neither seemed to feel the need to fill the silence.

The return journey seemed quicker than the drive to Killiney, and they were back at the apartment complex before Lainey even realised it. Shay pointed the zapper at the gates and drove down to the underground car park.

'Well,' he said as they walked up the stairs to ground level, 'thanks for inviting me. It was fun.'

'Glad you thought so,' she said.

'Absolutely,' he assured her. 'I met my secret idol, Darren Price. I bopped around like a sad old fart, but I enjoyed it. And I enjoyed being with you too.'

'I'm glad you weren't too bored.'

'Of course not,' he assured her. 'I got to meet Darren Price, didn't I?'

'And Bonnie,' Lainey added.

'Nice girl,' Shay said. 'She's a whole different generation to me, though.' He made a face. 'You don't think you're getting older, but suddenly you realise that you are and that you're not the same person you were when you were twenty.'

'I know,' said Lainey.

'If I'd known then what I know now . . .' Shay couldn't quite hide the sudden strain in his tone.

'What happened between you and your wife?'

It was as though she had no control over her own voice once again. The thought had popped into her head – had been in her head ever since she'd realised he'd been married – and she was itching to know the answer.

'The usual.' Shay's eyes clouded over. 'We got married without really knowing each other. We were very young. I thought I loved her. I guess she thought she loved me. But we were both wrong.'

'I'm sorry.'

'Water under the bridge,' he said briefly.

'Do you have kids?'

She knew by the spasm of pain that crossed his face that the answer was yes.

'I don't get to see them as often as I'd like,' he said tightly. 'And she wants . . . Oh, well, it's messy. I guess marriage break-up is messy full stop.'

'Everything about relationships is messy,' Lainey told him.

'Including you and Adonis?'

'His name's Ken,' she reminded him. 'He's a good guy.'

'I'm sure.'

'I didn't invite you tonight to make him feel jealous.' It occurred to Lainey that Shay might be thinking she had.

'If you'd wanted to make him jealous, I'm sure you'd've kept him in your apartment until I arrived.'

'I certainly wouldn't have done that.'

'You have an interesting life,' he said.

'Not really,' she told him. 'Like you, just messy.'

They stopped outside the entrance to her block. 'Well, thanks,' she told him. 'I appreciate you coming, and especially driving. It was very good of you.'

'No problem,' he replied. 'As I said, I enjoyed it.'

'See you around,' she said.

'Of course.'

He leaned forward and kissed her quickly on the cheek before turning away and walking across the pathway to his own apartment building. She waited for a moment to see if he'd turn back and wave. But he keyed in the code to the door and went in straight away. She entered her own apartment and tossed her bag on to the sofa before taking off her gold sandals. She rubbed the soles of her feet and then walked over to the window. He had to be in his apartment by now. She waited for a moment, expecting to see him turn on the lights. But the apartment remained in darkness, without even the blue flicker of a TV. She wondered why he wasn't bothering with the lights, why he was presumably sitting alone in the dark.

'It's none of my business,' she told herself as she closed the curtains and flopped on to the sofa. 'People are entitled to live their lives whatever way they like.'

Deanna was still at Feargal Wright's. Many of his guests had departed, but a few stragglers remained. They were all in the garden, bunched into disparate groups of three or four people.

Deanna had spent the last hour talking to Cliona Boyle about female news presenters, arguing that ageism in TV was unjust.

'Women are pushed off the screen as soon as they get a few wrinkles,' she said. 'But craggy-faced men can patronise viewers for ever.'

'Hope you don't mean Feargal.' Cliona glanced at him on the other side of the garden.

'He's not old yet,' said Deanna. 'But I bet he'll still be presenting when they've replaced you with a newer model.'

Cliona looked startled.

'I don't mean that they *should* replace you,' Deanna said. 'Only that they will.'

'That's the way things are,' said Cliona.

'But not the way they should be,' Deanna told her. 'Yet when we complain, we're told that we're shrill and turning ourselves into victims and . . .' She shook her head. 'We're countered with the argument that TV has become feminised, that schools have too and that men generally are unsure of their role in society. But despite all this, they're still there, cocking up everything.'

Cliona laughed. 'It's refreshing listening to you, Deanna. I read all your books, you know. I don't agree with everything you say, but I like the way you say it.'

'You should agree with me,' said Deanna firmly. 'Because I'm right.'

'D'you hate all men?' asked Cliona.

Deanna hesitated. 'I don't hate them,' she said finally. 'But I certainly don't trust them. Any of them.'

It hadn't been a case of trust with Jorge, in the end. But the reasons he hadn't come back were buried deep within the darkest recesses of her memory, and she didn't allow them space. She didn't want to think about them, to let the emotions of more than thirty years ago take hold of her again. Because she'd needed to be strong. She needed to be strong for her new life. She'd told herself that over and over as she sat in the bus on the journey from Monterey to Palo Alto for the start of her first semester. Strong for herself and for her daughter, and for every woman in the world. She wanted to make a difference. She promised herself that she would.

Deanna thrived in college. She loved the atmosphere, and the support that many women gave each other. She loved the fierce debates, the multiple societies, the belief that the world was there to be changed. Women were now knocking on the doors of business, expecting to be let in and expecting to be treated fairly. And it was people like her who were helping to make that happen.

Deanna focused on the inequality of women in the workplace, on how they were paid less for the same jobs as their male colleagues and on how they were discriminated against after they had children. It was at a rally for equal pay that she'd been arrested for the first time and then interviewed on a local news station, where she told the broadcaster that women physicians in California were paid 57 per cent less than their male counterparts, and that this was utterly wrong. Even in real estate, she said, they received 47 per cent less, which was a disgrace! But it was her passionate appeal to all women to fight for their rights and not to lie down and accept that they should be treated as second-class citizens that made people listen to her. Deanna didn't get caught up in rhetoric or ideological arguments. She pointed out that women were hard workers who deserved their money. And she demanded that they get it.

She knew that her success would be limited. Women were cheap labour for many companies, working hard and being productive but getting fewer of the rewards than their male colleagues. And getting fewer of the promotional opportunities too, because although many companies no longer asked about the choices a married woman might make with regard to her family, the bosses (usually male) would draw their own conclusions. Women would have babies, they decided. And they wouldn't be able to leave them with childminders. Naturally. So they'd leave work instead. Or, if they didn't, they'd be less productive, stuck in some kind of mommy-bubble that prevented them from giving their full attention to their job.

This attitude incensed Deanna, who had come to the conclusion that mothers were the most organised people on the planet, and that most of them combined their jobs and their family lives in a way that men couldn't even begin to understand. Many years later she wrote a book called *Multitask Mom*, which, when it came out, led to a rash of people wondering if Deanna Ryan had gone soft, because she'd admitted that some women wanted to be mothers as well as hard-hitting businesswomen, even though she also talked about the tyranny of trying to be the perfect mom. Deanna had been surprised that on publication of the book, nobody had challenged her about not having experience in the motherhood department herself. She'd been prepared to admit to having a daughter of her own back then, because she was now in control of the situation with nothing to worry about, but nobody had asked. Nobody had told her that as a single, childless woman, she shouldn't be writing about women who were married with children. Commentators instead focused on the key points of the book – that women's choices about how they raised their families should be respected. And that they shouldn't have to feel guilty all the time. It hadn't been her most successful book, though, and it disappeared off the shelves earlier than some of her other work. For her next book, *Career Casualties*, she returned to her main interest, which was in getting women to see that having a career was important and that sometimes you owed it to yourself to give it your best possible shot. Which could mean putting marriage and family on hold. If that was what you wanted to do.

Deanna hadn't initially expected that any of her books would be very successful. Her arguments weren't new, after all. But she wrote clearly, getting her points across concisely and reaching out to women in a way that engaged their attention. She was as amazed as anyone at the number of people who bought her work. And at the number of times quotes from her books were used in debates about women in the workplace. Whenever she heard the words 'as Deanna Ryan says in her book . . .' she felt a warm glow of satisfaction. And whenever she was asked to appear as a guest or panellist on a TV or radio show, she knew that she'd been right in the decisions she'd made.

But one of the things that she'd learned was that no matter how much women might want things to be different, there was no way they could have it all. What she was trying to do was help them decide which parts they wanted. And to get the best possible deal for whichever part they chose.

* * *

'Tell me about your daughter.' Feargal sat on a chair beside Deanna, who'd walked further down the garden when Cliona had left.

'No,' said Deanna shortly.

'Hey, that's no way to speak to an investigative reporter,' Feargal said in amusement.

'That's not what you are,' Deanna reminded him. 'You're a presenter. But very good at what you do,' she added. 'Sometimes I listen to your radio programme over the internet. It's informative, if a bit lightweight.'

'I can't interview you about your work without mentioning Lainey,' Feargal told her. 'It wouldn't be fair to the audience.'

'For thirty-odd years I've done interviews in which nobody has mentioned Lainey,' Deanna said evenly. 'Nobody has complained about it being unfair.'

'That's because they don't know she exists!' cried Feargal.

'She doesn't want to be part of my life,' Deanna said. 'You should respect her wishes.'

'She doesn't want it, or you don't?' he asked.

'If it were you talking about your work,' Deanna fixed him with a piercing look from her blue eyes, 'would people pressurise you to know about your children? Would they ask you questions about them? Would they feel they had a right to know?'

'Probably not,' he admitted. 'But that's different.'

'Why?'

'Well, because . . .' He was irritated. 'You're trying to trap me into some kind of feminist ideology.'

Deanna shook her head. 'I'm showing you there's double standards.'

'Not really.' His face brightened. 'You see it with politicians all the time. Wheeling out their children and talking about their family life.'

'To advance their careers!' cried Deanna. 'To try to make themselves look like people who give a shit about family values.'

'Sports people,' suggested Feargal, tacitly agreeing with her about politicians. 'Hugging their wives and girlfriends after matches.'

She snorted derisively.

'Men care about their families and their kids.' Feargal sounded defensive.

'Nobody – but nobody – ever asks a successful man how he copes with a career and a family,' Deanna told him. 'But everyone asks a woman that question.'

'You're a hard woman to talk to,' said Feargal.

'I'm a rational woman,' said Deanna. 'Men fail miserably when we're rational.'

'You're not going to tell me about her, are you?'

Deanna shook her head. 'It's not up to me to talk about my daughter to you. She's a grown woman.'

'Wouldn't it be better if you filled me in all the same?' Feargal made a last appeal. 'If I knew everything, then I wouldn't be curious.'

'I see no need to satisfy your curiosity,' Deanna said. 'If you don't think you can do the interview without encroaching into my personal life, then we can forget it. I want to publicise my documentary and my books, but not at the expense of my daughter's privacy.'

'Whose privacy are you more worried about?' asked Feargal. 'Hers or yours?'

'We're both private people,' Deanna told him.

'Yet both of you have ended up in a public medium,' Feargal reminded her. 'Not very private of you at all.'

'This obsession with the personal lives of public figures is beyond irritating,' Deanna said. 'And the comment isn't worthy of you.'

He raised his hands in a gesture of defeat. 'OK, OK. Private life off limits. I won't ask about your daughter . . . What about her father?'

'You won't ask about him either,' said Deanna.

'Satisfy my curiosity a little,' begged Feargal. 'Irish? American? Do you actually live with him?'

'It's none of your business.'

'I think that part is.' He looked thoughtful. 'You lecture women about how they should live their lives. Surely they have a right to know how you live yours.'

Deanna considered his comments. 'Perhaps. So if you want to go there, no, I don't and never have lived with Lainey's father.'

'Did you love him?' asked Feargal.

Deanna felt her stomach lurch. She breathed slowly through her nose.

Of course she'd loved him. That was why she'd slept with him. That was why she'd wanted to live with him. To marry him. To be with him for the rest of her life.

'I was very young when I met him,' she said calmly. 'It was never going to last.'

'And does the ice-cold Deanna Ryan know what it's like to have her heart broken?' asked Feargal.

'Honestly!' She looked at him as though he was an irritating child. 'Haven't you better things to ask me about?

I hope you do, otherwise the interview will be very boring.'

'I don't think it will,' said Feargal. 'Not one bit.'

He didn't want to interview Deanna Ryan for his arts and culture show. He wanted her to be one of the first guests on his new project, which was called *Private Lives Public Faces.* It was a half-hour interview with one well-known person every week, talking about topics they never normally discussed. He'd already recorded two sessions and had got interesting material from the high-profile subjects. But getting Deanna Ryan to talk about her daughter would be way better than anything he'd done so far. And he wanted it to happen. He just had to figure out a way of breaking down the barriers Deanna had so carefully erected around her. But breaking down barriers was what he was good at. Was what had helped him win the Broadcaster of the Year award for two years in a row.

Deanna left the party shortly afterwards, calling a cab and settling into the back seat. Feargal had seen her to the gate of his property and closed the cab door for her.

'I'll be in touch,' he told her.

'Fine.'

She would deal with Feargal Wright when the time came, she told herself as the car moved forward. But she would probably have to deal with Lainey a bit sooner.

The house was in darkness when Deanna arrived home and walked quietly into her bedroom. She was back in her old room now, the one Lainey had used when she'd been living in the Killester house. The previous times she'd come back to Ireland, Deanna had stayed in the guest room (on most of her trips Lainey had still been living with Madeleine), and she'd supposed that was where she'd be this time too. But Madeleine had insisted on her sleeping in her old room once more. Deanna was finding it a strange experience. On the one hand, it wasn't the same room she'd left behind all those years ago. It had been redecorated a number of times since, so there were no traces of the posters she'd stuck to the walls, no lingering scent of the Charlie perfume she'd worn back then. Sitting on the edge of the narrow single bed (she was finding it hard to sleep in it; she had a queen-size back in the States), Deanna felt herself stuck between the past and the present, remembering the plans she'd made in this room as a teenager, thinking now about the plans she had to make for the future. And wondering, too, what sort of plans her own daughter had made, sitting on the edge of the same bed while she, Deanna, made new plans that had never included Lainey. I did what I had to do, she murmured to herself. I made the right choice. For all of us.

She climbed beneath the sheets and stared sleeplessly at the ceiling above her. She remembered a return journey to Dublin when Lainey was about seven, when she'd sat on the bed beside her sleeping daughter. The ceiling had been covered with reflective stars and moons, which glowed a pale green in the dark. Lainey loved her star-studded ceiling. Before she'd fallen asleep, she'd explained to Deanna that Edmund had arranged them in constellations, so that they mirrored the night sky.

'The Plough,' Lainey had said. 'And Orion. The moons aren't exactly right, of course. But I like them anyway.'

Deanna had been struck then by her daughter's ability

to talk about the constellations in a practical way. She had high hopes for her. She wanted her to achieve her potential and have the life she deserved. One in which no man would ever tell her she couldn't do anything. And no man would ever break her heart.

At four o'clock in the morning, after some fitful sleep, Deanna was woken by the quiet hum of voices. She opened her eyes and got out of bed, wondering what was going on. She pulled her robe around her shoulders, eased the bedroom door open and walked silently to the living room.

It was Madeleine who was talking, sitting in her favourite armchair and looking at the empty chair where Deanna remembered her father always sat.

'It's hard work,' Madeleine was saying. 'I'm not sure I'll ever get it right.'

'What's hard work?'

Deanna moved into Madeleine's line of sight.

'What are you doing up at this hour?' asked Madeleine.

'I woke up,' Deanna said. 'What are you doing up yourself?'

'I always wake up at this time,' Madeleine told her. 'Between four and five. I make myself a cup of tea and then I go back to bed for a couple of hours.'

'And do you always talk to an empty room?' asked Deanna. She remembered Lainey saying something about it, but she hadn't ever heard Madeleine talking to herself before and had decided that her daughter was exaggerating just to make her feel guilty for not being around much.

'I'm talking to your father,' said Madeleine equably.

'Mom!'

'Why shouldn't I?' asked Madeleine. 'He's very wise, you know.'

'You're talking to a chair,' said Deanna.

'That's what you think.'

'That's what I know. Honestly, Mom, maybe you need to see a doctor . . .'

'Don't be silly.' Madeleine was dismissive. 'I talk to your father and sometimes he talks back, and I like it.'

'You can't possibly be talking to him.' Deanna looked at the chair. 'I accept you might want to talk to him and that you miss him, but you've got to face facts. Dad is dead and he's not talking to anyone any more.'

Madeleine's brow creased. 'Do you always have to be so practical?' she asked. 'Can't you accept that some things are possible no matter how unlikely they seem.'

'People use belief in the impossible as a crutch to get through life,' said Deanna.

'Your father says you should stop being so goddam obstinate,' said Madeleine. 'And stop being so angry. You've never really let that go. It's about time you did.'

'My father is saying nothing of the sort.'

Madeleine spoke softly. 'I need to talk to him,' she said. 'I miss him. You don't understand.'

'I . . .' Deanna had been about to say that she did understand, but that understanding didn't mean she should lose her critical faculties. But suddenly she saw her mother as an elderly woman who'd been left on her own. And who was doing the best she could without the man who had shared her life for so long.

'I'm sorry.' The words caught in her throat. 'I really am.'

Madeleine's eyes were bright with unshed tears as she held

out her arms to her daughter. And Deanna allowed herself to be held as she hadn't been since she'd been a small girl who'd fallen off a wall and scraped her legs and who'd run home to her mother for comfort.

Chapter 19

Castellanus: layers of cloud rising in distinct turrets with bumpy tops

Lainey was dreaming the dream. The one in which it was raining while she sat on the wooden steps of an unknown house and arranged the coloured bricks into little piles. She could hear the voices arguing again, and she waited for the man who smelled of aftershave to pick her up and hold her close to him. It was taking a long time. She could hear the voices more clearly than she ever had, but it all seemed wrong and out of sequence to her. She didn't feel as though she should be on the steps now, but the man hadn't come to find her yet.

'You hardly ever see her,' she heard him say.

She tossed uneasily in the bed, and in the dream she knocked over the coloured bricks, which scattered across the dusty ground.

'You're making rules about me seeing her?'

The words were clear. She'd never heard distinct words

before, only the sounds of heated conversation. She wiped the raindrops from her arm.

'I'm her mother.'

She recognised Deanna's voice. She recognised the tone and the inflexion of it, but she didn't recognise the vehemence with which Deanna spoke. Her eyes snapped open and she sat up in bed. She was drenched with sweat and her hair hung damply around her face. Her fingers trembled as she tucked the strands behind her ears. Then she swung out of bed and opened the curtains.

The sun poured into the apartment. She realised that she'd forgotten to open the window the night before, which was why the bedroom was now a furnace. She undid the catch and flung it wide, breathing in the balmy summer air.

The dream had never upset her before. It usually comforted her. She liked the way it ended, with the unknown man picking her up and holding her to him. Although she also thought of it as a memory, she'd never asked Deanna if the events had actually happened. She didn't want to hear that it was simply a figment of her imagination. Now she wondered if her imagination was working overtime, putting words into people's mouths. Although, she thought, as her heartbeat returned to normal and she felt her body begin to cool down, surely the words she'd conjure up would be better than the ones in her dream?

'I'm her mother.'

Putting those words into the dream were probably as a result of having met Deanna at Feargal Wright's and having her admit that they were mother and daughter. Deanna hadn't sounded as convinced in real life as she had in the dream, though. Which was why Lainey thought she was probably making it up. But it would be nice to think, she murmured to herself as she walked into the living room, that Deanna could feel that strongly about her. That Deanna could actually think of her as a daughter instead of one of her social experiments to try to produce independent-thinking women who would change the world. Lainey didn't want to change the world. All she wanted was to be happy. And for other people to be happy too. If everyone was happy with their lives, wouldn't that be enough for mankind?

She walked slowly into the bathroom and stood under the shower. She let the lukewarm water cascade through her hair, revelling in the feel of it against her bare skin and enjoying the massaging action on her forehead. Her head ached. Probably a hangover, she thought, as she got out of the shower. She spritzed her body with a moisturising spray before slipping into a cotton sundress. I shouldn't have mixed beer and wine yesterday; it's always a disaster. She ran a wide-toothed comb through her hair. She was going to let it dry naturally again, although this time it was by choice, not because she didn't have time to blow-dry it. Her shift at Met Eireann didn't start until eight that evening.

She went into her living room. Her balcony was currently in shade, but she opened the patio door as wide as it would go and then swore as a bluebottle immediately flew into the room. She picked up a newspaper and brushed it at the fly until it eventually found the open door and disappeared. She massaged the back of her neck (chasing the fly had worsened her headache), then filled the kettle and put two slices of bread in the toaster.

While she waited for the kettle to boil, she picked up her bag and took out the packet of ibuprofen she always carried around with her. She swallowed a couple of pills, then checked her mobile, which had been in her bag too. She had four missed calls. The first was from Ken. It had been made the night before, but she clearly hadn't heard her phone ring at the garden party. The second was from Feargal Wright, the third from Deanna and the fourth from Shay Loughnane.

She looked at her watch. It was eleven o'clock. Everyone but her was up early today. She dialled her voicemail.

'Hi, babes,' said Ken. 'Sorry I had to rush away. I'll call you.'

'Hello, Lainey,' said Feargal Wright. 'Just rang to say thanks so much for coming along yesterday. I'm still in shock with the news that you're Deanna Ryan's daughter. I'd really like to talk to you. Call me whenever.'

'Are you up yet?' asked Deanna. 'I wanted to meet with you to talk about the documentary.'

'Hey, Lainey,' said Shay. 'I was just ringing to say thanks for inviting me yesterday, I had a good time. But now I've just realised your curtains are still closed. Hope I didn't wake you. See you around. Sleep well!'

She was still holding the phone when it vibrated in her hand, startling her so much she dropped it. It slid under the sofa and yet another call went to her voicemail.

'How's it going?' asked Carla when Lainey played back the message. 'I was wondering about the hot date with the sexy neighbour? And the gorgeous Feargal Wright? Have you written your list of requirements yet? Give me a shout. See you.'

Lainey put the phone on the coffee table. She didn't feel like returning any of those calls right now. She glanced out of the window towards Shay Loughnane's apartment. He was sitting on the balcony. With him was the woman she'd seen earlier in the week. The woman with the two children. Lainey caught her breath. They were sitting so close together that their heads were almost touching. After Shay's bitterness when talking about her the previous day, she didn't think the woman could possibly be his wife. When he'd talked despairingly about his children, she'd felt sorry for him. And then she wondered if it was his sob story, the one he used to snare so many women. I'm a lonely, separated man and my bitch wife took my kids. It was a story that would appeal to most women's natures, Lainey reckoned. But she'd seen too much of him in action for it to appeal to her. So, to answer Carla's question, she'd had an enjoyable enough time with the sexy neighbour but fortunately kept her wits about her, because she didn't really know him and didn't think she ever would.

As for Feargal Wright – using Carla's criteria, he'd be a good catch, with that gorgeous house and landscaped gardens. However, she didn't fall for people because they had houses and gardens.

And Ken . . . She replayed his message. If she did have a list of requirements, what boxes would he tick?

She sat on the sofa and tucked her legs beneath her. She picked up a sheet of paper from the pile on the table in front of her, reached for a pen and began to write.

Attractive. Tick.

Interesting. Tick.

In love with me.

She looked at the question. Every relationship went through a tough patch. She'd been responsible for theirs by behaving foolishly, wanting commitment even though she knew that it freaked Ken out. But the thing was, he'd come back to her. Even knowing what she was like, he hadn't been able to leave her. If that wasn't love, what the hell was?

She liked the night shift. Especially on nights like tonight, when darkness was late in falling and the lights of the city were spread out in front of her. The weather was still holding up, although she and Alva were tracking some fronts building up in the Atlantic, and both of them reckoned that the end of the week would also bring an end to the fine spell.

'Not that I mind,' said Alva cheerfully. 'I'm off to the south of Spain for a fortnight, and it's looking good there.'

'Lucky you,' said Lainey.

'Have you got holiday plans?' asked Alva.

Lainey shook her head. Her week in Portugal with Ken and his friends was a distant memory now, but she wondered if maybe they could head off again sometime soon. If they got back together officially, it would be nice to go away and have the kind of week that they'd had before; one in which they'd spend their time lazing around, feeling content in each other's company. It would be good to regain that sense of relaxation she'd had with him. Maybe that was something she could add to her list. Relaxed together. Well, she thought, they'd had it before. They could get it again.

She sent both Carla and Val an email in the middle of the night telling them about Feargal Wright's party and Deanna's arrival at it. She told them about Ken's arrival at her apartment too. She didn't say that they'd slept together, but told them that she was playing it cool, which seemed to be working. She also said that she thought she was getting the hang of being low-maintenance at last.

It was almost six before she remembered that Deanna had

also been in touch. She sent her a text to say that she was on the night shift and that she'd call her later in the week. As she pressed 'send', she wondered if its arrival would wake her.

Deanna was already awake. She was an early riser and rarely stayed in bed after six thirty. In the summer, she was often awake an hour earlier and frequently got up to make notes on whatever project she was currently working on. Although most of her time at the moment was taken up with her tour and her documentary, she was also researching her next book, which she'd tentatively entitled *EnGendered* and which looked at the lack of respect often accorded to women in senior executive positions by the media. Successful men were referred to in a positive way as being 'steely' and 'determined', but these traits were somehow seen as being unfeminine and negative in their female counterparts. This infuriated Deanna, who remembered being called steely herself and liking it. Women had to be steely and strong and determined to cope with life, she thought, but people wanted them to be sweet and nice and caring too. Yet if they tried to be hard on the inside and soft on the outside, they were regarded as frauds.

Deanna thought of Lainey, whom she'd always considered far too soft for her own good. There was no possible way in which she would ever be considered steely. Deanna blamed Madeleine for that, thinking that her mother had overdosed on feminine things where Lainey was concerned, fearful, she reckoned, of turning out another female Ryan who was angry with the world around her. Deanna had begged Madeleine not to indulge in an orgy of pink and glitter when Lainey was small. She'd banned Barbie, My Little Pony and other cute toys from the house. She'd encouraged her mother to allow Lainey to wear shorts and T-shirts, to run around and scrape her knees, to be able to take the rough and tumble of life without complaining. Most of the time, Madeleine had acquiesced to her requests, sending photos of Lainey in her football gear, although sometimes too ones of her wearing dresses and with her hair tied back in ribbons. Madeleine was always at pains to point out that these occasions were special ones – parties or other events that required Lainey to look pretty. Deanna thought that there were no occasions on which a girl was 'required' to look pretty, but she never said this to her mother. The only time she openly fought with Madeleine about anything Lainey wore was when she'd sent her Bethany's wedding pictures, in which Lainey was trussed up in satin and silk and looked like a living doll.

'She had a great time,' Madeleine protested. 'She felt like a princess.'

'Oh for heaven's sake!' Deanna said. 'She needs to know that the princess thing is a myth.'

'Everyone knows that,' Madeleine said mildly. 'But it's nice to pretend sometimes.'

Deanna didn't believe in pretending. She didn't want things sugar-coated or glossed over. She couldn't help thinking that modern life tried to airbrush difficulties out of existence. That women somehow thought that if they looked beautiful, if they had perfect glossy hair and perfect white teeth and perfect round boobs, somehow they'd be rich and successful and happy. But life was more complicated than that. It always had been and it always would be. And in the end, Deanna thought, happiness was something internal. Not something that airbrushing could ever produce.

Am I happy? she wondered suddenly. Does being angry about things make me happy? It was hard to be certain. But it was a long time since she'd asked herself such a question, and it wasn't one she knew the answer to.

Chapter 20

Horseshoe vortex: a subtle cloud forming in a region of rotating air

Later in the week the rain swept in from the Atlantic Ocean and began its relentless downpour. Lainey made it to her desk just before the dark tumble of grey clouds opened overhead and the sheeting rain blotted out the view of the city.

She spent the day tracking the fronts that were continuing to build up mid-ocean, while at the same time preparing forecasts for the hourly radio bulletins and the commercial clients. She also had a couple of meetings with Martin about various projects the team was getting involved in. She was too busy to think about her personal life, even though aspects of it worried at the edges of her mind: the time she'd put aside to talk to Deanna later that day; the fact that Ken had called to the apartment the evening before and they'd made love again; Carla's unprompted suggestion that she visit her in Stockholm when she'd called the previous evening; receiving an email from Feargal Wright giving her his contact details and telling her that he'd really like to talk to her;

and, peripherally, that she hadn't seen or heard from Shay Loughnane since she'd replied to his message after Feargal's party. It wasn't that she especially expected to talk to Shay; it was simply that he seemed to have disappeared off the face of the earth. She hadn't caught sight of him on his apartment balcony all week, either with or without a girlfriend, and she realised that lately she'd grown accustomed to waving at him across the garden of the apartment complex and that she was missing that friendly moment in her day. But things change, she reminded herself, and her brief connection with her neighbour had clearly ended.

The turn in the weather had changed life at Laurel Park for all the residents. When Lainey returned home after work, there were no children running around the communal areas, no residents drinking glasses of wine on their balconies and no music drifting from open windows. The buildings, which had looked bright and cosmopolitan beneath the cloudless skies and hot sun, were now darker and gloomier, shrouded in cloud and rain.

She hurried up the stairs to her apartment and hung her damp coat on the rack inside the door. The return of the rain had also lowered the temperature dramatically, and she shivered as she pulled a jumper from her chest of drawers and slid it over her head. Then she made herself a large mug of coffee and checked to see how much time she had to clean the apartment before her mother arrived.

She'd made the arrangement with Deanna to come to her apartment and talk about her documentary a couple of days earlier. Her mother had never been to her home before and had sounded surprised when Lainey suggested it as a place to meet, but had accepted it as a good location. Lainey had decided to invite Deanna there because she wanted to show her that she was a perfectly competent independent woman with her own place and her own life and not the fluffy no-hoper she couldn't help feeling her mother considered her. She'd planned to tidy it ruthlessly the night before, but when Ken had unexpectedly arrived with a bunch of roses and a bottle of champagne, all thoughts of housework had vanished.

She'd spoken to him twice on the phone since Feargal's party. He'd followed up his voice message with another call asking if he'd annoyed her.

'Annoyed me how?'

'I called to see you and then I rushed off. I got the feeling you weren't too happy.'

'Leaving like that was a bit annoying,' she agreed.

'I'm sorry about that. It was thoughtless.'

'It doesn't matter.'

The next time he called to ask her about the weather. He wanted to know if it was going to stay dry for the next few days. He was doing outdoor training. She told him it'd be fine and he thanked her, said, 'I love you, babes' and promised to be in touch soon.

His arrival at the apartment, though, was unexpected, as were the flowers and the champagne. She was surprised, because he never gave her flowers. She took them from him and put them in the only vase she possessed, a cut-glass Louise Kennedy one that Val had given her as a house-warming present.

'They're lovely,' she said.

'I didn't really know if you were a flowers girl.' He eased the cork from the champagne bottle.

'All girls are flowers girls,' she told him as she arranged them in the vase. 'At least, we are when a man turns up with a bouquet of them!'

'They're by way of an apology for the last time,' he told her.

'You're forgiven.'

'That makes me feel better.' The cork popped and he poured the champagne into the pair of wine glasses she'd taken from a cupboard. He handed one to her and she took a sip before placing the glass on the table. She wasn't really ready to have a deep, meaningful conversation with him yet, but she had to ask.

'Does all this mean we're back together?'

'Of course.'

'What about Bangor?' she asked.

He exhaled slowly. 'I hate talking about this sort of stuff,' he said. 'I was pissed off with you in Bangor. And the truth is that I'm having to think about the whole marriage thing differently. But if I can't make it with you, Lainey . . .' He looked anxious. 'I just don't want to feel rushed into anything, that's all.'

'I understand.'

'So are you OK with that?'

She'd put a lot of her time and emotional energy into Ken. She didn't want to waste it. Relationships were all about compromise. Nobody was perfect.

'That's fine,' she said.

Ken put his arms around her, and then he was sliding his hands beneath the fabric of the cotton top she was wearing; and a couple of minutes later they were in her bedroom and making love again, and Lainey was telling herself that everything had worked out after all and that she'd ticked the right box on the list because he wanted to be with her.

Lying in the crook of his arm she felt secure and happy. She'd been wrong to beat herself up over him. She wasn't a loser after all. He loved her. He'd come back to her. And that was what she'd always wanted.

They were like an old married couple the following morning. Her shift started at seven, so her alarm went off an hour beforehand. She was in the shower when Ken poked his head around the door and said he was off because he had to get back across town to change. He'd call her, he said; he was sorry he couldn't stay. Although, he added, it was hard to walk out on a shower scene. She flicked some suds at him and he laughed. It was like it had been before, Lainey thought as he closed the bathroom door; it was getting to be fun again.

When she sat down at her desk, Alva Brennan looked at her speculatively.

'What?' asked Lainey.

'Someone's getting it.'

'Alva!'

'You're glowing, hon. There's a sparkle in your eye that I haven't seen for quite a while.'

'Don't be silly.' Lainey rustled some charts.

'Who's the lucky man?'

Lainey grinned. She couldn't help herself.

'Ken and I are back together,' she said.

'That's great.' Alva smiled. Lainey had always told her that it was thanks to her she'd met Ken in the first place, so she felt a little proprietorial about the relationship. She'd been sorry to hear that they'd split up. 'Have you got him exactly where you want him this time?'

'I hope so,' said Lainey. 'I hope this time it's for keeps.'

She was scurrying round in the frenzy of tidying that Ken's visit had sidelined when the doorbell sounded. She hastily plumped up the cushions and buzzed her mother in.

'It's dreadful outside.' Deanna shook raindrops from a bright blue umbrella as she walked into the apartment. 'For a while I felt as though I hadn't left California, but now I know I'm back in Dublin.'

'It's not that bad,' said Lainey.

'It's torrential,' Deanna pointed out.

'It's certainly heavy right now.' Lainey glanced out of the window. Although it was a term she sometimes used herself, there was no strict meteorological definition of torrential rain. The word was often used for unexpectedly heavy rainfall, the type that could lead to flash flooding. Today's rain wouldn't do that. It would ease later, the heavy downpour receding into the more usual gentle hiss of persistent rain. Torrential was more fun than persistent, though. It was more of a statement . . . Lainey gave herself a mental shake. This wasn't the time to be thinking weather thoughts.

'So this is your place.' Deanna looked around the neat room with interest. 'Nice.'

'Thank you.' Thanks to her rushed cleaning, the room smelt slightly of Windolene and furniture polish, although the scent of Ken's roses also lingered in the air.

'Not what I expected,' said Deanna.

'Oh?'

'I thought it would be more fluffy,' she said. 'Pinker.'

Lainey started to laugh as she looked around the room, which was decorated in neutral shades of mushroom, beige and grey and lightened by modern artwork in bright primary colours. And, of course, the red roses in the vase on the small dining table. 'You really have no clue about me, have you?'

'Of course I do,' said Deanna. 'I thought your personality would be expressed in your home decor. But it's not.'

'My personality?' Lainey looked at her curiously. 'You think my personality is pink and fluffy? In that case, why on earth do you want to talk to me for your documentary? Surely I'm far too lightweight for it.'

'The documentary isn't about your personality,' said Deanna.

'Fair enough,' acknowledged Lainey. 'But on a personal note, I'd like to point out that I'm not fluffy.'

'I don't want us to be personal today,' said Deanna firmly.

'You brought it up,' Lainey reminded her.

'For heaven's sake!' Deanna looked irritated. 'It was a throwaway comment. It's not important. Can we get on with the business in hand?'

'OK,' said Lainey. 'But would it be wrong of me to offer you coffee? Would that be stepping over the boundary into a level of friendliness that you can't allow?' She looked at her mother quizzically.

'I didn't mean . . .' Deanna broke off, then spoke again. 'Coffee would be lovely, thank you.'

Lainey made coffee for both of them. Though I'll be hopping off the walls later, she thought, as she swallowed a mouthful of the extra-strong blend. She'd already had five cups that day, because she'd needed the caffeine to keep her attention at a couple of interdepartmental meetings. She took a tin of foil-wrapped biscuits from the kitchen cupboard and put them on the table in front of Deanna. Her mother ignored the biscuits and took a spiral notebook from the big shoulder bag she'd placed on the floor beside her. She took a pencil from the bag too and tapped it a couple of times on the front of the notebook.

'I want this to be a serious discussion,' she told Lainey. 'I want to get the viewpoints of a lot of different women. I haven't made a final decision on the shape of the documentary yet, but the more research I do, the better.'

'Fine by me,' said Lainey.

'So I want to know what you think about the feminist movement and how it's contributed to your life, and what benefits you think it's had for you and—'

'Hold on a minute!' Lainey cried. 'I don't have answers to these questions.'

'You must,' said Deanna.

'It's not something I think a lot about,' objected Lainey. 'I don't get up every day and brood upon the injustices done to women in this world. I don't have an opinion on the ways we should change.'

'I can't believe that!' Deanna looked horrified. 'I can't believe a daughter of mine could be so shallow as not to care about other women.'

'I care, of course I care!' cried Lainey. 'It's just not an obsession, that's all.'

'You think I'm obsessed?' asked Deanna.

'Oh, come on!' Lainey was incredulous. 'It's your life's work. It's what gets you up in the morning. It keeps you going. It's who you are. It's why you left me with Gran and Gramps.'

'I thought we weren't going to get personal?' said Deanna.

'I'm not. I'm just trying to explain—'

'No,' said Deanna. 'You're trying to make your point. To let me know that I might be a good feminist but I'm a bad mother.'

'Don't be so silly!' cried Lainey. 'Why do you turn everything I say into criticism of you? I don't care about your mothering skills and the choices you made. Honestly I don't. Gran did a fine job for me and I'm happy about that. I don't have massive issues about it. You're the one who's taking everything personally, not me.'

Deanna said nothing. She tapped the pencil against her notebook again. 'Let's give this another chance,' she said eventually. 'What do you know about the feminist movement?'

I know that it's full of people who think they have the answer, thought Lainey, but if they're like the rest of us, they don't. Because nobody has the answer to anything. We all have our ideas and we're convinced we're right, but half the time we're completely wrong. And we're lucky if we learn from our mistakes. A lot of the time we actually end up making them all again. Like I do.

'I know that great strides have been made in the area of women's equality.' She spoke slowly. 'I know that I'm lucky to live now and not fifty years ago. I know that my voice can be heard. And I know that this is thanks to the pioneering work of many feminists . . .' Her words were clear and considered and at first Deanna made some notes. But then she stopped and regarded Lainey thoughtfully. However, her daughter wasn't looking at her, she was staring out of the window as she talked.

'Do you believe any of that?' Deanna asked when Lainey was eventually silent.

'Yes.' Lainey turned her dark blue eyes to her mother. 'I believe every single word of it.'

'You don't think that Betty Friedan and Gloria Steinem and Andrea Dworkin were right?'

'I believe that what they want is right for them. I'm just not entirely convinced that every other woman wants it too.'

'The freedom to choose?' Deanna sounded incredulous. 'The freedom to have a career? The freedom to be independent?'

'I know all that,' said Lainey. 'I want all that. I guess I more or less have it. But that doesn't mean you ever have everything you want. And of course now that we have these choices, we're racked with guilt over them.'

'How?'

'The choice to have a career or be a stay-at-home mother or to try to combine the two. No matter what you choose, you end up feeling guilty about it. I know. I work with lots of women. The married ones always feel bad because they're not there for their kids; then when there's an emergency and they have to rush home, they feel bad because they're leaving their colleagues in the lurch . . .'

'You put your finger on a point there,' said Deanna. 'The women are the ones rushing home.'

'Mainly yes,' agreed Lainey. 'Of course things aren't easy for men either.'

'Excuse me?' Deanna snorted.

'All that macho career shit,' said Lainey. 'Men feeling that they have to be out there cutting deals and being alpha. And maybe that's what they want. Staying in the office till late. Jetting around the world putting together massive deals. But then they don't have the family stuff. Nobody does when you put everything into your career, and anyone who tells you otherwise is bullshitting.'

'You could combine your career and a family perfectly well if that's what you wanted,' said Deanna.

'I don't disagree that some people might be able to. But *you* couldn't.'

'My circumstances were different.'

'Everyone's circumstances are different. You can't generalise.'

'I have to make generalisations. Please remember this is a research documentary. Not a personal one.'

'Maybe. But in the end, it all comes down to people. And most people end up making choices.'

'And because of the work of people like me, you have choices to make,' said Deanna triumphantly.

'Sometimes the choices are hard,' said Lainey. 'And because they have them, and because they think it should be simple, women beat themselves up over them. But they shouldn't have to.'

Deanna put her notebook on the table.

'What about you?' she asked. 'What about your choices?'

'I haven't had to make big choices.' Lainey looked dismissive. 'My most pressing issues are generally skirt or trousers? Hair up or down? Pink lipstick or a slash of scarlet?'

'Be sensible,' said Deanna sharply.

'I am.'

'Are you happy?' Deanna shifted her line of questioning.

'Are you asking me professionally or personally?'

'Would the answer be different?'

'I don't know,' admitted Lainey.

'Do you hate me?'

Lainey stared at Deanna. Her mother's face was expressionless.

'Of course I don't hate you. Why would I hate you?'

'I abandoned you.'

'Like I said, we all have to make choices.' Lainey's words were light.

'But you think I made the wrong ones.'

'I'm sure you made the right ones for you,' said Lainey.

'Are you always like this?'

'Like what?'

'Obstructive. Remote.'

Lainey shrugged, even though she knew it irritated Deanna.

'Give me something!' cried her mother.

'I don't know what you want from me,' said Lainey. 'I am who I am. You are who you are. We've always been fine like this. I don't blame you for the choices you made. You got pregnant by mistake and you were left in a difficult situation and you dealt with it the way you thought best. I don't understand why you're suddenly interested in what I think. Especially what I think of you. It wasn't important to you before, so it shouldn't be important to you now. What matters, surely, is that you're OK with your life. Which I have to presume you are, given that you've made such a blinding success of it. So what I think hardly matters, does it?'

'Of course it matters,' said Deanna testily. 'Why wouldn't it?'

A small frown creased Lainey's brow. Her mother didn't sound at all like herself. Lainey had never known Deanna to care what anyone thought before. And then suddenly it struck her.

'It's because of Feargal Wright, isn't it?' she said.

'Huh?'

'Because you had to admit to him that you're my mother.' The realisation dawned slowly. 'You're afraid that he'll talk to me about you and I'll say things that you don't want me to say. You're afraid that you'll come across as an uncaring mother who abandoned her child.'

'No I'm not,' said Deanna quickly.

'And it'll dent your image, won't it?' continued Lainey. 'It'll make the stereotype of you seem like the real person. Cold, uncaring – couldn't be bothered with her own daughter.'

'You're being silly.'

'Other women more important than leading feminist's own child,' proclaimed Lainey. 'I can see how that wouldn't go down well.'

'My questions have nothing to do with Feargal Wright,' said Deanna firmly. 'I wanted to know for myself.'

'But you've never asked me before.'

'There's always a first time.'

'Why now?'

'This is a good time to have a conversation,' said Deanna.

'This is supposed to be our professional discussion,' Lainey reminded her. 'There have been plenty of other times when you could have asked me if I thought you'd done a good job as a mother.'

'I always wanted what was best for you,' said Deanna.

'I'll accept everything else,' said Lainey. 'All your choices, all the things you've done. But I won't accept that you wanted what was best for me. You wanted what was best for you. Which is fine, because it probably turned out best for me. But don't lie to me, Deanna. Just don't.'

The two women looked at each other. And then there was a knock on Lainey's door. Which startled both of them.

Lainey got up to answer it.

'Ken,' she said as she looked at the man standing on the landing outside. 'What on earth are you doing here?'

'I said I'd be back.' Ken sounded aggrieved as he tapped his foot impatiently on the tiled floor. His frequent return visits to her apartment meant he knew all the codes now and hadn't needed to buzz her to get in.

'I know, but . . .'

'Is there somebody with you?' He peered over her shoulder, his eyes narrowing in suspicion.

'Well, yes . . .'

'Anyone I know?'

Lainey shook her head. 'My mother.'

'Oh.'

'Come in.' She stood back. Ken hesitated for a moment, and then walked into the apartment.

Deanna stood up and said hello. Lainey introduced Ken as a friend, which made Deanna glance between them quizzically.

'Did I hear you mention him before?' she said. 'In an email maybe?'

'I could have done,' said Lainey.

'Nice to meet you.' Deanna extended her hand, and Ken shook it.

'Am I interrupting?' asked Ken.

'You are rather,' said Deanna. 'Lainey and I were having a meeting.'

Ken looked surprised.

'But it's fine,' said Lainey. 'I don't think we're going to

get anything more done here today, Deanna. Why don't we talk again soon.'

'We got nothing done,' said her mother.

'We'll reschedule,' said Lainey firmly.

Deanna looked from her daughter to Ken. And then to the vase of roses on the table.

'I'm being bumped for a man?' she said incredulously. 'Who brings flowers?'

'Get over it,' said Lainey.

Ken looked uncomfortable, and Deanna frowned.

'Are you dating my daughter?' she asked him.

'Deanna, that's so not an appropriate question,' said Lainey. 'It's none of your business.'

'Are you sleeping with each other?'

'Deanna!'

'Don't do anything foolish.' Deanna looked at Lainey, and there was both fear and warning in her eyes. 'Don't lose everything over someone who doesn't matter.'

At her words, the temperature in the room fell a couple of degrees. Lainey could see a spark of anger in Ken's eyes, but Deanna appeared oblivious as she gathered up her things.

'I'll call you,' she told Lainey as she hitched her bag on to her shoulder. 'We need to have that discussion. And we need to do it properly.' She nodded briefly at Ken. 'Good to meet you,' she said, and then let herself out.

'Wow.' Ken scratched the side of his cheek. 'That's some woman.'

'Yes.'

'She's overwhelming.'

'She's a strong person,' said Lainey.

'A bit of a man-hater? Or just ridiculously protective? Or offensive?'

'All of the above,' Lainey told him. 'I don't think Deanna means to offend; she's built a reputation on being a straight talker.'

Ken looked at Lainey in sudden comprehension. 'Deanna Ryan? She's Deanna Ryan! The mad feminist bitch who thinks all men should be castrated at birth?'

'Why do men think that? She never said it.'

'Hey, I saw her on *Letterman* one night. I wouldn't let her near my valuables, thanks very much. I don't believe it. She's your mother!'

Lainey nodded.

'I've just felt myself shrivel,' said Ken, which made her laugh.

'Why on earth didn't you tell me who she was before?' he continued. 'You said your mum was a lecturer in the States. That you were brought up by your gran because she couldn't cope with being a single parent . . .'

'Pefectly true,' Lainey said. 'I hardly ever see Deanna. She's not a major part of my life. You can see why. She makes me shrivel too.'

This time it was Ken who laughed.

'So why are you here?' Lainey looked at her watch. 'I didn't think you'd be back today. It's a bit early for you, isn't it?'

'I was in the neighbourhood.' He moved closer to her and put his arms around her. 'I knew you'd have finished work so I thought I'd drop in.' He kissed her gently at the base of her neck. 'I've missed you.'

'Since this morning?'

'Hey, it's nearly twelve hours ago.'

She kissed him too. And as he put his arms around her, she thought fleetingly of Deanna, and felt sorry for her and the choices she'd made.

Madeleine had cooked Deanna's favourite childhood dinner – shepherd's pie with creamy potato topping nicely browned on top.

'It's good wet-weather food,' said Madeleine after Deanna had let herself into the house and remarked on the mouth-watering aroma wafting from the kitchen.

'I don't think I've eaten shepherd's pie since I left,' said Deanna.

'Well, you can get some inside of you tonight.' Madeleine eased herself up from the chair in the living room, where she'd been sitting watching TV. She grunted as she picked up her silver-tipped cane, and Deanna looked at her with concern.

'Are you all right?' she asked.

'Wet weather makes my bones hurt,' explained Madeleine. 'The stick helps.'

'I thought the idea of the operation was that you'd be able to walk properly.' Deanna followed her mother into the kitchen.

'I couldn't walk at all before it,' Madeleine reminded her. 'Lainey had to move back for a while to help me out. How did your chat with her go, by the way? And do you like her apartment?'

'It wasn't a chat, it was an interview,' said Deanna. 'And the apartment's fine. A bit small, but I suppose she's living on her own so it doesn't matter.' She pursed her lips thoughtfully. 'Why did she move out? You and she are so close – why didn't she stay here?'

'She's like you in more ways than you know,' Madeleine said as she began to set the table. 'Very independent. And very stubborn.'

Deanna was going to say that she wasn't stubborn, but she knew she was.

'Did you have a row?' she asked.

'Not at all.' Madeleine shook her head. 'In her second year at college some friends asked her to flat-share with them. She wanted to, but she was a bit worried that your dad and I would feel abandoned. I told her not to be silly and to go for it. It was good for her to be with girls her own age. She was picking up some very old-fashioned notions from us.'

'Old-fashioned? How?' Deanna straightened the knives and forks that Madeleine had put on the table.

'Your dad and I were very lucky,' said Madeleine. 'He was my second boyfriend and we had a long, happy marriage. Lainey seemed to think that this was normal.'

'It kinda was in Ireland,' said Deanna.

'The long marriage, yes,' said Madeleine. 'Not necessarily the happy marriage. A lot of people stayed married because they didn't have any options. You said that yourself on a variety of occasions.'

'Mrs Kintyre,' remembered Deanna. 'Her husband used to cheat on her. We all knew.'

'And women like her,' agreed Madeleine. 'But Lainey somehow managed to acquire very idealised notions. I thought moving out would be good for her.'

'Though it wasn't,' remarked Deanna. 'She got engaged.'

'Hmm.' Madeleine turned off the oven. 'Fortunately they both came to their senses quickly enough.'

'Didn't stop her doing it again. Though *she* came to her senses that time.' Deanna noticed the expression on Madeleine's face. 'She didn't? I thought she broke it off with him?'

'Not really,' said Madeleine.

'For God's sake.' Deanna was disgusted. 'How could I have produced a child like her? What's her problem when it comes to men? A guy turned up at her apartment while I was there. Bit of a sleazeball if you ask me. Good body but dim mind.'

'Ken?' Madeleine looked surprised. 'Short hair, gelled?'

'That's him.'

'She's got back with him so.'

'Oh?'

Madeleine explained about their break-up at Carla's wedding.

'She shouldn't be allowed to go to weddings!' cried Deanna. 'Horrible, soppy, sentimental occasions.'

'I agree with you there,' said Madeleine. 'They bring out her romantic gene.'

'She couldn't possibly have a romantic gene!' Deanna was scandalised at the thought.

'Unfortunately she has,' said Madeleine. 'And it lands her in all sorts of trouble with men. Maybe this time it's different. No one has ever come back to her before.'

'And you think that's a good thing?' Deanna snorted. 'I should've stayed a bit longer at her place. I should've found out a bit more about this specimen before leaving her alone with him. I had an opportunity to be a good mother to her for once in my life, and I blew it. If she ends up with that moron, I'll never forgive myself.'

'It's her life,' Madeleine reminded her daughter.

'I know, I know,' said Deanna. 'I just want everything to have been worthwhile.'

'She'll be fine.' Madeleine put a plate of food in front of her.

'I wish I could believe you,' said Deanna as she poked at it moodily with her fork.

Chapter 21

Isotherm: a line of equal temperature on a weather map

'So where exactly do you stand with Ken?' asked Carla. She shielded her eyes from the glare of sun off the water as she looked at Lainey enquiringly. 'What do you want to happen next?'

Lainey poured cranberry juice into the frosted glass in front of her while she considered her answer. When Carla had reiterated her invitation to join her in Stockholm for a few days, she'd always known that her friend would quiz her about getting back with Ken. On the flight over, she'd practised how she'd talk about him, how she'd tell Carla that he was all over her like a rash at the moment but that she was doing her best to be low-maintenance and take it easy. But when she'd used the phrase in front of her friend as they sat together on the deck of a sunny waterside café near the Vasa museum, it had sounded defensive and apologetic. Lainey didn't want to appear defensive in front of Carla, who seemed to have relaxed into married life with considerable ease. (Well of course I've relaxed into it, she had said with amusement when Lainey told her this. It's wonderful. And Lainey had to admit that it certainly seemed to be. She was staying in Carla and Lennart's enormous apartment on Strandvagen, in the exclusive Ostermalm district of the city, while Lennart was in Norway on a business trip. As well as the apartment, the Soderlings also had a small house about two hours outside Stockholm and a lodge in the heart of the country. Lennart likes being in different places, Carla had told her. It helps him chill out.)

'Lainey?' Carla nudged her. 'Are you listening to me at all? What about Ken?'

'Of course I am,' said Lainey. 'I'm just trying to . . . to give you the right answer.'

'There isn't a right or a wrong answer,' Carla said.

'I guess we're in the full flush of happiness again,' Lainey told her. 'Maybe this is why couples break up and make up. It's very exciting. But I know I have to be careful. I need to take it slowly.'

'Why?' demanded Carla. 'He dumps you at my wedding and then waltzes back into your life a few weeks later, and you want to take things slow?'

'It was me dragging the whole marriage question into it that broke us up in the first place,' said Lainey. 'I don't want to pressurise him this time.'

'Doesn't sound like you're pressurising him at all from what you've told me so far,' said Carla. 'You haven't gone out anywhere nice with him since you've got back together. He calls to your apartment when he feels like it. He tells you he loves you. You have sex. He goes home.'

'You're deliberately twisting it,' protested Lainey. 'He's around every second day. And the sex is amazing.'

'It must be,' Carla said grimly.

'Are you implying that having sex with a guy is simply doing him a favour, which should be rewarded by getting something else in return?' Lainey shook her head. 'By being brought to nice places? Bought dinners or something? I know you've made your peace about marrying for money and it's worked out great for you, but it's not what I want.'

'I didn't just marry for money,' said Carla. 'You know that. And it's quite offensive that you keep saying it. I married Lennart because I know he's a decent guy and I care about him. I know he cares about me too. I'm planning on staying married to him. We have good fun together as well as having good sex. Now I'm not sure how much more you think there should be in a marriage, but quite honestly I think I've got what I want here.'

'I'm sorry.' Lainey knew she'd said the wrong thing. 'I know there's more to it than the money. There's your list of requirements, which he's fulfilled.'

'I admit there was a trade-off,' said Carla. 'I didn't pick a man who makes me tremble with desire every time I see him. But I picked a good man who respects me.'

'Are you saying Ken doesn't respect me?'

'Lainey! He might have brought you flowers and champagne, but he's shagging you whenever he feels like it and ignoring you the rest of the time. That's not exactly respect, is it?'

'He's not ignoring me,' objected Lainey. 'I told you. He texts me all the time.'

'To ask where you are and what you're doing. And then he turns up unexpectedly on your doorstep. Which is frankly a bit creepy and controlling.'

'That's not true!'

Carla opened her mouth to reply but was interrupted by her mobile phone, which buzzed urgently on the table. She picked it up and her eyes softened as she started speaking rapid Swedish to the person at the other end.

'Len,' she said when she'd finished the call. 'Hoping we're having a good time and that I've brought you to see all the sights. I told him I'd dragged you through the Vasa, so he's happy that your cultural needs are being met.'

'I've had a lovely time,' said Lainey warmly, her annoyance with her friend forgotten in the realisation that Carla had looked after her very well.

'Except for right now when I'm giving you grief.'

'Oh look, I understand that you're concerned about me. I was just as concerned about you. But we have different views on what love and marriage are all about. We don't have to fall out over them.'

'Do a list,' begged Carla. 'Think about what you want. Really think about it.'

'I absolutely don't need to do a list. I know what I want.' Lainey didn't count the short list she'd already made.

'Can I just say one thing about that.' Carla took a deep breath. 'And please don't throw a wobbler on me. For as long as I've known you, the most important thing on your list has been getting married. It's your number one thing. But Ken doesn't want to marry you. So he doesn't tick the most important box on your list.'

'*Didn't* want to,' Lainey corrected her. 'Not when I put it to him like I did. We talked about it. He felt pressurised. I understand that. That's why I'm not pressurising him now.'

'Are you certain about him?'

'Of course.'

Carla looked doubtfully at her friend.

'Really,' insisted Lainey. 'All right, I worry a bit that this . . . this enthusiasm he has for being with me again will wear off. I worry that he might get bored. But . . .'

'I was never uncertain for a second about Len,' said Carla.

'That's because your list worked, I suppose.'

'But would yours, with Ken?'

'I have the chance to start again with him and that's what I want to do,' said Lainey firmly. 'Oh, Carla, I've had so many bad relationships when I've never had the opportunity to get another go at it and get it right. But with Ken, I can.'

'I just think you're blaming yourself entirely for the break-up and feeling guilty about it simply because you told him what you wanted. And now he's in the driving seat again and you don't know if he's really going in the right direction for you.'

'You know what I'm like,' Lainey said. 'You and Val both agree that I lose my marbles and get obsessed with the whole wedding thing. So it's not surprising Ken took fright.'

'I think you really have to sort out whether you're in love with a particular guy or in love with the idea of being married,' said Carla gently. 'If you truly love Ken then I understand why you'd want to give it another go. But if you're just thinking that you want to get back with him because you've got some history and you're further along the prospective marriage path . . . well I'm not sure that you're building your hopes on a very strong foundation. I like Ken, honestly I do. But I worry he's not right for you, hon.'

'You're not supposed to tell me that,' Lainey pointed out.

'Because when I do marry him, I'll remember you didn't really approve of him.'

'If you guys get married I'll be happy for you,' promised Carla. 'I'll come to your wedding and beg your forgiveness for ever doubting him.'

'I'll hold you to that,' warned Lainey.

'But if you want to cut your losses and walk away before that, don't feel that you'll lose face with me or Val.'

'I've never been the one to break up with anybody,' confessed Lainey. 'Every time I've gone out with a guy, he's been the one to dump me.'

Carla looked startled.

'Surely you realised that before now,' Lainey said. 'I never want to break up with my boyfriends.'

'Weren't there any of them that bored you?' asked Carla. 'Or who had annoying habits that you couldn't stand? Or who you just stopped caring about?'

'Sometimes,' replied Lainey. 'But usually that's my fault. I'm very impatient. I'm also serially dumped.'

'Because you won't admit you've made a mistake,' said Carla.

'That's not it!'

'It must be.' Carla spoke intently. 'You want to get married and you want to have picked the right person so it's impossible in your mind that you didn't. Therefore you don't dump them because you'd have to admit you were wrong.'

'In that case I'm always getting it wrong.'

'It's not wrong to want to find the right man,' Carla said. 'You've just got this idealised notion about them.'

'We all have to have ideals,' Lainey told her. 'Otherwise there'd be no point in anything.'

* * *

The following day they took a ferry to the nearby island of Fjaderholmarna, where they wandered around the pretty craft shops and watched the owners as they painted, knitted, worked metal or blew glass. Lainey bought a painting of the archipelago for Madeleine and a glass paperweight for Deanna. (It had taken her a lot of time to decide what to get for her mother. She wasn't really sure that Deanna would appreciate a gift at all, but it seemed wrong to bring something back for Madeleine and not for her too.) Afterwards they went to a city centre spa, where Carla insisted on treating Lainey to a Swedish massage.

'It was very good,' said Lainey as they sipped herbal tea in the relaxation area. 'The girl said I was knotted up with tension. But they always say that when you're having a massage. It justifies all the pampering.'

Carla, who'd elected for a body scrub instead, nodded in agreement. 'Though you've a right to be tense, what with all the turmoil in your life at the moment.'

'It's not turmoil,' said Lainey. 'Admittedly having Deanna in Ireland is a bit stressful, and I do have to get my head straight about Ken, but I'm OK really.'

'So how's Deanna's work coming along?' asked Carla.

'She's been back and forward to the UK and the rest of Europe interviewing people. And she's trekking around Ireland too, so I guess it's progressing.'

Lainey took another sip of tea and told Carla about Deanna's lecture in Galway and about her own conversation with her mother on the subject of feminism. 'And then of course there's this whole thing with Feargal Wright.' She'd already told Carla about the garden party and Deanna's arrival at it, and Feargal Wright's interest in talking to her about her relationship with her mother. And she'd told her of how uncomfortable Deanna had been discussing it at her apartment later.

'D'you really think she's worried that her whole relationship with you could be laid bare?'

'I think she's afraid of being held up as a bad mother and a fraud, which will set back the feminist cause. She's probably just as worried at having to be quizzed about my father.'

'Why?'

'She doesn't like talking about him, even to me and Gran.'

'Wasn't he just a one-night stand?'

'Something like,' Lainey said. 'He didn't give a shit anyway, that's all I know.'

And then the words of the dream, spoken by the man, suddenly came to her: '. . . my daughter.' She saw herself on the steps of the house again, felt the warm drops of rain on her bare arms.

'Lainey?' Carla clicked her fingers in front of her friend's face. 'You OK?'

'Yes. Yes.' Lainey focused on her again. 'Just thinking about something.'

'Maybe Feargal Wright would do an investigative thing. Find out about your dad. Have a massive reunion on his show.'

Lainey roared with laughter. 'It's an arts and culture show, not Jerry Springer,' she reminded Carla. 'Have you ever watched it? You might be able to get it as a download. He's good, but it's a bit too dry and worthy for me. So to be honest, I don't think Deanna needs to worry. He might try to link her work into the fact that she was a single mother, but that's all.'

'I wonder does she feel she missed out?' Carla looked thoughtful. 'I know she's been hugely successful and everything, but she gave you to your gran to look after while she did her thing, and now she hardly knows you. It must hurt.'

'Nothing hurts Deanna,' said Lainey confidently. 'She's convinced that she's utterly right about everything. Once she makes a decision, she sticks to it regardless. So I'm sure she's convinced that she was right about me too. Which, actually, she was. I had a great upbringing with Gran and Grandad. I wouldn't change it at all.'

'You're quite like her,' Carla said.

'I am not!'

'When you make a decision you stick to it regardless too.'

'Is this about Ken again?' asked Lainey.

'Maybe.'

'I swear to God if you weren't my best friend I'd hit you over the head,' said Lainey. 'I'm not trying to make it work with him because it'll make me right. I'm trying to make it work because . . .'

'Because?'

Lainey looked rueful. 'It would be good to be right once about a man,' she confessed. 'It would be good not to think that I chose the wrong one for all the wrong reasons.'

'You'll get it right,' said Carla comfortingly. 'And I hope you get it right with Ken if that's what you want. I really do.'

Lainey's return flight was from Skavsta, an airport a hundred kilometres outside Stockholm. Lennart, who'd returned from his business trip, drove her there, with Carla in the passenger seat beside him, because they were continuing on to their country house afterwards. Lainey had to admit that she liked

Lennart, who'd been a warm and friendly host. She couldn't help but envy the way he looked after Carla when they went out together, not fussing over her but nevertheless attentive to her. He was equally attentive to Lainey herself – she thought that perhaps he was one of the best-mannered people she'd ever met. But she could see too that there was a genuine bond between her friend and her new husband. And she thought that Carla might have been lying about simply following her list of requirements when it came to Lennart Soderling. The truth was, Lainey mused, that she could easily fall for Lennart herself. There was certainly something nice about being with a man who was very much in charge, as Lennart definitely was. She wondered if that was what had attracted Carla. If it was all to do with power and authority. Something that would incense Deanna!

I'll find someone like Lennart one day, she thought, as she kissed both of them goodbye and thanked them for a lovely stay. And then she frowned. Because if Ken was the man for her, she'd found him already. She wondered why she hadn't realised that straight away.

Chapter 22

Roll cloud: a long, low tube of cloud that seems to stretch from horizon to horizon

'At worst I want to have you on *Look Wright*.' Feargal named his arts and culture show. 'But it would be utterly wonderful to have you on *Private Lives Public Faces* instead.'

'Feargal, you know I don't want to sit there and have my life unnecessarily sensationalised,' said Deanna. 'I'm happy to talk about my work, but not anything else. I don't want my story to be a bigger one than what I do, which is certainly what'll happen if you try to sensationalise my stupid teenage pregnancy.'

'I wouldn't sensationalise it,' he promised. 'Anyhow, don't you think it would be inspirational? Women will know that having a baby doesn't put them at a disadvantage . . .'

'Oh for heaven's sake.' She looked at him impatiently. 'You know that's rubbish. It does put them at a disadvantage no matter how politically incorrect it might be to say that. The only reason I wasn't disadvantaged was because my parents raised my daughter. I'm happy to admit that to anyone who asks but I don't want a big issue made of it.'

'Think about it again,' begged Feargal. 'I'm sure it would be good for you and for Lainey. And it would give you more publicity than you dreamed of.'

'I will *not* prostitute myself on television for that sort of publicity.' Deanna's words were clipped. 'I will *not* appear on a gossip programme.'

'I promise you it's not gossip,' Feargal assured her. 'It's very serious.'

'Rubbish.'

Feargal sighed. He'd met Deanna in a small coffee shop close to the television centre. He'd phoned her twice to confirm the meeting because, following the revelation about her and Lainey at his garden party, he wasn't entirely sure that she would even appear as originally scheduled on *Look Wright*.

He desperately wanted her to change her mind and come on his new show instead. But even if he couldn't persuade her about that, he still wanted to interview Deanna Ryan. She was always good for provocative TV. The only other time she'd been on the show, on a publicity trip to Ireland, she'd been on a panel reviewing the then popular movie *The Devil Wears Prada*. While everyone had agreed on the brilliance of Meryl Streep's performance, Deanna had been the only one to complain about the ending of the movie, with the character of Streep's assistant throwing it all away to be a hack on a small newspaper. It would have been a better movie, she said, if the girl had ended up in a senior position working for a rival magazine and had become more influential than the Miranda Priestly character.

'And what about her boyfriend?' she'd added hotly. 'Whining and complaining because she had a great job with fabulous clothes and freebies. Making her feel guilty for coming home late. How many working men do that all the bloody time?' Hollywood, she said, was all about putting women in boxes and subjugating them, and just because Miranda Priestly didn't get shafted in the end didn't mean that the film wasn't totally judgemental about her.

Feargal had loved her reaction and the debate it had sparked afterwards. The ratings for the show had shot up. So it would do him no harm at all to get her on again, even though switching her to a single-interview programme would be far more interesting.

In his wildest dreams he hadn't imagined that the result of her turning up at his party would be to reveal a secret love child. Even better, a love child who'd turned out to be one of Ireland's favourite weather presenters! Feargal desperately wanted to break the story on TV. Nobody at the party seemed to have overheard Deanna's admission that Lainey was her daughter, but he was sure that sooner or later the news would come out. There was no way he wanted anyone else talking to Deanna Ryan before he did.

Although he didn't say it to Deanna at their meeting, Feargal was thinking of ways to get Lainey on the show too. People would have a real surprise when they saw them side by side. The two women looked so very different, and yet there was an on-screen confidence about Lainey that must have come from Deanna. At the same time, Feargal wanted to explore how much contact she'd had with her dad and what type of influence he'd had on her life. It could be riveting stuff.

'OK then,' he said, deciding to concede to her for the time being. 'As far as your work goes, people will be very interested to hear how your views have changed over time. I suppose this documentary will show them that.'

'The main purpose is to find out how women have engaged with feminism over the years,' said Deanna. 'Not necessarily how I've engaged with it.'

'But you must be pleased at how much progress has taken place.'

'Hmm.' Deanna was dismissive. 'There was a time when feminism was important, but it got lost in a capitalist culture that places making money above all else.'

'Don't you ever get tired?' asked Feargal.

'Of what?'

'Banging the same old drum.'

'It still needs to be banged,' said Deanna.

'But things have changed so much for the better.'

'Depends on your point of view.'

'That's what I like about you,' said Feargal. 'That's why you'll be a great guest. Because you don't sit back and accept that you've made advances. You still think that things are as bad as they ever were. You're still a man-hater. That provokes debate.'

'I don't hate men,' said Deanna. 'I just find it wearying that when men get into positions of power or influence they hang on like grim death. And they promote the same old agenda.'

'Like I said,' Feargal pointed out. 'Banging the drum.'

'Like I said.' Deanna looked at him coolly. 'Needs to be banged.'

'I'll get Bonnie to give you a call later in the week,' said Feargal. 'Firm up the date and that sort of thing.'

'Fine,' said Deanna, determined that any discussion on Feargal Wright's show would stick to the topics she wanted to talk about and that he wouldn't get the slightest opportunity to ask her about things that were none of his business.

She could always duck out of the show completely, Deanna conceded as she sat in a taxi on the way back to Killester, but that would mean caving in to pressure, and she never caved in. Besides, the self-promotion wouldn't harm her book sales and would certainly help the documentary. But she would have to be on high alert the whole time. She knew that Feargal was itching to drag Lainey into it somehow. And she wasn't going to let that happen. For Lainey's sake, and for hers too. Her daughter was known for her professional skill. Deanna didn't want her to be known for having a complicated personal life.

Thinking about Lainey's personal life made her frown. Her daughter was her polar opposite in so many ways. She was so beautiful, for one thing – Deanna could never quite believe how lovely she was. She'd clearly inherited every one of Jorge's attractive genes. And she was beautiful with so little effort. But the side effect of her beauty seemed to be her never-ending stream of boyfriends. Deanna didn't quite understand how Lainey didn't appear able to hang on to them, even when she got engaged to them. She hoped that each time it was because she had seen sense, but she wasn't convinced of that.

She'd never actually met any of Lainey's boyfriends until seeing Ken at her apartment, and she hadn't exactly warmed to him. She had to admit to herself that she didn't think she'd warm to any man Lainey decided to have a relationship with. There was too much heartache where men were concerned to believe that having them around was a good idea. She would have liked to spare Lainey that kind of heartache, although she realised she'd failed miserably at that. She'd had conversations with Madeleine about it over the years whenever her mother had called her to tell her that Lainey had locked herself in her room and was crying her eyes out over some unworthy boy.

Deanna had been utterly shocked when Lainey had called her to tell her about her first engagement. She couldn't believe that a girl who was barely out of her teens would consider getting married in this day and age. She hadn't even tried to sound enthusiastic about it, but had asked Lainey if she was completely off her head.

'Of course not,' Lainey had replied, her tone hurt. 'Ross and I love each other and we want to be with each other all the time.'

Deanna had derived some satisfaction in realising that 'all the time' had meant until the end of Christmas. But her relief had been relatively short-lived as Lainey moved on to new boyfriends. She hadn't been at all happy when she rang to tell of her engagement to Denis.

'Again?' she'd said, which had put a dampener on the conversation, because, of course, Lainey had been offended by her comment. Deanna hadn't meant to offend her, but she didn't see the point in pretending that she was pleased about another engagement.

Deanna wished she understood her daughter and her apparent need to have a man in her life. She wished she could explain that they simply weren't worth it. But she never seemed to be able to connect with Lainey and she knew that she was wasting her time even trying.

She wondered how serious this current relationship was. It had been odd, Deanna thought, to see Ken turn up at the apartment, when the previous week she'd seen Lainey at Feargal's party with someone else. She knew she should be pleased to think that Lainey wasn't having exclusive relationships. But she worried about it all the same.

If I'd kept her with me, she wondered, would it have been better for her? I know it wouldn't have been better for me, as she so eloquently pointed out. But for Lainey herself? Would it have been better for her to be with me, regardless of how crap I was as a mother? She stared unseeingly in front of her. How could it have been better when she'd have been struggling to pay the bills and for childcare and just about everything? How could it have been better when every day she would have seen Jorge's dark eyes reflected in Lainey's? And how could it have been better when she would have worried about her daughter every single day? She'd done the best possible thing for her, she was sure she had. Lainey had had a much better relationship with Edmund and Madeleine than she would have had with Deanna – a better relationship than Deanna herself had had with them, in fact. Apparently there weren't the blazing rows that had been part of her own life with them. Lainey had been sweet and loving and a far better granddaughter than she'd been a daughter. Which was maybe why Lainey and Madeleine shared so much.

I shouldn't question my choices now, Deanna told herself. I made them and I did what I did with the best motives. But the thought of other people questioning them . . . that made her flinch. And she knew that they would question them. Because nobody would ever be able to understand why she'd allowed her parents to return to Ireland with her daughter. Nobody would ever be able to understand why she'd thought it was the best place for her to be.

Lainey called to her grandmother's house after she got back from Stockholm. With Deanna staying there, she wasn't visiting as often as usual, and she missed her time with her grandmother. Carla had been full of useful and caring advice, but Madeleine was always unconditional in her love and support.

Madeleine beamed with delight when she saw Lainey on the doorstep and ushered her inside the house.

'Oh my God,' said Lainey as she looked around the living room. 'What's going on here?'

The room was full of papers and folders, books and photographs. The papers were piled high on Madeleine's two coffee tables, and the books were stacked higgledy-piggledy on the floor.

'Your mother's research,' said Madeleine drily. 'She's been doing a lot of work.'

'She's taken over the house altogether!' exclaimed Lainey. 'Oh Gran, it's such a mess.'

'It's back to the future all right,' agreed Madeleine. 'Deanna was always an untidy child.'

'I thought she was simply doing a documentary,' said Lainey. 'What does she need all this stuff for?'

'Research on the people she plans to include,' replied Madeleine. 'And information about the activities of Irish feminists in the 1970s. Deanna was growing up then but she doesn't remember much about things like the contraceptive train, so she's having to research it all.'

'The what?' Lainey looked flabbergasted, and Madeleine told her about the time a large group of Irish women went to Northern Ireland to buy contraceptives, because they were banned in the Republic at the time.

'They came back waving condoms in the faces of the guards,' recalled Madeleine. 'It was quite funny actually.'

'Banning condoms, though.' Lainey looked astonished. 'What was the point in that?'

'A belief that if you didn't talk about it, sex didn't happen,' said her grandmother. 'Lots of things were swept under the carpet in those days. Including unmarried parenthood.'

'Deanna was in the States when she was pregnant with me,' said Lainey. 'Was that because she was shunned here?'

'Of course not,' said Madeleine. 'She was already in the States when she got pregnant. You knew that.'

'I just wondered,' said Lainey. 'You get told lots of stuff as a kid, but sometimes it's not all strictly true.'

'I've tried never to tell you deliberate untruths,' said Madeleine slowly. 'But I suppose time blunts one's memory. Deanna meeting your father in the States is accurate.'

'He knows I exist.' Lainey spoke thoughtfully. 'Yet he's never tried to find me.'

Madeleine looked uneasy.

'I don't care,' Lainey reassured her. 'I know guys can be like that. Not want to think of the consequences of their actions. It doesn't upset me. But does it ever upset Deanna?'

'Deanna was upset about the whole pregnancy deal,' said Madeleine.

'Oh, clearly.' Lainey spoke with assurance. 'She'd hardly have dumped me on you and Gramps otherwise.'

'She didn't dump you,' said Madeleine.

'I think she did.'

'Don't judge her.' Madeleine sounded concerned.

'I do my best not to,' said Lainey. 'After all, she's not someone you can get away with judging.'

Lainey had left to return to her apartment when Deanna arrived back at Killester. Madeleine was taking some bread out of the oven, and the aroma of home baking hit Deanna as soon as she walked in the front door.

'You don't still bake bread?' She looked at her mother as though she was crazy. 'There's a bakery ten minutes up the road.'

'I like baking,' said Madeleine. 'It's therapeutic. And if you wait a minute or two you can have a slice and tell me that anything from the bakery up the road could be half as nice.'

'I know it won't be.' Deanna hung her jacket on the back of a chair. 'I remember your bread. Always delicious. I just can't see the point in slaving over it, that's all.'

'I don't see it as slavery,' said Madeleine. 'I enjoy it.'

'It's a symbol of oppression,' Deanna told her.

Madeleine snorted. 'No it's not. Loads of people like making their own bread these days. They've come back to it, in fact. It's a nice thing to do and I enjoy it. Same as I enjoy cleaning the house.'

'Oh, Mom, nobody likes housework!'

'I do,' said Madeleine. 'I like bringing order out of chaos. Speaking of which, you've turned my living room into a tip. I'd appreciate it if you'd tidy up.'

'It's my work.'

'I don't care,' said Madeleine. 'It's my house, not an extension of your office.'

Deanna bristled for a moment, then her shoulders sagged. 'All right,' she said. 'Loads of people would love to have me working in their home, but I realise you don't see it like that.'

'Sweetheart, I'm delighted to have you working here, but I'm terrified to move anything and the room needs to be dusted and vacuumed,' said Madeleine.

'It's fine, you know.'

'In your eyes. Not mine.'

'You've been conditioned into thinking that your house has to be spotless.'

'I haven't,' said Madeleine. 'I like it that way.'

'Oh all right.' Deanna turned towards the living room. 'I'll tidy up like a good little girl.'

'Thank you,' Madeleine called after her. 'And if you do a really good job, I'll spread your bread with home-made jam.'

Deanna poked her head back around the door. 'You still make jam, too?'

Madeleine nodded.

'Blackberry?'

Madeleine nodded again.

'I feel like I've stepped into my childhood life,' said Deanna.

'Was it so terrible for you?' asked Madeleine sadly.

'No.' Deanna's smile was sudden and genuine. 'It was me who was terrible. And I'm sorry.'

'Ah, get away.' Madeleine grinned at her in return. 'You had a mind of your own. That was a good thing, Deanna. And I'm proud of you for it.'

'You are?'

'Of course I am.'

Deanna was astonished to find that her eyes had flooded

with hot tears. She turned back towards the living room so her mother couldn't see them. She'd never realised that Madeleine was proud of her. She'd always thought she'd been nothing but a worry.

Chapter 23

Kelvin-Helmholtz: a wave cloud appearing at all three cloud levels, caused by wind shear

The thing about the States, Deanna often thought as she pursued her life and career there, was that it was a place that allowed you to be the person you wanted to be. Not the person someone else thought you should be. She'd realised this after returning from her second visit to Ireland. Back home she felt as though she'd instantly regressed, that people still treated her as Edmund and Madeleine's wayward daughter. The neighbours would smile at her and ask her how she was, but she couldn't help feeling they were wondering when she was going to come home, get a proper job (maybe even be lucky enough to find a nice boy who'd marry her) and start looking after Lainey properly. In later years, after each visit home, she'd felt more and more distant from the country of her birth and more and more distant from both her parents and the person her daughter had become. She hadn't especially wanted that to happen. She hadn't wanted to reject Lainey or make her feel unwanted.

She regularly wrote her letters and sent cards with inspirational messages. But she realised that in leaving her with Edmund and Madeleine, in deciding that her career in America was more important than being a mother to the little girl, she had naturally made Lainey feel that she wasn't all that interested in her. Lainey had no such qualms about Edmund and Madeleine, who adored her. Deanna knew that she adored both of them in return. She was OK with this, thinking that perhaps when Lainey was a little older the two of them could have reasoned discussions with each other about the choices she'd made and her reasons for making them. But Lainey always seemed singularly uninterested in having those discussions.

When her daughter was fourteen, Deanna asked her to visit her in California. Although she now lived near the university, she liked to return to Monterey during the summer months and she usually rented a small house as close to the ocean as possible. She would meet up with Lexy and Fawn (whose shop had grown over the years and now had a stylish restaurant attached) and she would visit Maya, who'd married a local businessman and lived on the exclusive 17 Mile Drive in a smart modern house with five bedrooms and four bathrooms, even though she and Frederick still hadn't any children and so didn't need all the space. Deanna thought Lainey would like Monterey. And she wanted to give her a taste of a different culture, to show her that not everywhere was like Ireland. It would be educational, as well as fun, she wrote in a letter to Lainey, and she hoped to see her soon.

Lainey hadn't wanted to go. She'd read the letter aloud to Madeleine and Edmund, and when she finished, she'd wrinkled up her nose at the 'educational' part and said that she'd much rather stay with them. Besides, she'd added, Val's family was going to Majorca and Val was begging them to let Lainey go too.

'If Val's parents ask about Majorca, then we'll see what can be done about that,' said Madeleine. 'But I think you should visit your mother, Lainey. It's good of her to ask.'

'What d'you mean, it's good of her?' Lainey demanded. 'She's my mother! She should ask to see me sometimes. But I don't care. I'm not going. It'll be beyond boring.'

Madeleine smiled. 'You need to get to know her,' she said. 'It's important.'

'It's not,' said Lainey obstinately. And the thing is, Gran . . .' she looked shamefacedly at Madeleine, 'I don't really like her very much. She's not a lot of fun.'

'I understand that,' Madeleine said. 'But when you get to know her a bit better, you'll feel differently.'

Lainey was sceptical. She simply couldn't see the point in going to California and spending time with a woman she hardly knew, despite the fact that she knew a lot *about* her.

Deanna was now a prominent women's rights advocate in the States. Madeleine had a folder of newspaper articles Deanna had sent her, including one in which she was named Monterey Woman of the Year. There were pieces about her in the international papers too, and Lainey had read her occasional columns in *Time* and *Newsweek* magazines, although she hadn't yet ploughed through either of Deanna's books (her second, *Tit Power*, had come out a few years earlier and had made a much bigger impact than *Get Off Your Back*).

'OK, can I be honest?' Lainey turned her luminous eyes on Madeleine. 'She scares me, Gran. She's always telling me what I should want, what I should do, what I should like. And she makes me feel that if I don't want to do it, there's something wrong with me. It's a real pain.'

'She's not *always* telling you things,' Madeleine said mildly. 'You're not in touch that often.'

'She writes once a month,' Lainey said. 'And I don't understand half of it.'

Madeleine wasn't surprised. She'd read some of the letters. Deanna didn't seem to realise that she was writing to a child.

'Why does she want me to spend time with her now?' demanded Lainey.

'I expect she feels sad that she's missed so much of you growing up,' Madeleine said. 'She wants to make up for it.'

'But you can't, can you?' Lainey asked. 'When time is gone it's gone. You can't make it up.'

Madeleine didn't reply. Lainey might have inherited her looks from Jorge, she thought, but her obstinate streak was pure Deanna.

In the end, though, Lainey had gone to California, because her grandmother wouldn't take no for an answer. Deanna had been annoyed by her daughter's initial reluctance to travel and had asked Madeleine what on earth was the matter with her. Surely, she said, any fourteen-year-old girl would love the idea of a fortnight in one of California's most breathtaking locations.

'With her friends maybe,' Madeleine had told Deanna. 'But you're asking her to travel all that way on her own to stay with an adult she doesn't know very well. And it's not like you have other children, or friends with children she can pal around with. She's afraid she'll be at a loose end.'

'I'm sure she's perfectly capable of finding people her own

age to pal around with,' said Deanna briskly. 'I came here on my own, didn't I?'

'You were nearly five years older,' Madeleine pointed out. 'You were grown up. Lainey is still a child.'

'She's fourteen,' said Deanna. 'And in the last photo you sent me she looked older.'

'Fourteen is still a child,' said Madeleine. 'No matter how grown up she might look.'

Although she was expecting to see a young adult, Deanna was stunned when she saw Lainey walking into the arrivals hall, dragging her suitcase behind her. Despite the fact that she hadn't yet reached her full height, Lainey was already taller than Deanna, and she carried it well, not stooping as so many teenagers did but walking with her back straight. She was wearing sequinned flip-flops, stonewashed jeans, and a light jacket over a white cropped top. Her long hair fell loosely around her shoulders, although a sparkly pink slide kept it out of her eyes. She was looking around her with a faintly bored expression, and as Deanna walked over to her, she yawned widely.

'Hello,' Deanna said. 'It's good to see you.'

'Hi.' Lainey knew better than to try to kiss her. Not that she wanted to anyway. She was here under sufferance.

'The car's outside and the weather's glorious. Mam says it's cold at home.'

'It's average for the time of year,' Lainey said. 'Cloudy today, though and easterly winds. That's what's making it feel cold; the wind chill is knocking a couple of degrees off it.'

Deanna looked at her in surprise. 'Thank you for that rather detailed information.'

'It's interesting,' said Lainey. 'Ireland usually gets south-westerly winds, which are warmer. Our weather is dominated by the Atlantic Ocean. Here, of course, it's the Pacific. That's why you get so much fog.'

The fog was the one thing about Monterey that Deanna didn't like.

'It's why the summers here are generally cool and dry too. Although because the US itself is located within an area of disturbed westerly winds, it gets a lot of weather extremes.'

'I see.' Deanna was startled by her daughter's conversation. 'You're interested in winds, are you?'

'Weather,' said Lainey.

'Really?' Deanna led her to the car park and her bright yellow Corvette. 'You think there's a career path for you in weather?'

Lainey shrugged.

'Please don't do that,' said Deanna. 'It means nothing.'

Lainey shrugged again.

Deanna opened the car door. It was going to be a long two weeks.

It was certainly more difficult than she'd anticipated. The last time Deanna had seen Lainey, in Dublin three years previously, she'd been quiet and helpful and still slightly in awe of her. Now, as far as Deanna could tell, Lainey regarded her as an obstacle to her doing whatever she wanted to do. Which, it seemed, was to wander down to Fisherman's Wharf and sit there all day staring at the ocean. Sometimes Lainey would go into the aquarium and watch the marine life, which meant more staring at things. Deanna couldn't understand how anyone could spend so much time doing nothing. When she'd been Lainey's age she'd been out and about, into everything, talking to her friends, wanting to change the world. Lainey seemed perfectly happy with it the way it was. Deanna had planned to drive down to the college and show her where she worked, but Lainey wasn't interested in that. She also wanted her daughter to have coffee with Patsy Fuller, who still lived in the same house in the town, but Lainey said that she knew enough old people, thanks very much.

She did, however, allow Deanna to drive her to Big Sur, insisting on her mother stopping every few miles so that she could take photographs of the mist rising from the water, and surprising Deanna by chattering happily about the rapidly changing weather as they moved from sunlight to fog and back to sunlight again. That, and a visit to Lexy and Fawn's restaurant, where they also met Maya, were the most successful days they spent together. Lainey laughed and joked with the girls, who fussed over her madly, Lexy and Fawn giving her pretty jewellery from the store and Maya telling her stories about when she and Deanna had travelled around Europe, and the early days in Monterey. The stories were always funny, although Deanna grew edgy when they talked about smoking pot or drinking too much. She had already told them that there was to be no discussion of Jorge, and they respected her wishes, although they'd talked among themselves beforehand and wondered what they would say if Lainey herself asked about him. But despite the fact that she opened up when talking to them, the question of her father never arose.

'Do you remember being here at all when you were small?' Deanna asked on the night before Lainey went home, when they were sitting in the small garden outside the house.

Lainey shook her head. 'Gran showed me some photos but they didn't ring any bells. I guess I was too young.'

'Do you want to see the hotel where you stayed?'

'I probably already did,' said Lainey.

'Why are you being so bloody difficult?' Deanna's patience suddenly snapped. 'I've done my best for you, I really have. I've tried to make it interesting and nice but all you've done is wander off on your own and ignore me whenever possible. You're a young woman. It's not that long since I was your age myself! There must be some point of contact between us.'

Lainey's jaw jutted out and she said nothing.

'I want you to understand my life,' Deanna told her. 'I want you to realise how important my work is and why I have to be here.'

'You don't need me to understand you,' said Lainey. 'Loads of people do already. Me and Gran read the pieces in the magazines. You're a sort of famous crusader person.'

'Women need me,' said Deanna. 'They need someone to stand up for them and champion their causes. Everything I do is for women. And that means it's for you as well.'

Lainey picked at some dry skin on her ankle.

'Don't you get that?' demanded Deanna. 'Don't you see how women have to fight?'

'I don't see why you have to be angry all the time,' mumbled Lainey.

'I'm not.'

'You are. You're angry with . . . well, I don't know . . . all men. Other women? And you're angry with me.'

'I'm not angry with you.'

'You don't like me very much, though.'

'Don't be silly. And don't be sentimental. That's another problem with the world these days. Everyone is so damn sentimental. All this stuff about being in touch with your emotions is ridiculous. Too many decisions are made because of sentiment rather than reason. There's far too much emphasis on how we feel and not on what's right to do.'

'How did you feel when you found out you were expecting me?' asked Lainey quietly.

'Shocked,' said Deanna after a pause.

'And how did my dad feel?'

'I don't know how he felt,' said Deanna. 'I only know how he behaved.'

'Abandoned both of us without a second thought.' Lainey suddenly sounded much older than her years.

'He didn't live up to his responsibilities.'

'Neither did you.'

'In fact I did,' said Deanna. 'I made a rational decision based on what I knew about myself and my parents and I didn't allow soppy sentimentality to get in the way.'

'Did my father ever try to get in touch with you? Did he ever want to help?'

Deanna hesitated. 'Not in any meaningful way,' she said eventually. She had no intention of telling Lainey about Jorge's second visit. There was no point in bringing it up now. It hadn't come to anything in the end.

'Did you love him?' asked Lainey.

'Briefly,' said Deanna.

'If he came back now, would you be nice to him?'

'He's not coming back,' Deanna said.

'I know. But if . . .'

'There's no point in talking about ifs,' said Deanna.

'Is it because of him you hate men?' asked Lainey.

'Of course not. I don't hate men either, but I don't respect very many of them.'

'Why?'

'Because they've had it too easy for too long.'

'Have you got a boyfriend?'

'Don't be silly.'

'Have you got a girlfriend?'

'Lainey!'

'What?' Lainey looked at her innocently. 'You must have friends.'

'You met my friends.'

'Have you got friends at college?'

'I have colleagues,' Deanna told her.

'But people you go out with? Have a laugh with?'

'My life isn't about having a laugh,' said Deanna.

'Why not?'

'You know why not. I've told you why not. I have an important job to do.'

'I don't see why you can't have fun doing it.'

'I don't want you to grow into the sort of person who thinks that having a laugh is the most important thing in life. Or who wants nothing more than to be "happy". That's another one of these sentiment-driven statements. Very few people are happy.'

'I'm happy,' said Lainey.

'Are you?'

'Most of the time.'

'What makes you happy?'

'I dunno. Songs. Clothes. My friends.'

Deanna managed to keep her disappointment out of her voice. 'And what makes you unhappy?'

'Girls at school mainly.'

'Why?'

Lainey told her about the hard time she sometimes got because she was considered too pretty.

'Do they bully you?' Deanna's eyes glinted.

'They try. But I'm OK with it. I can look after myself.'

'I'm glad to hear it. And those girls are worth nothing.'

'I thought you were supportive of all women.'

'There are always exceptions. If you have trouble at school, tell your grandmother.'

'She knows already.'

'Oh.'

Lainey stretched her long legs in front of her. 'Don't feel guilty,' she said. 'I understand you have a different sort of life. I'm not emotional about it.'

'So what do you want from your own life?' asked Deanna.

A mother who talks to me about ordinary things, thought Lainey. Someone who chats rather than lectures. Someone who'll laugh at silly stuff with me. Who'll come shopping with me and buy pretty dresses. Paint her nails and mine. Nothing much.

'I don't know,' she said out loud. 'To do well at school. To get a good job. To get married.'

'You want to get married?'

'Why not? Gran and Grandad are very happy together. So I'd be happy if I was married. If I meet the right person, of course. Not someone like my father, someone who leaves.'

'Don't rush into getting married,' warned Deanna. 'It's not all it's cracked up to be.'

'How do you know that?' asked Lainey.

'I work with married women. Many of them feel trapped.'

'I'll make sure I find the right person.'

'You've got to get the most out of your life while you can,' said Deanna.

'How can there be more to it than being happy with someone you love?' asked Lainey.

'Love isn't everything,' said Deanna. 'Sometimes it just blinds you to the truth.'

Lainey stood up. 'I'd better go and pack,' she said. 'We'll have to leave way before breakfast to get to the airport tomorrow. I want to make sure I have everything.'

'Of course.'

Deanna watched as she walked into the house. Well, she thought, I gave it a shot. I tried to be a mother for a while. I had my daughter stay with me. And I don't know who hated it more, me or her.

Chapter 24

Lacunosus: a fleeting cloud formation, with a honeycomb appearance

On the days when she was rostered to do the prime-time TV forecast, Lainey usually went to the hairdresser in the morning. She didn't have to be at the studio until around 1.30 p.m., which gave her lots of time for a leisurely breakfast and a relaxing half-hour at the salon, where she would chat to Suzie, her stylist, who always brought her up to date with the latest in celebrity gossip.

'Did you hear that Feargal Wright is supposed to have someone new in his life?' Suzie asked as she twirled Lainey's hair around a styling brush. 'The word is he's besotted, although nobody knows who she is yet. Probably a younger version of Sadie. They always go for the younger models, don't they?' Suzie started on another section of Lainey's hair. 'How come men seem to manage to move on so much quicker than women after a break-up?'

Lainey thought of Shay Loughnane and his never-ending stream of girlfriends. Despite how badly he professed to feel at the ending of his marriage, he wasn't spending his time moping and being miserable. He was out there enjoying himself.

'We always seem to try so hard when men don't bother, and yet . . .' Lainey shook her head in mock despair. 'I'm the worst person in the world to ask, Suze. You know that.'

'Well, you'll set hearts fluttering again tonight,' her hairdresser told her as she switched off the dryer. 'You look lovely.'

'Thanks.' Lainey stood up and put on her jacket. 'See you next week.'

'Take care.'

There was a spring in Lainey's step as well as a bounce in her curls as she strolled back to the apartment and made herself a cup of coffee. Maybe everything in her life wasn't perfect, but the sun was shining, which always cheered her, she loved her job, and having her hair done made her feel good.

She'd just washed her cup and put it on the drainer when Carla phoned.

'How're things?' asked Lainey breezily. She hadn't spoken to her friend since returning from Stockholm. 'Did you have a nice weekend in your country house?'

'Yes. But not since then.' Carla's voice was shaky.

'Why?'

There was a pause.

'What's wrong?' asked Lainey. 'Are you OK?'

'Sure I am,' said Carla. 'Only . . .'

'What?'

'Lennart has a girlfriend.'

'He . . . what!' Lainey sat down with a thud. 'You've got

to be kidding me. He seemed mad about you when I was there. He can't possibly be having an affair – sure you're only married a wet week, for heaven's sake!'

Carla sniffed. 'He says . . . well, it's not exactly an affair. But there's a woman in his life. Her name's Jannike. Apparently she's one of his best friends.'

'Did you know about her? Had he introduced you to her? She wasn't at the wedding, was she?'

'No,' said Carla. 'He never mentioned her before.'

'Funny sort of best friend in that case.'

'I know.'

'So what's the story?'

'They went out together when they were both in their twenties. Then Jannike got married. And divorced. And married again. All this time they kept in touch. When she was between marriages they started going out together again. But according to Len, neither of them wanted to marry each other. He says they're not compatible enough to live together. He says . . .' Carla's voice trembled, 'he says it was about the sex really. Apparently they were really hot together. But the thing now is . . . she's getting divorced again. And he's been seeing her.'

'Without telling you?'

'Of course without telling me! At least, what he said to me was that he was meeting a friend. Jeez, Lainey, I'm so stupid and trusting. I thought he meant an old male friend. I didn't for a second think it was a woman.'

'But you must have talked about his previous relationships?'

'Only vaguely,' said Carla. 'He told me that as a man of over fifty he'd obviously had relationships but that none of them had been important enough for him to want to spend the rest of his life with that person. I was OK with that. I've had relationships too, after all. Naturally he'd have old girlfriends. I just didn't expect them to start popping out of the woodwork now.'

'So what exactly is the problem?' asked Lainey. 'Is she getting a divorce because she wants to be with Lennart?'

'He says not. He says that their marital difficulties are nothing to do with him.'

'But you don't believe him?'

'Lainey, he was away with her overnight!'

'No!'

'He was in Gothenburg last week. She was too. I couldn't get him on his mobile, so I phoned the hotel. She answered the call in his room and handed it over to him. Obviously I freaked, but he talked about it as though it was perfectly reasonable.'

'They were staying together at a hotel and he thinks that's perfectly reasonable?' Lainey was incredulous.

'He says they weren't actually staying together. He went to Gothenburg for a conference. The company she works for has offices there too. They decided to meet up. Lennart had a suite in the hotel – he always gets a suite when he can. So there was a living area too, which is where he says they were having a drink together. I looked up the hotel website straight away and there is a suite like this, but for God's sake, Lainey, he's a married man and he shouldn't be sharing suites with soon-to-be-divorced women.'

'No, no, I understand that.' Lainey exhaled slowly. 'Is he denying that he's sleeping with her?'

'Yes. But he says that even if he was, I shouldn't be getting into such a heap about it. He says that we had an arrangement in our marriage. That we both knew what we were getting into. That I have everything I wanted.'

'Does he have a point?' asked Lainey tentatively.

'No he bloody doesn't! He's my husband!'

'Whom you only half love.'

'I don't only . . . I had a list! It was all about security. But it doesn't mean love doesn't come into it.'

'Whatever love is.' Lainey echoed the words Carla had spoken on her wedding day.

'It's being faithful, surely.'

'He says he has been.'

'I don't believe him.'

'Yes, well, neither would I, to be honest. So what are you going to do about it?'

'I don't know.'

'Have you been faithful to him?' Lainey's tone was quizzical.

'What sort of question is that?' demanded Carla. 'Of course I have.'

'How much *do* you love him? How much do you care about him and your marriage? Enough to ignore it? Enough to forgive it? Enough to pretend to believe him?'

'I don't know that either.' Carla sounded miserable. 'Oh Lainey, I think I've managed to get it all wrong.'

Lainey said nothing.

'I thought I would be OK with it,' muttered Carla. 'I thought there might be times when . . . well, it happens, doesn't it? No matter how good the relationship. But the thing is, I don't want him to be seeing other women, even if they are just friends. Which clearly she's not. And even if by some miracle she *was* just a friend, she's a better friend than me. He's known her more than half his life. He's known me less than a year.'

'He didn't marry her, though,' Lainey pointed out.

'So why did he marry me?'

'You said it was because he wanted to settle down with one person.'

'Maybe he's suddenly decided that one person is Jannike.'

'Maybe he wants the settling person to be you but he has other plans for her,' said Lainey. 'Perhaps he thought you'd be OK with that.'

'You're not being very supportive!' cried Carla.

'I'm sorry, I'm sorry. It's just that – well, most times when stuff like this happens it's a major disaster and everyone is devastated because hearts are broken. But you didn't give him your heart, did you? You married with your head. So I'm trying to figure out whether you're emotionally upset or if you're just annoyed with him.'

'I'm more than just annoyed!'

'I know.'

'I thought I'd figured it out.' Carla sounded tired now. 'I thought I'd picked the right person for the right reason. But now . . .'

'Now?' prompted Lainey.

'I don't know if I've picked the right person for the wrong reason or the wrong person for the right reason.'

'Um. OK.'

'Sorry, I know that's babble.' Carla sniffed.

Lainey paused before she spoke, and when she did, she chose her words carefully.

'So does it matter?' she asked. 'After all, if you chose him for reasons that weren't entirely to do with love, should you get upset if there are other people in his life?'

'We're married,' said Carla obstinately. 'There shouldn't be anyone else.'

'I know, I know,' said Lainey. 'I'm trying to look at it in a sort of pragmatic way. You said you got what you wanted. And so did he. But maybe he didn't want to give up something he had either.'

'Are you on his side?' demanded Carla. 'After all, you didn't totally approve of my reasons for marrying him, did you? Are you feeling sorry for him now, is that it?'

'Of course not. I'm trying to understand his actions. Maybe he thinks it's perfectly OK to see an old friend in the way he did. Maybe he thought you'd be OK with it. Maybe those are the signals you sent out.'

Carla was silent.

'He says he loves me,' she said. 'I think he does. But as a wife. Not . . . not as a lover.'

'Isn't that how you feel too?' asked Lainey. 'You said he didn't make you tingle with excitement.'

'I know. But it didn't mean I was going to rush off and find an old flame who did!'

'D'you want to come and stay with me for a while?' Lainey asked. 'Take a bit of time out?'

'No. At least, not yet, though thanks for asking.' Carla sighed. 'I have to decide what's best to do.'

'I'm so sorry,' said Lainey.

'Me too.' Carla sniffed again. 'I thought I'd worked it out, Lainey. I thought I'd got what I wanted. I thought I was being sensible about it. But now . . . now I'm not sure about anything at all.'

'Is there anything I can do?'

'No,' said Carla. 'Unless you want to say "I told you so".'

'I don't want to say that. I don't even think that. I hope you and Lennart can work it out.'

'So do I,' Carla said. 'But I don't know if that's possible any more.'

Lainey stared unseeingly in front of her after her friend had hung up. She couldn't believe that Carla's marriage was in trouble already. There was a part of her that had wondered if, sometime in the future, Carla might not have found another man. If the whole marrying for security thing wouldn't have been enough for her in the end. It had never occurred to her that it might not have been enough for Lennart either.

She was in the coffee room at the TV studios, leafing through the newspaper but still thinking about Carla's news, when she saw the feature about Deanna's documentary, flagging her forthcoming appearance on *Look Wright*. Two photographs of Deanna accompanied the piece; one of her delivering a talk at a seminar for International Women's Day and another sitting outside her house in Monterey. It was the same house where Lainey had stayed as a fourteen-year-old. Deanna had eventually bought it with the royalties from her third book, *Women in Waiting*, which she'd published a couple of years after Lainey's visit. In the photo, Deanna was standing against the wooden frame of the house, dark-rimmed glasses perched on top of her head. She was wearing a black leather jacket over her usual jeans and T-shirt, and was looking straight into the camera lens, a challenging expression on her face. Lainey thought that anyone else having their photo taken in such lovely surroundings (because the house was picture perfect) would have looked cheerful and happy. But not Deanna.

Ever since their encounter at Feargal Wright's party, Lainey realised that she was thinking of her mother in a different way. She'd been in awe of Deanna all her life. Even if she didn't agree with her, she couldn't help deferring to her powerful intellect and the strength of her personality. But she'd found the chink in her armour when Deanna had had to admit to being her mother. She had seen a flash of fear in Deanna's eyes and a worry that she would be judged by the people she judged herself. Because mothers were supposed to put their children first, and Deanna hadn't done that. She knew people would judge her for it, and in that judging she might be found wanting. Which wasn't entirely fair, Lainey reasoned, because none of them knew the situation Deanna had found herself in. If you truly weren't ready for a child, looking after it must be the most difficult thing in the world. Deanna had done what she thought was best. And although in the past Lainey had sometimes wondered if she had only considered her own best interests, she now thought that Deanna probably had had her daughter's best interests at heart too. Because the truth was it would have been a nightmare to have lived with Deanna in California. Her life had been far more peaceful with Madeleine and Edmund.

She looked at her watch. Deanna would arrive at the studio soon to do the interview for the documentary. They hadn't met up since the afternoon in Lainey's apartment. Instead Deanna had emailed her with a list of questions that she would probably (but not definitely) ask, and said that they wanted to film her at work if at all possible.

'You want to have me on camera? For sure?' asked Lainey.

'We might as well film it,' Deanna said. I can't promise we'll use it.'

'In that case it's probably best to come to the studio,' suggested Lainey.

'Good thinking,' Deanna said. 'Though I'd like to get a few shots of you at Met Eireann all the same.'

Lainey wasn't all that convinced about letting the cameras into what she regarded as her 'real' workplace. But she said she'd talk it over with Martin anyway. Martin said he'd be delighted to help out in whatever way was possible, and then looked anxiously at Lainey.

'You won't say anything about what I said to you when you were going for the presenting slot, will you?'

'Huh?'

'Well, you know.' He looked embarrassed. 'About you being photogenic.'

She winked at him. 'My lips are sealed regarding your blatantly sexist comment.'

'It wasn't meant to be sexist.'

'I know,' she assured him. 'I'm not one of those people who decide to get offended by something like that.'

'Thanks.' Martin looked relieved.

'You're welcome.'

Lainey wondered how Deanna would have reacted in the same circumstances. She felt that her mother was one of those people who made a conscious decision to be offended no matter what. Lainey couldn't help feeling that life would be a lot easier if fewer people got fired up about things in the way Deanna did. But maybe, she acknowledged, progress in some areas would be a lot slower.

She folded her paper and made her way back to the small office in the television building. It was a miniature version of her work area in Glasnevin, although as well as the computers it also had a monitor showing what was on TV and the time till her next broadcast, which was the main evening forecast after the news. She'd be telling people that the area of high pressure would last for another day but would sadly be replaced by a front bringing some grey skies and drizzle.

She glanced at herself in the mirror on the wall. She was wearing purple today, a shade that suited her colouring. She'd briefly considered dressing entirely in pink, but she didn't want to piss her mother off altogether, and besides, she wanted to appear as a strong, independent woman, which she didn't think she would if she was in head-to-toe pink. It was a pity, she thought, that one of her favourite colours seemed to have become inextricably linked with airheads everywhere.

She reached into her bag and pulled out the list of potential questions that Deanna had emailed to her earlier. She wanted to go through them again. There were questions on career, aspirations and marriage. She wondered whether her answers would mark her out as a determined woman, bubblegum airhead or sad singleton. Maybe she was a mixture of all three, although, she reminded herself, she wasn't exactly a sad singleton right now, even though Ken hadn't been to her apartment since her return from Stockholm. He'd texted a couple of times, saying that he was busy at work and equally busy training. He didn't have time to drop by but he was missing her, he said, and hoped she wasn't too lonely without him.

Actually, she was relieved he wasn't around. Since her stay with Carla she'd been trying to look at her relationship with Ken more critically. She'd accepted that she might appear needy and a bit pathetic to allow him back into her life. Or maybe not so much into her life as into her bed. They still hadn't actually gone out anywhere since he'd come back to her. Having listened to her friend, Lainey had been forced to think that maybe what Ken had missed most when they were apart was sex. At first it seemed odd to her that wanting to sleep with her would have driven him back into her arms, because Ken was an attractive man who would surely find someone new without too much trouble. Yet he'd always said that she was the best in the world between the sheets. She'd dismissed that as just talk, but maybe he'd actually meant it. In the last few days she'd weighed what seemed important to Ken and what seemed important to Lennart, and found Ken wanting. She hadn't been able to help herself comparing him unfavourably to the older man. But since Carla's phone call earlier, she was beginning to think again. Given what had happened, Carla's relationship advice could be taken with a large dose of salt. All that stuff about making lists and knowing what you wanted hadn't done her any good in the end, had it?

She looked at the clock. Deanna would be here any minute. She glanced at the first few questions and then pushed the papers to one side. There was no point in getting too analytical about it. She took out her make-up. It might be shallow in Deanna's book to look good, but it was important nonetheless. She wasn't going to appear on her mother's documentary looking anything but her best.

She'd just capped her strawberry lip gloss when there was

a tap on the door and her mother walked in. Deanna looked around her curiously.

'It's very small,' she said.

'We don't need a lot of room in here,' replied Lainey.

'I'm just worried that we won't have space to set things up . . . Jason?' She turned to the cameraman. 'What do you think?'

'No probs, Deanna,' he said. 'I'll set up over here, and you can sit at the desk there beside Lainey and ask her questions. I just need to be sure of sound . . . Give me a couple of minutes or so.'

'Fine.' Deanna perched on the edge of the desk, in front of Lainey's computer. 'Well then, what's the weather going to be like?'

Lainey told her about the clouds and the drizzle and Deanna looked glum.

'I'm missing the sun.'

'It isn't always sunny in California,' Lainey reminded her.

'True. I remember some terrible storms . . .' Deanna's voice trailed off as she recalled the storm the day that Lainey had been born, the rain lashing against the hospital windows while the wind howled around the building.

'And there's the fog,' said Lainey. 'From the ocean or in the valleys.'

'But it's the sun you think of most,' said Deanna.

That was true. When Lainey had stayed with Deanna, the days were gloriously sunny. Sitting on the beach watching the surfers, or going to the harbour to look at the sea otters and feeling the sun on her shoulders had been wonderful. She knew that Deanna had been annoyed with her for sloping off on her own so much, but she hadn't cared. She hadn't wanted to let Deanna think that spending time with her was important. Which, in the end, it hadn't been anyway.

Jason continued to set up his lights and cameras while Lainey scrolled through some computer screens. Deanna stood up, and as she did so, she knocked papers off Lainey's desk, including the list of questions. She apologised and picked them up, pausing as she looked at one of the sheets.

'What's this?' she asked.

Lainey looked at the paper and blushed. Bloody hell, she thought, I must have picked it up with the others by mistake. Deanna was holding her list of requirements for a boyfriend.

'Oh, something one of my friends was talking about,' she said.

'No "good sense of humour"?' asked Deanna drily.

'It's not . . . it doesn't . . .' Lainey was flustered.

'"Someone I can live with for the rest of my life"?'

Lainey had added that requirement after returning from Stockholm.

'Always aspirational,' she murmured.

'Please don't tell me you want all this,' said Deanna. 'And don't tell me you're rating that man I met at your apartment on the basis of it.'

Out of the corner of her eye, Lainey saw Jason, who was still fiddling with his camera, glance at them.

'Of course not,' she said. She reached out and took the paper from Deanna's hand. Then she crumpled it and threw it in the bin.

Deanna said nothing and began to flick through her notebook. Lainey tried to get over her embarrassment. Of all the people to see the list – a list she hadn't even wanted to make – the last person she would've wanted to look at it was Deanna. Her mother was no doubt thinking that she was pathetic. And she didn't really blame her; she'd always thought the list was a bloody stupid idea. She watched as Deanna drew her pen through something in the notebook. Maybe it's me she's crossing out, thought Lainey. Now that she's seen my list, she's decided I'm not worth having in her documentary.

'Are you nearly ready?' Deanna looked over at Jason.

'Any minute,' he replied.

She might be still going ahead with it, thought Lainey, so that she can put me into her sad loser category.

'Have you interviewed many people for this?' she asked as Deanna flicked through a sheaf of papers.

'Quite a few,' replied Deanna. 'You're the last.'

'I'm ready now,' said Jason. 'Lainey, I need you to put on the mic.'

'Right.' Lainey fastened the mic into position on her lapel.

'Do you want to start, Deanna?'

'Yes.' Deanna turned to Lainey. 'Of course this will be edited and moved around within the documentary. It won't come out as one long interview with you. We might only use a sentence, you know.'

'I see. Like a talking-heads thing?'

'Yes,' said Deanna. 'Are you comfortable with starting now?'

'Let's rock and roll.'

It was a completely different Deanna now that she was filming, Lainey realised, as her mother asked the first question – the rather vague query about what feminism had done for Lainey. She was crisper and sharper, but more professional too. Suddenly she wasn't her mother at all, but simply a woman doing her job. Lainey didn't feel as though the questions she was asking were direct barbs at her and her choices. It was more like Deanna was mining for information, truly trying to find out what Lainey thought. It was a strange and interesting experience and she couldn't help responding with more thought and enthusiasm than she realised she possessed. For the first time in her life she understood why her mother was so successful in what she did. (Although, she reminded herself, Deanna didn't usually interview people for film. Which just proved how multitalented she was too!)

'So when you look at older feminists now, do you just think of them as tired old grey-haired hags preaching a dead message?' asked Deanna.

'Sometimes,' admitted Lainey. 'It's probably the fact that they're so driven and they want all of us to be driven too. And that's a lot to live up to. Part of me thinks that now we have too many choices and it's not always possible to make the right one.'

'Women have always had to make choices,' said Deanna.

'But in the past some were made for them. Getting married and having kids was something you pretty much had to do. Now you decide to do it. Which is better, of course, I know that. It's just that we have to be so responsible ourselves for everything now . . . choosing the right career, the right man – all such important decisions. All our own to make.'

'But women are good at responsibility,' said Deanna.

'Umm . . . maybe too good.' Lainey had completely forgotten that they were being filmed now. She smiled suddenly at her mother. 'We're so responsible that we find it hard to let go. And hard not to blame ourselves if something goes wrong. Actually, if something goes wrong there's a feeling of letting down women everywhere, you know?'

'Absolutely,' said Deanna. Her eyes met Lainey's and both

women looked at each other with a flash of understanding before Deanna turned to Jason and told him that she thought they'd managed to get everything they needed and that they'd better wrap up now.

'Okey-doke,' said Jason. 'You looked lovely, by the way,' he told Lainey. 'You've got great camera appeal.'

'Thank you.'

'What time do you finish tonight?' asked Deanna.

'Ten,' Lainey replied.

'Probably too late to meet up again.'

'Do we need to?'

'I thought it would be nice to buy you dinner. Say thank you for your participation.'

'Thanks for the offer, but yes, it's a bit late to eat. Maybe another time?'

'OK, I'll give you a call,' Deanna told her. Then she put her notebook in her bag and followed Jason out of the room.

It was twenty past ten when Lainey finally got in the cab to go home. She arrived at her apartment block another twenty minutes later and didn't bother turning on the lights when she walked into the living room. She was feeling unexpectedly good about herself, and good about the interview with her mother. She'd anticipated being sandbagged by Deanna, but with every passing minute she'd felt herself grow more and more confident. It was as though Deanna's passion for women being positive and proud of themselves had transmitted itself to her, so that she didn't say things like she'd been lucky to get her job like she usually did, but instead emphasised that hard work and study had paid off. Nor had she felt, as she so often did when talking to her mother, that Deanna was being critical of her, or thinking that she could do better. Deanna had spoken to her as one professional person to another. Which had actually been quite exhilarating. By the time they'd finished, she'd felt even more convinced of her own abilities and more assured in herself. It was an extraordinary sensation.

She stood in the dark and enjoyed the self-satisfaction that was still enveloping her. I'm good at what I do, she told herself. I've done well in my career. I'm reaching my potential. And maybe that is due to people like my mother who fought hard for me to be taken seriously. Because they do. I know that. It's not all about my hair and my face. It's about what I say, too.

The rap on her door made her jump. She looked at her watch. There was probably only one person who would be looking for her now without having called in advance. And that would be Ken. The thing was . . . There was another rap at the door, more insistent this time. She stood immobile in the centre of the living room. Her phone, set to silent for the interview, began to vibrate. She went into the bedroom, closed the door softly behind her and answered it.

'Hi,' said Ken. 'Where are you?'

'Why?'

'I'm outside your apartment.'

'Are you?' She lowered her voice.

'Yeah. I thought I'd drop by.'

'Oh.'

'Where are you?' he repeated.

'I was doing the weather tonight.'

'I know. Saw you. You looked fantastic. I thought I'd come over, see you in the flesh.'

'I was delayed,' she said. 'I had to do some extra stuff afterwards.'

'I'll pop round the pub and wait for you.'

'No.'

'Huh?'

'I'm . . . I'm meeting friends.'

'You never meet friends after doing the telly.' Ken sounded surprised.

'I am tonight,' she lied.

'You mean I came all the way over here to see you and you're not coming home?' He sounded incredulous.

'Sorry,' she said. 'You should have called me first.'

'I shouldn't need to.'

'I do have a life besides you,' she told him.

'Hey, no need to get narky with me. I'm sorry if you're busy and it pisses you off.'

'Being busy hasn't pissed me off,' she said.

'Well you sure sound annoyed.'

'Maybe because you just assumed I'd be here . . . at home,' she said.

'You usually are.'

He was right about that.

'I'm sorry,' she said.

'So am I. Wasted bloody journey across town.'

'You should have called,' she repeated.

'I guess so.'

'Well, look, I've got to go.'

'All right. Maybe I'll come round tomorrow.'

'Text me before you leave.'

'I get the message,' said Ken tightly.

'That's all right then.' And she hung up.

* * *

She waited for nearly ten minutes before walking out of the bedroom again, her phone still in her hand. She'd never hung up first before. But then she'd never felt the sense of irritation she'd had talking to Ken before either. What made him think he could waltz over to her apartment any time he felt like it and expect her to welcome him with open arms? Didn't he realise she didn't spend her every waking moment wishing he was with her?

And then she realised that she did. Or at least, she had. At some level she'd always known that, of course. It was the way she was, after all. With Ken, as with all of her other boyfriends, she'd felt that every moment not with him was somehow lacking. She'd always been prepared to change her plans to suit any of them. Because she didn't like being on her own when she could be with them instead. But tonight . . . tonight she didn't want anyone else muscling in on her life, no matter how much she would have wanted it in the past. And she especially didn't want Ken coming to her apartment, making love to her and then rushing out again either later that night or early the next morning because he needed to be somewhere else in a hurry.

She rubbed the back of her neck. She knew that Ken cared for her. At the beginning of their relationship, especially, there had been moments between them of utter tenderness. When he'd said 'Love you, babes' she'd known he was speaking the truth. She'd believed him then and she wanted to believe that he still loved her now, because otherwise why would he have come back? And why would he keep on wanting to be with her and to sleep with her if he didn't love her?

She opened the doors to the balcony, wanting to stand in

the open air while she put her thoughts in order. She hoped that Ken actually had gone home and that he wasn't standing Romeo-like beneath her balcony waiting for her to return. Her heart jumped as she saw a solitary figure walking along the path towards the block opposite. Then she realised it was Shay Loughnane. She almost called out to him, but stopped herself. She didn't want to talk to any man tonight, not even Shay. Which was possibly just as well, as she realised that he was walking unsteadily. Maybe his latest girlfriend, the one with the football-playing children, had given him the push. Perhaps he'd been drowning his sorrows. Although he shouldn't have been, should he, because he'd told her he wasn't supposed to drink too much. But when you were miserable you often did things you weren't supposed to. She couldn't blame him for that.

She stayed standing in the shadow of her balcony until she saw the light come on in his apartment. Shay walked slowly across his living room, took off his leather jacket and threw it over the back of a chair. Then he shuffled towards the kitchen.

He's forgotten about closing the curtains, Lainey thought. Forgotten that we can see too much of each other's lives. Though he can't see me, because tonight I'm living my life in darkness! She went back into the apartment and made herself a cup of coffee. She still didn't bother to turn the lights on in her living room; the gentle glow from the kitchen light was enough. She sipped the coffee thinking that it didn't matter if it kept her awake, because the day after a couple of TV broadcasts was a rest day, so she didn't have to get up early in the morning. She could sit up all night drinking coffee and trying to deal with the fact that she was feeling very differently about her life right now. And that this seemed to be due to the interview with her mother. Which, from her point of view, was difficult to believe.

If I suddenly feel like this after talking with her professionally, she thought, warming her hands on the big mug, what would I have been like if I'd lived with her all my life? Would I have turned into a man-hating feminist bitch too? She paused in her thoughts. And what would have happened to Deanna if my father had been someone who'd stayed around? Would she have become a man-hating feminist bitch anyway? Or would her views on men be completely different? Although, Lainey said to herself, she's not really a bitch. She's just determined. Why is it that we see all determined women as bitches?

She drained her coffee and looked out of the patio windows again. And stared. Because Shay was standing in the middle of his living room, a juice carton in his hands, struggling to twist the cap. As she watched, the carton slipped from his grasp and he sank slowly to his knees. Then, to her horror, he toppled sideways on to the floor so that he was sprawled motionless across the pale mushroom carpet.

Chapter 25

Cumulus humilis: a small convective cloud formed after a rising thermal reaches condensation level

Lainey didn't hesitate. Even if Shay had simply passed out because he was drunk, she couldn't leave him like that. He had an underlying medical condition and he needed help. She picked up her mobile and called the emergency services; then – too impatient to wait for the lift – she ran down the four flights of stairs from her apartment and hurried across the garden to Shay's block.

She let herself in and ran up his stairs too. Breathless (and thinking to herself that deserting the gym hadn't been a good idea), she rapped on the door of his apartment. She didn't know if he'd manage to open it, but she was hoping that he might call out. There was no sound from within, so she rapped again a little harder. The blocks in Laurel Park were designed so that two apartments shared one landing. She half expected the door opposite to open and Shay's neighbour to emerge and ask what all the noise was about. But either there was nobody in, or they didn't care about crazy people banging on doors late at night.

She heard the distant sound of the ambulance siren and was relieved at their speedy response, although part of her worried that they might be annoyed at her for calling them, especially if it turned out that Shay was simply in a drunken stupor. But she couldn't have left him there, she just couldn't. She hit the button on the lift, which was already at the fourth floor. It seemed to descend far more slowly than her frenzied running, but she told herself she was imagining that.

When she reached ground level, she ran to the gates to open them for the ambulance. She told herself that it might have been more sensible to wait in her own apartment, where she could simply have observed Shay and then buzzed the ambulance driver into the complex. But it felt better to be actually doing something, even if it had turned out to be pretty futile.

'He's not answering his phone or his door,' she told the paramedic breathlessly as she keyed in the code to open the door to the block, thinking it was fortunate that she was good with numbers and had remembered it from the night he'd invited her up to his apartment for a glass of wine. 'I know I might be creating a big fuss over nothing, but . . .'

'Better safe than sorry,' the paramedic replied as he and his colleague followed her into the building.

As soon as they were outside Shay's front door, Lainey banged on it a number of times, calling out his name, but there was still no answer.

'Let me.' The first paramedic, in a convincing impression of Sylvester Stallone or Arnie Schwarzenegger in their prime, kicked the door, which flew open.

Lainey had a fleeting moment of thinking that the doors to the apartments were far too flimsy and worrying that she could easily be burgled by someone with the paramedic's physique, before following them anxiously into the room.

Shay had moved. He'd dragged himself into a seated position, his back supported by the sofa. His eyes were glazed and there were beads of perspiration on his forehead.

The paramedic knelt in front of him and immediately reached for the juice carton, which he opened quickly.

'Come on, mate,' he said. 'Drink it.'

The other paramedic was preparing to give him glucose. Shay was shaking and he looked confused.

'What's his name?' the first paramedic, whose name was Joe, asked Lainey.

She told him.

'Come on, Shay,' he said. 'Your blood sugar is way too low, buddy. We've got to get it up. You know that, don't you?'

Shay nodded feebly.

'Good man.'

Lainey watched anxiously. She knew nothing about Shay's illness other than that not taking medication or eating the wrong sorts of foods could cause problems. But Shay seemed to be otherwise healthy, and he'd said that he kept his diabetes under control. So what on earth had caused him to have an episode like this? She watched as the paramedics worked with him, hoping that he'd be all right. She knew that it was important that he didn't slip into a coma.

'Will you check the bathroom?' Joe asked her. 'See what medication is there?'

'Sure.'

Shay's bathroom was very male – black and white and with none of the fruit- and blossom-scented gels and shampoos that she used herself. No fluffy coloured towels either – the ones on the rail were slate grey with black detailing around the edges. His bathroom cabinet was neat and tidy (surprisingly so for a man, she thought, remembering the mess that was Ken's); as well as toothpaste, shaving gel and foam, it contained two packets of ibuprofen, a throat spray and a packet of Durex. She blushed as she saw the condoms, suddenly thinking of the women he brought back here, and wondering if he replaced the contraceptives weekly, because a single packet surely wasn't enough to keep him going. She didn't see any other medicines there.

She went into his bedroom feeling voyeuristic and slightly embarrassed, noticing that this room, too, was essentially male – the duvet cover on the bed was a plain dark green, matched by the pillowcases. The furniture was a stylised black brushed steel and the walls were painted (like her own) in neutral shades. But on the low table beside the bed was a collection of photographs in plain frames. The photographs were of two children, fair-haired boys with impish grins and happy faces. Lainey recognised them as the boys who'd been in his apartment before.

There was also a packet of pills beside the bed. She picked them up and brought them in to the paramedics.

'Other than ibuprofen, this was all I found,' she said as she handed the packet to them.

Joe studied it.

'Will he be OK?' asked Lainey fearfully.

As she spoke, Shay focused his eyes on her.

'Lainey,' he said, his voice slurred. 'How lovely. What are you doing here?'

'You went into shock,' Joe told him before Lainey could say anything. 'We're bringing you to hospital.'

'I'm fine.' This time Shay's voice was stronger and he tried to sit up straighter.

'You will be,' agreed Joe. 'Come on, mate, let's get you on to the stretcher.'

'Do you still need to bring him to hospital?' asked Lainey. 'Given that he woke up?'

'Yes, we do.'

'Will I come too?'

'If you want.'

'OK.'

She followed them out of the apartment and pulled the door closed behind her (it didn't lock properly, but she hoped it would be all right). Once outside, she climbed into the ambulance. She watched anxiously as they hooked Shay up to an array of monitors. He groaned and opened his eyes again.

'Shay?' said the other paramedic. 'How're you doing now, pal?'

'I feel like shit.'

'You'll be grand.' The paramedic looked at a readout from one of the machines. 'They'll check you over when we get you to the hospital.'

Lainey looked at Shay and then took his hand.

'You'll be fine,' she said. 'I know you will.'

But Shay had closed his eyes again and didn't say anything.

She hadn't been in an Accident & Emergency department since the time she'd broken her leg. She couldn't remember much about that time, but she was sure that it had never been as crowded and dismal as it was now. The waiting area was full of people sitting listlessly in seats; one man had a cut over his eye, another broke into spasms of coughing so intense that Lainey was sure he would choke in front of her. Others had less obvious complaints, but all of them looked tired and dispirited and Lainey wondered how long they'd been waiting.

Shay had been admitted immediately, but Lainey wasn't sure what they were doing to him or how long it would take. She had a vague feeling that once he got the sugar he needed he could recover quite quickly, but she couldn't be certain about that. Besides, he'd been practically comatose, and that, she knew, could be very serious. They might need to observe him for a while. She wasn't sure if anyone would keep her up to date on his progress. But she couldn't go home until she found out if he was all right. So she joined the ranks of people sitting on the uncomfortable seats and waited.

The coffee she'd drunk earlier kept her alert for a while, but sitting around aimlessly was inexplicably tiring. From time to time she shivered, although she knew this was from worry about Shay, not because it was cold. Nevertheless she rubbed her hands together and got up every so often to walk around the waiting area. There was a small TV on one wall that was tuned into Sky News and so repeated the same stories over and over again until she could have given the reports herself. She perked up each time the presenter did the weather forecast (she had a professional interest in that, after all), but otherwise she was bored with the blanket coverage of the latest celebrity to admit to a 'drugs shame'.

After a while she went to the receptionist, who told her that Shay was still being treated but that she didn't know when he'd be released.

'Go home,' she advised Lainey. 'It could be a while before he can leave. There's no point in you staying here.'

. . . and clogging up the reception area, Lainey added to herself. There were a lot of people in the relatively small space and she knew she was in the way. But she felt bad about leaving without him. She gave the receptionist her name and number and asked them to call her when Shay was ready to go himself. She wasn't entirely sure they would. There was a system, she knew, and ringing neighbours with news of patients probably wasn't part of it.

She got a taxi back to Laurel Park. Before going to her own block she let herself into Shay's again. The door of his apartment was as they'd left it, closed over but not shut tight. She opened it and peeped inside. Nothing had been disturbed, but she was concerned at the fact that there was both a laptop and an iPad on the living room table. They'd be easy pickings for a burglar, she thought, while at the same time telling herself that as nobody had reacted to the commotion caused by the arrival of the paramedics, nobody would realise that the apartment was unlocked and unoccupied. Nevertheless, she decided to take both laptop and iPad with her. Shay might have personal information on either of them and she didn't want to leave them lying around. She switched off the light, which she hadn't thought of doing earlier, and pulled the door to again. She didn't know how to secure it properly, but she hoped that at a casual glance it looked as though it was shut.

She was suddenly very tired. She walked out of Shay's block and back to her own. She went into her bedroom and began to wipe her face with a cleansing tissue. It's a good thing, she told herself for the hundredth time, that she didn't let Ken into the apartment. Because if she had, she wouldn't have noticed Shay until much later. If at all.

She realised that she was shaking and she knew that this was just reaction setting in. While she'd been sitting at the hospital she'd kept wondering what would have happened if she hadn't seen Shay collapse. If, instead, she'd been in her own bedroom making love to Ken. Would Shay's condition have deteriorated rapidly? Would it have been critical? She shivered. She hoped he would have managed without her. But she was glad she'd been able to help.

There were advantages to living in close proximity to people, she told herself as she finally got into bed. Even if they sometimes saw more than you wanted them to. Even if you sometimes saw more than you wanted yourself.

Chapter 26

Refraction: the bending of light as it passes through areas of different density

Although she was utterly exhausted, it took her an age to fall asleep, and she snapped awake again at eight. She got out of bed and looked across to Shay's apartment. The curtains were still open and the juice carton was on the coffee table where Joe, the paramedic, had put it. It looked as though Shay hadn't yet come home. She checked her phone, but nobody from the hospital had called. She wasn't entirely surprised at that; the emergency department had been chaotically busy and she was sure they were spending time treating patients rather than phoning anxious neighbours, but she was worried about him. Of course, she thought, he might have contacted a family member from the hospital and gone home with them instead. He might not have wanted to be alone.

By the time she'd had a shower, washed her hair and got dressed, there was still no sign of him. She was concerned about the fact that his apartment door was unlocked. She knew this worry had been bred into her by Madeleine, who was always very strict about securing her home and not, as she put it, making things easy for prospective burglars. Lainey wondered if she was being unnecessarily anxious. After all, the complex itself was relatively secure. Nevertheless, there had been break-ins in the past. She'd check it out, she decided, and bring the laptop and iPad with her in case the door could be locked. If it couldn't, she'd hang on to them until Shay returned.

The apartment door was slightly ajar. She knocked tentatively, in case Shay had come back after all, but there was no reply, so she pushed it gently and peered inside. She called out an uncertain 'hello' and was met by silence. She walked over the threshold, still half expecting to see someone despite being subliminally aware that the apartment was empty.

She looked around. Nothing had been disturbed. Nobody had made off with the TV or the speaker system or Shay's Xbox and PlayStation. Boys and their toys, she thought as she placed the laptop and iPad on his table. This is such a bachelor pad! Ken's house had been too, she remembered, until she'd started to leave her bits and pieces around. And until she'd cracked one day and tidied up. It had been an absolute tip thanks to the weights, training equipment and mucky clothes scattered around, as well as PlayStation games and a vast selection of DVDs. In Ken's case there was also his top-of-the-range bike and all the equipment that went with that too. He hadn't been as grateful as she'd expected for her efforts, though. He'd demanded to know what she'd done with all his stuff and had been less than enthusiastic when she'd told him that it was just as easy to put things away as leave them in a heap on the floor. Although after she'd found some old training manuals he'd been looking for for ages, he'd conceded she might have a point.

Shay's apartment wasn't messy at all, just overloaded with technology. She'd meant to ask Ken if he'd ever been treated by her neighbour. But she'd forgotten.

'What on earth are you doing here?' Shay's voice startled her and she whirled around.

'I'm just . . . I came to . . . Are you all right?'

'I'm fine.'

'You weren't last night,' she pointed out.

'No. Of course. I'm sorry.' He ran his fingers through his hair, which was already standing spikily on end. 'Sorry if I gave you a fright, too. I'm a bit jumpy right now.'

'That's OK.'

'I should be thanking you, not snapping at you. They told me at the hospital that a neighbour had called the ambulance. I forgot it was you. It's all a bit blurry.'

'I'm not surprised.' She looked at him, a crease of concern in her forehead. 'You're sure you're all right?'

'Absolutely.'

'Good. Well, look, I just came to check on your place because of the state of the door and to bring back your computer and iPad. I didn't want to leave them lying around in case they were nicked.'

'That was thoughtful of you. Thanks.'

'Now that you're here, I'll go. Let you rest.'

'I won't be resting much,' he said ruefully. 'I'll be getting a locksmith. Or a carpenter. Or maybe both.'

'A bashed door isn't the worst that could have happened,' she said.

'No indeed. Thanks again, Lainey.'

'You're welcome.'

He was still standing in the middle of the room rubbing

his head when she left. She just hoped that he really was OK.

Madeleine was watching TV when she arrived later that afternoon as she'd promised.

'I know it's desperate to be looking at it during the day,' she confessed, 'but I just love that Judge Judy woman. So much straight talking, and she takes no nonsense.'

'You're entitled to watch what you like when you like,' said Lainey. 'Besides, Judge Judy is great. Sit down again and I'll make you a cup of tea.'

'That'd be lovely,' said Madeleine. 'No cupcakes today.'

'I don't just come for the cupcakes.' Lainey gave her a kiss. 'I like your company too. Also, I brought this back for you from Stockholm.' She took the small painting out of her bag and handed it to her grandmother, who looked at it with pleasure.

'Thank you,' said Madeleine. 'It's lovely.'

Lainey took Deanna's paperweight out of her bag too and left it on the table.

'Where is she?' she asked her grandmother.

'Meeting with that Feargal Wright man.'

'Again!'

'Yes. Something to do with his programme.'

'He invited her to his party, and they met up before now . . .' Lainey chuckled. 'Maybe he fancies her.'

Madeleine looked thoughtful. 'Well, that'd be a turn-up, wouldn't it?'

'Yes. Though more likely he's trying to worm information out of her. He's very taken by her being my mother as well as a feminist icon.'

'Hmm. She told me all about you meeting at his garden party.'

'Nightmare.' Lainey shuddered.

'Don't exaggerate. She also said that you did a good interview yesterday.'

'Did she?'

'Yes, she did. She was very impressed.'

'Well, I was impressed with her too,' Lainey conceded. She told her grandmother how she'd felt afterwards. 'I guess empowered is a good word for it.'

'That's Deanna's skill,' said Madeleine.

Lainey nodded. Then she related the events of the previous night.

'You did the right thing,' said Madeleine.

'I would've liked to stay at the hospital until they discharged him, but given that he only got home this morning, there was no real point in my hanging around.'

'No,' Madeleine agreed. 'You'd only have been in the way. I watch those programmes where they have cameras in hospital A&E departments. I don't know how they keep up sometimes.'

'The paramedics were great, too.'

'Front-line medical staff usually are,' Madeleine said. 'The poor man, though. Is he the one you brought to the garden party?' She had to call out the question because Lainey had gone into the kitchen to make the tea. She repeated it when her granddaughter returned with a tray and cups.

'Yes.'

'Deanna said he was very attractive.'

'She noticed?'

'So . . .'

'So nothing, Gran. I asked him to Feargal Wright's on the spur of the moment. He's got a girlfriend. Actually, he has plenty of them. You don't have to worry, I'm not going to ask him to marry me because I feel sorry for him.'

She went back into the kitchen, made the tea and came back with the pot and some dainty macarons she'd found in a tin.

'You don't think you could secretly be in love with him and he might whisk you away?' asked Madeleine wickedly. 'Like in those romantic novels you like so much?'

'Don't be silly.' Lainey poured the tea. 'He's not that sort of man. He's more of a friend than anything.'

Madeleine looked surprised. 'You don't have friends who are men.'

'Give me a break.' She handed the cup to her grandmother. 'What about the guys in Met Eireann, they're my friends. Anyway, good news, Ken and I are back together.'

'Oh.'

'So I'm all fixed up in the boyfriend department.'

Although even as she said the words, she remembered how irritated she'd been with Ken when he'd phoned her from outside her door. She'd felt taken for granted. As though she was supposed to be there for him whenever he wanted. Which, she had to admit to herself, was how things had been with every one of her boyfriends before. Not only had she always been there when they wanted; she'd been there when they didn't want her to be too! It was no wonder, she realised suddenly, that they got annoyed with her when she phoned every day or turned up outside their offices unexpectedly, saying that she missed them. They obviously felt as she'd done – irritated that she wanted to take over every part of their lives.

Oh my God, she thought. No wonder I'm so bad at relationships. I've been getting things wrong from the very start. I've been an absolute fool.

'You all right, honey?' Madeleine had been watching the changing expressions on her granddaughter's face.

'Just thinking,' said Lainey. 'Just figuring something out.'

'Figure away,' said Madeleine easily and settled back in her chair.

Deanna and Feargal Wright met in Davy Byrne's pub off Grafton Street. When Feargal said that the city centre would be a convenient place for them to meet, Deanna had suggested the pub where, over thirty years ago, she'd made her decision to leave Ireland and to leave Lainey.

She hadn't been there since then, and it seemed to her that it hadn't changed very much at all. She knew it was a landmark pub (of course, half the pubs in Ireland were landmarks of some description, and any time you asked an Irish person for directions, they'd always include a pub as a navigational aid), but even so she felt herself being pulled back through the years as she waited for Feargal to arrive. She remembered sitting on one of the seats just inside the door, sipping her Bacardi and Coke, her plane ticket in front of her. She'd been nervous but quietly excited. She hadn't felt one bit selfish about what she was doing. She'd told herself (and she knew she was right) that she had no other choice.

There was a glass of sparkling water in front of her today. She didn't drink spirits any more, and even her consumption of beer and wine was fairly limited. She didn't like the out-of-control feeling that came with alcohol. She liked to know she was on top of things at all times. If anyone is ever truly on top of things, she thought, while nevertheless congratulating herself that she usually was.

Feargal pushed the door open and saw her immediately. He sat down opposite her, the marble-topped table between them.

'Nice to see you, Deanna,' he said.

'You too. Why did you want to meet?' Deanna didn't believe in faffing about with pleasantries.

'Down to business, huh?'

'Why not?'

Feargal beckoned to the barman and ordered a glass of Guinness.

'This wasn't really a business thing,' he said casually to Deanna. 'I wanted to have a chat with you. We won't get to chat on live TV.'

Deanna looked at him in puzzlement.

'I don't see why we need to chat.'

'We don't,' said Feargal. 'I just wanted to anyway.'

'So this is nothing to do with the TV show?'

'Nope.' He shook his head.

'I'm confused.'

'The show is about your work, we've said that before. But I wanted to know you, Deanna Ryan the person.'

'Flattering though that might be, I don't see the point. I'm not appearing on your touchy-feely confessional programme, so you don't need to know me.'

'I told you. You're interesting.'

She looked at him through narrowed eyes.

'What's this really about?' she asked abruptly. 'Are you trying to soften me up so's I blab about my past anyway and give you something that you can drag into the interview later?'

'Is there something worth blabbing about? Something you're afraid of giving away?'

'Of course not,' she said.

'Oh, look.' He shrugged. 'I'm intrigued, that's all. And, being honest, I want to know all about you and Lainey.'

'There's nothing to know.'

'You left her while you went to work abroad,' said Feargal. 'That must have been a very difficult decision to make.'

'Funnily enough, I was just thinking about that,' Deanna said. 'And telling myself that it was an excellent decision.'

'Still doesn't make it easy.'

'Still doesn't make it any of your goddam business.'

'Tell me about your life in the States, then,' said Feargal. 'You live in California, don't you? Or do you spend more time in New York these days?'

Deanna drank some of her water. 'These days I have an apartment in Manhattan and a house in Monterey. Manhattan is for business. Monterey is home.'

'Is there anyone waiting at home for you?' asked Feargal.

'Why do you want to know?' she asked.

'Curious.'

'I'm an independent person,' she said. 'I don't need anyone waiting for me.'

'Nobody special?'

'I don't need anyone special.'

'Was Lainey's father special?'

'I was very young at the time. Young girls think all men are special. It takes us a while to realise that none of them are.'

'So . . . you don't do men?'

Deanna laughed. 'Contrary to what you might think, I do, in fact, have male friends, but regrettably they always like to think they're more important than they actually are. It's a constant source of amusement to me that men seem to think that having a penis is an actual achievement in itself.'

He grinned. 'D'you really think a world driven by women would be any better?'

'Oh, absolutely,' she said. 'But that doesn't mean I don't think men have their uses.'

'What?'

'Well, sex for one thing,' she replied. 'It's much better with a man.'

He paused, the glass of Guinness that the barman had brought over a moment earlier halfway to his lips. 'You've tried both?'

'What d'you think?'

'You know, with you I just don't know what to think,' said Feargal.

'Excellent,' she told him. 'That's how I like it.' She looked at him thoughtfully for a moment. 'Just for a change,' she said, 'let's do things the other way round. Tell me about yourself.'

'I don't talk about myself that much,' said Feargal.

'Humour me,' said Deanna. 'Do you live in that huge house all by yourself?'

Feargal explained about his split from Sadie.

'She left me,' he told Deanna. 'Everyone thinks that I left her, but she was the one to walk away. She said she wanted to get married one day, but that with me she'd always be the appendage on my arm and that's not what a partnership should be.'

'Did you want to marry her?' asked Deanna.

'It had never been top of my agenda,' Feargal admitted. 'But when she said she was leaving . . . I asked her then and she said no.'

'I don't see you as the marrying type,' Deanna observed.

'Neither did I,' Feargal told her. 'But to tell you the truth – and I know you'll laugh at me – I don't want to spend the rest of my life alone either. I don't know anyone who really does.'

He wondered later that night what it would be like to live with someone like Deanna Ryan. A nightmare probably. She was too opinionated and too self-confident and too unlikely ever to put his career and his concerns ahead of hers. Ultimately, of course, Sadie hadn't wanted to do that either. But all of the time she'd lived with him, she had deferred to whatever he wanted, so that in the end he'd taken her for granted. Feargal didn't think any man would ever be able to take Deanna for granted. She wouldn't let him. It would be a constant battle of wills. Not peaceful and relaxing. Anything but. It would be permanently challenging.

Feargal smiled to himself. He liked a challenge. In fact, he liked Deanna. Far more than he'd expected. Which surprised him very much indeed.

Chapter 27

Radiatus: a layer of cloud extending in long lines towards the horizon

Lainey was still at the house when Deanna arrived back four hours later. Feargal had insisted on bringing her for something to eat, and because she was hungry, but also because she was unexpectedly enjoying his company, Deanna had agreed. They'd gone to Captain America's for burger and chips. Feargal had been taken aback, saying that he was happy to bring her somewhere a little more upmarket, but Deanna said that she'd always liked Cap's, which was buzzy and vibrant and had been an occasional haunt of hers when she was a teenager. Afterwards Feargal had offered to drive her back to Killester, but she pointed out that she could get a cab at the top of the street and be home in fifteen minutes. And that Killester was on the opposite side of town to him. She thanked him for the meal (she'd allowed him to pay the bill) and told him she'd see him soon. Then she'd hopped into the taxi and come home, smiling each time she recalled the verbal spats that had been a feature of the time they'd spent together.

She was surprised to see her daughter sprawled on the sofa while Madeleine sat in the armchair, both of them watching an ancient episode of *Miss Marple* on Alibi.

'We meet again,' she said to Lainey, who hushed her because, she said, all was about to be revealed.

'I can't believe you're—'

'Shut up, Deanna,' said Madeleine. 'We want to know whodunnit.'

'I can tell you that,' said Deanna.

'Don't you dare!' Lainey shot her a daggered look. 'Hah!' she exclaimed as Miss Marple revealed the culprit. 'You were right, Gran. It was the owner of the house after all.'

'I guessed as much,' said Madeleine triumphantly.

'Oh for heaven's sake,' Deanna exclaimed. 'You read all those books when I was small.'

'Your father was the Christie fan, not me,' Madeleine reminded her. 'I had to work it out myself.'

Deanna said nothing as she sat down in the armchair opposite. She put a small square box on the table beside her.

'Cupcakes.'

Madeleine looked surprised.

'I know you both like them,' said Deanna, 'even though they're not really my thing.'

Lainey gave a snort of laughter.

'What?' asked Deanna.

'Gran told me you finished them off yesterday. That's why we're on macarons today.'

'One.' Deanna's tone was injured. 'In all the time I've been here, one.'

Madeleine raised an eyebrow.

'Maybe two,' conceded Deanna, which made Lainey smile.

'I appreciate them, thank you,' said Madeleine. 'So where have you been all day?'

'Out.'

'You sound just like a teenager. Are you going to tell me where, or do I have to drag it out of you?'

Lainey couldn't help laughing at her mother's face as Madeleine spoke.

'I told you I was meeting with Feargal Wright,' said Deanna.

'All day?'

'We had a lot to discuss.'

'I thought you'd have covered it all by now,' Lainey remarked. 'What was the topic of conversation this time? Was he trying to extract more information on your life in the States? Did he want to find out if you had any more unknown children lurking in the background?'

'Actually, yes,' said Deanna. 'But then he realised I wasn't going to play ball, and so he bought me dinner and told me about his sad love life instead.'

'Deanna!' Lainey looked at her in mock astonishment. 'You let a man . . .'

'. . . pay for me, yes, of course, why not?'

'Surely it's against all your principles?'

'Sometimes when I go out with my friends we split the bill. Sometimes I treat them. Sometimes they treat me. No difference.'

'I think there is, dear,' said Madeleine.

'Not as far as I'm concerned. The whole thing is not to treat men differently. And I didn't. If he'd been a woman producer who'd offered to meet me and buy me dinner, I'd have allowed her to pay. Besides,' she added, 'we only went to Captain America's, so it wasn't exactly going to stretch him to his financial limit.'

'I still think it's . . . interesting,' said Lainey. 'And what's the story on his love life? Is he on the hunt again after dumping Sadie-in-Waiting?'

'You've got the dynamics of that break all wrong,' Deanna told her.

Lainey looked at her sceptically. 'Don't tell me he fed you a "poor me" line. You're the last person I'd expect to fall for that.'

'I've far more sense than that!'

'Do you fancy him?' asked Lainey with amusement. 'Wouldn't it be a turn-up if you found a boyfriend in Ireland!' Her eyes sparkled. 'My hairdresser said he's supposed to be seeing someone. Is it you?'

'Don't be so silly.'

'I don't think it's silly.'

'Hmm. Well I don't have time for finding boyfriends, as you put it. I'll be far too busy working with the editing team on the documentary for the next few days. I think it's going to be great.'

'So when are you planning to head back to the States?' asked Madeleine.

'Soon,' Deanna said. 'Don't worry, Mom, you won't have to put up with me for much longer.'

'I'm not putting up with you,' said Madeleine. 'I'm enjoying your company.'

Deanna looked startled. 'I thought I was messing up your home.'

'You're getting better at tidying up. And it's nice to have someone else around.'

'Are you all right on your own, Gran?' Lainey sounded concerned. 'Are you too lonely?'

'Not too lonely,' Madeleine said. 'But sometimes it's good to have a real person to talk to.'

'As opposed to Dad,' said Deanna.

'Your dad is very wise and offers me excellent advice.' Madeleine's tone was relaxed. 'He told me to stop nagging you about your papers, Deanna.'

'Oh, Mom . . .'

'And he was right, because when I stopped asking you to tidy, you started doing it. But that's always been your way. I should've known from the start.'

Lainey chuckled and they both looked at her.

'It's fun to hear you sparring like this,' she said. 'It's as though you're actually family.'

'Of course we are,' said Deanna.

'But you never behaved this way before. Like you belong.'

Deanna looked at her impatiently. 'Don't try to psychoanalyse me,' she warned. 'I've got a much greater knowledge of that than you ever will.'

'I know, I know!' cried Lainey in sudden frustration. 'You're my brilliant, intellectual mother, and no matter what, I'll never be good enough for you.' She stood up. 'I'd better go, Gran. It was lovely seeing you. I'll call round again soon.'

'Oh, for heaven's sake, Lainey.' Deanna was irritated. 'There's no need to head off in a huff.'

'I'm not in a huff.'

'What about our dinner?' asked Deanna. 'We have to arrange that before I go.'

'Let me know what suits you,' said Lainey. She picked up her bag and slung it over her shoulder. 'Oh, by the way,' she said, 'I brought this back for you from Sweden.' She handed the paperweight, wrapped in delicate white paper, to her mother.

'I . . . Thank you.' Deanna unwrapped it and ran her fingers over the smooth glass. 'Thank you very much.'

'Take some cupcakes with you,' said Madeleine.

'It's OK,' said Lainey. 'They're not the same as home-made.'

'Take some,' ordered Madeleine.

Lainey hesitated, then took a couple from the box. She went into the kitchen and came back with a paper bag into which she put them carefully.

'Thanks,' she said.

'You're welcome,' said Deanna.

'I was really saying thanks to Gran, but thank you too.'

Then she kissed Madeleine on the cheek and left the house.

'She's as moody as be-damned!' exclaimed Deanna when they heard the front door slam shut.

'Like mother, like daughter.'

'Oh, don't you start.'

'She's bound to have inherited some of your characteristics,' said Madeleine.

'I'm not bloody moody.' Deanna shook her head and Madeleine chortled.

'Of course you are,' she said. 'You were the moodiest kid on the block because you took everything so seriously.'

'I did not!' Then Deanna's shoulders slumped and she looked remorsefully at Madeleine. 'You're right. I did. Was I a pain to live with?'

'Not enough of a pain that we ever wanted you to leave.'

'I had to,' said Deanna.

'I know. And I know you have a great life over there in the States. But, sweetheart, it's nice to have had you home.'

'Don't get all maudlin on me.'

'I'm being factual, not maudlin.' Madeleine stood up and stacked the empty cups on the tray. She lifted it from the table, but Deanna stood up too and took it from her.

'I'll do that,' she said. 'You shouldn't be carrying things.'

'I have to when I'm on my own,' said Madeleine. 'And I can. I'm not a helpless old dear, you know.'

Deanna grinned suddenly. 'I never thought you were.'

'Darling, you thought I was a helpless old dear before I was forty,' said Madeleine. 'As far as you were concerned I was a sad, oppressed woman who knew nothing about anything.'

'You're right,' Deanna admitted. 'Yet when I left, you were younger than I am now. But,' she added with a touch of determination, 'you were less questioning than me. More set in your ways.'

'And you're not now?' asked Madeleine. 'Set in your ways of having to be a certain type of person? Of always showing your hard side?'

'I don't have a soft side,' said Deanna.

Madeleine looked at her appraisingly. Deanna turned away and took the tray into the kitchen. She put the cups into the dishwasher and switched it on. She'd never had a soft side, she thought to herself. She was too strong for a soft side. Madeleine might think she knew her, but she didn't. Not really. No one did. Or ever would.

The following morning Lainey embraced her inner domestic goddess and cleaned the apartment again. Although she didn't mind a bit of untidiness, she liked knowing that surfaces were clean and dust-free, something she hoped was simply hygienically-minded of her but which she secretly conceded might be a little obsessive. She couldn't help feeling that this was something else Deanna might not approve of; after all, her mother hadn't fought for women's rights to have them chained to a bottle of Domestos, but cleaning was strangely therapeutic.

She was listening to Mariah Carey while she worked and almost didn't hear the knock on her door over Mimi's highest notes. She turned down the music and hesitated. If Ken had arrived again and managed to get into the complex without calling her first, she'd be really annoyed with him. Surely it wasn't too much to ask to give her advance warning of his visits? Besides, she didn't want to meet him while she was hot and sweaty from scrubbing the bath. But she couldn't pretend she wasn't in this time. He would have heard the music. She looked through the spyhole of the door. Shay Loughnane was standing outside.

'Hi,' she said as she opened it.

'Hello.' He handed her the enormous bouquet he was carrying. 'These are for you.'

'Oh, thank you. They're lovely.'

'It's me who should be thanking you.'

'D'you want to come in?' She stood back to let him enter. 'I was just doing a bit of a tidy-up,' she explained as she saw him notice the bottle of bleach sitting on the table.

'Sorry if I'm interrupting you.'

'Not at all.' She went into the kitchen, filled the sink with water and put the flowers in it. The bouquet was too big to simply thrust into the vase that had previously contained Ken's wilted roses. 'Can I get you a tea or coffee?' she asked.

'Coffee would be lovely, thanks,' he told her.

She filled the kettle and took the cupcakes from the bag on the worktop. They weren't going to be half as good as her gran's, she thought, but they looked pretty with their swirl of creamy icing and glacé fruit on top. When the kettle boiled, she made the coffee and brought it and the cupcakes into the living room, where Shay was sitting on her sofa looking out through the open patio doors to his own apartment.

'Thank you,' he said as she put a mug and a cupcake in front of him. 'You didn't have to go to any trouble. You've done enough already.'

'No trouble. I can't vouch for the cupcakes, I'm not sure where they were bought. Usually I eat home-made.'

'Wow.' He looked surprised. 'You're a baker, too! Is there no end to your talents?'

She explained that it was her grandmother who normally looked after her sweet tooth. 'My domesticity extends to cleaning and supermarket ready-meals,' she said.

'I can't say I'm much better,' confessed Shay. 'Though I was traditionally good at spag bol in my younger days.'

'Weren't we all.'

'Anyway,' he said, 'I just wanted to say that I appreciate everything you did for me. I was a bit rude and distracted yesterday and I don't want you to think that I was ungrateful for your help. You saved my life.'

'I'm sure you would've been fine,' she said. 'I was afraid I'd overreacted.'

'No I wouldn't.' He looked sheepish. 'I was beyond

stupid. I hadn't checked my sugar levels, I hadn't eaten and I'd had a few drinks. That's not something I should do. I usually manage my condition really well so that it's never a problem.'

'Why not this time?' she asked.

He replaced the mug on the purple beaded coaster on her table.

'I was stressed,' he said. He said the word with a touch of embarrassed defiance.

'Oh.' From her observations, Shay's life seemed remarkably stress-free. It was all about dating women, playing with his electronic gadgets and loafing around. And as far as his work was concerned, she couldn't see how his post in a sports injury clinic could lead to high levels of pressure. But then again, what did she know? People didn't think that forecasting the weather could be pressurised either, but not so long ago the coldest winter in years had arrived, bringing unheard-of amounts of snow and sleet and almost paralysing the country. The pressure had been on then to accurately predict when and where the snow would fall and how long it might be before a thaw set in, because local authorities had to know how much grit and salt they might need for the roads before their attention would have to switch to the inevitable burst pipes that would occur when the thaw set in. And the media had been on to the office every hour looking for updates and trying to get them to be more specific about how much snow to expect and how far the temperatures might plunge. Lainey knew that everyone wanted accurate information, but the sort of detail they were being asked for was almost impossible to provide. The meteorologists had become more tense and irritable by the hour as they tried to ensure that their forecasts were accurate without turning themselves into hostages to fortune.

Stress was relative, she reminded herself. Perhaps in Shay's job it was accurately deciding whether someone had a strain or a break that caused them to feel the pressure.

'It's my kids,' he said abruptly.

She looked at him, startled.

'Joel and Aaron,' he told her.

She recalled the photo of the fair-haired boys beside Shay's bed, the same boys who'd been playing football on the grass.

'Great kids. Wonderful kids. They're my life. They're my ex-wife's life too, of course.' His tone was flat. 'I understand that. She's a good mother.'

'But?'

'But she's met someone else.'

'And you don't approve of him?' A tricky situation, Lainey thought. It wasn't up to Shay to have an opinion on his wife's new partner.

'It's not that,' he said. 'It's that he's French.'

Lainey was startled. What was wrong with the French? She liked France. She'd spent a number of holidays there. Admittedly, like the rest of the Irish nation, she'd gone ballistic the year Thierry Henry had handled the football and ended up scoring a goal in a vital World Cup qualifying match that destroyed Ireland's hopes of reaching the finals, but although she'd given up her breakfast croissant for a week in protest, she'd got over that.

'And he wants her to move to Paris with him.'

'Oh.'

'Which would mean moving the kids.'

'I see.'

'Which I absolutely refuse to allow to happen.'

There was a hint of steel that she'd never heard before in Shay's voice.

'They're my kids too,' he said. 'Whatever happened in our marriage, the boys need two parents. And I'm a good dad, I know I am.'

'I'm sure you are,' said Lainey.

He looked at her warily. 'You think?'

'Yes.'

'Women don't generally,' he said. 'They don't think that fathers care about their children as much as mothers do. They don't think that our hearts are broken when we're the ones who have to leave. And usually we are. No matter what's happened, the wife hangs on to the family home and the man is shoved out into the wilderness. Bad-mouthed by everyone and suddenly a stranger to his own children. It's not fair.'

'I know that happens sometimes,' she agreed.

'More often than you like to think,' he said. 'About a third of parents – usually dads – lose touch completely with their kids after divorce. That's a horrible statistic. I don't want to be one of those dads.'

There was raw pain in his voice.

'I've been having a legal battle with Rachel over the kids for the past six months,' he continued. 'It's taken over my life. She was being obstructive about letting me see them in the first place, and then she dropped this bombshell about heading off to Paris with Olivier. I'm trying to stop her, but of course that's turning me into the bad guy.'

'I'm sorry,' said Lainey.

'I was having trouble sleeping. Having trouble with

everything, to be honest.' Shay sounded embarrassed again. 'I was tense and grumpy and I felt I couldn't cope. Very unmanly not to be able to cope. Made me feel worse actually. Meant I started to drink more than I should, which isn't good for me. Then I heard that Rachel had gone to Paris with the children.'

'No!' exclaimed Lainey.

'Just for a few days,' Shay said. 'But clearly they were making plans . . . I called around to the house when they got back. We had a row. The kids were there. I was trying not to fight with her, I really was. But I called her names and the kids got upset and she said she was going to get a barring order against me. A barring order! It makes me out to be some kind of monster. But I wasn't violent. I was just angry.'

Lainey looked at him cautiously. He'd always seemed like a relaxed, carefree man to her, with his selection of girlfriends and his easy-going lifestyle. But she knew nothing about him. And maybe the whole reason his wife had thrown him out was because he'd been seeing those other women while he was married to her. Maybe he had a quick temper. Maybe, despite what he was telling her now, he was violent. She didn't think so, though. She was sure that he was a decent person.

'It's stacked against men in situations like this,' he told her. 'Everyone believes what the wife says. Somehow we're always the ones at fault. I know we can be bastards. I know we can be fools. But we're people too, and we don't turn into monsters overnight.'

'Is there no chance of the two of you getting back together? You said before that you married too young, but perhaps . . .'

'Too young and without knowing each other,' Shay said.

'My fault really. I was mad about her. The minute I saw her I was infatuated. She was the most beautiful girl I'd ever seen. Tiny, five feet nothing. Gorgeous blond hair. The bluest of blue eyes. All I could think was that I wanted to take her away and make her mine. I wanted to marry her straight away and protect her.'

Lainey knew what wanting to get married straight away was like.

'Obviously I didn't,' said Shay. 'I just asked her for a date and, you know what, I was almost sick with excitement when she said yes. I thought she was too good for me, you see. I thought I was punching above my weight.'

She understood that feeling too.

'Where did you meet her?'

'Like me, she's a physio,' Shay told her. 'I met her at a conference. And then, after we got married, we set up our own practice. We were living in Milltown at the time and we set it up in our house. Maybe not a good idea in retrospect. It meant that we were together all the time and that we never really left the house.'

The mention of Milltown had startled Lainey. She'd been to a physio in Milltown whose name was Rachel. A pretty young blonde (although not, in her view, the bombshell described by Shay). Nevertheless, it had to be a coincidence. Ken visited her regularly, and when Lainey had pulled a muscle using the cross-trainer in the gym, he'd recommended Rachel. But her name wasn't Rachel Loughnane. It was Rachel Ferriter.

'Ferriter was her maiden name,' said Shay when Lainey said this. 'She changed it back the day I left. I can't believe you've actually met her.'

'She seemed . . . nice enough,' said Lainey carefully.

'Of course she's nice enough!' cried Shay. 'She's not a total bitch, really she isn't. I loved her. More than anyone. But when it went wrong, she became . . . oh, vengeful, I guess. Angry that things hadn't worked out.'

'And why would she have become vengeful?' asked Lainey. 'Would it have been because you did the dirty on her, by any chance?'

Shay looked mildly irritated. 'I suppose it's inevitable you'd ask a question like that,' he said. 'With your background.'

'My background?'

'Well, your mother is the woman who thinks all men are simply a waste of the earth's resources. I guess some of that rubs off and you're immediately prepared to think the worst of us.'

'You already know I hardly see my mother,' she reminded him. 'And you know that I have a boyfriend. Hardly something that would make you imagine I'd think the worst of men all the time.'

'All the same . . .' Shay sounded sceptical.

'Truly not,' she said. 'When it comes to men – well, let's say I haven't exactly covered myself in glory. Somehow I never seem to last the distance. So why didn't you and Rachel?'

'We fell out of love,' said Shay simply. 'That's all there is to it. We grew tired of each other. Tired of the work and home thing being so intertwined. There was no desperate catalogue of rows or affairs or anything like that. Which somehow makes it all the more difficult, really. We were crazy about each other when we married but then all the little things we were crazy about became things that annoyed us. Sometimes I wish it had been something awful, then everything we're going through now would have a definite reason.'

'But why has it all become so confrontational?' Lainey looked at him enquiringly. 'Surely you could have split up amicably if the break wasn't over something drastic?'

'When you fall out of love with someone, you stop wanting to understand them,' said Shay. 'You don't give them leeway any more. The biggest row was over the practice.' His expression was grim. 'I'd done just as much to build it up but suddenly it was all hers – it was in her house by then, after all, and although my solicitors argued that she had to buy me out, it became part of the settlement in the end. Then I got the job at the sports clinic. I like it there, though I preferred working for myself. But I didn't have the time or the resources to build up another practice. I resented how things had turned out. That somehow she'd ended up with everything. The house. The business. The kids. All the same, I accepted that. I got on with it. But now she's met The Frenchman and she wants to change everything to go off and live with him. She even offered to sell the business back to me!'

'Ouch,' said Lainey.

'Yeah, well.' Shay's voice was controlled. 'I could've got my head around that, but I can't get my head around my kids being taken away from me. I know women think men can't care for children as well as they can. It's a myth you perpetuate. But it's not true. I love my boys and I'm perfectly capable of looking after them. I don't want them to think I don't care about them as much as their mother. I don't want them to become strangers to me.'

'Of course you don't,' agreed Lainey. 'Will you work it out, d'you think?'

'I've no idea.' Shay sounded weary. 'All the arguing is doing my head in. I can't sleep and that's making me irritable and cranky. Forgetful too. Sometimes I can't remember if I've taken my medication or not. After I'd had the row with Rachel, I was so keyed up I nearly ran over an elderly woman at a pedestrian crossing. I got a terrible fright. So did she, the poor dear. Though the language out of her . . . Anyway, when I came home, I went out again to the pub. I decided I needed a few drinks to relax me, but I ended up dizzy and disoriented. I was close to passing out when you did your Florence Nightingale thing.'

'You looked awful,' admitted Lainey. 'I was really frightened.'

'It didn't take me that long to recover,' he told her. 'But you know how it is when you're sucked into the hospital system; it took ages for me to get out again. Now I'm afraid that her solicitors will hear about it and say that I'm unstable and not fit to be a parent and she'll get her way. She'll go to France and I'll be airbrushed out of the picture.' He sounded despairing.

'That won't happen,' said Lainey with more confidence than she felt.

'I don't want it to happen. But the courts favour the mother.' He released his breath slowly. 'Anyway, I'm keeping my fingers crossed. And being more careful about my medication, too.'

'I don't think they'll let her whisk your kids away. I'm sure it'll work out. And I do understand how you feel, your boys are lovely,' added Lainey.

He looked at her questioningly.

'I had to go into your bedroom,' she admitted. 'The

paramedics asked me to check for drugs. I didn't touch anything,' she added, 'but I saw the photographs. And I remembered them playing football when they were here last.'

'Of course.' He nodded. 'Lisa brought them over.'

'Lisa?'

'My sister. She picks them up and delivers them home.'

Lainey had been wondering about the woman on his balcony. When Shay had started talking, she'd assumed it was Rachel, although she didn't match her memory of the physio.

'Rachel doesn't like me coming to the house,' Shay continued. 'Which is another reason the other day was such a mess.'

'What's her problem with that?'

'She thinks it upsets the kids. And she thinks I'm trying to break her and Olivier up, so she doesn't want to see me.'

'Are you?'

'No! Well . . .' He looked shamefaced. 'I want her to be happy. But I don't want her to go to France with the boys. I know it's putting a strain on their relationship too, but what can I do about it?'

'I wish I could tell you,' Lainey said. 'Life is a mess, isn't it? You think it should all be simple, that we should have the job we want and meet the person we love and live happily ever after, but we don't. Or we make a mistake and we end up paying for it all our lives.'

'Everything will work out fine for you,' Shay assured her. 'You're that kind of person.'

'You think?' She looked doubtful. 'I suppose I'm fortunate that I didn't get married and have kids and fall out of love – not that I thought it at the time.' She told him about her two engagements. 'I'm totally hopeless,' she admitted. 'But hopefully one day I'll get there.'

'With Adonis?'

'Maybe.'

'Well, best of luck,' he said.

'You too.'

They looked at each other awkwardly for a moment, then Shay said he had to go and Lainey told him she had to get on with the cleaning. Shay hesitated for a moment, looked as though he was going to say something, but then just smiled and moved towards the door, saying goodbye as he opened it.

'Goodbye,' Lainey said. 'And good luck.'

Then she turned up the music again and went back to her polish and sprays.

Chapter 28

Fibratus: high ice-crystal clouds drawn out by the wind into long, fine filaments

Feargal Wright made a last-ditch attempt to get Deanna on to his new talk programme instead of his arts and culture show. He asked her to meet him once more and selected the bar in the Westbury Hotel as the place to make his pitch. (He told himself that his reasons for wanting to meet her once more were purely professional, but he couldn't help looking forward to seeing her too.)

'I don't know why you're wasting your time and mine on this yet again,' she remarked as he outlined the reasons for wanting her to change programmes. 'I've never spoken about Lainey without her permission and I don't intend to start now.'

'Have you ever asked her permission to talk about her to anyone?' enquired Feargal.

Deanna looked at him steadily. 'No.'

'Maybe she'd like to be on the show. She's in the public eye. It must be difficult for her to field questions about her private life. This will give her an opportunity to do that.'

'As far as I'm aware, the only person asking questions about her private life is you,' said Deanna. 'So she's not under any pressure. And I'm quite certain she'd like to keep it that way.'

'Perhaps it would be good for you both to talk about it,' said Feargal. 'Cathartic.'

'Oh, please.' Deanna looked contemptuous. 'That's unworthy of you.'

'Sorry,' said Feargal. 'I have to try.'

'Stop trying,' advised Deanna. 'Do your job. Talk about my work. Talk about my documentary. Tell me that women have it all. Allow me to point out that they haven't. Whip up a bit of controversy. Insult me if you like. But steer clear of my daughter.'

'You care about her a lot, don't you?' said Feargal.

Deanna took a sip of the still water in front of her. 'I don't want to mess up her life,' she said as she replaced the glass on the table.

'Do you think you already have?' asked Feargal, who thought he'd seen a fleeting expression of regret cross Deanna's face as she raised the glass to her lips.

'I'm sure all children think their parents have messed with their lives,' she said steadily. 'And all parents think they did what was right.'

'Talk to me about it,' urged Feargal.

'You've got to be kidding me!'

'As a friend.'

'Oh, come on!'

'I mean it,' he said. 'I think . . . well, we're friends, Deanna. Aren't we?'

'No.'

His shoulders sagged slightly. 'I thought we were. I thought this was more than me being an interviewer who was trying to worm information out of a subject.'

'I didn't.'

'You're a hard woman, Deanna Ryan,' said Feargal.

'I'm a woman who looks after herself,' she told him. 'Not hard. Not soft. Just practical.'

'I was hoping there might be more to you and me,' Feargal said abruptly.

'Really?'

'There's a connection. Don't you feel it?'

'Feargal, I'm a fifty-one-year-old unmarried woman. I didn't manage to stay this way by giving in to every random feeling I've ever had.'

'You don't have to be the hard-hearted, hard-headed feminist with me,' Feargal said. 'Really you don't.'

'But that's who I am,' Deanna told him. 'It's who I'll always be.'

'You could change.'

'I don't want to.'

'Why do you cut yourself off from people?' asked Feargal.

'I'm not cutting myself off from anyone,' said Deanna firmly. 'You seem to think that I'm a frigid old bat with a sad life. Nothing could be further from the truth. I'm happy, Feargal. I truly am.'

'But having a relationship with someone would surely make you happier.'

'Why?'

'It's nice to have someone on your own wavelength to share things with. Like me, for instance. We have interesting conversations. We enjoy each other's company . . .'

Deanna roared with laughter and Feargal looked affronted. 'We do, don't we? You meet me whenever I ask.'

'Why wouldn't I meet you?' asked Deanna. 'You're promoting my work, after all.'

'Nevertheless . . .'

'Do yourself a favour and stop talking,' she said. 'We have a professional relationship. Don't mess with it. Don't say anything you'll regret.' She stood up. 'You know what? I'll go now and save you from yourself.'

She didn't look back as she walked out of the hotel, leaving Feargal staring after her.

Lainey hadn't been to dinner with Deanna since she'd visited her in Monterey as a teenager. Deanna had insisted on going out most evenings back then because she thought it would be easier for them to eat in the company of other people rather than at home alone. Lainey vividly remembered a restaurant on Cannery Row where everyone seemed to know her mother and where they fussed over her whenever she came in. Deanna had introduced her as Lainey-from-Ireland. She hadn't said they were mother and daughter, nobody had asked in what way they were connected and Lainey didn't try to tell them either. As far as she was concerned, Deanna was more like a distant aunt than a mother. She'd enjoyed all the eating out, though, and particularly the Cannery Row restaurant, which was cheap and cheerful and decorated with hurricane lamps, fishing nets and shells. She'd had clam chowder, she remembered suddenly, hot and flavoursome. Funny how that's come back to me, she thought, as she waited for Deanna to arrive at the very different venue her mother had chosen for their dinner together. Funny how sometimes you get such a jolt from the past that you can almost believe you're back where you once were.

It would be better fun to be at the beachside restaurant now, she thought. She'd felt intimidated as soon as she'd walked in the door of the Michelin-starred venue Deanna had chosen for their mother/daughter dinner. Or, she amended to herself, their interviewer/interviewee dinner. She wondered if this was where her mother had brought the other, more important Irish women she'd interviewed, and if they'd enjoyed it. She was sure it was lovely, but she didn't normally do the sort of fine dining that it boasted on its website. She preferred simple food in simple places. She rather thought that Deanna did too, but maybe her mother was trying to prove a point. Trying to show that she was rich and successful and trying to underline how meagre Lainey's own career was by comparison. At my age, Lainey thought, as she sat at the table with its brilliant white tablecloth and gleaming silver cutlery, Deanna had already published two books and cut a swathe of mouthy men down to size. She'd proved herself. Whereas, Lainey murmured to herself, it's the men who've cut me down to size, and I've proved nothing at all.

The door opened and her mother walked in. She was wearing a plain black shift dress, accessorised with a gold-coloured chain belt and a chunky gold necklace. It was a sixties retro look and it suited her. Lainey tried hard to think of any previous occasion on which she'd seen Deanna in a dress and simple court shoes, but she couldn't. Lainey had elected to wear a dress herself; it was a red wrap-over, which clung to her trim figure. She was also wearing the high-heeled black shoes with red bows she'd worn to Carla's wedding and which she'd since had repaired. So far she'd managed not to fall over.

She stood up as Deanna arrived. Her mother kissed her on the cheek and sat down opposite her, then glanced around the restaurant. Her eyes flickered over the other diners, who were mainly men in suits. Lainey was sure she was going to make some disparaging comment about them, but Deanna simply asked her if she'd had a good day.

'Not bad,' Lainey replied. 'I'm working on a long-term forecasting model. Everyone knows long-term predictions are extremely tricky, but it's a kind of holy grail of forecasting to be able to say what the weather will be like in a month's time.'

'Given that you can get it wrong for the following day, I wouldn't exactly be holding my breath,' remarked Deanna.

'Of course we get it wrong,' agreed Lainey, 'but not as often as we used to. No matter how good the technology, though, wind direction can suddenly change, a storm can slow down or speed up and suddenly it's not raining where you thought but a couple of hundred miles further north or south. I like the unpredictability, but I also like trying to make it predictable.'

'Is that how you like your life?' asked Deanna. 'Predictable?'

'Sometimes.'

'Just like your gran.'

'Is there something wrong with that?'

'No,' said Deanna. 'But it's nice to rock the boat sometimes.'

'If you're someone who always rocks the boat, is being calm and reasoned your bout of unpredictability?'

Deanna laughed. 'Maybe.' She opened the menu.

The waiter came and took their orders and then Deanna sat back in her chair.

'Feargal Wright called me this morning,' she said.

'Again?' Lainey stared at her mother. 'Is there something going on between you two?'

'Of course not. Like most men, he thinks I'd be flattered by a man taking an interest in me.'

'And you aren't?'

'I'm way past that.'

'You're still a young woman,' said Lainey. 'Why shouldn't you be flattered by someone who says nice things?'

'It's sweet of you to think that fifty-one is young.' Deanna looked amused. 'In the context of relationships, in any event. But Feargal was really hoping I'd cave in and agree to come on his new show.' She told Lainey about his pleas for her to tell people about her daughter on *Private Lives Public Faces.*

'Tell them if you like,' Lainey said. 'It doesn't matter to me, Deanna. I realise that somehow nobody has ever managed to dig up the story of your unwanted pregnancy, but sooner or later they probably will. If you want to deal with it on your own terms, that's fine by me. It doesn't affect me.'

'It's not as simple a story as all that,' said Deanna. 'I don't want them poking and prying because Feargal Wright sensationalises it.'

'Oh, people always think things are complicated. That their own stories are special. But they're not really. No matter what the complications are, the basic fact remains that you were very young when you got pregnant, you couldn't cope and my dad didn't want to know. That happens all the time. And being raised by grandparents happens a lot too. The only difference with us is that they raised me in Ireland while you stayed in the States.'

Deanna played with the corner of her napkin and then lifted her eyes to look directly at Lainey.

'I've wanted to talk to you about this for a while, but there's never been the appropriate opportunity,' she said as she tapped her fingers gently on the table. 'I haven't been entirely honest with you about your father.'

'Not honest?' Lainey's expression was bewildered. 'How?'

'I didn't know how to tell you before,' said Deanna awkwardly.

Lainey's heart was beating faster. She'd always accepted what her mother had told her. A brief fling that went wrong. He hadn't even believed that he was her father. She'd lived with that version of events all her life and was comfortable with it. Her voice shook. 'Tell me now.'

Deanna took a deep breath. 'It truly is complicated. I hope you'll understand.'

It hadn't seemed at all complicated on the day Edmund and Madeleine left for Ireland, taking Lainey with them. All it had seemed then was that, once again, and despite his protestations about wanting to be involved, Jorge had abandoned her and abandoned their child. However this time Deanna was relieved. The idea of having to share custody of Lainey with him while she tried to carve out a life for herself in the States was almost too much to contemplate. If he tried to take things further, she would have to be involved in so many decisions she didn't want to have to be involved in. Men on their own were useless with kids. It would be madness to think that Jorge could look after Lainey. Not that she'd trust him to anyway. Despite the spruced-up look and the alleged brokerage job, Jorge was a drifter at heart. Who knew what he might decide to do with his life and how it would affect Lainey. Sending their daughter home with her parents was the best choice to make. And it was *her* choice to make. But she didn't know if Jorge would come back again sooner or later and ask about her. And she didn't know what on earth she was going to say to him if he did. Anyway, she told herself while she waited, every passing day showed her how right she'd been not to trust him and made her more confident in her own decision.

It was two days later before she discovered the reason he hadn't returned. She was sitting on the deck of the house, skimming through the local newspaper, when she saw the news story. At first it meant nothing to her, but as she read further, she felt her mouth go dry.

Body of man washed ashore identified, said the headline. And beneath: *Parents of George Reeves arrive in Monterey.*

> George Reeves (also known as Jorge Reyes, the name under which he played the guitar semi-professionally) was the only child of Anthony and Annabel Reeves. Anthony Reeves is the flamboyant owner of the Cockatiel Hotel and Casino in Las Vegas and was involved in the so-called White Linen money-laundering case last year in which over $1 million cash, thought to be the proceeds of drugs crime, was found in a Vegas warehouse. Henry Carney, the financial controller at the Cockatiel, was sentenced to fifteen years' imprisonment on charges of fraudulent transactions. Reeves was acquitted in the case, although investigations into his financial affairs are

ongoing. Police have not yet determined the cause of death in the case of Reeves's son and it is not known whether he was still alive when he went into the water.

The words danced in front of Deanna's eyes and she had to put the paper down on the deck because she couldn't hold it steady any longer. She smoothed it with trembling fingers and read on:

'My son was a good man with his life ahead of him,' Anthony Reeves was quoted as saying today. 'He was an accomplished musician and a regular visitor to Monterey, where he had a number of friends. We are devastated by this news.'

According to the report, Annabel Reeves had collapsed on being told of her son's death and had been rushed to hospital. The reporter went on to say that George had been estranged from his family for a period of time but in the last few months had been working with a brokerage firm owned by a subsidiary of the Reeves Corporation, the family company. The Reeves Corporation had, like its founder, been under investigation.

George Reeves was staying alone at a motel in the town and had checked in for a number of days. There is no known reason for his visit here, although sources suggest that his death may have been due to a drug-related incident. Reeves Jnr had two previous convictions for possession of banned substances. Police are asking anyone who might have seen anything unusual in the coastal area on Thursday or Friday night to get in touch with them.

Deanna's tears plopped on to the paper in front of her. She didn't know if her tears were for Jorge or for herself. Or for her baby daughter, who was, thankfully, back in Dublin and away from any possible connection with the Reeves family. She'd heard of them before, of course, because Anthony Reeves's activities had been reported in the newspapers, but she certainly hadn't made any connection between Jorge and the notorious crime family.

She was still sitting on the step when Maya arrived home. Her friend took one look at her and realised something was badly wrong.

'Are you sorry she's gone home?' she asked. 'Do you want her back?'

Deanna said nothing. She was still shaking. She handed the paper to Maya.

'Oh my God,' said her friend as she read the piece. 'Oh my God.'

'He was a drug dealer.' Deanna's teeth chattered and she wrapped her arms around her legs and rested her head on her knees. 'Jorge was involved in drugs. He was murdered.'

Maya sat on the deck and put her arm around her. 'We don't know that he had anything at all to do with drugs. That's just speculation.'

'He smoked pot. He was arrested for possessing drugs.'

'Jeez, Dee, we all smoke pot.'

'Maybe he left me because he was involved in the other stuff with his father. Maybe this money-laundering thing was drug-related.'

'His father was acquitted . . .'

'Oh, come on.' Deanna's voice was suddenly sharp and she sat up straight again. 'He might have got off, but that doesn't mean he was innocent. They're still investigating his company. And Jorge started working for him after the financial controller guy went to jail. Maybe he was helping out.'

'He never seemed like a hardened druggie, though,' said Maya. 'And even less the kind of guy who'd get involved in trafficking or dealing.'

'How do I know that?' asked Deanna. 'We were only together for a short time, after all. He never said anything about any of this. He never told me his name was really George Reeves. He let me think he had Latin American heritage. Probably afraid I'd make the connection otherwise. I didn't really know him, Maya. I didn't ask any questions. He told me he never spoke to his parents. Maybe that was true then, but how do I know that over the last couple of years he hasn't been involved in his father's empire? And there's more to this than meets the eye. The financial controller is clearly the fall guy for what was happening. Money-laundering is serious stuff. What if there's some kind of gang warfare going on between this Anthony Reeves guy and other people? What if they know about Lainey? Oh God – what if she's in real danger?'

'Stop it, Deanna!' Maya caught her by the hands. 'Of course Lainey isn't in danger. Even if Jorge was involved in some kind of deal that went wrong, or if it's anything to do with his family, there's no reason to think that anyone is looking for Lainey.'

'It's like in *The Godfather*,' said Deanna shakily. 'They kill people to teach them a lesson.'

'You're freaking out and I understand that. But you're overreacting,' said Maya.

'OK.' Deanna nodded furiously. 'Let's say there's nothing on the drugs side. But what about his family? Did he tell them about Lainey after meeting her? Will they come looking for her because she's Jorge's daughter? Will they come looking for me?'

Maya was silent. She wasn't able to answer that question. Deanna started to cry.

'I loved him,' she said. 'I really did. And although I was angry with him when he came back and worried about him messing up my life, I was happy to see him again. Happy to think that he hadn't forgotten about me altogether and pleased that he wanted to know Lainey, even though I wasn't convinced about how we should deal with that.'

'I know.'

'And now he's dead.' Deanna's teeth were chattering again. 'And I don't want to be involved.'

'You don't have to be.'

'What if the police find out he was here? What if they think I've been involved too? I'll either be arrested or kicked out of the country! Whatever happens, it means that people will find out about Lainey, if they don't know already. I don't want the Reeves family to find out about her. It was bad enough that Jorge and his parents might get involved when I thought they were ordinary people. But a crime family? I can't have anything to do with that, Maya, I can't.'

'Of course you can't.'

'And I can't have Lainey thinking that her father was a criminal who was murdered. That's not the kind of start she needs in life.'

'You don't know that he was a criminal. Or that he was murdered.'

'What else can I think?'

'Oh, Dee, Jorge was one of the gentlest men I knew. OK, he treated you badly, but he tried to do the right thing in the end.'

'It doesn't matter.' Deanna was shaking her head so hard it was making her dizzy. 'There can't be any connection between her and him. There just can't.'

'I know,' said Maya comfortingly. 'I know. Please don't worry, Deanna. We'll sort it out. We won't let anything happen to you. Or to Lainey.'

The following day, Deanna and Maya went to Patsy Fuller and told her the story. The older woman looked at her in shock. Then she gathered herself and told Deanna not to worry. Lainey's father was officially unknown. There was no way that anyone could find out anything different. And Lainey was now safely out of the country. Meantime Deanna herself would be starting college soon. Patsy arranged for her to go to Stanford straight away, instead of waiting for the beginning of the college year. She could stay with a friend of hers, Patsy said. Patsy and Maya would stay alert, see if anyone was asking awkward questions about possible girlfriends or children that Jorge was supposed to have in Monterey.

'We'll keep in touch,' Patsy told her. 'If we hear anything at all, I'll let you know straight away.'

But there was no further news. The post-mortem on Jorge revealed that he'd been alive when he'd gone into the water and that there were traces of cocaine in his system. There were no signs of previous injury. Nobody had seen or heard anything. Nobody came to Monterey asking questions about him. The newspapers ran a story saying that it appeared to have been a tragic accident, and Deanna eventually accepted that this was probably the case. Jorge, careless or disoriented because of the coke, must have stumbled into the water and drowned. It seemed too simple and sad a way for his life to have ended, and yet it also seemed the most likely thing to have happened.

The media lost interest in the accident. After a few more colour pieces about the Reeves family the story faded from the newspapers, replaced by more current news and events.

Patsy, Maya, Lexy and Fawn kept in contact with Deanna while she was at college and confirmed over and over again that nobody had come looking for her or for Lainey. Eventually she felt able to relax. It seemed that Jorge hadn't told anyone about her or their child. She kept alert for any stories about the Reeves Corporation in the media. There weren't many. She made a determined effort to put the past out of her mind and concentrate on the future instead. And she worked hard to make her future the one she'd always wanted. A future in which no man would mess with her life ever again.

Nearly ten years later, after Deanna had published *Get Off Your Back* and *Tit Power* and had made a name for herself as a prominent feminist, another story about the Reeves family broke. She saw it first on the nightly news and then read about it in the papers, and she felt herself begin to shake once more. Anthony Reeves had been arrested again and was to be charged with narcotics crimes, as well as identity theft and firearms offences. Deanna immediately flew to New York, where Patsy was currently lecturing in Gender Studies at New York University.

'It doesn't concern you,' Patsy told her. 'The police never contacted you after Jorge's death and there's nothing to link you to the family. Not that it would matter if there was. This is an investigation into criminal offences and nothing to do with you.'

'I know,' said Deanna. 'It's just that I feel linked. Any time I see anything about them I start to panic.'

The Reeves Corporation had occasionally featured in the newspapers over the intervening years as various charges against it were dismissed in the courts, but until now there had been nothing personal about either Anthony or Annabel.

'There's no need to panic,' Patsy assured her. 'You'll be fine. Lainey will be fine too.'

And they were. Anthony Reeves was eventually found guilty of wire fraud and other offences and sentenced to twenty-five years' imprisonment. The newspapers revisited the story of his previous acquittal, as well as Jorge's drowning. They said that the family's luck had run out the day Jorge died.

Three weeks after beginning his sentence, Anthony Reeves suffered a heart attack and died instantly. Annabel took an overdose of sedatives after she heard the news. The two of them were buried together. As far as the newspapers were concerned, it was the end of a bad family. And everyone had got their just deserts.

Lainey's food was practically untouched on the plate in front of her. She couldn't believe the story her mother had just told her. It was as though the axis on which her world revolved had shifted and she was looking at everything she knew about herself from a completely different angle.

'You lied to me,' she said eventually. 'Gran lied to me. Over and over.'

'We didn't tell you the whole story,' admitted Deanna. 'But we tried not to lie.'

Lainey thought of all the times Madeleine had talked to her about her father. No matter what questions Lainey had asked, Madeleine's answers had always been the same. That her father had left and not come back. Which was true. But she'd never said why he hadn't come back. That he hadn't been able to come back because he was dead. She'd told Lainey that she'd never deliberately lied to her, and that was true, but nevertheless she'd allowed her to believe that he was out there somewhere, not caring.

'Why didn't you just tell me he'd died?' she asked. 'You didn't have to give me all the gory details about his family, but you could've been honest about that part of it.'

'You'd have wanted to know more about him if we'd told you that,' said Deanna. 'You know you would. I didn't want you to find out. I didn't want you to know that your father came from a family led by a rotten thug, which is basically what Anthony Reeves was. I didn't want you to think you had blood like that in your veins. That your father had left you that sort of legacy. I didn't want you to think that you should find out more about them or involve yourself in any way with them.'

'That wasn't your decision to make. Gran's either.' Lainey's voice was cool.

'Not now,' agreed Deanna. 'But back then, when you were small, we were trying to do what was best. Jorge had walked out on me before. He had said that he didn't want to know. Simpler to leave it that way and forget he'd ever come back.'

'Did it rain?' asked Lainey suddenly.

'What?' Deanna was startled.

'The day he came back. Did it rain?'

'I can't remember.'

'I have a memory.' Lainey told her about it. 'Is it real?'

'I think . . .' Deanna tried to recall. 'It was a muggy day. It probably rained.'

'He picked me up,' said Lainey. 'He held me in his arms.'

Deanna bit her lip. 'Yes.'

'He cared about me.'

'There and then,' said Deanna. 'On that day. Yes.'

'He wanted to know me, to look after me. He got a job. He came back so that he could be part of my life.'

'His job was in his father's corporation. Which was a criminal empire.'

'He hadn't spoken to them for ages. He'd even changed his name. Maybe this job was perfectly legitimate. Maybe he took it so that he could look after us.'

'Maybe.'

'He didn't walk out on me for ever.'

'No.'

Lainey swallowed hard. 'You should have told me before now.' She pushed her chair away from the table. 'I've got to go.'

'Lainey, please . . .'

'I can't be with you right now.'

'I'm sorry I didn't tell you sooner,' said Deanna. 'I couldn't.'

'I've got to go,' repeated Lainey, and walked out of the restaurant leaving Deanna looking helplessly after her.

The memory kept spinning through her head. The rain. The arguments. The man picking her up. The scent of his after-shave.

Her father. Dead.

Her grandfather. The head of a criminal empire.

Her grandmother. Suicide.

A family secret.

She'd never thought they were a family with secrets before. Growing up with Madeleine and Edmund had been reassuringly normal. They used to call themselves The Three Musketeers. All for one. One for all. It was a joke, of course. But she'd believed in the closeness. Believed that they all cared about each other, looked out for each other. Yet they'd lied to her. It didn't matter why. They'd known things she didn't know and they hadn't wanted her to find out. It was wrong. She'd deserved to be told the truth about her father before now. It didn't matter what their reasons were. Jorge had come back for her. He'd loved her. And they hadn't told her.

She got a cab back to Laurel Park. A cool breeze tugged at her jacket as she entered the code on the security pad for the pedestrian gate. She shivered and walked rapidly along the narrow cobbled pathway. It was as she turned towards her block that she felt the heel of her shoe catch between the cobbles and she pitched forward, landing with a thump on the freshly mown lawn.

'Bugger!' She yelled the words out loud. 'Bugger and shit and bloody, bloody hell!'

She sat there for a moment, unable to move. She'd fallen right out of her mended shoe, which was still lodged between the cobbles. She leaned forward and picked it up. The heel hadn't broken this time. All the same, she thought, unlucky shoes. She kept ending up on her arse because of them. Her dress was probably dirty too. It was futile trying to do sophistication, she told herself. Every time she did, it ended in disaster. Both sartorially and personally.

'Are you all right?'

It was Shay's voice. He was leaning over his balcony, looking down at her.

'Yes. Sure. I'm fine.' She scrambled to her feet. Falling had been a shock, but at least this time she hadn't hurt anything. Nevertheless she tested her foot gingerly before putting her weight on it.

'Hang on. I'll be down in a second.'

There was no need to hang on. She was perfectly all right. And she didn't want to talk to Shay. Not right now.

The contents of her tote bag had spilled out on to the grass and she gathered them up quickly. But Shay arrived before she'd put the last item, her strawberry lip gloss, back in the bag.

'I saw you fall,' he said. 'It was quite a tumble. Are you sure you're OK?'

'Yes. Yes.' She spoke quickly. 'It probably looked worse than it was. I do this a lot. No need to worry about me.'

'My turn to be neighbourly.' He smiled at her. She looked away.

'Lainey?' He touched her shoulder. 'Is everything OK?'

'Yes. Of course. I just . . . It's only . . .' And then, to her horror, she started to cry. She hated crying. She'd had practice at it, of course, every time she split up with someone. But she hated it all the same. Because once she started, she found it hard to stop.

She swallowed a few times and brushed her hand across her eyes.

'Don't mind me,' she said. 'Being a bit girlie today. Nothing to worry about.'

'Are you sure?' He sounded concerned.

'Oh, absolutely.'

'This isn't because of Adonis, is it?' he asked. 'Has he upset you somehow?'

She smiled shakily. 'No.'

'Would it help to talk about it?' His expression was faintly embarrassed. 'I know that men aren't so good at the talking thing, or apparently the listening thing either, but if you want . . . Why don't you come up to my place? Have a coffee? Or a drink if that's what you need?'

She was going to say no, that she wanted to be alone with her thoughts, but she realised after all that she didn't. Right now she wanted someone to look after her. She nodded.

'Indoors, I think,' said Shay. 'This wind is a bit chilly.'

She sat on the comfortable sofa. Shay pressed play on his iPod and the room was filled with the upbeat tempo of Taylor Swift. He lowered the volume, went into the kitchen and returned with two coffees as well as a glass of wine.

'I haven't drunk alcohol since you picked me up from the floor,' he told her as he sat down beside her. 'But you look as though you could do with it. It's nice for me to have the opportunity to repay you.'

She took the glass from him, and set it down on the table in front of her, then picked up the coffee.

'How are you?' she asked. 'Are you doing OK?'

'I'm fine,' he told her. 'But what's more important right now is how are things with you? Can I help?'

'It's not something I need help with,' she said. 'It's just something I need to put into context.'

He watched her while she cupped her hands around the mug. Her glossy hair shielded her face. Her shoulders were tense. Then, as he watched, she released the breath she'd been holding and started to speak. She told him what Deanna had revealed to her, and of her shock at realising that information about her father had been kept hidden from her. She said she felt betrayed. By Deanna. By Madeleine. And by Edmund.

'I understand how you'd feel that way,' said Shay.

'I know why they did it,' said Lainey. 'But that's not the point, is it?'

Shay shook his head.

'I had a right to know. I should have known that my father came back. That he wanted to be part of my life.' Tears slid down her cheeks and she put the mug on the table before wiping them away. 'I realise his walking out on Deanna was a terrible thing to do. I've always thought he didn't care and as far as I was concerned he was a shit and so it didn't matter. But he *did* care, even if he showed it a bit late. Then something truly terrible happened to him. And they've blotted it out as though it never took place. As though it was never important. But it was important and it does matter. At least, it matters to me!'

'What do you want to do?' asked Shay.

'I've no idea.' Lainey took a tissue from her bag, blew her nose and gave him a watery smile. 'It's not that I want to search out my criminal genes and discover I have a talent for tax evasion or drug dealing. But I need to know about those people. And I want to find out more about Jorge. My dad.' Her voice trembled. 'He came back,' she whispered. 'He wanted to know me. So I want to know about him too.'

Shay put his arms around her and held her close to him. 'It's OK to want that,' he said. 'He's part of you no matter what. You're linked to him and you always will be.'

She stayed in his arms for almost a minute and then slowly pulled away.

'Thank you,' she said.

'You're welcome.'

'I understand better how you feel about your boys now,' she told him. 'Why it's so important to you. Why you don't want to lose them.'

'Of course I don't want to lose them,' said Shay. 'Your dad – well, maybe it would've worked out. Maybe not. Maybe everything else would have been too much of a problem. But at least now you know that he tried.'

'Yes.'

'Don't blame your mum, or your gran either,' said Shay. 'After all, they were only trying to protect you.'

'I know that, I really do. I can't imagine what might have happened if Deanna had contacted the Reeves family and told them about me.' She looked thoughtful. 'They might have thought she was trying it on, of course. But they might have wanted to be a big part of my life too. That could've been a disaster. I'm a quiet-living girl at heart and I can't see myself being involved in money-laundering and drugs . . .

I still can't quite believe it, to be honest. Yet it's part of me. *They* were part of me. I can't ignore it either.'

'Are you going to try to find any relatives you might have?' asked Shay.

'I want to know about Jorge's family,' said Lainey. 'That doesn't necessarily mean I want to chase down distant relatives. Anthony, Annabel and Jorge are all dead, so it's not as though there's anyone close to talk to.'

'There must be others, all the same.'

'I'm sure,' Lainey agreed. 'I guess Deanna would've kept up to date with what went on with any of them.'

'You need to talk to her about it again.'

'Yeah.' Lainey sounded doubtful. 'We're not that good at the talking thing.'

She took a final sip of coffee. 'Thanks for this. But I need to go home now.'

'Sure you don't want the wine?' he asked.

She shook her head and stood up.

'No wonder you fell,' said Shay as she slid her feet into the high-heeled shoes. 'How on earth can you walk in those?'

'Clearly not very well,' she admitted.

'They make you very tall.'

'I know. I quite like that.' She smiled. 'When I was younger, being tall bothered me. But now I like looking down on the little people.'

He laughed. So did she.

'Thank you so much for being around,' she said.

'Any time.'

'I'll be off.' She picked up her bag.

'Well, see you,' she said.

'See you,' said Shay.

And she left.

When she got into her apartment, she kicked off the shoes and swore never to wear them again. She walked over to her window and looked over at Shay's. She'd planned to wave to him. But he'd closed his curtains. She closed hers too. She sat in the dark for nearly an hour before she went to bed.

Chapter 29

Thermal: a small rising parcel of warm air

She was dreaming the dream again. But this time it was different. This time when the unknown man picked her up and held her to him, she put her arms around him and hugged him tightly. She knew he was her father. She didn't want him to let go. But the rain was getting heavier and heavier and she could hear it thudding against the ground beneath them. She could hear the wind too, howling through the spindly trees in the garden, eerie, high-pitched and disturbing.

Her eyes opened abruptly. She could still hear the screech of the wind and the rhythmic drumming of the rain, but this time it was real. The forecasts they'd made earlier in the week had been accurate, and the predicted stormy spell had now hit the east coast. She shivered and snuggled down beneath her duvet. But she was utterly unable to sleep. Her mind was racing again with thoughts of Deanna and Madeleine and how they'd kept such important information from her. She accepted that they might have had the best of reasons. She understood their feelings. But she couldn't forgive them for lying by omission.

At five thirty she slid out of bed and pulled on her dressing gown. She padded into the living room and opened her laptop. Then she Googled George Reeves and Jorge Reyes.

The only information that came up related to old news reports on Anthony and his trials. They told the story that Deanna had given her, painting him as an unprincipled criminal who'd been heavily involved in money-laundering and narcotics. The reports talked about the loss of his son, George, in an unexplained drowning in Monterey, something from which neither of his parents had ever really recovered. There were two photographs: one of Anthony and Annabel at a formal function, in which they beamed at the camera; she was beautiful, dressed all in white, with russet hair tumbling in loose curls to her shoulders; he was wearing a tux and reminded Lainey of Al Pacino. The other photograph was a grainy one of Jorge, in which he looked engagingly at the photographer, the faint grin on his face partly hidden by his beard. He was wearing a striped polo shirt.

It was the first time she'd ever seen a photograph of her father, and her heart was thumping as she stared at the image on the screen, recognising herself in Jorge, realising that it was all true and that this man was a part of her. And she could see herself too in the way Annabel's hair fell around her face, and in her smile, and how she had turned in the photograph to Anthony. She had a similar photograph herself, taken when she and Ross had got engaged. She'd been looking at him in exactly the same way as Annabel was looking at Anthony. Happy. Excited. Trusting.

My grandparents, she thought, as she traced her fingers over the screen. My father. Photos on a screen, though, not real-life people. Yet they had been real-life people. She was as much a part of them as she was of Edmund and Madeleine. It was hard to take in. And Jorge, her father, had been part of them too. But she didn't know, would never know, if he'd been a good person or not, if knowing about him would have made a difference.

She closed her eyes and the images of her dream returned. She felt the splash of the rain and then the hold of the once-unknown man's arms around her; she felt the touch of his lips as he whispered into her ear: 'I love you, Lainey.'

He'd never said that in her dreams before. She didn't know if he'd said it to her in real life either. But she remembered the security of his arms and the warmth of his breath, and she knew that he'd cared. In her dreams, she'd always known.

Madeleine and Deanna were having breakfast together. Usually Deanna didn't bother with it; she was either out and about early or sitting at the dining room table, her laptop open and a cup of black coffee beside her, by the time Madeleine appeared. But this morning the two women had both got up at the same time and Madeleine had made buttery toast, which she'd put in front of Deanna.

'I can't eat,' Deanna said, but she started nibbling on the toast anyway. 'Oh, Mom, I've made such a mess of things.'

'It probably wasn't the best way to tell her.' Madeleine repeated the words she'd said the previous evening when Deanna had come home and related what had happened. 'You should have broken it to her here, Deanna, not in some impersonal restaurant.'

'I thought it would be easier with people around us,' Deanna said. 'I thought we could be practical about it that way. I'm useless with this touchy-feely stuff.'

'I know,' said Madeleine.

'But you're good at it. I should have let you tell her.'

'I should've told her years ago,' said Madeleine. 'It's as much my fault as yours.'

'I asked you not to say anything.'

'I wouldn't have anyhow.'

'D'you think she'll want to go to Vegas?' asked Deanna. 'D'you think she'll want to find out more about them?'

'You did,' Madeleine reminded her. 'You wanted to know too.'

Of course she'd wanted to know. How could she not? It wasn't enough for her to go to the college library and trawl through microfiches of old newspapers, looking for information about Anthony and Annabel Reeves. She had to go to Las Vegas, to the source of Anthony's empire. She hadn't been able to contemplate it at first. She'd been too frightened. But when Anthony was arrested, she decided that the time had come to see his hotel for herself.

Maya came with her. They booked into Caesar's Palace, because Deanna hadn't wanted to stay in Anthony's hotel. She hadn't been sure, either, that the police wouldn't have closed it down, but when the two girls walked along the noisy, glittering strip later that evening, they saw the huge glass building that was the Cockatiel, with its distinctive emblem of the tropical bird in big neon lights that changed colour every few seconds.

Inside, the hotel was big and bustling and the atmosphere intense as throngs of people tried their luck in the casino.

'Didn't work out all that lucky for Anthony,' murmured Deanna as they gazed upon the room full of slot machines.

'Maybe his luck just ran out,' Maya said. 'This is awesome, isn't it? I've never seen anything like it in my life before.'

The two of them walked through the vast slots area, where people sat in front of machines feeding them coins with unblinking concentration.

'It's pure chance,' remarked Maya. 'I dunno why they're looking at those machines as though they can influence them.'

'Maybe they feel they can.' Deanna led the way towards the roulette table. 'But the house always wins, doesn't it?'

As though to make a liar of her, there was a sudden piercing alarm and multicoloured lights began to flash at one of the slots. A middle-aged woman was jumping up and down shouting, 'I won, I won,' and people had gathered around while the machine spilled coins in front of her.

'One winner, hundreds of losers,' said Deanna. 'All there to give Anthony his money or to help him launder what he already has.'

'I wonder what'll happen to this place if he's convicted?' mused Maya.

'I don't know. I hope they shut it down.'

Maya glanced at Deanna. There were tears in her friend's eyes.

'Hey, c'mon,' she said. 'Everything's OK. You know it is.'

'I can't ever let her know about this,' said Deanna. 'It's the polar opposite of everything I believe in.'

'You surely don't care if the men who come here lose money,' said Maya.

'I care that it's probably men who are making it,' Deanna said grimly. 'Feeding on people's hopes and dreams. Selling them bullshit.'

'You can only be sold bullshit if you want to be,' said Maya.

'I guess you're right.' Deanna took her by the arm. 'Let's get out of here. I can't believe that this is where Jorge came from. He was always so chilled and laid-back. How could he ever have been a part of it?'

'Maybe he wasn't,' said Maya. 'Maybe he was trying to get away too. Maybe that's why he wanted to be Jorge, not George. Did you ever think of that?'

She hadn't. That was the truth. She'd been angry with him for leaving her (nobody could possibly be expected to be forgiven for that), then furious with him for returning. But she hadn't thought of his feelings at all. She hadn't considered the man she'd fallen in love with, whose life was music and the simple things. Who'd loved her, at least until the news of her pregnancy. Maybe he'd had his own reasons for not wanting to be involved at first. Maybe he hadn't wanted to include her and their baby in his complicated family life. Maybe, when he'd got the job with his father's company, he'd believed that things had changed. Perhaps that was when he'd written the song for Lainey, the song she'd never had a chance to hear. And now nobody knew she was the mother of his child. Of Anthony and Annabel's grandchild. Nobody knew anything at all. Certainly nobody in Vegas knew or cared about Deanna Ryan. Nobody in Vegas knew or cared about her daughter, who was now in Ireland. And despite Anthony Reeves's position as a player in the town, nobody really cared about what happened to him either. Vegas was way bigger than all of them. Only the gambling mattered. And Deanna was very happy to keep it that way.

* * *

She didn't plan ever to return to Las Vegas, but eventually she did. Twice. After Anthony's death, she came back to research a chapter of her third book, *Women in Waiting*, which dealt with how women were treated by big businesses, as both customers and entrepreneurs. As far as she could see, the Vegas casinos didn't care whether their gamblers were men or women and treated them both equally. But, of course, there were more high-rolling men than women. Which meant that more men than women got the best suites and the best service. And women were used as glamorous adornments in the casinos too. There weren't many women in senior positions in Las Vegas. She hadn't expected there would be.

This time she stayed in the Cockatiel, which had been sold and given a makeover and was now even more ostentatious than she remembered. Although she was vehemently opposed to the gambling culture, she wanted to experience the feeling, so she exchanged some money for chips. It didn't take her long to lose at the craps table, and she moved to the slots instead. Feeding money into the machines reminded her of the time her parents had visited her during her Gaeltacht stay. They'd brought her to an amusement arcade in Salthill. After she'd lost half her pocket money, she'd decided to stop.

She was on her tenth spin when the Cockatiel Dream Machine lined up five in a row and paid her $5,000.

People nearby whooped and hollered, but Deanna simply took the money and went to the bar, where she ordered the Cockatiel Special, a red and orange cocktail that she decided was just a Tequila Sunrise in disguise. She sipped it slowly while her eyes wandered over the room. Five thousand dollars, she said to herself. From the Cockatiel. For Lainey. That seemed fair. She'd wire it to Madeleine straight away.

'Mind if I join you?'

The man who came over to her table was, she guessed, in his mid-thirties and was casually dressed. She didn't usually allow strange men to sit down beside her. But this was Vegas. Normal life went on hold in Vegas. So she gestured at the empty seat and he sat down.

'Saw you win at the slots,' he said. 'Saw you walk away.'

'Of course I walked away.'

'Not many do.'

'Depends on whether you're a real gambler or not.'

'Funny thing . . .' The man looked at her thoughtfully. 'You look like a gambler. You look like the sort of woman to take a chance.'

Her heart began to beat faster. She was in Anthony's hotel, after all, and even though it had actually been sold to another consortium, and even though Anthony himself was dead, she couldn't help feeling a frisson of fear.

'Chris McConaghie.' The man held out his hand. 'I'm a customer relations executive here at the Cockatiel. And I have the jump on you, because I recognise you.'

'You do?' This time her heart was racing.

'My sister bought your first book.'

'Oh.'

'I didn't think this would be your kind of thing.'

'It's not.'

'I'm hoping you're not here to trash our hotel in print.'

'Not specifically,' she said.

He looked relieved.

'Hey, this is your business,' she said. 'I don't care much

for it, but if people want to spend their money, it's up to them how they do it. I'm just interested in how Las Vegas treats women.'

'Much the same as anywhere else, I guess,' said Chris. 'Plus they do damn well in our shows. People like Cher and Bette Midler have made a lot of money here.'

Deanna looked sceptical. 'I'm sure not all the girls do so well.'

'They do OK,' said Chris. 'And the shows are tasteful.'

'Hmm.'

'Let me bring you to one of them,' he offered.

She never went out with men. But this was Vegas. So she agreed.

She'd forgotten that men could be fun. Jorge had been fun at the start. Falling in love with him had been the mistake. In the intervening years she hadn't allowed herself to get close enough to a man to fall in love with him. Besides, her research with Patsy and at college made her think that falling in love seldom worked out as well for women as it did for men. She didn't need to fall in love to feel happy and fulfilled. Her studies and her career did that for her.

But she realised as she sat in the bling-bling surroundings of the MGM with Chris (he said that everyone frequently visited each other's hotels and casinos) that she'd forgotten how nice it was to talk to a man. She'd talked to plenty of them in the past few years, but only as colleagues or interview subjects. Not as people. Chris McConaghie reminded her that not all men were bastards, not all men were criminals and not all men wanted to break a woman's heart.

* * *

She slept with him. She knew that she didn't love him and wasn't going to fall in love with him, but she wanted to sleep with him. He was good in bed. Better than Jorge. Maybe, she thought, just before she fell asleep in the crook of his arm, maybe it was better to sleep with someone you didn't love. Maybe that way you kept a piece of yourself that nobody else could touch.

Chris became one of her closest friends. He was the person she rang when she wanted to hear a male voice and the person she ran to when she needed a man's arms around her. She knew there were other women in his life, and that was fine by her. One day, she thought, he'd meet someone who would want him exclusively. But until then Deanna was happy for him to be there when she needed him and to be there when he needed her. He knew nothing about her past life. She knew nothing about his. As far as she was concerned, it was the perfect relationship.

The day that Deanna learned about Lainey's second engagement was also the day that Chris told her he was getting married. To one of the singers in their latest show, he admitted a little ruefully. He'd been seeing her for the last few months and he knew this was different. He loved her in a way he'd never loved a woman before. She loved him too.

'I don't think I'll ever be friends with a woman the way I was friends with you,' he told Deanna over the phone. 'But Chantelle needs me. You don't. And I guess we won't be in touch any more.'

All men needed to be needed, Deanna thought, as she slowly replaced the receiver and scratched Chris's name from her Filofax. They wanted to believe that you couldn't cope without them. But of course you could. She was living proof of that. She wasn't hurt that Chris had dumped her in favour of the other woman. It had been nice to have him in her life, but she hadn't fallen for him in the way she'd fallen for Jorge. She was pretty certain that she'd never allow any man to get that close to her again.

No man was worth the pain.

Chapter 30

Velum: a thin horizontal patch of cloud above a group of large convection clouds

The weather pattern was complex, Lainey thought, as she sat in front of the screens in the television centre office. There were competing fronts coming from the Atlantic and from northern Europe, and they were bringing high winds and rain. It was difficult to predict, though, which would dominate over the next few days, and Lainey knew she was going to have to give a forecast that included a bit of everything. She hated those sorts of forecasts. She liked things to be more cut and dried.

She was tracking the Atlantic weather system, thinking that although it would be settled for a day or two longer, the outlook was likely to be stormy later in the week, when her mobile phone rang.

'Hi, Carla,' she said as she answered it. 'How are things?'

'Not so bad,' said Carla. 'Still in Stockholm.'

'Is that a good sign?'

'I hope so,' said Carla. 'Coming home seemed like running away, and I didn't want to run away.'

'Were you afraid he'd change the locks or something?'

'Not at all.' Carla was positive. 'I just thought . . . well, I married him, didn't I? It's up to me to stay here and decide how to work it out.'

'And have you?' asked Lainey. 'Decided?'

'Yes.'

'And?'

Carla cleared her throat. 'You know, when I did the check list of what I wanted, I forgot to put fidelity on it.'

'I guess you kinda expect that,' said Lainey.

'Why?' asked Carla. 'We're bombarded with images of infidelity all the time. Why should we think it's the norm?'

'Because it should be,' Lainey said. 'If you love each other.'

'I wasn't getting married for love,' Carla reminded her. 'I was doing it for security. And so that I didn't die a sad old maid.'

'Carla!'

'You know it's true. But the stupid, stupid thing is that I did love him after all. I just didn't admit it to myself.'

'Love him? As in, *in* love with him?'

'Not your way,' said Carla. 'Not bells and whistles and moons and Junes sort of love. But all the things I thought were good in a husband, well, they're the things I love about him.'

'So what are you going to do? Put up with him having . . . what's-her-name in his life?'

'Jannike. No, I'm not. I can't be that detached, Lainey. I thought maybe I could be, but I can't.'

'Where does that leave you, then?'

'I told him I loved him. I told him I was his wife and I wanted to stay married to him. I also said that if he wanted to have a single female friend as his best friend in adjoining hotel rooms, then I couldn't stay with him.'

'And what did he say?'

'He said he wanted to be married.'

Lainey could hear the relief in Carla's voice.

'He says he loves me too and that he only wants to be married once. He says that it's important for him to know how much it matters to me. And if it matters that much, he won't stay in touch with Jannike.'

'Do you believe him?'

'He's the most honourable man I've ever met,' said Carla. 'I trust him completely. There won't be any more flits to Gothenburg.'

'That's a result, isn't it?'

'It's a compromise,' said Carla. 'I was scathing about compromising before, but I don't want to throw it all away. I have to know that I've made the right choice, and he has to be sure he's done the right thing.'

'Of course it's the right thing,' said Lainey. 'You've admitted you love him. And he loves you!'

'Before we got married, I thought I wouldn't be too bothered about friends of his of either sex because I had the lifestyle I wanted,' Carla admitted. 'But in the end it's not about the lifestyle, it's about the person.'

'I'm glad you think that way,' confessed Lainey.

'Hmm. Well, I feel a bit stupid actually. I wanted to be analytical about my marriage, but I've ended up being soppy about it.'

'Soppy can be good,' Lainey said.

'We still have to make it work. Despite our best efforts, it might not.'

'I hope it does.'

'So do I.'

'D'you want to come and stay with me anyway?' asked Lainey. 'A few days, perhaps?'

'I'll let you know,' said Carla. 'Len and I need to be with each other for a bit more before I feel good about leaving him again.'

'I understand. But you said you trust him.'

'I know,' said Carla. 'He's got to trust me too, though.'

'I'll light a candle for you.' It was a promise Madeleine always made when she wanted to let someone know she was thinking of them. Lainey thought it was a comfort.

'Thanks.'

'It'll work out.'

'Fingers crossed. Anyway, in the meantime . . .' Carla cleared her throat and spoke brightly. 'How're you? How's everything going on with Ken, your mum, and the hunky neighbour and all that stuff?'

'I've lots to tell you. But it'll keep.'

'No it won't!'

'It'll have to,' said Lainey. 'I'm doing the evening bulletin shortly. And I need to get my head together for that.'

'Oh, OK,' said Carla. 'Sorry if I distracted you. Call me soon.'

'Will do,' promised Lainey as she double-clicked on one of the isobars on the chart in front of her. 'And then we can have a good girlie gossip about life and love and all that jazz.'

* * *

She looked at herself in the monitor as she waited for the signal that told her she was live on TV. She was wearing the magenta-pink jacket again, and it occurred to her that maybe it was becoming overexposed. Perhaps it was time to hit the shops and get a new TV wardrobe. She hadn't done a serious clothes shop since before Carla's wedding. Now that summer was drawing to a close, she'd need a few autumnal shades to reflect the season ahead. She'd go into town on her next day off, she decided, as she clicked through the weather charts in front of her. It was a while since she'd indulged in some retail therapy. She was still thinking about shoes rather than showers when she realised that she was on screen.

She immediately focused on her first chart and started to talk about the competing fronts and the mixed bag of weather they were bringing to the country, although she didn't think she'd entirely managed to get control of her presentation. Nevertheless she finished exactly on time with a comment that it would be changeable over the next few days, and wished the viewers a good night.

She slipped back into her shoes (despite the fact that as she'd worn ballet pumps that day there was no real need to remove them), then scurried to her office. The live TV feed showed the ad break that followed the weather. And then the intro music to Feargal Wright's show began. Lainey watched as the camera panned into the studio. Deanna was sitting on the sofa opposite Feargal. She appeared cool and composed, wearing a grey wool dress and black shoes, a heavy silver chain around her neck. A splash of colour would have flattered her more, thought Lainey, but the grey lent her an air of gravitas. She looked like someone who meant business.

Lainey sat down on the chair beside her desk and turned

up the volume on the TV. She'd known that Deanna would be on the show tonight and had set up her digital box to record it, because she hadn't decided whether she'd watch it live or not. But now that the programme had started, she couldn't walk away.

'. . . author, feminist and women's advocate, Deanna Ryan,' Feargal was saying. 'Here to talk about her latest project, an analysis of feminism over the last couple of decades.'

She might look grave, Lainey thought, but her mother came alive on television. There was an intensity about her that kept your attention completely fixed on her. As Feargal asked his questions, Deanna sparkled. She rebutted his arguments, made cutting ones of her own, scored points off him and generally gave the impression of someone who was completely in control of herself and her subject.

'Oh, look,' she was saying to Feargal, who'd asked if she was totally anti-man, 'I'm not anti-anyone. But I'm anti-pressure. And women are pressurised to please men. They always have been and they always will be. Women like to please other people. That's how we're programmed. Unfortunately, the people we please least is ourselves. We all have body issues and career issues and family issues and we worry endlessly about them, whereas men simply look around to find someone else to blame for the things that go wrong in their lives. And they usually blame the nearest woman.'

'Isn't this boring old feminist claptrap?' asked Feargal.

'Just because something has been true for years doesn't mean it's boring or claptrap,' Deanna told him. 'I want men and women to be friends. I want them to have equal opportunities. But no matter how far we've come, there's still a lot further to go. Not necessarily in the legal framework of things, but in the mindset of both men and women. We deserve more. We'll get it.'

Feargal told her that he was absolutely sure she always got everything she wanted, and she said unfortunately not but she'd keep trying, and he remarked that she certainly didn't seem the kind of woman to give up, at which she laughed and agreed that she wasn't.

There was a definite chemistry between them, thought Lainey as she watched and listened. Even when Feargal was trying to provoke Deanna, and even when her responses were barbed or spiky, it was clear that they were both enjoying the encounter. Feargal tried to itemise the gains that women had made over the past thirty years, Deanna came back with the things that made their lives harder. Feargal said that the fact she'd become so well known surely showed how much respect was now given to the women's movement; Deanna retorted that men were condescending towards prominent women. Feargal mentioned the power of women's internet groups like Mumsnet, reminding Deanna that politicians had fallen over themselves to answer their questions. Deanna replied that they still hadn't managed to talk to women without trying to patronise them first. Most men, especially prominent men, thought that their very appearance was enough to placate women; they forgot that women were perfectly capable of having independent views.

'D'you remember when the novelist P.D. James skewered the director general of the BBC in an interview?' she asked. 'He seemed to have made the common mistake of underestimating the intellect of an elderly woman. The unfortunate thing is that no matter what our age we often underestimate ourselves too.'

'I'm sure you don't,' said Feargal. 'I'm sure you've never underestimated yourself in your life.'

Deanna faltered for the first time in the interview.

'I don't underestimate women,' she said eventually. 'But I do know my own limitations.'

'You have limitations?' There was a challenge in Feargal's eyes.

'Everyone does,' she said, recovering. 'The trick is knowing the ones that you actually have and the ones that other people have forced on to you.'

Lainey continued to watch as Feargal quizzed Deanna further about her work and her beliefs. But as he'd promised, he didn't ask her a single thing about her private life. Lainey felt a sense of relief as the closing credits started to roll. In the end, the past wasn't important. Who'd done what so many years ago didn't matter any more. But she wouldn't have wanted Deanna to have to publicly answer questions about her feelings and her actions as a nineteen-year-old away from home and faced with an unwanted pregnancy, and about the subsequent story of Anthony and Jorge. Her mother would have come under a barrage of criticism for keeping the details from her. Ultimately, what had happened was nobody's business but their own, and Lainey thought it was right to keep it that way.

She put her bag over her shoulder and walked out of the studio. Halfway down the stairs she heard the buzz of voices, and she hesitated for a moment as Deanna and Feargal came into view. Deanna looked at Lainey, startled.

'What are you doing here?' she asked.

'The weather, obviously,' replied Lainey.

'This late?'

'I stayed to watch you, of course.'

'Oh.'

'You were good. You too,' she added, glancing at Feargal. 'You gave her plenty of opportunities to make her case.'

'And to make me look foolish,' said Feargal. 'She ran rings around me most of the time.'

'That's my job,' said Deanna.

'You're better at yours than I am at mine,' Feargal told her. 'You got what you wanted. I didn't.'

'What did you want?' asked Lainey.

'The personal, not the political,' said Feargal.

Deanna looked amused by his twisting of the well-known feminist slogan.

'You know that eventually people will realise that Lainey's your daughter,' said Feargal. 'I should have said something tonight. I was going to. But I backed off. That was a mistake.'

'It's not a mistake to respect people's private lives,' said Lainey, aware that Deanna was looking at her with a hint of apprehension. 'As for me – I want to do my own thing. I don't need to be Deanna Ryan's daughter.'

'Oh, Lainey, you very much are,' Feargal told her. 'The trouble with you two ladies is that I can't seem to resist you.'

Lainey looked at him sceptically.

'Your mother somehow manages to wrap me round her little finger,' continued Feargal. 'And I think you're doing the exact same thing.'

'Rubbish,' said Lainey. But she laughed.

'I was going to ask Deanna to join me for a drink,' said Feargal. 'Would you like to come too?'

'You know, Feargal, I think I'll just head off, if you don't mind,' Deanna told him. 'I'm tired and I've an early-morning flight to London tomorrow.'

'You do?' Both Feargal and Lainey looked at her in surprise.

'I'm speaking at a Women in Business meeting in the City,' said Deanna.

'I didn't know that,' said Lainey. 'Are you off for good this time?'

'Not quite,' replied Deanna. 'After London, I have to go to Paris. Then I'm back for a day or two to get my things together. I've wrapped up all the stuff I need to do here.'

'I hope we have a chance to meet one more time before you go,' said Feargal.

'Why? Now that you're finished with my interview, you don't need to talk to me at all.'

'I'd like to,' he said.

Deanna hesitated. 'I'll call you,' she told him. 'Right now, though, I'm going home.'

'There's a cab waiting for me outside,' said Feargal. 'You two are going in more or less the same direction, aren't you? So take it if you like. I'll get them to send another for me.'

'Thank you,' said Deanna. 'Does that suit you, Lainey?'

'Well . . . yes, thanks.'

'Excellent.'

The three of them walked to the foyer of the studios. The monitors on the walls were showing the current programme, a political question-and-answer format where the panel (all men) was discussing the latest economic news. Deanna gave them a black look and glanced outside. The cab was waiting.

'You're sure you don't mind us nabbing this one?' asked Lainey.

'Not at all,' said Feargal.

'In that case, thanks again,' she said.

'Hopefully I'll see you around,' Feargal told her. 'And maybe you could come on my other show yourself some day?'

'I don't think so,' she said lightly. 'But never say never.'

'Good night, Lainey,' he said and kissed her on the cheek. Then he turned to Deanna. 'Call me?'

'I said I would,' she told him. 'I always keep my promises, no matter how rash.'

'Good.' He kissed her too. Then both Lainey and Deanna walked outside and got into the waiting cab.

Lainey gave the driver directions, but as they drove towards the city, Deanna turned to her and asked if she wouldn't like to come to Madeleine's for a while.

'Now?' Lainey looked at her watch. 'It's very late.'

'I know,' said Deanna. 'But your grandmother would like to see you. And you know she doesn't go to bed early. Besides, she was staying up to watch me tonight. Well, I assume she watched both of us; she always watches you when you're doing the weather.'

'Your appearance was far more interesting than mine,' said Lainey.

'Perhaps. But don't you think it's nice for her to see both her daughter and her granddaughter on screen? Two successful women?'

'I'm just presenting the weather,' said Lainey. 'It might be nice for her to see me, but it's hardly success, is it?'

'You're an expert at what you do.' Deanna sounded frustrated. 'You both forecast it and present it. Why do you always put yourself down in front of me? What is it that stops you from admitting that you've done well?'

Lainey stared at her. 'Me? Done well? As far as you're concerned? Are you kidding me?'

'No,' said Deanna.

'I thought you looked down on what I do,' Lainey said.

'Have I ever told you that?' demanded Deanna. 'You're a smart, intelligent girl and you're doing a good job. That's exactly what I would've wanted for you. Why on earth wouldn't I think you were a success?'

Lainey didn't know what to say. She'd always felt that it was impossible to live up to Deanna's expectations.

'Your grandmother thinks you're a success too,' Deanna said.

'Of course she does,' Lainey agreed. 'That's because she thinks anyone who's on the telly is successful.'

'Are you going to come and see her with me or not?'

'I guess so.' Lainey didn't feel like a successful woman right now. She felt like a teenager being ticked off by her mother.

Deanna gave the new directions to the driver and sat back in her seat.

Neither of them spoke for the remainder of the journey to Killester. When they arrived at the house, it was Deanna who unlocked the door and went in first.

Madeleine was sitting in the armchair in front of the television. She was watching the political programme that had followed Deanna's appearance on Feargal's show, but she turned down the volume as her daughter and granddaughter walked into the room. She smiled at both of them, told Deanna she'd been brilliant and told Lainey that she was glad to see her.

'I'm glad to see you too.' Lainey sat on the sofa.

Deanna moved some books out of the other armchair and flopped into it.

'I know you're angry with me about your father,' Madeleine said gently to Lainey. 'Your grandfather always said that you would be one day.'

'Did Grandad want to tell me about him?' asked Lainey.

'He didn't know what was best,' Madeleine replied. 'Neither of us did. The thing is, honey, there didn't seem much point in discussing Jorge. By the time you were old enough to understand, his parents had passed away too. We couldn't see what would be gained by talking about it.'

'Except that I would have known,' Lainey told her. 'I would have known that he cared. And it doesn't matter what *his* father was like; it was *my* father I would have wanted to hear about.'

'You always insisted you didn't care,' Madeleine reminded her.

'Because I thought *he* didn't,' protested Lainey. 'If you'd told me he'd come back, then I would've wanted you to tell me everything about him.'

'There wasn't really an awful lot to tell,' Madeleine said. 'He didn't stay with your mum for long. It was a brief fling, that's all.'

Deanna's face reddened. 'It was long enough,' she protested. 'At least at the start.'

'Tell me about it now,' demanded Lainey.

Deanna exhaled slowly. Then she closed her eyes.

'He was the love of my life,' she said slowly. 'I never felt for anyone what I felt for Jorge. I don't think I ever will again.'

She opened her eyes again and slowly began to talk about the day she'd met him, and the days after that. Days when they'd walked hand in hand along the shore, sat on the deck together while he played his guitar, talked about the meaning of life, their dreams and their hopes and their aspirations. Lainey had never heard Deanna speak like this before, never known her to become emotional over a man.

'Of course he always said that he was an artist,' said Deanna. 'Back then, his music was the most important thing in his life. He wrote a song for you.'

Lainey looked startled.

'He died before he could play it.' Deanna's jaw tightened. 'I wish I could've heard it. I regret very much that I didn't. He wrote beautiful songs. But then he went to work for his father. The notion of him working in a brokerage firm is one I can't even begin to get my head around. I was totally shocked when he told me. He must have been influenced in some way by Anthony, because he'd never have done it otherwise.'

'Unless he did it for me,' Lainey pointed out. 'Because he wanted to provide for me.'

'Perhaps,' agreed Deanna. 'But I can't help feeling that working for his father wasn't the best choice.'

'Maybe he would've got a job somewhere else eventually,' said Lainey. 'Maybe he had plans for us together.'

'I've often thought about that myself,' Deanna admitted. 'But the thing is, Lainey, after he died, I was terrified that he might have told someone else about whatever plans he had. And I couldn't take a risk with you . . .'

'So the reason you left me with Gran and Grandad was because you were afraid for me?' Lainey sounded hopeful.

'Not because I was a burden to you? Not because I interfered with your life?'

Deanna was silent. She got up and walked to the window. Lainey and Madeleine watched her as she stood with her back to them. It was almost a full minute before she turned around to face them.

'I can't lie to you, Lainey,' she said eventually. 'I really, really want to, because I know how much it means to you. I didn't realise it before, but I know now. You want everything to be like a fairy tale. You want two people to fall in love and be together and live happily ever after. You want their children to be needed and loved and for them to live some kind of Disney life. But real life's not like that.' She took a deep breath. 'I was afraid for you, yes, absolutely. I certainly didn't want you back in the States, because I didn't know what was going on with the Reeves family. I worried that Anthony Reeves knew about you and would want to take you, to replace the son he'd lost with a granddaughter. That was a genuine fear. But the truth is . . .' she moistened her lips with the tip of her tongue, 'I did what I hoped was the right thing, but not for the reasons you'd like. I didn't want my life messed up by you. I wanted desperately to go to college, and I couldn't see how I could do that with a small child. Even now, when there's so much more help available, it's bloody difficult to be a single parent. And I didn't want to be a parent at all. I knew Mom and Dad would do a much better job with you. As far as I was concerned, the whole Reeves thing was just an extra reason not to keep you with me.' She held up her hands helplessly. 'I know you'll think that's heartless and selfish. I accept that. But I can't sugar-coat it and pretend any different.'

'Your mother is only partly right.' Madeleine looked at Lainey, who was stony-faced at Deanna's words. 'She was always concerned about your welfare, and she did ask you to come and visit her after Anthony died. She thought that perhaps you might want to stay. But I have to be honest, Lainey, and tell you that your grandad and I were glad when you came home.'

Lainey remembered the summer she'd visited Deanna. The summer she'd spent staring at the ocean, resenting being dragged away from her friends and missing the holiday in Majorca with Val and her family. She'd remembered being impressed by Deanna's conversation and intellect, but thinking she'd be glad to get home to Madeleine's warmth and gossip. She'd been relieved when the fortnight was over. But it would have been different, surely, if she'd been brought up by Deanna. In that case they'd have bonded like a mother and daughter should.

'I'm glad you have the decency to be honest with me now,' she told her mother. 'But Gran's wrong. I don't think you wanted me to stay when I visited you.'

Deanna gave her the ghost of a smile. 'You were a truculent teenager,' she said. 'I guess I had idealised notions before you came. They were knocked out of me pretty damn quick.'

'What notions?'

'I thought we'd connect. That you'd suddenly understand me. That you'd want to be like me. I thought that we'd hang out together, but of course I was wrong about that. You wanted to do your thing. You wanted to be on your own.'

Lainey recalled her solitary days at Fisherman's Wharf or the aquarium wishing she was back home with Madeleine and Val and the people she loved.

'But you inspired me,' added Deanna.

'How?'

'I used to think I'd make the world a better place for all women,' she said. 'I'd think about you and tell myself that I wanted women of your generation to have more than women of my generation. But I thought about it in broad brush strokes. After your visit, I realised that I had to narrow my focus, deal with individual issues. And so I concentrated on women in the workplace, what it was like for them, what it should be like for them . . . I wrote *Women in Waiting* as a result. And it was my best-selling book.'

'Glad to be of help.' Lainey didn't look at her as she spoke.

'I'm sorry,' said Deanna. 'I'm sorry I was a shit mother and I'm sorry you didn't get what you wanted from me or from your father. I'm sorry that I continued to be a shit mother and will always be a shit mother, and I'm sorry you hate me so very much. I'm sorry I'm the woman I am, but I can't help that. And I can't help wanting to do things that you don't like or don't approve of.'

'I never said I didn't approve of your work,' said Lainey.

'But you see me like so many women of your age,' Deanna said. 'Out of touch, out of date, out of ideas . . .'

'Don't all children think of their parents like that at some point?' asked Lainey.

'Usually when they're teenagers,' Madeleine interjected. 'By the time they're your age, they've generally come to realise that their parents aren't quite so ancient and stupid after all.'

'I admire you,' Lainey told Deanna, who looked surprised and opened her mouth to speak. But Lainey held up her hand to stop her. 'I admire everything you've done. I admire the fact that you got your scholarship and that you published so many books and that people come to your lectures and that you've been to the White House and got your Legion of Honour medal and all of those things. I'm proud of you for that. I admire the fact that you don't give up and that you keep on and on reminding women that we have to work twice as hard to earn half as much and that the glass ceiling might have cracked a bit but it's still there. I like the fact that you hate Barbie dolls and mindless celebrities and glamour models. All those things make you who you are, and I wouldn't change that.'

'You wouldn't?'

'Of course not,' said Lainey. 'Oh look, Deanna, there's no use pretending I wouldn't have loved a mother like Val's, who talked to her about hairstyles and fashion and boyfriends and relationships and all that sort of stuff. I wanted a mother to read me books and hug me when I was unhappy and dry my eyes when I cried. But that's not you, and Gran did a good job of the reading and the hugging and the eye-drying and stuff like that. I love her for that. I also love you for who you are.'

'I didn't think . . .'

'I love you because you're my mother. I don't always like you,' she added. 'I think you're opinionated and dismissive and you have tunnel vision about loads of things. But you're also brainy and passionate and determined, and those are good qualities in a person.'

'They might be good qualities, but they make me sound terrible,' said Deanna.

'Not terrible,' said Lainey. 'Just not . . . not . . .'

'Not a mother,' Deanna finished.

'Don't concentrate on what Deanna's not,' advised Madeleine. 'That's what Grandad's saying. Concentrate on what she is.'

'Mom!' Deanna looked at Madeleine in exasperation. 'We're not even in the kitchen. Dad can't be in the living room too.'

'Why not?' asked Madeleine. 'Even when you were in America, we could feel your presence here. Just because your dad has gone somewhere further doesn't mean we can't feel his presence too. He was a very wise man. You didn't always appreciate it at the time. You should appreciate it now. You should listen to him. Both of you.'

Deanna shot a look at Lainey, whose lips held the ghost of a smile.

'You'll never get the better of Gran,' she told Deanna. 'She's had practice at bringing up two generations of Ryans. She always gets the last word. She always will.'

Chapter 31

Iridescence: bands of colour appearing as sunlight or moonlight passes through thin cloud

The following day, Lainey phoned Ken and asked him to meet her. She realised with a jolt of surprise that she hadn't called him since they'd got back together – in the last few weeks he'd always been the one to get in touch with her. Or to arrive at the apartment unexpectedly.

'Sure, babes,' he said. 'I'll drop over later tonight.'

'I'd really like to meet you in town,' she told him.

'But why?' he asked. 'It's far more comfortable in your apartment.'

'I need to go into town,' she told him.

'In that case . . .' He sounded disappointed.

'See you at eight,' she said and hung up.

She was standing at the bus stop when the now-familiar blue Golf pulled up beside her.

'Want a lift?' Shay asked.

'If you don't mind.' She opened the door and got in beside him. 'How're you feeling?'

'Are you going to ask me this every time we meet?' He glanced at her questioningly.

'Sorry,' she said. 'Are you getting bored with people worrying about you?'

'I hope you're not worrying about me,' he said. 'I don't want to be thought of as the hopeless basket case who can't look after himself.'

'You look perfectly capable of looking after yourself,' she admitted.

He grinned. 'Thank you.'

'Any word about your wife and children?'

He shook his head. 'These things take for ever. It's not like the legal people ring me up every day. Rachel did at the start, but they have her under control as well. Our lives are being run by other people now.'

'How horrible.'

'You get used to it.'

'It'll work out,' she said warmly. 'Truly it will.'

'I tell myself that,' he said. 'I also tell myself that it doesn't always. All the same, I'm not going to lose contact with my boys. I'm not.'

Lainey could hear the determination in his voice. His kids clearly meant a lot to him. She hadn't realised how deeply men felt about their children before, because her own experience hadn't been like that. Edmund, of course, had been a warm and loving presence in her life. But her father . . . Jorge. She'd got used to the idea that he hadn't wanted to know about her. She'd lived with it all her life. Yet it hadn't been as clear-cut as she'd always believed. She wondered how things would've turned out if Jorge had been like Shay from the start; a man who wouldn't let go. What sort of person would she have become as a result?

Once again the dream – no, she reminded herself, the memory – flashed through her mind. The rain, her father, the strength of his arms, the warmth of his body. Jorge. Who'd come back for her in the end.

'Will this do?' Shay's voice broke into her thoughts and she realised that they were in Capel Street. 'I'm turning up the quays towards Heuston. Going to see Lisa,' he added.

'This is fine, thanks. I appreciate it.'

'No problem.'

She opened the car door. 'See you around.'

'Sure. I'll wave across at you later.'

'I look forward to it.'

She pushed the door closed. Then the lights changed and he drove off into the evening traffic.

Thanks to the lift from Shay, she was in town earlier than she'd planned. She was meeting Ken in The Old Stand, one of his favourite city centre pubs. They often met there on the days of rugby internationals, where they'd cheer on the Irish team with the rest of the highly partisan crowd. The pub was on the other side of the Liffey, about a ten-minute walk away. She strolled leisurely southwards, pausing for a moment on the Millennium bridge and looking west towards the setting sun. The sky was a dusky pink, reflected in the water of the river.

Red sky at night, shepherd's delight. Or sailor's delight. Both of the phrases were familiar to her. The colour was due to the scattering of light through the atmosphere. A red sky in the evening meant that the light was coming through a high concentration of dust particles because of high pressure and stable weather. Not for much longer, she thought, as she recalled her charts. The skies would change. But right now they were beautiful.

She glanced at her watch. She didn't want to be at the pub before Ken. In the past, as a result of her desire to be punctual, she'd often arrived at meeting points before him, but she was going to be late tonight. Not very late; she was incapable of being very late. But a few minutes would be fine. So she continued to walk slowly, diverting through the cobbled streets of Temple Bar, which were still bustling with tourists, until she turned towards Dame Street. She crossed the road and looked at her watch again. It was past eight o'clock. She quickened her pace.

There were about half a dozen people sitting at the bar when she arrived at the pub a couple of minutes later. She looked around but couldn't see Ken. He didn't have the same attitude towards punctuality as she did. She hesitated for a moment, then went to the Ladies', where she ran a brush through her hair and reapplied her lip gloss. When she returned to the bar he was there, sitting at a table, a bottle of sparkling water in front of him.

He waved at her and told her she was looking great.

She was wearing her favourite pair of skinny jeans, which made her long legs look even longer, and a white shirt over a cerise top. She sat down beside him.

'What'll you have?' he asked.

'A bottle of Miller would be nice.'

He got her drink and brought it back.

He was looking good himself, she thought. He'd had his

hair cut since she'd last seen him, and his face was smooth-shaven, which she liked. Ken liked to flirt with stubble; he thought it gave him a more masculine appearance, but it always brought Lainey out in a rash. She used to insist that he shaved at the times when she was presenting the TV forecasts. She didn't want to appear on the nation's screens with a red face.

'So how've you been?' asked Ken. 'Sorry I haven't been over for a while. Training hard.' He nodded at the glass in front of him. 'That's partly why I didn't want to come to a bar tonight. It's difficult to drink nothing but water.'

She hadn't thought of that. She'd just decided that she wanted to be out, not stuck in the apartment with him.

'Maybe we can head to your place later?'

She smiled but said nothing.

'How was your trip to Stockholm?' he asked.

It seemed like an age ago, and it was hard to believe she hadn't actually seen Ken since her return, only spoken to him briefly on the phone or by text.

'Enjoyable,' she replied. She didn't tell him that Carla's marriage – which had seemed so solid then – was now under repair.

'I liked it when I went there for a triathlon event.' He started to talk about the competition and how well he'd done. Then he moved on to talk about the one he was currently in training for. 'It's a strong field, but I've a good chance of a top-five finish,' he concluded.

'Great,' she said.

He looked at her, a trace of irritation in his eyes. 'What's the matter?'

'Nothing.'

'Oh, God.' He groaned. 'Nothing? That means I've done something terrible, doesn't it?'

'No.'

'Of course it does. Nothing is like the ticking time bomb. Women lob it into the conversation when they want it to explode.'

'That's not true.'

'Good.'

They were silent for a moment.

'It's just . . .'

He groaned again. 'I knew it.'

'Do you love me?' she asked.

Ken sighed. 'Of course I do.'

'But things have been different between us since Carla's wedding.'

'Better,' said Ken. 'Less pressured.'

'This is the first time we've been out together since then.'

'Is it?' He sounded surprised.

'Ken! Yes. All we've done in the last few weeks is be at my apartment. We have a drink, we go to bed. You leave. Sometimes we don't even bother with the drink.'

He looked at her. 'And because I come to your apartment and stay with you and make love to you, you need to ask me if I love you?'

'Yes.'

'I brought roses,' he reminded her.

'I know. But—'

He interrupted her. 'I've said I love you, that should be enough.'

And it should, she thought. He was right. He'd come to her; she didn't have to go to him. He brought flowers

He stayed. Not every night, of course. But he always came back. So why did she need to ask him? Why didn't it feel right?

She sighed. 'Don't mind me. I've had a bad day.'

Which wasn't strictly true. She'd had a busy day, with very little time to brood on Deanna and Jorge and their doomed relationship. She was beginning to put it into perspective, seeing things through her mother and grandmother's eyes. Understanding their course of action. She was still angry with them, but her anger was beginning to disappear like hoar frost beneath the morning sun.

'What's a bad day in weather forecasting?' asked Ken. 'Blue skies and sun or clouds and storms?'

'Getting either of them wrong,' she said.

'Well, why don't we make your day better?' He finished his water. 'Let's go back to your place and I'll do things to you that'll cheer you up no end.'

'No,' she said quickly. And then added, 'Thanks.'

'Huh?'

'I don't want to go back to my apartment and have sex with you,' she said.

'I knew it.' He looked at her wearily. 'You want to have some over-long deep and meaningful conversation again.'

'Yes,' she said. 'I do. But not a long one. Honestly.'

'All right.' This time his look was challenging. 'Say whatever it is you want to say.'

She hadn't thought about what she wanted to say. She didn't really know. Part of her was aching to tell him that she loved him and wanted to marry him and be happy with him. She wanted to put her arms around him and have him put his arms around her and she wanted to feel safe and secure and loved. Another part of her wanted to say all that but add that he couldn't take her for granted. He couldn't assume she'd always be there for him, ready to slip out of her clothes and twine her legs around him whenever he asked. She wanted to ask him why he'd come back to her after Bangor. She wanted to know if they had a future together.

But she didn't say any of these things. Because it was as though the clouds had parted to reveal a blue sky. She knew for sure why she'd asked him to meet her that night. She knew what she needed to say.

'You were right to break up with me,' she told him. 'I was crazy about you, but for all the wrong reasons.'

'Excuse me?' He stared at her.

'I wanted to marry you,' she said. 'I thought you were . . . well, The One.'

'And now you don't?'

'*You* don't,' she reminded him. 'You don't want to marry me and you don't want responsibilities, and you're right.'

'I am?'

'Yes.'

She thought she could see a glimmer of relief in his eyes.

'But of course I want those things,' she told him.

His expression changed. Now he looked hunted.

'Not with you, though,' she added. 'Because that's pointless. But with someone.'

'Maybe in the future . . .'

'Don't say that.' She shook her head. 'Please don't. You came back to me because you enjoyed sleeping with me. Which is fair enough; I enjoyed it with you too. But that's not enough in the end. Especially when . . . especially when it's always when you want. You turn up at my place when it suits you. You stay when it suits you. Coming out with me tonight was a major effort on your part.'

'Make me sound like a total bastard, why don't you?'

'Hey, it's not your fault,' she said. 'It's mine. For wanting someone, anyone so much that I was happy when you turned up again. I thought it meant something.'

'It does mean something.'

'What? That you're not getting it from anyone else?'

'Lainey!'

'You came back to me because I was a habit.'

'I came back because I missed you.'

'Not really,' she said. 'You missed the sex.'

'Didn't you?'

'Yes. But not that much.'

'Thanks a lot.' He sounded annoyed. 'Now you're saying I wasn't the best you ever had.'

'It was good,' she agreed. 'Great, even. But it's not good any more. And that's because I want different things.'

'So you're breaking up with me?' He looked incredulous. 'You? Are breaking up with me?'

'Yes.'

'If I walk away, I don't come back,' he warned her. 'It's finished. For good.'

'I know.'

'I don't understand you,' he said. 'You wanted to be with me all the time.'

'I did,' she told him. 'Now I don't.'

'Right.' He stood up. 'I see why you didn't want me to come to your place tonight.'

She said nothing.

'Is this anything to do with your mother?' he asked as he

put on his jacket. 'The man-hater? Has she been filling your head with feminist nonsense?'

'No,' said Lainey. 'This is to do with me. Filling my own head with common sense. At last.'

She'd broken up with someone for the first time in her life. It was a strange feeling. Disappointment and sadness. But relief too. And a sense of achievement. Plus a growing sense of freedom. She didn't have to worry about Ken any more. About being there when he wanted. About saying the right thing. About not upsetting him. She didn't have to be a perfect girlfriend. She didn't have to pretend to care about his damn triathlon events. Or going to the gym. Or making sure that her apartment (or at least the bedroom) was always tidy. Not that he'd ever noticed, really. It was only she who'd cared.

She began to smile. She was a single woman. Unmarried. Unengaged. And OK with that. At last.

She took out her phone and opened her contacts list.

'Hi,' she said when Deanna answered her call. 'I just thought I'd let you know. I've dumped my boyfriend. It was the right thing to do. But if it hadn't been for you, I don't know if I'd ever have done it. So thanks.'

'That's OK.' Deanna sounded surprised. 'You mean that guy I met at your apartment?'

'Yes,' said Lainey.

'He wasn't good enough for you,' Deanna said.

'I know.'

'I'm glad you realised it.'

'So am I.'

'Plenty more fish in the sea,' her mother added.

Lainey chuckled. 'I know that too. I do a lot of fishing.'

'I suppose one day you might find one you don't want to throw back.'

This time Lainey laughed out loud. 'I've never thrown one back before. It was a liberating experience.'

'Good,' said Deanna.

'So . . . thanks again,' said Lainey.

'You're welcome.'

Lainey was smiling as she ended the call. She thought Deanna was too.

Chapter 32

Cloudbow: an optical effect seen from above low and mid-level clouds, caused by sunlight reflecting and refracting from the tiny droplets that make them up

It was two in the morning, and most of the apartments in Laurel Park were in darkness by the time Lainey got home. After Ken had left, she'd sat on her own in the bar for a while, then she'd phoned Val to tell her what she'd done. Val, sounding anxious, had asked if she was OK, and despite Lainey's assurances that she was absolutely fine, had begged her to drop over. Lainey had dithered about it, but then walked up to St Stephen's Green and caught the Luas to Dundrum.

Val greeted her on the doorstep and looked at her anxiously.

'I really am OK,' Lainey said a little impatiently. 'It's a break-up, that's all.'

'Yes, but before . . .' Val couldn't help her worried expression. 'You've always been so upset before. And this is the second time with Ken.'

'But the first time for me.' Lainey sounded triumphant.

'Pathetic and ridiculous though it may be, it's my inaugural break-up night. I'm celebrating.'

'Really?'

'And truly,' she assured Val.

When Val realised that Lainey actually was happy about it, she insisted on opening a bottle of champagne.

'You keep champagne on ice?' asked Lainey, who'd followed her into the kitchen.

'I was keeping it for later in the week,' admitted Val. 'We're having the next-door neighbours in for dinner and I thought it'd be nice to have champagne. But we have another bottle. They were on offer in the local off-licence and Nick picked them up. He won't mind sharing this one tonight.'

And so Lainey allowed her friend and her husband to toast her on her first successful break-up. They did it with much laughter and clinking of glasses, and Val repeated Deanna's comment about the number of fish in the sea. Then Lainey sat down and told them all about Jorge and Anthony, which left them open-mouthed.

'So how do you feel about all this?' asked Val anxiously.

'Still dealing with it,' Lainey confessed. 'But I'm doing all right.'

'You look it,' agreed Val.

'You always do,' said Nick, and Val punched him lightly in the side.

Lainey smiled at the interplay between Val and her husband. She could see that they were friends as well as lovers. Which is how it should be, she told herself. And what I'll find one day, hopefully. But not quite yet. Right now I'm rather enjoying being an unattached woman.

Nick had gone to bed at eleven, and Val and Lainey had

spent time talking together, not only discussing Lainey's family history again, but also discussing Carla's situation.

'I hope it works out for her,' said Val. 'But I have a horrible feeling it might not.'

'So do I,' said Lainey. 'All the same, Carla's a very practical woman. Lennart is a practical man. Maybe they'll simply be practical about it together.'

'Maybe,' agreed Val. 'Still, I'd kill Nick if it were him. And he knows it.'

It was after one by the time Lainey phoned for a cab and headed home. As she said goodbye to her friend, she realised that although she was happy for Val and delighted that she was content in her marriage, she herself didn't feel the tug of envy that normally bothered her after an evening at her friend's house. She didn't feel as though she was a failure, nor, she told herself as she let herself into her block and ran lightly up the stairs, did she feel sad about being on her own.

She was tired, but not ready to sleep yet. So she stepped out on to her balcony and leaned on the iron railing. Then she looked up at the sky.

The clouds were scudding across the full moon, which shone silver-white. Away to one side of it she could see the bright light of the planet Jupiter. Without a telescope she couldn't make out its string of moons, like diamonds chipped from a massive stone. She remembered the first time her grandfather had shown them to her, beckoning her to take her place at the telescope and look deep into the night sky. When she'd finished, he'd lifted her into his arms and hugged her, and she'd felt safe and secure. She'd always felt safe and secure with Edmund.

A light came on in Shay's apartment. These days he usually

kept his curtains half closed, so she didn't see him walk through the living room. But then the curtains parted and he pushed open the patio doors and stepped outside. Lainey didn't know if he'd seen her, until he raised his hand in acknowledgement.

'You're up late,' he called softly.

'So are you.'

'I stayed at Lisa's for longer than I intended. Now I can't sleep.'

Lainey hesitated for a moment. 'D'you want to come over for a while? I don't think I can sleep either.'

'Sure. Give me a a few seconds.'

He disappeared back inside his apartment. A couple of minutes later she buzzed him into her block and then opened her apartment door. He appeared at the top of the stairs carrying a box containing two large cupcakes.

'Got the taste for them with you,' he said. 'But did the man thing of buying far too many. Thought you might like some.'

She took the box from him. 'Would you like one with a coffee?'

'Are you mad, woman? There's no chance I'll sleep if I drink coffee.'

'I have decaff. Or tea,' she added. 'A nice camomile blend. That's supposed to help with the zzzzs.'

'Why do girls always have this kind of stuff?' he demanded. 'Camomile tea. Decaff coffee. I have ordinary tea, a big jar of instant, and heavy-duty Java beans for when I need a decent caffeine hit.'

She looked amused. 'For the same reason we have loads of different shower gels and shampoos. We like the notion of being pampered.'

'I'm not sure camomile tea is pampering. More sissy,' said Shay.

'You're afraid of showing your feminine side?'

'A bit. But I'll risk it.'

'Camomile tea it is so,' she said cheerfully. 'Sit yourself down and I'll bring it to you.'

She went into her galley kitchen, made the tea and put the cupcakes on a plate. When she came back, Shay was on the sofa, his legs stretched out in front of him.

'Your apartment is very cosy,' he said. 'I like mine, but it's more . . . more functional, I guess.'

'Another girlie thing,' she told him. 'A woman's touch.'

'I guess you're right.' He sat forward and took the tea from her. 'Still, I'm glad this is a mug. I'd have been far too much in touch with my inner woman if you'd offered me a china cup on a saucer to go with my frosted-icing cakes.'

'I only do cups for special occasions,' she told him.

'I'm not a special occasion?'

'God, no. You're just the neighbour popping in for a cuppa.'

'Even if it is in the middle of the night.'

'It's all the same to me,' she commented. 'In a couple of days' time I'll be working through the night.'

'Is that weird?' he asked.

She shook her head. 'You get used to it. Anyhow, we're all 24/7 now.'

'When I wake up in the middle of the night I feel as though I'm the only person in the whole world who's up,' he confessed. 'It freaks me out.'

'Call me next time you feel like that,' she said.

'That's sweet of you, but I don't think you'd thank me for ringing you at two in the morning.'

'If I've been doing the TV forecast, I'm often still awake at two myself. I'd welcome someone to talk to.'

'I'll bear it in mind.'

'Any fresh news about your kids?' she asked after a moment's silence between them.

His face lit up, although there was still tension around his eyes.

'We're meeting next week,' he said. 'Me and Rachel and our solicitors. She got in touch with them again. She says she wants to work something out. Something we'll all be happy about.'

'That sounds like good news,' said Lainey.

'I don't want to get too excited.' Shay's voice was cautious. 'But I'm hoping that this time we'll find a way. Rachel isn't a bad person. I don't want her to think I am either. But you know how it is. You get stubborn. It becomes a battle, and it shouldn't.'

'I'm sure it'll work out,' she said.

'We have to make it work out,' said Shay. 'The most important thing is that the boys know they have two parents who love them.'

'I'm sure they know that already.'

'I'm always afraid they'll forget me,' admitted Shay. 'It's not the same when I'm living away from them.'

'I remembered my dad even though I thought it was a dream. I still remember him. And I was very angry with Deanna and Madeleine for keeping the story from me. If he was alive, I would've wanted to find him. Your boys already know you and love you. They won't forget you or let Olivier take your place.'

'I wish I could be sure of that.'

'Believe me,' she said, 'you won't be one of those fathers who loses touch with his children, no matter what happens.'

'When I moved out, I thought I'd lost everything. I wanted to find a woman to take Rachel's place. I went out with a string of them, looking for what I had before. Of course I was being silly. You can't get something like that back.'

'I suppose it's not about getting things back. It's about how things fit into the future.'

'You're right. And I was being selfish, because those women meant very little to me. I didn't much like myself whenever I thought about them.'

'We all do selfish things, but sometimes for the best of reasons . . .' Lainey's voice faltered as she thought of Deanna, who tried so hard to justify her decisions.

'The best of intentions sometimes don't work out exactly how you plan,' remarked Shay. 'They didn't for your mum, either.'

'Indeed.' She twirled a strand of hair between her fingers. 'Funny, it's changed how I feel about Deanna, too. She'll always be a self-centred woman, but I can imagine what it was like for her. And I sympathise.'

'She's not generally the kind of person you think needs sympathy.'

'She was only nineteen when she got pregnant and twenty-one when Jorge died. It must have been awful for her. Especially when she found out everything else. I'm not sure how I would've coped.'

'Brilliantly,' said Shay. He drained his mug and put it on the table. 'You're definitely a coper. You saved my life, remember?'

'All I did was call the ambulance,' Lainey reminded him.

'I probably would've thrown a complete wobbler if I'd been in Deanna's shoes back then.'

'I guess we all want to think we'd do the right thing or the best thing under every circumstance. But we probably wouldn't.'

She nodded and put her mug on the table beside his. Then she curled her legs up beneath her. 'It's funny how life becomes complicated,' she said. 'You want everything to be smooth and easy and you can't see why it shouldn't be, and yet somehow events conspire against you. And you fight it, but sometimes it doesn't do any good.' She closed her eyes. 'You just have to hope that it works out in the end.'

Shay didn't reply, which was OK with her. She could feel herself drifting into sleep, and she told herself that she should ask him to go so that she could head off to bed. But she was too comfortable on the sofa to bother.

She didn't know how much later it was when she suddenly awoke. She realised her head was resting on Shay's shoulder and she jerked upright. But he didn't move. His eyes were closed and his breathing was regular and even.

'Shay?' She spoke softly. 'Are you awake?'

He didn't reply.

She got up from the sofa and brought the two mugs into the kitchen. She put them in the sink, then walked back into the living room. He still hadn't moved. She watched him for a moment, uncertain whether to wake him or not. He didn't look uncomfortable sleeping upright on the sofa, but she couldn't help feeling that he'd have a crick in his neck if he stayed like that. Nevertheless, sleep might be what he needed. He was still going through a hard time.

She went into her bedroom and took a soft woollen throw from the top of the wardrobe. She draped it over him, half expecting that it would wake him. But he simply gave a gentle sigh and settled further into the sofa. She was amused by the notion that this was the first time she'd ever had a man in her apartment who'd slept on the sofa.

She stood in front of him and watched the gentle rise and fall of his chest. I can't believe I'm doing this, she said to herself. Standing in my apartment watching a sleeping man. A man who's a neighbour and a friend and who I like but about whom I feel so differently to anyone else I've ever known. Mainly, she reminded herself, because we don't have a 'relationship'. Even though he'd given her lifts into town, even though he'd come to Feargal's party with her, even though he'd been there for her when she needed him – and, more importantly, she'd been there for him when he needed someone too – they weren't a couple. Each time she saw him, she didn't wonder if this was the start of something special. She didn't try to make it something special herself. She didn't have wedding fantasies about him. And yet, she realised, she liked him. She liked being with him. She liked him being here with her. Even if he was asleep. And snoring softly.

'The first time you slept with me, I realised you snored,' she murmured softly. 'But it didn't matter.'

She went back to her bedroom and crawled sleepily into bed. She tried to conjure up a picture of walking down the aisle with Shay, but it wouldn't come. She didn't really want it to. She was newly unattached and she needed to stay that way for a while. Besides, she murmured to herself as she pulled the duvet around her, I've never thought of Shay as someone I want to marry. Just as a friend. It's nice to have a friend who's a man.

She realised she'd always woven dramas about the men she knew, turned her time with them into the most important part of her life. But the important part of her life was how she dealt with things herself, not how she tried to get other people to deal with them.

Que sera, sera. What will be will be. Madeleine used to sing it to her as a lullaby when she was small. She'd always liked it. But she'd never taken the words to heart before. Now, as she drifted into sleep, she did.

Chapter 33

Rainbow: formed by light being refracted and reflected by moisture in the air into concentric arcs of colour

Lainey was at Madeleine's house when Deanna arrived back from her trip to Paris. It was a wet day; rain had been falling steadily all morning, although the forecast was for the sun to break through later in the afternoon. But it was still hissing down when they heard the key in the lock and Deanna called out that she was back.

'Heavens above.' Madeleine looked at her in surprise when she walked into the room. 'You're looking good. Did everything go well for you?'

Deanna blushed, a sheepish expression on her face, while Lainey gave a low whistle.

'I am *so* liking this,' she said. 'Definitely.'

Deanna glanced at herself in the mirror over the mantelpiece. She still hadn't got used to the new colour in her hair, a gentle honey-blond that suited her skin tone and knocked at least five years off her age.

'That's not why I got it done,' she told Lainey when she

told her this. 'I went into a salon in Paris looking for a wash and blow dry. Obviously my schoolgirl French isn't quite as good as I thought, because the next thing I know she's tut-tutting and loading colour on to my head.'

Lainey roared with laughter. 'And what about the outfit you're wearing? Is that a result of schoolgirl French too?'

Deanna was clad, as usual, in jeans. But instead of her normal white blouse and black jacket, she was wearing a soft blue top that reflected the sapphire of her eyes. And her jacket was raspberry cord.

'What can I say?' She shrugged. 'It was Paris, for heaven's sake. The shopping was great and I couldn't help myself.'

'You look fabulous,' Lainey told her. 'You really do.'

'Hmm.' Deanna glanced at her reflection again before sitting down. 'Looks aren't everything.'

'Of course not,' said Madeleine, who'd been to the hairdresser herself that morning and was wearing her own hair in her favourite elegant up-do. 'But there's nothing wrong with making the most of what you've got.'

'Why?' Deanna sounded slightly despairing. 'Why does it matter so much?'

'Sometimes it matters too much,' agreed Lainey. 'But when you look good outside, you feel good inside.'

'You must always feel great so,' said her mother.

Lainey's eyes widened. 'Is that a joke?' she asked.

'No,' said Deanna. 'A compliment. I was checking out the documentary on my laptop last night. You looked stunning.'

'Thank you.' Lainey was unexpectedly overcome by her mother's comment.

'Really, you did,' said Deanna. 'And you came across very well too.'

'All that TV experience,' Lainey told her as dismissively as she could. 'Has to be good for something.'

'I wondered, would you like to add a little bit to the end?' asked Deanna.

'Like what?'

Deanna said nothing for a moment. Lainey watched her quizzically. There was no doubt, she thought, that her mother looked a different person now. Softer, and less angry. Looks, however, were deceiving. She was probably just the same as ever inside. And God only knew what she was cooking up for the documentary now.

'I wondered if you'd talk about motherhood with me,' Deanna said eventually.

'Huh?'

'I don't want you to think I'm doing this as a hook for the documentary,' said Deanna quickly. 'It's not that at all. But I can't have you in this film and not say that you're my daughter.'

'Nobody will care about it,' said Lainey. 'Don't worry.'

'I care,' said Deanna.

'Oh.'

Lainey didn't know what else to say.

'I've thwarted Feargal Wright with his every attempt to make our relationship into some big story. But sooner or later it'll become news. Better we deal with it ourselves than have it happen in a way we don't want.'

'It'll be a one-day wonder,' said Lainey.

'I know. But I'd rather it was *our* one-day wonder.'

'So do you want to tell them everything? About Jorge?' Lainey looked anxious.

'What do *you* want?' asked Deanna.

'It hardly matters . . .'

'Whatever you want,' Deanna told her. 'Whatever you decide. That's what we'll do.'

Lainey stared at her in astonishment.

'Why have you changed your tune so much?' she demanded. 'Why is it suddenly about me?'

'It should always have been about you,' Deanna told her. 'I was wrong before.'

'No.' Lainey looked sympathetically at her mother. 'I understand why it wasn't. I really do.'

'I was selfish,' said Deanna.

'Maybe,' acknowledged Lainey. 'But you accomplished so much. You helped a whole generation of women. You did important work.'

'Don't you think the most important work would have been making sure my own child was happy?' asked Deanna.

'I *was* happy,' Lainey reminded her. 'Very happy. I still am. Oh, I get miserable from time to time. I get it wrong from time to time too. But I turned out OK.'

'Thanks to your gran.'

'Not entirely.' Lainey glanced at Madeleine, who hadn't spoken. 'Gran's been wonderful to me,' she said. 'But you were always there to drive me on. To make me try harder. You were someone to live up to.'

'Not someone to live with, though.'

'We can't have it all,' Lainey reminded her. 'You've said that yourself.'

'I should have done things better,' said Deanna.

'Everyone can say that,' Lainey told her. 'But life is about doing the best we can.'

Deanna swallowed hard.

Lainey got up from the chair where she'd been sitting.

'I have to go,' she said. 'I'm due at work later. I'll happily do that extra bit for you. I'll have a think about what I want to say. But we'll agree on it together.'

'Thank you,' said Deanna.

'When will you be heading back to California?'

'Next week,' said Deanna. 'I've been away a lot longer than I expected. But it's been worth it.'

'Will you be meeting Feargal before you go?'

'Maybe.' Deanna's voice was carefully non-committal.

Lainey smiled at her mother as she draped a cerise scarf with gold embroidery around her neck and picked up her bag. 'Well, enjoy yourself if you do, and let me know when it suits you to do the interview stuff.'

'Will do,' said Deanna. 'See you soon. Perhaps I'll even see you in California again some day?'

'That would be nice,' Lainey told her.

She turned to Madeleine. 'Bye, Gran. I'll see you soon too.'

'Goodbye sweetheart,' said Madeleine.

Lainey paused with her hand on the doorknob. She looked at Deanna. Then she went back and hugged her.

'Bye, Mum,' she said, and let herself out.

The rain had stopped. The dark grey clouds were disappearing. And as Lainey got on her bike, she could see a brilliant rainbow arcing across the sky.

Read on for a preview of Sheila O'Flanagan's fabulous new novel, BETTER TOGETHER, available in 2012 from Headline Review

Prologue

Sheridan Gray knew that the piece she had written, full of tragedy, drama and long-kept secrets, was one of the strongest she'd ever done. It was a compelling story and she'd got the balance just right. She'd been sympathetic where sympathy would be expected, and critical where it was important to criticise. It was everything she'd been asked for and more. It would change the lives of the people concerned for ever.

And it would change hers too. At least that was what she hoped. That was why she'd written it. To change everything. Back to the way it was before. Back to when she'd had everything she'd ever wanted.

Well, almost.

She stared unblinkingly at the computer. Was it ever possible to go back? And would she ever be able to forget the people about whom she'd just written? People who had become part of her life.

She had to. Because that was the only way to be a winner. She'd always wanted to be a winner, and with this story, she was.

The only problem, she realised, as she saved the document and closed her laptop, was that she didn't know if the prize was worth it. Or even if it was the prize she truly wanted any more.

Chapter 1

Sheridan was so engrossed in the newspaper report she was writing that she dismissed the notification about a new email in her inbox without even thinking. Her fingers continued to fly over the keyboard as she described the carnival atmosphere in Dublin the previous night, where an unprecedented crowd had turned up to watch the Brazil women's national soccer team play a friendly match in the city. It had been a fun evening, full of colour and good humour, helped by the unexpectedly balmy weather which, as Sheridan now wrote, the Brazilian women had brought with them – along with their footballing skills, cheerful personalities and undoubted good looks. A large portion of the sizeable crowd had been teenage boys following the footballers' every move, and every time the glamorous striker got the ball, the stadium had been illuminated by thousands of flashlights as they took yet another photo of her. After the match the ladies had posed for more photos on the pitch, much to the delight of the supporters.

From Sheridan's point of view it had been a lovely assignment, in sharp contrast to the times when she was sent to the back of beyond to watch dour men's matches in torrential rain. She wanted the readers of the *City Scope* – Dublin's biggest newspaper – to absorb the atmosphere too and, she admitted to herself, she wanted to present women excelling in what was generally seen as a men's sport in the most positive light she could.

So she was taking special care about the piece, making sure she got the balance exactly right. It wasn't until Martyn Powell, the sports editor, pushed a pile of papers out of the way and sat on the edge of her desk that she glanced up from the screen in front of her.

'Looks like D-Day.' Martyn's naturally long face was even gloomier than usual, his drooping moustache adding to his hangdog expression. 'It's from the top.'

Sheridan felt her heart beat faster as she opened the email, which was headed 'The Future of the *City Scope*', and scanned its contents.

Rumours about the paper where she'd worked for the past five years had been circulating for weeks. The staff had listened to every one of them and come up with some ideas of their own too, but nobody really knew what the fate of the thirty-year-old newspaper would be. Changes would have to be made, they all acknowledged that. The newspaper industry was in a precarious state and the *City Scope* had been -haemorrhaging money over the past year. Everyone knew that something had to give sooner or later. The reporters had been gossiping for weeks. Now it looked like the time had come.

'What d'you think?' asked Martyn.

'I haven't a clue.' Sheridan pulled her flame-red curls back from her face and secured them with a lurid green bobble, which she took from her desk drawer. 'I suppose they can try some more cutbacks.'

The paper had introduced a raft of cost-cutting initiatives a few months earlier, most of which had irritated the journalists without delivering the required savings.

'I hope it's only cutbacks,' said Martyn. 'And not anything worse.'

'Well yes. So do I.' Sheridan tightened the bobble. 'But we're an institution, Marty, they have to come up with something.'

'Huh. So far all they've come up with is reducing expenses. Ours, not theirs, of course.'

Sheridan grinned. Martyn was a man who liked to take full advantage of his expense account.

'How's the piece going?' Martyn nodded at the open document on her computer screen.

'Nearly finished.' She glanced at it herself. 'It was good fun and nice to see the ladies on the pitch for a change.'

'There were some real crackers there all right.' Martyn had been looking at the photos earlier.

'Skilful athletes,' Sheridan reminded him, and he nodded even though she knew he only paid lip service to women's sporting abilities. 'And not a diva among them.'

'I wonder will we all still be here to report on the European Cup qualifiers?' asked Martyn, who enjoyed talking football with the paper's only female sports reporter.

'I hope so.' Sheridan looked worried. 'Ireland has a great chance this time. I want to get the *Scope* totally behind the team.'

'You're supposed to be impartial.'

'Get lost, Powell.' She roared with laughter. 'When was the *City Scope* ever impartial about football?'

Martyn's smile still wasn't enough to rid him of his gloomy

expression, but the conversation had temporarily taken their minds off the contents of the email. Which had said that there would be a meeting of all staff in the boardroom at noon. Everyone was expected to attend.

The boardroom of the *City Scope* wasn't really big enough to accommodate all of the newspaper's staff, so they stood shoulder to shoulder in the limited space as they waited for the arrival of the management team. There was a buzz of chatter as people speculated on the news that Ernie Johnson, the managing director, might bring. But Sheridan wasn't talking. She was considering all the possible outcomes and not liking any of them.

The worst, of course, was that the newspaper might close down. But that was utterly unthinkable. The *City Scope*, with its extensive sports coverage, had been in existence all of her life. Even before she'd joined the paper, reading it had been a major part of her week. When she'd finally landed a job there, she hadn't quite been able to believe it. And it had turned out to be the best job in the world. Even though she'd originally studied journalism to get away from sport. Even though she'd wanted to carve a very different career for herself.

Sheridan Gray had grown up in a sports-mad family. Sitting down in front of *Match of the Day*, *Sportsnight* and *Grandstand* was practically mandatory in the Gray household (as had been the daily purchase of the *City Scope*, widely regarded as the paper with the most authoritative sports section in the country). Sheridan's father and her two older brothers played both soccer and Gaelic football, and her mum was a PE teacher. But Sheridan wasn't obsessed in the same way as her parents and her brothers, and (being perfectly honest about it, although she wouldn't dream of saying so out loud) she disliked competing against other people. This was in contrast to everyone else in the family, who didn't believe that it was the taking part and not the winning that counted; as far as they were concerned, winning was the most important thing of all.

Sheridan didn't know why the competitive gene that ran so strongly through her parents and her brothers had passed her by, but the truth was that her favourite sporting activity was simply running by herself, not trying to beat anyone, not even the clock. She enjoyed jogging, which she found relaxing, and she needed relaxation because the Gray household, caught up as it always was with matches that the others were involved in, was rarely a relaxing place to be.

For most of her childhood it had been a given that she would spend weekends with her mother, Alice, on the sidelines of a pitch, wrapped up in a quilted anorak, warm gloves and knitted hat against the biting cold, while shouting encouragement at the men in her family. Afterwards there would be endless, sometimes heated, discussions about the match. The coach's selections were analysed, as was the team's performance, the opposition's tactics and even the level of support that both teams received. Sheridan would listen to the conversation without taking part. As far as she was concerned she'd done her bit by screaming until her throat was sore.

Matt and Con, her brothers, were picked to play for the Dublin Gaelic football team when they were old enough, which was the pinnacle of success as far as everyone in the family was concerned. They threw a huge party the day the announcement was made and Alice (not normally known for her baking skills) produced an enormous rectangular cake, which she'd decorated to look like a football pitch. Plastic figures wearing green shirts were placed in each goal mouth to represent Matt and Con, while a referee in the middle took the place of their father, Pat.

It was unfortunate, Sheridan thought, that her brothers' time with the Dublin team had also coincided with a slump in its fortunes, otherwise there would have been even bigger and better parties to celebrate more success. However, the Gray boys, as they were known, were always given high praise by the media for their unstinting efforts on behalf of their county, and indeed for their local club too, which regularly won the league, more often than not due to a spectacular shot from one or other of the boys.

It was when these reports (always from the *City Scope*) were being solemnly read out that Sheridan felt both proud of and yet disconnected from the rest of her family. She couldn't understand why being beaten totally devastated Matt and Con, and left them stomping around the house, slamming doors and impossible to talk to. Both Alice and Pat seemed to think that this was perfectly normal behaviour, but Sheridan asked herself why on earth they didn't just get over it. She was used to hearing people say 'it's only a game', but as far as the Grays were concerned, it seemed to be so much more than that.

As she grew older, she became impatient with their obsessions. She wished that she lived in a house where she didn't fall over football boots as soon as she walked in the door, and wasn't greeted by a forest of drying sports shirts in the kitchen every day. She longed to have discussions on hair and make-up from time to time (something she knew woefully little about) instead of listening to constant arguments about disallowed penalties and professional fouls. But there was nobody to have these discussions with. Alice wasn't the sort of person who devoted much time to hair and beauty. She was a tall, trim woman who kept her greying hair short and whose main beauty product was an industrial-sized jar of Pond's moisturiser which she kept on the bathroom shelf, between the cans of Lynx and tubs of Brylcreem. And the truth was that Sheridan couldn't categorise herself as the kind of girl who knew a lot about beauty either. Despite her weekly jogs, she didn't have the lean, wiry build of a runner. She was as sturdy as her brothers, broad-shouldered and statuesque rather than thin and elegant, and infinitely more comfortable in jeans and jumpers than dresses and high heels. From time to time she went on a blitz of fashion shopping with some of her friends, but more often than not the micro miniskirts or tight boots that had seemed like a good idea at the time ended up unworn in the back of her wardrobe, a testament to the fact that her thighs were the body feature she disliked the most.

Her relationship with the opposite sex was, in many ways, as comfortable as the clothes she preferred to wear. Unlike many of her female friends, she didn't get tongue-tied in the presence of a boy she'd never met before, because she was accustomed to a constant stream of beefy soccer and GAA players traipsing in and out of the house, and she was perfectly at ease talking to any of them – especially as their conversation was generally about their matches, and she'd been to most of them. She knew that men weren't mysterious creatures who would magically change your life. She knew that they could get anxious and worried just like girls – although, in fairness, usually about different things. Matt and Con were rarely anxious about their dates; they were more concerned about their matches. Nevertheless, when Con was stressing about where to bring the lovely Bevanne Dickinson the first time they were going out together, Sheridan was the one to suggest that taking her to see *Jerry Maguire* in the warmth of the cinema would probably be better fun for her than standing on the terraces in the rain watching a League of Ireland match; and when Matt was at a loss to know what to get for his girlfriend's eighteenth birthday, she told him firmly that Melissa would prefer a dainty watch to the bulky thing with multiple functions and two different timers he was considering. The boys were always surprised when she came up with girlie tips but always grateful for what was generally the right advice. In turn, they steered her away from men they regarded as messers and not good enough for her (even though she didn't always agree with them and didn't solely judge prospective boyfriends on their footballing prowess).

In the end, most of the guys she eventually dated were people she'd met at one sporting fixture or another. They generally knew her parents and her brothers, and seemed to regard her as more of a friend than a girlfriend. They usually brought her to rugby matches (which she enjoyed) or to dark and gloomy bars (which she didn't quite as much – she preferred the trend for bright, modern gastro-pubs that was beginning to hit the country). Most of them, at some point or another, would tell her that it was great to go out with someone like her, a decent sort who liked a laugh, could talk soccer, rugby and GAA and could get ready for a date in less than ten minutes.

Sheridan wasn't insulted by being regarded as a decent sort rather than a sex symbol. After all, she didn't think her body could ever be regarded as sexy, and her interest in make-up and clothes was fairly minimal. She didn't mind a dash of lip gloss before she went out, but the idea of spending absolutely hours in front of the mirror, like some of the girls she knew, bored her beyond belief. Besides, she couldn't help thinking that it was far better to be someone that men felt comfortable talking to, and who got on with them all (even if most of her relationships petered out after a couple of months), rather than one of the group of air-headed, giggling women who seemed to regard them as creatures that they would never understand and who were a prize to be won if they only knew how. Sheridan felt that she had a lot to be thankful for in that respect and was glad that the opposite sex wasn't a mystery to her; in fact there were times she felt that she knew far too much about them and their interests. However, there were also times when she felt a bit of an outsider among her friends because she was never at ease participating in breathless conversations about fanciable guys. She wondered if she'd ever meet someone who would fill her every waking thought, or turn her legs to jelly, or make her think that an evening spent waxing her legs and plucking her eyebrows was worth the pain. Somehow she doubted it.

That feeling of being an outsider extended to her home life too, although the reasons were different. But she couldn't help feeling distant from the rest of her family whenever she looked at Matt and Con's trophies, the symbols of their success, which were proudly displayed in the huge walnut cabinet in the corner of the room, and totally dwarfed the only award she'd ever won. This was a plastic medal for the under-10s girls' five-a-side football tournament (which wasn't a proper tournament at all but was designed to give the girls the chance to kick the ball around and wear themselves out, while their mothers sat in the clubhouse for a cup of tea and a chat, and for which all of the young participants had received a medal).

She didn't want to be an airhead but she didn't always want to be the fallback girl that men dated when they couldn't get anyone else either. (Matt's friends in particular used her as a last-minute date whenever they needed someone, knowing that she'd enter into the spirit of whatever the occasion was.) She didn't need to be a winner but nor did she want to be the perennial loser in her testosterone-filled family home. Most of the time she was comfortable in her own skin, but occasionally it was hard to be the one who simply didn't match up, no matter how hard she tried.

Matt and Con both went to college after school, choosing to study business while hoping to get jobs that would allow them plenty of time to devote to playing for their football club. Sheridan knew that she didn't have a business brain and wanted a job that could become a career. Alice suggested that she follow in her footsteps and become a PE teacher (you mightn't be all that good at competing yourself, she told Sheridan, but you know how it should be done). Sheridan had scotched that idea immediately. She wanted to do something dramatically different from the rest of the family. She needed to break out on her own.

She decided to study journalism on a whim, mainly because one of her teachers complimented her on a report she'd done on the school fashion show. Miss Kavanagh said that it had been a vivid piece of writing that had brought the show to life for anyone who read the piece. Was Sheridan very interested in fashion? she asked.

It was a question that reduced Sheridan to fits of laughter, and Miss Kavanagh, realising that designer dresses were intended for women who looked like a half-decent puff of wind would blow them over rather than well-built girls like Sheridan, looked suitably embarrassed. Sheridan told her not to worry, that she'd enjoyed writing the piece because it was about something so alien to her, which led Miss Kavanagh to sigh with relief; although then Sheridan remarked that nobody would take seriously as a fashion journalist a woman who liked her food and had never been on a crash diet. Miss Kavanagh tried to convince her otherwise but Sheridan knew that she was wasting her time. All the same, she thought, maybe she could become an investigative reporter and one day have her name in big print beneath a story that could be added to the enormous file of cuttings that Alice kept documenting Con and Matt's successes on the playing field. And maybe then she'd finally feel like a success in her own right too.